AERIE

A Fantasy Novel

Broken Wings Duet
Book 1

S. E. Wendel

To Jeanne, whose Disney reference saved this book.
Thank you for your patience, your kindness, and your wisdom.

I

Turning her destrier, Lady Maddalena Montcaer buried her nose in the fur lining of her cloak, understanding suddenly why man had settled the forest, the marshes, even the desert before settling the mountain. The jagged peaks speared the skyline like an eyetooth, mist curtaining the steep crags and running in rivulets down to frigid streams. There was a wildness this far north, this far into the rock. If she listened past her horse Yvain's hot puffs, she imagined she could hear the steady thrum of the earth's heart.

It was a gentle, sure beat, drumming life into the ground beneath Yvain's hooves, its tendrils racing south into the foothills and beyond, into the southlands of Vagora with its wide plains, gentle hills, and rich soil. Vagoran vineyards stretched as far as rivers, its cities as wide as lakes. The rain and snowmelt gathered here and surged south along six different rivers to feed the land, watering Vagora's farms and pastures. All flowed from the northern mountains.

She found all of it rather desolate. But then, Lena had had enough of cold craggy mountains to last a lifetime.

She sighed, and the cold gripped her tight as a fist.

"Take the air wherever you go, Lena," her father always said, his voice a rough rasp in his damaged windpipe. *"Breathe in the land. Feel it in your lungs, taste it on your tongue. See what it tells you."*

But all Lena breathed was more mist, tasting like a mystery on her tongue. It felt just like it should, sucking a cloud into her lungs, and all it told her was that—

"It's *freezing*!" came echoing up the mountain path, bounding off the rocks to make it sound like a whole army of disgruntled squires, when really it was only the one.

Lena sighed and twisted in her saddle. "I thought her throat would have rubbed raw forty leagues ago," she grumbled to her horse.

She looked down the mountain path to behold her squire trudging up behind, looking damp and glum. A scrap of a girl, most of Alixandre was buried beneath furs and cloaks, the bottom half of her face wrapped in a voluminous knit scarf. Startling jade eyes narrowed into slits at Lena, daring her to grin at her misery. With her untamable ebony curls wet and plastered to the hard contours of her face, Alix looked to Lena like a soaked kitten. Just barely fifteen, Alix had begun their journey with gusto, singing all the bawdy pub songs she knew. While she hadn't grown any quieter through the journey, her words turned markedly sour as the land around them had begun to rise and the air took on a mountainous chill.

Between the palfrey Alix rode and the two packhorses she led, three pairs of ears lay flat against skulls, no doubt wishing they were deaf. Yvain pranced beneath her, as if he wanted to outrun Alix again.

"Ho' muff longer?" came slurred through Alix's many layers of knitted wool.

"Not long." She peered at Alix as the girl pulled down her scarf just enough to be intelligible. "It'll only be getting colder from here. Winter hasn't even set in yet."

Alix shrugged. "Not like we'll be spending another night outside."

Lena drew in a long breath of mountain air, the cold burning her from the inside, to voice the same question she'd asked since they set out from Highclere, the capital of Vagora, almost three weeks ago. "Won't you turn back?"

Alix avoided her eyes by readjusting her mittens. "No," she said and kicked her palfrey back into motion.

Lena knew it was too late to leave Alix behind, knew she'd never convince the girl to turn back. That hadn't stopped her from arguing the point. She'd asked Alix to turn back every day of their journey. She'd begged Alix not to share in her fate after the king passed sentence from his high throne, encased in his ornamental gold armor that made him glow like a sun god and his frown all the more terrible, a deity displeased. She'd told Alix to abandon her, to run, to take everything and go to ground the night she cut the hand, the right hand, the sword hand, off her new liege lord. Alix had seen her do it, had watched Lena lay the accusations of abuse at Lord Balderak's feet, watched Lena describe his many crimes against the serving maids and scullery maids and the house-keeper and village women and merchant women, watched Lena throw away everything her parents taught her when she drew her sword on her liege lord, when she betrayed her liege lord, left him there bleeding and felt nothing, no guilt, no pride. Lena pled with Alix to abandon her that night, had known what the consequences would be, but the girl had refused. "*If it were me, it would've been his cock,*" was all she'd said.

She turned away from Alix so the girl wouldn't see the hot tears threatening to leak out. Lena gave an irritated huff to find there were tears left to shed; she'd cried her fill already. The memory of that night sat heavy in Lena's breast, a soreness that never went away. Alix's pres-ence—difficult, saucy, aggravating as she may be—was a relief, light and welcome, like taking armor off after days of marching, feeling that first wave of fresh air after peeling it from your skin.

It was too late, and Lena had easily given in to her own weakness, keeping Alix with her. It was supposed to be *her* exile, not Alix's. It was she alone who should suffer this two-year sentence to the northernmost reaches of the kingdom, where the winds were bitter and the snow thick-er than mud. But it was too late, Alix had insisted, and Lena was grateful for it.

Alix had stood with her when King Artemian condemned Lena to exile and demanded now to stand with her through it. The girl had proven herself loyal a hundredfold the past year, never more so than during the mess with Lord Balderak. A hot well of frustrated tears clutched at her at the thought of *that man*. Because of that man, scores of women lived in terror and pain within his demesne; because of that man, Lena had done what she knew to be right, accused him of the heinous crimes he committed; because of that man, Lena had stood before her king in chains as he passed sentence while Balderak looked on, free.

"Prove to me that you aren't a danger to this kingdom," King Artemian had declared that awful day. *"Prove that you will uphold the vows you took as a knight."*

I already have! cried Lena's heart of hearts, just as it had that day and did again now as she and Alix made their way deeper into the north mountains. Lena had tried defending the innocent, the abused, just as she vowed to. She'd vowed to be Vagora's sword and shield, its justice and defense.

And where had it gotten her? Condemned, exiled. Just barely a knight anymore. A person to scorn, to spit at in the street. Her mother was so ashamed.

Lena tightened her hold on Yvain's reins and pushed those thoughts away. They served no purpose now, for she knew, even as she made her way further from her former life, from any sort of honor or respect she'd gained through the years, that she'd do it all again for those women. What was done was done—today she would reach her place of sentence, would serve her two-year exile. She would prove herself a good knight, a trustworthy knight, and then return to service, to defending the kingdom and her people, something she'd trained her whole life to do. She would prove herself, for there was no other choice.

———•◆•———

The low-hanging clouds brushed her face as the horses climbed. Wisps clung to her cloak as Lena led her little band onto a narrow plateau overlooking an equally narrow valley. Pines and shrubs stood starkly green against the delicate, puffy gray of the mist and harsh slate of the mountain. A dark alpine stream cut through the center of the valley, running through hardy reeds and spindly berry bushes.

At the far mouth of the valley sat the town of the Longbourne, named for the numerous long houses situated on stone platforms. Sheep and mountain goats bleated in separate paddocks, and rugged mountain ponies wandered throughout the valley, their multicolored manes fluttering in the cold breeze. Pillars of blue smoke rose from chimneys and smoke holes, and even from across the valley Lena spotted the soft glow of fires through leaded windows.

"Thank Matella and all the Maidens!" Alix crowed. "*Tell me* they got a pub."

"I should think they do. Most folk want for the same things."

"Well, this folk wants an ale."

Lena nodded resolutely. The squire deserved an ale. "Let's go, then. Somewhere there's a fire to welcome us."

Alix let out a lover's groan.

Leading the way through the valley, Lena took note of the livestock and orchards of mountain apples. The people here lived a rugged life, what with the steep slopes of their mountain meadows and the wind that howled through the night, but their animals were fat and crops hearty, so life here could be good.

A light shower dampened their heads and shoulders by the time their horses passed the first line of houses. Townsfolk sat on porches, sheltered beneath the deep awnings of their houses' steeply slanted rooves. The crossbeams ended in animal heads, shaped like rams, bucks, bulls, even dragons.

"Good evening, mistress," Lena said to a woman smoking a pipe.

"And to you," the woman said, her jaundiced eyes moving over the knight and squire with cool shrewdness. Lena preferred the mountain mist moving over her skin to this.

"I've business with your mayor. Could you point the way?"

"And what business might that be?"

"King's business, mistress. I can't say more than that."

"There's only one thing a person on king's business comes here for." Leaning forward in her chair, the woman lifted her chin and grinned. "You're the new warden."

Lena said nothing. It probably didn't matter who knew their business; everyone would soon enough, as she and Alix would be living near Longbourne for two years. Still, her orders were to talk to the mayor first, and then the current warden and relieve him of duty. And she had no choice but to live by her orders now.

She'd made a vow once, a vow to uphold the knightly code of honor, chivalry, and duty. All her life she'd trained to be a knight, joining her parents' academy at the age of five. She'd trained there until the age of twelve, squired until twenty, and then, finally, earned her spurs. The king knighted her at age twenty-one. That day, nearly six years ago now, she'd promised her father, a famed knight whose service was cut short when he was nearly assassinated with a garrote, that she would do what he could not and devote her whole life to king and country. She had promised her mother, the most famous, the most beloved knight in Vagora, that she would uphold the family name and honor by never wavering, by always fulfilling her duties. She had promised herself that one day, she would surpass both.

She'd forsaken those vows, thrown away her parents' good name and the merit of her own years of service, yet she would not take it back. Perhaps there had been a better way, but she would never regret accusing Balderak. Perhaps others now wouldn't turn a blind eye. It was all she could hope for, and because she wouldn't take back her actions, she sat in her saddle, taking this old crone's sneer with a bland face.

"Take this path," the old woman said in a cloud of sweet tobacco smoke, "turn left at the town square. The mayor's house is there."

"Thank you."

Bowing her head, she motioned behind her back. Alix often needed a reminder.

"Why should I be courteous to someone who isn't back?" Alix had asked after narrowly missing a gauntleted cuff from a less patient knight.

"Because knights are expected to have manners," Lena explained.

"They're also supposed to be great warriors. I've been with you a week and I haven't seen you fight anyone."

"That's a good thing, Alix."

The girl's look—dubious eyes, slanted brows, pinched mouth—told Lena she begged to differ.

"And just who is it I should be fighting? I haven't exactly come across any grievous injustices this past week."

Alix had shrugged. *"I don't know. That butcher yesterday was definitely getting away with robbery."*

Heading into the town square, Lena stopped before the largest long house. Two beaked griffin heads adorned the crossbeams, forked tongues snarling. The roof was newly thatched, the hay sweet smelling, and the beams of the porch polished to a high shine. Finely carved posts formed a railing around the perimeter of the porch, and three huge slats of wood made steps up to the wide landing.

Lena's heavy boots had barely met the packed earth before she heard a woman say, "No need, warden. I can point you on your way."

Turning, Lena beheld a woman in her middle years, sturdily built, with wide shoulders and strong arms. Her face was ruddy, as if she'd just come from the fireside, and her coppery hair, streaked with silver near the temple, was scraped ruthlessly back into a nondescript coif at the nape of her neck. Rolled up sleeves revealed muscular forearms used to work, yet laugh lines marked the edges of her eyes and mouth.

"Mistress," Lena said with a nod, "I'm looking for the mayor of your town."

"You've found her. I'm Tilda Yarlsson, Mayor of Longbourne."

Clicking her heels, Lena executed a courtly bow, required for the woman's rank. Pulling the sealed packet of papers from her jerkin, she said, "Mayor Yarlsson, I am Lady Maddalena Montcaer of Lindenfaire, knight of His Highness King Artemian of Vagora. With me is my squire, Alixandre of Highclere. I am here to serve as Warden to Castle Finhöln and all the prisoners therein. I trust you'll find everything in order."

"I'm sure it is, warden," the mayor said.

Mayor Yarlsson held out her hand for the papers, her lips pinched as if she'd suddenly tasted a lemon. Lena handed them over, and they promptly disappeared into a pocket.

Lena couldn't help looking at the pocket. "Forgive me, mayor, but it is my duty to ensure everything is as it should—"

"You're the sixth warden to come to Longbourne. Let me reassure you, I've got everything in hand."

"But—"

"You're here to take your wardenship, that donkey's ass Sir Ollander will leave—thank the Maidens—and everything will be as it always is for us."

"Yes, mayor." What else was there to say to such an unwelcoming greeting?

She heard a squeak of protest from Alix, but the girl muffled anything further under all that wool. Lena had to stop from grinding her teeth or scuffing the toe of her boot. The mayor had that look on her face Lena dreaded, the one that said Lena was barely worth the mayor's time, that she was barely better than the grime the mayor scraped from her nailbeds. Like Lena was herself a criminal, sent to watch over other criminals. She did her best to swallow down her ire, promising herself that one day soon, she'd change the mayor's mind. She certainly had time.

"If it isn't too much trouble, it's been a long day and my squire is tired. Do you have a pub we might visit before heading for the castle?"

"The pub's across the square. Just follow the smell of ale. But I'd suggest you start up to the castle now, lady. You've a climb yet and the day's getting late. Night comes fast in the mountains." And with a swish of skirts, the mayor disappeared back into her long house, Lena's orders still unopened.

Lena swung back up onto Yvain, ignoring Alix's loud guffaws.

Lena led her small, soggy band out of Longbourne, the gaze of the townsfolk prickling along her spine. She didn't know why she expected a better greeting—wardens of Castle Finhöln were disgraced knights, sent by the king to serve penance for crimes. The good people of Longbourne already had to suffer prisoners as neighbors.

Still, she wished a warm fire and a deep cup of ale could have been found for Alix.

The path up the mountain cut through shrubs and berry bushes, and the horses nickered in protest when led too close to the thorny brambles. The rain relented, and the path began to switchback, ascending a steep crest. Atop, through the pines, Lena spied the foundations of Castle Finhöln.

The brambles soon gave way to rubble, stone and mortar laid by the wayside of the path leading up to the barbican gate. The path took them along the south wall, and Lena's mouth nearly dropped open at the state of the castle. It barely stood!

Great sections of wall had crumbled away, and in one place, a hole gaped so large that a well-trained horse could jump through. Her dismay only grew when they came to the gate and found the iron portcullis, showing signs of extreme rust, disuse, and possible uselessness, drawn all the way up.

Ducking down over Yvain's back as they crossed through into the inner bailey, Lena clenched her teeth against a wave of despair that burned the back of her throat with bile. The courtyard was a disgrace, remnants of barrels, carts, tables, chairs, and all manner of wood scattered about. One corner had been devoted to refuse, jealously guarded over by a large raven, who cawed and croaked at several challengers.

She surveyed the bailey from her perch atop Yvain, suddenly wary of dismounting. She didn't want to let her feet touch the cracked cobblestones, didn't want to face anymore of this sad place. Somehow, to dismount was to resign herself to this, to sign her name to a contract she hadn't agreed to. It would be real the moment her foot touched the ground.

As she looked about the bailey, searching for but finding nothing to ease her disappointment, she couldn't help but think of Lindenfaire, the manor her parents had converted into a martial academy. From its white-washed walls to the barracks-turned-dormitories, everything had been so clean, so well-kept there, her father keeping the staff working like a well-trained army. It was one of many such beautiful estates throughout Vagora, the defenses and buildings and fountains and landscape all mixed together to create a defensible, aesthetic wonder. But Finhöln...

A flick of temper ignited in Lena's belly, and she welcomed it. She'd fought her despair ever since that night she confronted Balderak, when her world had crumbled as surely as this castle was. She wouldn't give into it, instead embraced her anger.

How could this place be called a prison? The walls could barely stand up, let alone keep prisoners inside. How could no one have reported this, or started repairs? How could she submit Alix to such an awful place?

Lena spotted movement, and out of what she assumed was the stables came a lean young man in brown homespun. Looking as unkempt as the castle, the man was unshaven, unwashed, and, if Lena had to guess, unpracticed.

"Squire!" she snapped. The man nearly lost his footing, just catching his balance before skidding across the cobblestones. "I was under the impression this was a prison."

The man looked her up and down, spared a glance at Alix, and then returned to her for a shrug. "You must be the new warden."

"Lady Maddalena Montcaer of Lindenfaire. And you are?"

"Lor. But you'll be wanting Sir Ollander."

"By all means. Hopefully he'll be more informative."

The man merely shrugged again and strolled off in the direction of the main hall, leaving them in the dilapidated bailey.

Lena nearly threw herself off Yvain, pacing up and down the courtyard, boot heels clicking on cobblestones. Every time she had to dodge a missing cobble her temper mounted.

Behind her, Alix shifted her considerable bundle of blankets and dismounted, making for the stables.

"Oh, hells!" Alix yelped from the stable door. "They actually put the animals in here. I wouldn't put the meanest fuckers in Cheapside here, let alone warhorses."

"Language," Lena grumbled. She waved at Alix. "Lead them out."

Lena's temper spiraled when she heard the unshod tread of the warden's horses as they were led into the bailey. They were well fed, but their winter coats could use a good grooming and their heads hung low.

"What are you doing with my horses?"

Pivoting, heel scraping, Lena rounded on an older knight. Dressed in leathers, somewhat better maintained than his squire, Sir Ollander stood half a head taller than Lena, his graying beard an unpleasant yellowish color—whether from being blond once or from ale, she wasn't sure.

"Taking pity on them," she clipped. "Sir Ollander?"

"Lady Maddalena."

"You're relieved of duty, sir."

"Glad to hear it. This hellhole's yours now. May you find as much joy in it as I have."

"The king's instructions were vague, as this prison is a secret one. But judging by the state of things, I'm beginning to think you have no prisoners at all. Unless your horses qualify."

Sir Ollander shared a look with his squire that Lena couldn't quite define but certainly didn't like. There was nothing good in it; part cunning and part spite.

"Prisoner. Just the one."

Lena bit down on her scoff.

"So," Sir Ollander said conversationally, easing his arms across his wide barrel chest. "What're you in for?"

"Excuse me?"

"Innocents aren't sent to Finhöln. Takes a special kind of scoundrel, committing a special kind of *crime*," he said, the last word spilling from his mouth like oil. He watched her with shrewd eyes, set far back in his skull.

"You're correct, this is a place of penance for wrongdoers. Warden and prisoner."

"And what are you seeking penance for, lady? Lose a squadron? Taunt a duke? Spill wine in the king's lap?"

Lena tipped her head back, assessing him. Lena was considered tall for a woman, making Sir Ollander just above average for a man, but he made up for it in the blocky width of his shoulders. She suspected, when fit, he could do quite a bit of damage with a war hammer. In a fight, she'd have to use her speed and strength of her shoulders to get in close. There was a softness about him, though, and she could see the past two years hadn't been much of a physical trial for him. She avoided looking at his rounded gut—the day she didn't fit into her stiff steel cuirass, currently buckled around her chest and back, she didn't deserve to be a knight.

"Insubordination," she said carefully. "And you?"

Silence trickled around them until finally he said, "Had unpopular opinions about the southern front."

Lena didn't let her eyebrows rise in surprise, though it was close. The war with the southern barbarian tribes came in waves, quiet one year but hot the next. Vagora fought over a riverplain, pushing and being pushed across the River Dyne year after year. It was unending, the southern Vagorans growing fat and rich in times of peace but always under threat of a new campaign. The southern front seemed doomed to perpetuity, making any new soldier hope for assignment on the eastern campaign instead. Although, her mother was there now, quickly returning to her command after the disgrace of Lena's trial. Perhaps the famed Lady Margot would finally win the forever war to make up for her daughter's shame.

Lena and Sir Ollander considered one another again. His gaze held mild interest, as if he wanted to pry further, as if he sought a kind of camaraderie with her, but Lena widened her stance and squared her shoulders, putting an end to any such notions. From Mayor Yarlsson's words, she suspected Sir Ollander and his predecessors weren't well-loved and she could guess why. She wouldn't be like him or the other wardens; she wasn't his comrade.

"There's a castle to inspect, sir. Shall we?"

"I suppose Lor and I should show you around. Tradition and all. There are only a few important bits. Shouldn't take long."

"Lead on, then."

One of Sir Ollander's bushy eyebrows rose. "So eager, lady?"

"I don't believe in wasted time or breath, sir. My orders are to take the grounds with you and then relieve you of wardenship. I would've thought, judging by the state of the castle, you'd be pleased to leave this place and take your new post, wherever the king decides that may be."

"You've a penchant for speeches, you know that?"

Lena knew better than to grace that with a reply.

Shrugging his meaty shoulders, Sir Ollander turned on his heel and strode for the castle without further comment, a smirking Lor close behind. Assigning Alix to see to the horses, she followed the two into the castle proper.

"So few torches," Lena couldn't help saying, though it was probably strategic in hiding the moldering rushes covering the ground.

"Not much to see," was Sir Ollander's explanation.

A wide foyer led into what, in its time, would have been a magnificent great hall, worthy of royal visits. Great arching timbers scaled from the stone walls to form the roof, resembling the boning of a ship's hull. One section had caved in, violent cracks and splinters gouged through so that a little afternoon light, and much of the day's rain, poured into the hall below. *Need to fix that before winter comes,* Lena thought with a groan.

The high table upon the dais, directly in front of the great hearth, was the room's only adornment, and instead of the finely carved chairs for the lord and their family to sit upon and hold court, four rickety replacements sat at the center. The two smaller hearths along the east and west walls were cold with small hills of ash and dust, cobwebs running thick as cloth up the chimneys. The floor was unswept, bearing no carpets except for two mangy wolfhounds lounging at the foot of the dais.

She followed Sir Ollander and Lor down a winding staircase. *Could use more sconces. It's so dark you could trip on every other step.* The steps spilled into the kitchen, where two men in their middle years sat over a meal of stew at a heavy carving table. The room was noticeably warmer than the hall, and Lena thought it a tolerable kitchen. She'd seen far worse.

The younger of the men scraped back his stool and stood, bobbing his head to them; the other looked over his shoulder and grunted. Sir

Ollander gave his stool legs a kick.

"Up you get, steward—what'll the new warden think of your inso-lence?"

Heaving a mighty sigh, the man stood, bringing his bowl of stew with him. The two men shared the same meaty jaw and tea brown eyes. But where the older, taller man looked mean to his core, eyes narrowed, mouth sneered, the other seemed pensive, wary eyes looking between Lena and Sir Ollander. Those eyes missed nothing, though the man's shoulders hunched, as if he could make himself smaller and disappear.

Sir Ollander motioned at the man eating his stew. "This here's Mal-thus. He's been the castle steward for over twenty years and knows it like the back of his hand. Don't you, man?"

"Best if you don't move anything," Malthus said into his stew.

"I'll bear that in mind," said Lena.

"And this is his brother, Pol. Decent cook. He was born stupid, mind you, deaf and doesn't speak much. If you have to communicate with him, Malthus knows his hand gestures. Pol likes to be accommo-dating, but you'll have to tell him through Mal what you want. Right." Sir Ollander turned for the stairwell and exited the way they'd come.

Glancing between the two brothers, Lena settled her gaze on Pol, who offered her a tentative smile. Nodding to the both of them, she said, "Gentlemen. I'll be back this evening to discuss particulars. In the mean-time, I'd appreciate it if you'd see something sent for my squire. I left her in the bailey."

The deaf brother watched her mouth intently and then looked to his brother. After settling himself back at the table, the older brother made a few gestures with his hands. The man named Pol smiled at Lena and nodded.

"Excellent. Thank you."

Nodding to the brothers again, Lena hurried to catch up with Sir Ollander. He was waiting for her on the dreary landing, and when she arrived, he wordlessly led the way down another dark corridor. The air grew colder the further they walked, heading into the castle and, eventually, into the mountain itself.

"Malthus has a place down in Longbourne and stays there most nights. Pol sleeps here. So, it's just you three and our prisoner here."

"And they are...?"

Again, that malicious look flitted across Sir Ollander's face, making a shiver run through Lena that she felt in her fingers, chest, and behind the knees. Whatever came next, the man liked this part of the castle.

"He's down there, waiting." He nodded at the end of the corridor, where a wrought iron door stood open before a dark chasm leading down into the bowels of the castle.

"I see. The cells are down there, then?"

"The prisoner has free range of the castle."

Lena stiffened. "What?"

"He's...unusual. He's allowed the run of the place, just not allowed to cross the curtain wall. Your job is to see he doesn't and track him down if he does."

"And what prisoner wouldn't run, with the state of the wall and the gate wide open?"

Sir Ollander ushered her towards the iron door. "Shall we?"

The stairs to the dungeon were steep and slick, the air moist. She tasted the foul air on her tongue, an aftertaste of iron burning the back of her throat. Evenly spaced torches lit their way, each flickering sickly, the air almost too dank for even fire.

The narrow descent saw them to the mouth of a short corridor, one wall rough-hewn rock and the other lined with six cells. The first on the right glowed with torches, the barred door yawning open.

Dread gnawed at the bottom of Lena's stomach, and instinct told her not to enter that cell. Sir Ollander's gaze was heavy behind her. Gripping the hilt of her sword, she stepped inside.

The acrid air hissed from her mouth in shock.

Seated backwards in a chair in the center of the cell sat an avian. A young avian. Seven Hells, he couldn't have been older than Lena's twenty-seven years.

The avian was a prime example of his species, his human-like body strong, his bird wings wide and heavily feathered. Waves of hair the color of burnished gold gleamed in the firelight, veiling his face. At his nape, hair gave way to down, tracking in two lines down his shoulders to the mass of muscle, cartilage, and bone that made up the wing joints. He hid his face in his arms, wrapped around himself to shelter his bare torso from their sight. Even so, Lena saw the muscles of his massive avian chest twitch as he shifted, cringing at their entrance, the skin of his bare back pebbling in the damp, bitter air. Shoulders twice as wide as any human man's curled around a chest that was three times as strong.

And his wings. There wasn't a sight in Heaven or the Seven Hells like avian wings. Mottled brown at the base, his feathers ended in pure white at the tip. They sat folded against his sides protectively, but when raised for flight, each had to span eight feet at least.

But there was something wrong with his right wing. He held it low, at an odd angle, almost as if...

Sir Ollander strolled into the cell, giving the avian's back a friendly slap. The avian cringed away.

"This here's Bel. I'll leave you to make your own introductions—you already have a speech, I assume. What you need to know is that this wretch is the king's favorite prisoner. In exchange for free movement within the castle, he does little tasks for King Artemian. It works well enough. But the wretch is young and must be reminded of his place."

In a move that had her lurching for her sword, Sir Ollander grabbed the avian's right wing, straightened it, and smashed his elbow through the radial bone. The avian barely cried out, just wrapped his unhurt wing closer around himself, his fists clenching at his sides.

At Lena's shock, Sir Ollander smiled a greasy smile, showing off all his teeth, and said, "He's a prisoner, not a guest. Our orders are to keep him grounded for life. Sometimes this one gets a mind to set the break and let the wing heal. If he does, it's your duty to break it again."

Her mouth opened again, to shout she'd do no such thing, but her orders weighed heavy in her breast. She tried to swallow the refusal down, but the horror of the break choked her. How could she do something so appalling? Who could call themselves a knight and do *this*?

"You'll find all this written out for you in the warden's office. The directive lists all your duties and outlines all the wretch can and cannot get up to." Smacking the back of the avian's head, Sir Ollander said, "Well, boy? Going to greet your pretty new warden?"

The avian drew in a shuddering breath before the muscles in his great back eased. He straightened, vertebrae by vertebrae, his chest expanding, golden skin tight. He stood swiftly on powerful legs and swept his unhurt wing back, crowding Sir Ollander against the far wall.

All of him unfurled; stance wide, hands in fists, he glared down at Lena with large, wide-set eyes that burned so blue, they were turquoise. Standing, he was taller and wider than Sir Ollander, and Lena wondered how the old knight had had the gall to attack such a strong avian.

As if he could feel her assessing him for weakness, the avian's mouth twisted in a sneer, and then in two long strides he was out of the room, sweeping past Lena in a rush of feathers.

2

Hell. Bel was in hell. The humans thought there were seven hells, but he knew better. There was one, and this was it.

The castle echoed long into the night with the scurrying and banging of the new residents. Bel lay on his stomach, listening to the foreign noises slither beneath his door and slip through his walls. It reverberated in his sensitive, pointed ears, making them feel hot and too large.

He'd watched the newcomers from one of his favorite nooks as they bid farewell to Sir Ollander and his squire. Needless to say, Bel didn't join them. Bel hadn't disliked a warden as much as Ollander since his first warden, Hallan, the one who first broke his wing, down by the joint. That break was the worst and had never healed properly. Even now, with five breaks and four secret resets, he could barely hold his right wing outstretched because of that first break.

The new warden didn't seem to care much for the old one either. She had watched Ollander leave with a stony face, her squire flanking her in silence. They had that in common at least.

How could two people make so much noise? Twilight had come and gone and still they were about, their voices, bodiless and incoherent, bounding down the empty corridors. Did they intend to tear the castle down on their first night?

If the curtain wall fell, would his prison boundaries still stand?

He swallowed back the ironic sound that wanted free from his throat. Even if the whole castle crumbled, Bel sometimes thought he'd never leave. Ten years he'd been here. He hadn't tried to run since the first year. His back prickled with the memory of Hallan's beloved whip-lashes. If Ollander's treatment of his horses were anything to go by, he too was fond of the whip, and Bel had kept himself in line and well away from the old warden because of it. Not to mention the hungry looks those bloodthirsty hounds gave him.

He shifted, flinching as a wave of pain, bright, echoing, snaked along his wing, making his shoulder ache and his feathers twitch. He tongued the edge of a pillow and drew it into his mouth. Biting down, he held his breath for two counts, breathed for three. Soon he found a rhythm, brea-thing in counterpoint to the pulse of pain emanating along the curve of his wing.

Bel waited until even the nightingales sought their nests before ris-ing. He felt rickety, his breath broken and his tendons moldering, skin too tight, clothes too clingy. Blood swirled in his head, making his skull feel viscous and momentarily unattached to his spine. The dizziness passed when he started his rhythmic breathing again, the blood pooling once more in his shoulders, creating a steady but manageable thrum.

Unfurling his healthy wing, he began the process of binding the broken one to his side with the gauze strips he'd squirreled away weeks ago. Round and round the wad wound, around his ribs, around his wing, around his back. He pulled tight, wincing through the move—and breathed a sigh of relief when everything, chest, wing, blood, bones, sett-led into place.

He eyed one of the tunics he'd altered to accommodate his wings but left the bedroom without one. It wasn't worth the effort, or the pain. Who did he need to dress for?

The cold damp of the castle stuck to his skin in an oily cloak, coating him in a slick layer of chilled sweat. No torches illuminated the way, but then, Bel hadn't needed a guide in over nine years. He'd learned it always paid to move through the castle noiselessly—especially with a new, unknown warden under his roof.

As Bel descended the stairs to the kitchen, the damp burned away in warm wafts smelling of melted butter and yeast. A hearty fire greeted him in the kitchen hearth, snapping and crackling merrily, finally unencumbered by any cauldrons, skillets, or pans.

At the heavy carving table sat Pol, his chin dipping to his chest as he snored, his fingertips whitened with flour. A steaming kettle sat nearby a pewter goblet, as always.

Bel took an unsteady breath, aching all over again. Always Pol knew just what he needed. Always Pol looked out for him, even under the suspicious eye of a new warden.

Pouring himself a cup from the kettle, he downed the first serving of Pol's willow bark and lavender tea in one gulp, ignoring the poppy milk's bitter aftertaste, then measured a second. The movement roused Pol, and with a little start, his gaze found Bel's.

He lifted the cup and nodded his gratitude, avoiding the sympathy saturating Pol's gaze. It very nearly dripped from his eyes, the rims watering, seeping into wrinkles long and defined that fanned towards his temples.

Bad? Pol signed with a tentative gesture of his hand.

Not bad, Bel signed back.

After the year it took Bel to swallow the fact that no rescue was coming for him, that his cousin, King Dartegn, would be leaving him here to rot just as he deserved, he'd finally gotten smart and learned Pol's signing. Relying on Malthus for translations was always precarious, and Bel, the human king's avian translator, knew all about the hazards of mistranslation.

Pol and Malthus had been here longer even than Bel, the last remaining heirs of the fallen family who used to be lords of Finhöln and the mountains beyond. The castle had been decaying for decades, and the brothers intended to see the end of their family line and therefore the end of their family shame. The castle would finally fully revert to the crown, no longer bearing any heirs who could tell the story of how, a hundred years ago, Finhöln had failed to defend the north against what Bel's people called the Great Reunion and what the humans called the Bloody Spring. After seven years of conflict, the avians struck a killing blow to the Vagoran army and retaken their ancestral lands in the Hollenheim Mountains, ending the Third Avian War. What followed was an uneasy thirty years of peace between the species, but Castle Finhöln would never again regain the crown's favor or trust.

The first thing Bel had figured out about Malthus was the man's boundless loathing for the castle. He could rarely stomach sleeping under its roof and never helped Pol with those small minor repairs that made the castle livable. He took immense pleasure in flouting his first-born duty to produce an heir, ensuring the ending of their line.

Pol, however, cared about the moldering timbers and stones. It was rare to find him away from his kitchen, but Pol's touch was everywhere salvageable in the castle, in the clean main rooms, in the steady supplies of necessities, in the smell of sage and lavender and lemon permeating his portions of the castle. Bel sometimes wondered if Pol had ever been off this mountain but doubted it. Sometimes he comforted himself with that fact, that Pol felt bound to Finhöln by blood, by duty, by his own deafness, and would never leave it. Would never leave Bel.

Should I set it? Pol asked.

Bel looked deep into the bottom of his cup, heart aching all over again.

Too soon, he replied, making the gestures small out of habit. The break was fresh in the new warden's mind—to set it would draw her attention. These first weeks were always the worst for Bel, enduring the break, waiting for it to eventually fade from the warden's mind, and finally, finally setting it—which usually meant breaking it all over again.

When Bel went for a fourth cup, Pol put his hand on the rim and shook his head.

Enough. You will make yourself sick.

I need to sleep.

Yes. But not like this.

Grudgingly he relinquished his cup, waiting as Pol instead filled it with another soothing concoction, this one of lemon and honey and chamomile and a splash of his precious supply of rum. It burned Bel's tongue, but by the time it hit the back of the throat, it went down like liquid sunshine.

Pol ran his thumb along the rim of his own mug of ale, eyes vague and unfocused as Bel drank down the mix.

Malthus and I spoke with the warden tonight. She is different, Pol finally signed.

We never had a woman before.

Pol shook his head. *Not that. She is kind. I do not think she will hurt you.*

W-i-s-h-f-u-l thinking, he replied, having to spell out *wishful.*

Again, Pol shook his head. *She is honorable, I think.*

Then what is she doing here?

Pol sucked in his cheeks, an expression that belonged on a boy but was endearing on him. Bel ignored the frown that accompanied the look.

Bad ones are sent here, he reminded Pol. *She is a bad one, too.*

Maybe. Maybe not. It has only been a day.

Two years will not change much.

This could be your chance, Pol signed, his gestures slow. He watched Bel's face carefully, making sure he watched. *Bel, you have been here so long. Maybe this time—*

He shook his head, ignoring Pol's words as he downed the last of the rum-honey mixture.

Thank you, my friend. You are too kind to me.

Pol huffed. *A little alcohol and you are all compliments.* He regarded Bel through narrowed, considering eyes for a long moment before he sighed. *To bed with you.*

He'd have no argument from Bel. Already the poppy milk and rum were muddying his mind, making each thought sluggish, as if swimming through thick cream. Giving Pol another nod, he ascended back into the dark castle. By the time he reached his bed, his wing and the accompanying pain felt detached from his body, there but transient, and he sank face-first into his nest of blankets.

Bel drifted on that drugged haze for a pleasant eternity before slipping into sleep. His last thought was the hope he hadn't taken enough of Pol's concoctions to sleep through sunrise. Broken limb or no, new warden or no, he'd a schedule to keep.

3

Lena's first morning as warden began with a gray dawn that promised a misty morning and a soggy afternoon. It suited her mood.

Thin gray light eked into her drab bedchamber from a small slit window in the east wall. There was little in the room worth illuminating. The single bed stood against the south wall, dividing the room into two narrow spaces just wide enough to turn around in. A nightstand with two drawers and topped by a chipped porcelain washbasin was the only other piece of furniture to grace the room. A laughably small fireplace sat in the north wall, and Lena doubted it could do much about the cold.

All in all, the bed may have been lumpy, the feather tick questionable, but Lena had had much worse. Five years of fighting on the eastern front at the crown prince's side against the avians had taught Lena about gritty hardship and stark living. On campaign, a bed was where you laid your head, be it a pillow or a thatch of grass. On campaign, you didn't ask what was served, just ate the questionable chunks of meat and colorless vegetables and tacky bread. On campaign, you wore clothes and armor and a thick layer of dirt and sweat and grime, baths too time-consuming a luxury.

The accommodations were actually better than Lena had expected, given the state of Finhöln. There was more space to be had in the warden's suite, but after taking one look at the mess Sir Ollander left behind, she'd thought it prudent to bunk with Alix in the old servants' corridor.

The suite was a disintegrating den of old papers and clothes, used candle stubs, and half-finished goblets of cheap ale. And the smell. Unwashed man with a tangy undercurrent of week-old whore. She hadn't decided if it was even worth cleaning out the suite when there was a perfectly useable room here.

Leathers buckled, sword strapped, hair pulled into three thick braids bound together at her nape, Lena braved the corridor.

It was cold and damp, the stones of the opposite wall weeping into cracks and crevices, feeding the bountiful arrangements of moss. It was also empty.

Pounding on the last door along the hall, she called, "Up with you! The day has started and so should we."

From Alix's room, she heard something that sounded suspiciously like a pillow hitting the door. Lena gave it another few knocks just to be thorough.

"I'll see you in five minutes for breakfast. I don't expect Master Pol to wait around for you."

Making quick work of the stairwell, Lena soon found herself in the much more agreeable kitchen. Unlike many of her fellow knights, Lena preferred staying in or near servants' quarters; not only were the spaces less fussy, they always had quick access to the kitchen.

A tidy fire roared in the main hearth, a cauldron already bubbling with what smelled like the base for a hearty dinner stew. From the sideboard, Master Pol marked her entrance with a shy smile and dip of the head. Lena returned the gesture, happy to see it was just the two of them. She already suspected she'd have a much easier time with the younger brother.

"Good morning, Master Pol," she said. "I trust you slept well?"

Pol nodded and eagerly flew into a series of lively hand gestures. Lena had learned in her meeting with him and Malthus last night that, unsurprisingly, Sir Ollander had severely slandered Pol's communicativeness. Not only was he adept at reading lips, he had also made a whole language for himself using his hands. While it would take a while for her to learn all of it—as Pol seemed to have a gesture for everything—it was a challenge she looked forward to.

Pol ushered her over to a steaming skillet and began heaping a plate high with buttered toast, creamy scrambled eggs, and blood sausage.

"Master Pol, if this is the fare every day, we'll become quite spoiled."

Blushing furiously, Pol rationed her another slice of toast and waved her towards the thick carving table in the center of the kitchen, ringed on two sides by tall stools. Taking her seat, Lena tucked into the food, relishing the freshness of the eggs and butter.

Soon, the unmistakable clomp of barely awake squire's boots echoed from the stairs. She was surprised to see Alix looking well-rested and spritely.

"Something smells great," Alix said with an appreciative sigh. She quickly fetched a plate for Pol to pile high. "Master Pol, you and I are going to be friends."

Pol made a huffing sound that Lena took to be his laugh. The rest of the food was bestowed upon the squire, and Alix lost little time depositing breakfast into her mouth.

"Sleep well?"

"Asleep before my head hit the pillow," Alix replied around a piece of toast, her fingertips glossy with melted butter.

"Good. From now on, I expect everyone to be up a half hour sooner. We'll have a short training session today, but I want to get you back on schedule. Afterwards, you'll begin work on the stables."

"And where will you be?" Alix asked.

"I've a prisoner to acquaint myself with."

Alix's eyes burned with curiosity, and she could already see her calculating how to follow Lena from the stables and sneak a look at the prisoner. Lena had shared what little she knew last night; that there was only the one prisoner, a young male avian. Being from Highclere, far to the south and comfortably nestled by the western sea, Alix had never seen an avian.

"Why's he here? What'd he do?" Alix had asked over dinner.

"We're at war with them," Lena answered. *"He fought against us. That's all the reason the king needs."*

As far as she knew, Castle Finhöln had been running as a prison for ten years now. Had the avian been here all that time? King Artemian's war with the avians had been going on, intermittently, for over twenty years now, so Lena supposed it was possible. He must have been captured quite young. Barely at an age to fight. But where had he been captured? And why this avian? Lena had witnessed many avians being taken prisoner; they were poor captives, lashing out at anyone who drew near. They'd lost many soldiers to captive avians, and so the human army now took as few as possible.

The king's latest crusade against the avians had begun five years ago, just as Lena entered service. It had been promising in the beginning, the Vagorans taking large swathes of land as they moved through the territory like wildfire. The border had swelled well past previous conquests, finally pushing into the avian homeland. King Artemian claimed a victory few of his ancestors had ever dared hope for—the avian capital of Aeriand was captured, forcing what remained of the avians to flee southeast to their stronghold of Hadria.

And that was when the campaign turned against them. The troops had been euphoric at their success—Lena remembered feeling invincible, like the river that had carved up the mountain, as she'd walked the wide streets of Aeriand in the crown prince's elite guard. But the campaign quickly ground to a halt at the base of Hadria. A mountain fortress, the walled city sat two hundred feet up, carved into the very mountain itself. Inaccessible without wings.

That had been more than three years ago now. Aeriand was still theirs, along with the Hollenheim Mountains and the western third of the Grass Sea, but still Hadria and the avian King Dartegn stood defiant. With the cliffs at his feet and the treacherous Gogona Mountains at his back, the avian king had good reason to feel confident.

From his perch, King Dartegn enjoyed raining destruction down upon the ranks. Lena had too many memories of seeking cover from the arrows and projectiles that came down like hail, ferocious and pounding. Sometimes all she'd had was her shield and a sliver of luck between her and death. She tried not to remember those times, saving them for her nightmares, pinned down, having to wait, just wait, pray that a stray arrow wouldn't find just the right angle. There had been such screaming, human and horse, and the *thwack-thunk, thwack-thunk* of arrows finding their mark. *Cowards, cowards,* Lena had chanted in her head, *they won't face us like warriors.* It'd been almost a year since Lena left the front and still she cringed at the whistle of an arrow in flight.

"How big are his wings?" Alix asked for the third time, scraping all the little bits of egg left on her plate for one last forkful. Lena had met few people who ate as fast and thoroughly as Alix. Even living her life with soldiers, who wolfed food down, Lena hadn't seen anything like it. Despite almost a year of hearty meals, Alix was still slight, still small for her age.

"They're bigger than you," Lena said.

"That's not saying much," Alix laughed.

When Lena had sensed someone easing the few coins from her pocket that overcast afternoon, she'd struck fast, grabbing a wrist so thin it nearly slipped her gasp. She'd held fast, feeling bones as delicate as bird wings, crushable. The feeling of those narrow bones had made her stomach turn. Lena still remembered the feeling of Alix's wrist held in her calloused hand. She remembered the dagger blades of Alix's eyes, defying her slim wrist and little hand, as she demanded Lena "*Fuck off*!" Those eyes weren't so hollow or sunken now, but they were no less sharp.

Sometimes Lena forgot, but the streets had raised Alix for fifteen years. She had to hope she'd do a better job, even from Finhöln.

With breakfast finished, she herded Alix towards the kitchen door, away from the larder. Small she was, but Alix could decimate a kitchen if given time. Bidding Pol farewell, Lena followed her squire out into the chill morning. The damp air hovered around her exposed face, leaving a cold sheen to her neck and cheeks. Mist plunged from the mountain, falling in languid wisps through the treetops and over the curtain wall.

She thought she caught a glimpse of white wings fluttering through the mist on the other side of the bailey, but it was gone before she could blink. Shaking out her gloves, Lena pulled them on with an uneasy feeling twisting her gut. It didn't sit well, a prisoner walking freely about. She'd trained Alix rigorously, but this avian was strong, and she knew well how lethal they could be in combat, what with six limbs rather than four. She'd taken enough hits from avian wings in hand-to-hand combat to know that a wing strike to the gut knocked the wind out of you just as effectively as any kick or punch.

Rather than leading them on a light jog to warm their blood, Lena and Alix instead tidied the bailey, hauling soggy wood, metal bits and pieces, and unidentifiable refuse into the corners, leaving the inner courtyard clear. With that accomplished, Lena led Alix through their forms.

⸻ ◆ ⸻

When they'd finished their third spar, Lena waved Alix off to her tasks for the day. The squire made a bit of noise about wanting to meet the avian too, but Lena held firm. This one was strong and in pain—in a word, unpredictable.

As a member of Crown Prince Arion's elite guard, Lena hadn't had to oversee avian prisoners, but it'd always set her teeth on edge when the prince insisted on interrogating the avians himself. There always seemed to be a cunning edge to avians' eyes; for a being who could both run on land and soar through the sky, there were many opportunities for escape. She'd never seen an avian on the defensive; even with their lands besieged, they attacked first, aggressive and brutal.

She steeled herself as she walked back into Finhöln, aware of Alix's avid gaze at her back. The castle stood utterly silent, not even the sound of rats scurrying along the floorboards to break the cold stillness. It gave Lena the impression the castle was still asleep, covered as it was in the light blanket of mist.

Venturing into the small wing Sir Ollander said the avian used, Lena headed down a narrow hall, stopping at a peaked doorway. Sir Ollander had just shrugged when she turned down his offer to show her the avian's rooms yesterday; after enduring a broken wing, she hadn't wanted to agitate the avian as he nursed his wound.

She knocked—and knocked again after a long moment of nothing. She tapped her foot, trying the latch. It opened easily, and she supposed she shouldn't be surprised—prisoners, even those with freedom of movement, certainly weren't allowed locks.

Behind the door lay a realm of scholarly bliss. One wall was devoted to bookshelves, the vellum bindings dyed deep burgundy, forest green, and sapphire, and the gilt embossing gleamed in the pale light streaming in from the bay windows set into the opposite wall. A fire roared in the hearth, keeping out the worst of the chill, and dozens of candles marched across the mantle, wax dripping in stalactites to the scuffed floorboards. Legs were the only clue that a table stood in the center of the room, the top covered in all manner of paper stuffs, ink, quills, stoppers, magnifying glasses, a lectern, cloth scraps, and texts. The massive piles of material lay in uneven slopes, several looking less than structurally sound.

Despite her training, a horrified squeak escaped her throat at the mess.

A shuffling sound drew her attention to an arched threshold without a door. A bedchamber lay beyond, and from the glimpse she caught, the space fared worse than the little library.

Massive wings and broad shoulders swiftly blocked her view. The avian stalked into the room, a scowl adorning his brow.

Lena held her ground, widening her stance. "Good day," she said.

The avian blinked at her before surveying her from head to toe. He said nothing, jaw clenched, the pulse at the base of his throat beating rapidly.

"There was no time for introductions yesterday as..." She cleared her throat. "My name is Lady Maddalena. 'Lady' or 'warden' will do perfectly well."

She waited expectantly, but the avian offered her only another slow blink of his unsettling eyes. She almost thought she saw his pupils dilating, sharpening that penetrating gaze. His wary silence made Lena's unease grow, and she assessed him as he did her, measuring the strength of his body, calculating the thoughts flickering behind his eyes. For a prisoner, he was certainly healthy and fit, making Lena all the more suspicious and cautious.

"Bel," he said finally.

"Very good, Bel. I have a squire with me, but she will stay well out of your way." Looking over the piles he had strewn about, she extracted a packet of papers from inside her jerkin. "I've brought new orders from King Artemian. As you can see, still sealed."

She held them out, impatient when he didn't immediately take them. Instead, he assessed the space between them before moving the smallest amount possible to take the papers. As he moved, he kept his wings behind him, well out of her reach. He'd bound the broken one to his side with gauze, his feathers cascading down his side and pant legs. She looked anywhere but at the broken limb, uneasy at the sight of it.

He broke the seal and scanned the top document.

Lena waited while he read. She recognized the scrawl of runic, the avian's written language. She knew little of it herself, but her interest piqued at knowing the king could write avian script.

His gaze flicked to her a moment, clearly wondering why she was still there.

"Everything's in order?"

"Looks to be."

"Excellent. When will you be finished?"

The corner of his mouth twitched. "Wardens take the translations when they leave."

"I see." Sir Ollander must have collected the last batch before his hasty retreat to Longbourne as dusk settled last night. "Two years is a long time for translations."

He remained silent, looking between her and the open door behind her shoulder.

Lena cleared her throat again. "My squire and I will be making necessary repairs in the weeks to come, but it's a large enough castle. We shouldn't all be under each other's feet."

Again, he said nothing, and though Lena had stared down dozens of haughty generals and sometimes a stubborn crown prince during her service, she felt herself beginning to squirm. She kept the rising heat from showing in her face with sheer will, tensing all the muscles in her body. Though he'd the longer tenure here, *she* was warden. She wouldn't give apologies or excuses.

"Well, then. We've both our tasks to see to—I'll leave you to yours. Good day."

He gave her the barest of nods, and her mouth pursed to see the relief wash over his face.

Clicking her heels, Lena left the prisoner, her long strides devouring the narrow corridor. Only when she'd made it back to the bailey did she begin to wonder who exactly had won that little exchange.

Grimacing, she suspected it wasn't her.

4

Sweat trickled down the column of Bel's throat, running into the thin linen shirt hanging from his shoulders. The day was hot, especially for this high in the mountains. The sun seemed larger in the mountains, like he could reach out and grab it in his fist.

It was nothing to holding the sun to his chest, high above the clouds. So high up, there would be nothing but sun and sky and the beat of his wings, holding him aloft, defying the sun in her realm. The humans said that was why the avians were doomed to destruction—Matella, their goddess of the sun, would one day smite all those who dared defile her realm. Bel knew better. So high up, he thought she must like seeing something up close for once.

But those days were long past him. It had been seven years since Bel took to the sky. Some days he couldn't remember the sharp cut of wind across his skin as he thrust into the sky; he'd grown weak, his muscles incapable of the strength it took to push off the ground.

At the thought of flight, his left, healthy wing twitched, pebbling with anticipation. He tossed his shoulder, sending the wing into tingles.

Bel strolled along the crumbling battlements, watching the sky ripple with color as the sun began dipping behind the jagged line of the mountain. Off to the south, the sky looked a saturated lilac, heavy with rain. Nearer, golds and roses infused wispy clouds, remnants of that morning's storm.

The castle still glistened from the heavy rain, puddles numerous and treacherously deep.

A movement from the stable caught his eye, and Bel watched the squire navigate the bailey, scowling at each unassuming puddle. When he spied Bel's reflection watching him from above, he turned his scowl on him and barked, "Don't get any ideas up there."

"Such as?"

Jaw thrust out as if to bat away Bel's taunt, the squire made for the hall, leaving Bel alone again.

It was almost a year into this new squire and warden, but Bel had stopped learning names that weren't offered. It was always Warden and Squire. They were the fourth pair to come watch over him and this decaying castle. There was no point to familiarity when, in a year's time, they would leave and he would remain and it would all start over again.

For how long?

Bel pushed that thought away. It did him nothing, just made something suspiciously like hope choke in his gullet. He'd been so impatient his first year, so desperate to heal and escape. If he'd kept his head, perhaps his wing wouldn't have been broken so badly. Hallan, the first warden, had been happy to discipline Bel—usually by aggravating the break he'd so dutifully inflicted his first day of service.

His body unconsciously shuddered at the memory of Hallan, his hard, black eyes and sharp narrow jaw set, always set, as if he found Bel, the castle, everything distasteful. Well, perhaps he did. He never failed to show his displeasure, either.

Escaping the memory, Bel's eyes swept over the bailey again, making sure everyone else was within. No Malthus slinking off to sell castle goods for a tidy profit in Longbourne. No Pol feeding the sparrows week-old breadcrumbs. No Warden spying, no Squire scowling.

Turning to face the rugged, alpine terrain to the east, Bel's gaze lifted skyward eagerly. It should be coming any day now.

Sunlight glinted over the mountaintop, catching his eye. *Ah, there.*

Riding an air current over the mountain came the stalwart form of a golden eagle, the symbol of the avian royal house. Winding down in a wide spiral, the eagle descended towards the castle, wings shimmering in the late day sun.

Bel's breath caught each time he saw the symbol of his nation flying free. The eagle's wings cut through the air like a blade, reminding him of a time when the sky was not so blue and not so empty, filled instead with beating browns and blacks and golds and whites and reds.

A pine overlooking the west corner of the curtain wall bowed under the weight of the eagle alighting. The sound of needles and branches snapping grated against his skin, and as the eagle folded her great wings, Bel checked the bailey below again.

Still alone.

Bel wedged himself into the corner and flared out his good wing for balance. Pulling the branch to him, he clucked his tongue, catching the eagle's attention. Fluffing and arranging her feathers like any good courtier, the eagle shuffled along the branch to him. Just out of reach, she bowed her head.

A hard knot of pain lodged in Bel's throat.

"Don't bow to me, friend," he murmured. "I'm not a prince anymore."

The eagle squawked and ruffled her feathers again, her sharp eyes dubious and unblinking. A moment passed. Carefully, the eagle extended her right claw, a long gray feather clasped in her talons.

Bel slid the feather free and tucked it safely away. Holding the branch steady, he thanked the messenger.

"Go, my friend. You're too beautiful, and they'd kill you for it."

The eagle peered at him, and Bel's chest ached.

"I'd like your company, but I don't want you taken from the sky. Believe me, it's a terrible fate."

Bowing again, the eagle gave him a sorrowful look before unfurling her magnificent wings. The last rays of sun gleamed along the barbs, burnishing the wings a bright bronze.

Wings outstretched, the eagle cooed at him and took flight with a mighty flap, bark and pine needles scattering in the sudden gale.

Brushing debris from his hair, Bel watched the messenger soar higher and higher, challenging the tall mountain peaks.

Bel stayed until she disappeared over the mountain, safe and out of Vagora. Longing rose in him, sharp and hot, tugging low in his gut. His next breath came out ragged, catching in his throat. Clutching the craggy parapet, Bel wrapped his arm and wings around himself, trying with his limbs to keep everything together and in place when all he wanted to do was shatter.

A breeze flowed over the wall, ruffling the downy feathers at the base of his wings. A shiver ran through him, the need to take flight a living, writhing thing just beneath his skin.

Darkness came on quickly as it always did in the mountains, the night visibly crawling along the treetops, cooling the air and the fever sluicing through Bel. When he felt able to lock away his hurt, he loosened his wings, draping them about his shoulders. It hid the small movement of pulling the feather from his pocket. He only glanced at it, assuring himself of the small runes carved down the center shaft, before tucking it and his hand into his pocket.

As he walked along the battlements, he began to run his thumb down the length of the shaft. All avians learned to read runic through touch as well as sight. He pressed the pad of his thumb deep into the grooves, needing to be sure; messages were so rare, so precious.

The messages had started to find him a year into his captivity. It had given him such hope in the beginning—Dartegn, his cousin and now the avian king, knew where he was, had to be planning his escape. But years slipped by and Bel's only connection to his people dwindled to the two or three engraved feathers smuggled to him each year.

It had taken him years to finally swallow that he didn't deserve more. Not when it was his own fault he'd been captured and crippled. Not when it was his fault that Maddok, Bel's brother, Bel's king, Bel's hero, had died with all his guard in an ambush seven years ago.

If it wasn't for Eamon, the warrior who'd taken charge of Bel's education and training when Maddok went to war against the human king, Bel doubted he'd even get these small messages. Sometimes he wondered if Dartegn even knew that Eamon still sent him news at least once a year. Sometimes he wondered if Dar liked the thought of Bel locked away by the human king, if he thought it was Bel's due for what had happened to Maddok. Bel certainly thought it was his due.

Bel and Dartegn had always been jealous of each other, both anxious to be by Maddok's side. Though he was twelve years younger than his brother, Bel had dreamed away his childhood imagining the glory he'd win beside his brother, how together they would defend the Adiiron name, Aeriand, and the avian nation from the gluttonous, heartless humans. Only a few years younger than Maddok, it was Dartegn who got to stand by Maddok's side, got to win the glory, and now he sat on Maddok's throne. Dartegn hadn't wanted Bel to go on that night mission with Maddok and his guards, had argued Bel wasn't ready. Bel had been anxious to prove Dar wrong, to prove himself to Maddok, so anxious that he'd missed the human ambush waiting for them.

When he came to the end of the message, he stopped walking and turned northeast, toward his homeland. He ran his thumb over the shaft again.

AERIAND TAKEN. FALLEN BACK TO HADRIA. MESSAGES NO LONGER SAFE. ON YOUR OWN LITTLE HAWK. EAMON.

Bel's heart skipped before beating, drumming, pounding so loud he thought the stones beneath him must shudder with the din. His hands trembled, his chest heaved, tears gathered in his eyes as a shout ripped from his lips.

How could Dartegn lose Aeriand? Maddok wouldn't have lost Aeriand! Bel wouldn't have...

The feather snapped in his shaking grip, splintering and biting into his palm. The pain brought him back, centered him on that curtain wall when his heart wanted to break from his chest and fly away, fly home.

There is no home anymore. Aeriand is taken.

The truth drew bile to the back of his throat. The stronghold of Hadria would hold. It had to. Dar just needed to regroup their forces. Hadria had never been taken. None could get to it without wings.

Bel sucked in a ragged breath and drew himself up. He let the wind snatch the shards of feather from his open palm, ash gray barbs rippling like a starless night.

Evening had descended upon the mountain by the time Bel shut himself up in his rooms. He looked about the small library where he spent his days scribing, eking out the small favor of continued existence from the human king.

Hot rage replaced the cold dread hollowing out his chest, suddenly tempting him to set fire to all the translations, all the books and charts and maps. Set the whole castle alight.

No. Bel had to be smart this time. He came here a sixteen-year-old fledgling, angry, scared, guilty. He was still all of those things, but now he was smarter. Now, his people just might need him.

The human king always corresponded in runic, which only a handful of humans could read. Bel had years of tracking the king's mind, seeing what texts he wanted translated next. That information had to be worth something. He had to try.

Clearing away space in his bedchamber, Bel shoved papers and blankets and empty dishes to the corners until he could take a steady, wide stance and stretch his wings. He bent his knees and unfurled his wings, no matter how much the muscles prickled and pulled. He positioned himself, arms out, legs planted, in the first of the ten *ariant* forms, the basis for all avian martial arts.

He would build his strength. He would train and watch, making himself strong. No more waiting. Dartegn and his people may have forgotten about him here on this mountain, but Bel knew he needed to escape. He needed to fly to them.

Until then, he'd bide his time.

5

The last of the ten *ariant* forms was of course the hardest. It demanded the wings be completely unfurled, legs locked, arms relaxed so that the wings kept the body in balance. It was all the harder when there was only one wing to help balance, the other still splinted to his side.

Bel's shoulder burned, the wing joint aching, but he gritted his teeth. He wouldn't fall, wouldn't even list. Tilting, listing, falling was the first year of training. He was stronger now, his body once again that of a trained avian warrior.

Well, for the most part.

Bel hadn't seen battle since the night of the ambush ten years ago, the night that took his brother and left him crippled. He'd thought he successfully scouted ahead. He'd thought the narrow pass was clear, his night vision much better than any human's—surely good enough to spot one, let alone a whole contingent, hiding amongst the rocks and crags. He'd thought it was true when he told Maddok it was safe.

He tried not to think like that, tried not to see his brother's proud smile when Bel reported back. It only welcomed pain in his chest and bile in his throat.

He'd make it up to Maddok, somehow. He'd fight for his brother's kingdom, any way he could, until he hadn't any strength, breath, or feathers left. He didn't know what awaited him beyond Finhöln, didn't know how his people would feel about a shamed prince. He didn't think

Dartegn would welcome him back, but his people needed him. He thought he knew the human king's mind; he could be of use to them finally. Dar might not welcome him back, but it was a risk Bel had to take.

He'd prepared for that day, that risk, for years now, building his strength slowly, doing the forms to mastery in the time it was supposed to take. Bel had nothing if not time, and instead of watching it pass like a curse, he used it. It'd taken patience to understand the new ways he had to move—compensating for his weaker side and his full-grown height. He'd come to Finhöln sixteen and gangly. Even after years of training with Eamon, he'd been scrawny for an avian, especially a royal. He'd topped out at his full height only a few years ago and weighed at least two stone more.

Necessary for the brute strength to defend himself, but it doused any small hope he'd harbored for flying again. His right wing just couldn't take the weight for longer than a short glide, if he was lucky. And Bel had never been lucky.

Bel shifted his weight forward, making the form a little harder. His shoulder and wing joint prickled and ached, and if he let it, the pain would make him think of all the individual tendrils of muscle drawn taut and beginning to fray like rope fibers. But he didn't let it.

Instead he focused on the cool of the dawn, pictured the wide-open sky, empty of even the sun this early. The last resilient stars clung to the rounded edge of the sky, their shimmer slowly veiled beneath a sheen of purple.

The rough tread of boots nearly sent him off balance. Anxiousness made a tight know of his guts as he came out of the form to the avid audience of the new squire.

Damn. After nearly being caught that first morning, he'd neatly avoided the two of them for days now. For three years he'd been training without a hint of detection, keeping to odd hours. It helped that the wardens and squires usually lazed about. Three perfect years, ruined. Damn, damn.

The knight came up behind the squire, her eyes measuring his movements and the strength of his back. He felt assessed, her gaze running from head to toe, leaving behind a prickling sensation.

The new warden couldn't have been much older than him, if at all, but that was still plenty old enough to have fought in the war. Had she been at the fall of Aeriand? Helped take it? The bottom fell out of his stomach at the thought.

He returned her gaze, noting potential weaknesses. She kept her hair long, though it was scraped back mercilessly in a knot of coils and braids. Bel wasn't above using it to get a good grip. She was tall for a human female but still a head shorter than him. He was wider, much wider, but that was true about all humans compared to avians. He thought he could exert more brute force, but there was something sharp about the warden, a lithe strength that hinted at speed and craftiness. If she got in his guard, she could do plenty of damage. She was hidden under layers of clothes, leathers, and a well-polished cuirass, but from the way she moved he knew a hard warrior's body coiled beneath. Her skin was tanned from the sun, though he thought much of it must be her natural color, and perhaps, to the human eye, she might be considered attractive with her thickly braided hair and full mouth and painfully green eyes, but there was something cold, edged about her. Something hawkish.

They took the other's measure for long moments over the head of her unabashedly curious squire.

"No wonder he's so big," said the girl.

"*Alix*," the knight warned.

"Is he even allowed to train?" she asked, throwing the question over her shoulder at the warden. Then, louder, to him, "Are you even allowed to train?"

Bel only grunted, not sure what would get him out of this both fast and unhurt.

The knight's gaze flicked down to the practice sword he held. His grip tightened instinctively.

He'd had the wooden sword for years now, adding weights to mimic the heft of a blade—avians liked their swords broad and heavy, all the better to swoop down from the clouds and cleft an unsuspecting enemy in two.

Pol had given it to him when he'd begun training. He suspected Pol had had Malthus filch it from the fourth warden's squire, but as usual, Bel never asked, just felt grateful.

A tendon in the knight's jaw ticked, as if she struggled to keep it shut instead of issuing demands. She seemed to weigh her words carefully when she said, "Who taught you to fight?"

Did she think a warden had deigned to teach him? He sneered at the idea.

"My brother," he finally said. It was something of a lie, one he liked to tell himself, but she didn't need to know that.

If anything, that made her tense more.

Bel felt himself tensing too, readying for a fight he wasn't allowed to defend himself in.

"Are you allowed to be training?"

He didn't know how to answer, but settled on, "I've never heard a rule against it."

With a bemused frown she said, "Wait right here," and turned on her heel, disappearing back into the castle.

Bel's mouth hung open as the echo of her boots faded. Was she honestly going to go check? The squire smirked, making him think so.

He angled himself away, keeping his weak wing out of sight. In his experience, squires could be just as cruel, if not crueler, than their knights.

The girl was the first to break the silence hanging heavy over the bailey. She was a slip of a thing, barely coming to the middle of Bel's chest, and something about her reediness made him anxious, as though if he moved too quickly he might accidentally break her.

Loping down the last two steps, she asked without pause for breath, "How often do you train? Were you a soldier? Have you been to the front? When do you train? Want to show me some moves?" Before he'd digested half the verbal onslaught, she'd taken a loose fighting stance, her eyebrow cocked in either invitation or challenge—Bel was rusty at reading facial expressions.

"I know you can talk, avian," the girl said when Bel still didn't make a move.

Of course, he could talk. Humans weren't the only intelligent beings. His early education included tutoring in the five languages of the continent, including both high and low Vagoran. The girl spoke low Vagoran, emphasizing her vowels and almost swallowing the last syllables.

"And?"

"So talk!"

"Why?"

She blinked at him. "Because that's what people do."

Bel decided she was a strange creature.

She tried a different angle. "Lady Maddalena says your name's Bel."

He grunted again.

"That short for something?"

"What?"

"Names like that are usually shortened from something else, to save time. Like Alix. Alixandre is a lot and I could be run through before I got it out."

"Why would you be telling someone your name who was about to run you through?"

She shook her head and gave him a pitying look, as if she thought him slow. "Because when you're facing down a rival in a duel, you're supposed to taunt them with your name, the one who's about to beat them."

"Is that what you do? Duel?"

"Oh, no," she replied, her grin sharper than a dagger's edge, "I fight too dirty for dueling."

This conversation was going in circles, leaving Bel exhausted by what the little human seemed to think was pleasant banter. Her eyes sparkled with a mischievous twinkle, and he suspected she'd gotten much more out of the exchange than he did.

Suddenly she hitched up her chin. "You didn't answer my question. Is 'Bel' short for something?"

"Yes." *Arubel. Prince Arubel Adiiron.* But he sure as hell wasn't about to tell a human that. Perhaps it was vanity to think even this scrap of a human might know his name, his full name, but he'd learned from his years with Hallan that there was safety in anonymity. People liked punishing princes.

He almost grinned to see the irritable frown transform her face. She opened that wide mouth of hers to protest yet again when the light slap of the knight's boots on the flagstones interrupted her.

Bel watched the knight approach with a hard face, but other than the quick cut of her eyes, he couldn't read her. She stopped on the landing, folding her hands behind her back. With her feet planted shoulder-width apart, it made her seem taller, as if she was about to address a whole contingent rather than just Bel.

"There's nothing in the directive stipulating a prisoner isn't allowed to train," she said.

Was she disappointed by this? She said it with a neutral air, hands still folded, stance still wide.

Bel nodded slowly, not sure what else she wanted from him.

The knight held his gaze for another moment before surveying the otherwise empty bailey. The space looked better than it had in a long while, perhaps the best Bel had ever seen it. The refuse and grime and gravel had been swept away, missing cobblestones filled in. The squire spent her afternoons rethatching the stable roof.

With the bailey clean, the knight had turned her attention to the great hall. He knew from Pol that she was trying to devise a way to fix the large hole in the timbered roof that leaked snow and sleet and rain throughout the year. The eastern floorboards needed replacing because of it. There was timber to harvest and cut and the not insignificant challenge of mounting the hall's roof. It was a steep ascent and the rotting wood looked rickety at best, even from the ground. It would take balance and a light touch.

It would be an easy enough task for Bel, but he said nothing. The knight was remaking the castle to her liking and he wanted nothing to do with it. The thought of her turning her attention to his meager, if messy, chambers nearly made him shudder.

"We've plenty of space," the knight said finally. "We won't disturb you." And with a tap to the shoulder, she had the squire moving to the opposite side of the bailey.

The girl watched him as long as she could, her head cricked so far back she looked like an owl.

Bel resumed the tenth *ariant* form. He knew there was little point—with that long of a rest, he should start over again. The scuffle of boots and intermittent clack of practice swords didn't fool Bel. He had an audience.

He held his position, wings flexing in the steadily growing light. For a few moments he didn't hide them, instead showed them to their best effect. He knew the brown base captured the light, burnished bronze by the sun; he knew the white tips glowed like fresh snow, almost painful to look at, they gleamed so bright.

He felt her eyes sweeping the length of his wings, leaving behind a prickle of awareness. She would watch him closely. He felt it in the weight of her gaze.

He swept his wing up and down twice in a long stretch before snapping it closed. The practice sword held tight in his fist, he turned away from the humans, disappearing back into the castle.

Bel had seen the knight's ilk before—hardened, strict warriors whose faces aged into a preternatural scowl. They lived for the routine, the code of their order. No insubordination or original thoughts for them, no whores or wine. They were respected but rarely liked, made fine generals but poor friends.

The knight waged war on the castle itself, on the vermin and grime it safeguarded. There was a relentlessness to her; none but his first warden had cared for upkeep. Most gave up training in the first month. Bel doubted it would be so with her.

She needed to be kept occupied. The castle presented a challenge, would keep her plenty busy. But would it be busy enough? As Bel shouldered the door open to his library, he worried she would eventually turn her full attention on him—not something he wanted.

He needed to be vigilant with her. Watch her even more closely than she watched him.

He sat in his chair, staring at the only empty space of his worktable. It was about a paper's width of space, surrounded on all sides by books, scraps, maps, and parchments. Ink bottles, some empty, most half-full, a few with their wax stoppers still intact, served as weights. A collection of quills lay strewn about. They were of his own making; when a bird willingly gave up a feather, he took it as a gift, carved and shaped the tip himself. The human king provided him with the best ink and quills, sent the supplies up with the food shipments every few months. But the best quills were made from avian feathers; long, multicolored works of beauty—unwillingly taken, harvested and cut away from broken avian wings for greedy human hands.

Bel picked up one of his quills, running a hand over the mottled gold and brown. It had come from an eagle back in spring, given as she flew north, flew home for the warmer months.

His throat tightened.

He should have left the castle when it was still under Sir Ollander's watch. The man could be vicious, but he was also lazy, complacent.

Bel remembered the new warden's sharp gaze, eyes burning so green it was like looking at new shoots of grass erupting into the sunlight. Set in her hard, hawkish face, those eyes brooked no complacency, no laziness or trust. She would be watching him, and she would pursue him into the mountains if he took his chance.

His training was almost done. He was almost ready. It didn't matter. She would be watching, waiting for his escape. Bel raked a hand through his hair, pulling at the tangles his fingers met. There could be no escape, not under the eye of this warden.

Two more years to train. Two more years in this hell.

Damn, damn, damn.

6

Excitement fizzed in Lena's chest, bubbly and bright. She wondered if this was what it was to be drunk. She felt as if her feet weren't touching the ground, that instead she floated down the carpeted aisle. An ornate crowd flanked her on either side, curious eyes watching her progress down the aisle their bodies made, waiting to see what her parents, Lady Margot and Sir Warrek, had created.

The thought skittered through her mind, making her feel the give of the carpet beneath her booted feet, but even the thought of her mother couldn't dampen this day. Perhaps Lady Margot had been knighted by age eighteen. Perhaps it had taken Lena a few years longer. That didn't matter today. Amongst the glittering crowd, with their sparkling jewels and glimmering gold and gleaming eyes, she felt herself a sun among stars. Where the ladies wore fine dresses draped from their shoulders and the men sported bright doublets of all shades, she was encased in armor, silver and gold metal in a sea of garish color.

The suit had been a gift from her father and when she'd first seen it, with its elaborate shoulder guards framing her head, the family crest with prancing winged horses emblazoned across the front, and the intricate etchings of starbursts along the gauntlets and greaves, she'd balked. *"Surely not—surely it's—are you sure?"* she'd babbled.

"Of course," he'd rasped. *"You've earned this, Lena."*

An unfamiliar sense of triumph had surged through her veins like liquid fire at his words, and Lena thought, almost didn't dare to think but couldn't help it, that she had finally, finally proven what a knight she would make. She'd done it, done everything asked of her, and today she joined the hallowed ranks that included her parents.

Despite the folded steel, the suit was still heavy. Lena had worried, only minutes ago, that she would clink and clank down the palace's wide basilica, that the polished marble and sandstone would reverberate with the sound of her inelegant stomping. Her mother always did say she was never light enough on her feet.

But instead, when the last buckle had been buckled, the last tie tied, she'd felt light, as if she would fly to meet the king. Most new knights were given their spurs together in one large ceremony, but that wouldn't do for the daughter of the two most celebrated knights in the kingdom. Sir Warrek trained many of the knights and soldiers who filled out the king's army; Lady Margot had singlehandedly saved many battles for the Vagorans. Ballads were written about how Lady Margot had never lost a battle, undefeated in combat both in the lists and the battlefield. Both were unparalleled strategists and it was whispered that if the king truly intended to intensify the war with the avians, they surely couldn't lose with the Montcaers at the helm.

Lena heard a small clink against her shoulder guard and remembered to keep her head as still as possible. Within the knot of braids and curls that had been made of her hair were seven long gold hair pins, one for each of the Maidens, framing her face. She herself was Matella incarnate, the goddess of sun and war, life and peace. She felt Matella with her, the divine presence hovering in the airy arches of the basilica, looming in the colored shafts of light slanting down from the stained glass. It made her fingertips tingle.

The basilica was resplendent in the bright afternoon sun, high arched windows letting in Matella. A breeze with a salty tang came in from the sea, mixing with the incense burning at intervals down the length of the great stone basilica. The smell was heady, filling up Lena's nostrils and separating her from her body. She didn't feel her footfalls, didn't see the crash and ebb of faces vying for a look at her. Her heart beat a staccato rhythm at the thought that today, she walked with a goddess.

Before her, on a wide dais, stood the royal family. King Artemian seemed to draw the light, the windows on the far side strategically angled to blaze sunlight onto the monarch and the throne. Mounted above the throne, catching the full brilliance of the sun, was a pair of gilded avian wings; it was rumored they were King Maddok's wings, taken after he was slain in battle and dipped in liquid gold to preserve them. They hung above King Artemian, framing his wide shoulders. His hair was unbound, falling in rich brown waves, held back by a coronet blazoned with rubies. Graying hair around the temples framed a face that was both weathered and bright, skin browned by the sun and eyes that sparkled with interest and intelligence. A crooked nose added intrigue to a face that was otherwise somewhat stern. His ceremonial armor blazed like molten gold, making it almost painful to look at him.

On his right sat Queen Ilona, draped in artful folds of ruby silk and brocade. The color matched her painted lips and the jewels shimmering along her forehead. A gold cuirass sheathed her chest, molded to her body to show a strong, feminine form. With her hazel eyes and golden hair, Lena thought the queen looked like a lioness, content in her leisure but always watching. On her lap was the king's ceremonial sword, sitting snugly in its gem-encrusted scabbard.

On his left stood Crown Prince Arion, a younger version of his father. The prince was close in age to Lena, but he'd already accomplished so much, leading the Vagoran forces against the avian-controlled Hollenheim Mountains. Lena felt her face flush to look at the young, handsome prince. It was no wonder women, from duchesses to scullery maids, threw themselves in Prince Arion's way on the rare occasions he was home in Highclere.

Other attendants stood along the wide, shallow steps of the dais, making an arrow of her path. She felt ushered along by the multitude of gazes on her back, as if momentum carried her not her own feet. That bubbly feeling had lowered to a simmer deep in her gut and her breaths came quick and shallow.

She was disembodied yet hypersensitive now; at once one with the goddess, her giddiness and excitement overwhelming, but all too aware of her body, of the sweat trickling down her spine to soak her hauberk, of her hands that shook and her gut that clenched. For a terrifying moment, she had to remember how to put one foot in front of the other.

Nearest the king on the left were her parents, clad in their best suits of armor. Lena was the image of her mother, similar armor, same dark hair and hawkish face—though, not as tall, face not as hard.

It was everything the three of them had worked Lena's whole life for. Her mouth ran dry and she had to suck on her cheek to form saliva.

Her mother stood nearest the king, tall and forbidding, her deep-set eyes watching the length of Lena's stride, measuring her gait. Those iron-hued eyes missed nothing.

Her father, on the other hand, was the one smiling face. Lined and pockmarked, tanned and weathered, Lena had always taken great comfort from her father's face. It was the face of understanding, of tolerance and patience. His had always been the steady hand at her back, the shoulder she cried on in those most desperate moments of weakness.

She took a deep breath, feeling the press of her cuirass against her chest, and was the better for it. She adjusted her gait, hoping it looked natural, and shot her father a half-grin.

Warrek was her father, her friend, her mentor. She'd left their manor home at a tender age, but Warrek had always tried to make a home for them at the academy, filling their chambers with plush chairs; eiderdown quilts and tapestries to keep the warmth inside; ballads and folklore and legends to entertain them; maps with crinkled edges to bring the world to them; and dogs to keep them company and cats to chase the mice away. When it came time to squire out, she'd wished her father was still in active service—he'd even considered it when Lena turned twelve. But, as in all things, her mother had had the final word, and it was to Lady Margot Lena went.

Lena liked to tell herself it had been for the best; her mother was the best knight in the land and her father, despite his love for her, hadn't wanted to serve again. Ever since the attempt on his life, he kept to Montcaer lands. Even now, he wore a high-necked gorget beneath his cuirass, and what the metal didn't cover a snowy white cravat did. All to hide the angry red line circling his throat, a deep divot in the flesh. The garrote-wielding assassin had yet to be caught.

Her eyes flickered from her father to the royal family and back again. The king was still too bright to look directly at, and she didn't dare stare too long at the prince. The queen had the same watchful eyes as her mother, as if waiting for Lena to find the one fold in the carpet and come tumbling down.

Finally she made the dais, finally she was ascending the steps. She stopped before the throne, careful to watch an empty space over the king's right shoulder. She thought the prince might be throwing a smile her way, but she couldn't be sure; she didn't dare to check.

An overwhelming hush fell over the basilica as hundreds watched the king rise from his seat. Fractals of light slanted off his great breastplate as King Artemian retrieved the ceremonial sword from his queen.

The king approached, and Lena held her breath. When he flicked his wrist, she kneeled, relieved when not even the smallest hinge squeaked. She didn't dare breathe yet could barely hear over her blood rushing as the king taking the sword from its scabbard. Its ring echoed through the basilica, and a satisfied hum burst from the crowd.

Lena kept her eyes on the king's knees, watched them bend slightly to—yes, she heard the sweetest sound, the small clink of the sword on her shoulder, could feel it press into her, not the edge or the blade but the weight; it settled over her, a cool sensation like sinking into and leaving a pool all at once. It was surreal, it was breathless. A slice of air whispered across her face as the king pressed the sword to her other shoulder, the blade ringing against her pauldron.

That giddy feeling returned, swelling inside Lena's chest. She was an ingot, hot and molten, ready to take shape.

Lena heard the king take a sharp inhale through his narrow nostrils. "I, King Artemian III, fifteenth of my line, recognize Maddalena Montcaer as knight of the realm. May she serve long and well. May she uphold the honor of her family and of her king. May she be my shield and my sword against all those who would threaten our realm."

Another whisper of air and the sword was replaced in its scabbard. Another sigh from the crowd and it was over.

Lena's heartbeat claimed the silence and she wondered if all could hear it. This was everything, everything they had worked for, wanted. This was too much and not enough—she felt hungry for that cool sensation to wash over her again, that sense of rightness and fullness. Instead the fluttering in her chest sank to her stomach, coalescing into a nervous knot.

She couldn't think anymore—there wasn't time—the king was reaching for her—she was taking his hand. She rose, and with the king holding their clasped hands high, she turned.

The sea of faces looked at her. A noblewoman near the front had on so much mismatched jewelry Lena wondered if she was actually robbing others and hiding in plain sight. A man three rows back was one of the few not looking at Lena, instead brushing a handkerchief along a slop of wine staining his doublet.

Lena could only stare back.

The gloved hand holding hers squeezed, a little too hard. Lena tried not to jump, let the king lead her in a slow turn about the dais. A cacophony of applause swelled, making the basilica pulse with the din.

Everywhere smiles were thrown at Lena, then flowers and garlands and wheat sheaves.

"To Lady Maddalena Montcaer!" the king boomed.

"To Lady Maddalena!" the crowd chanted back. The sound assaulted her ears, the tide crashing against the rocky shore.

Everywhere were smiles, even on her mother's face. Lena met that iron gaze and for the first time in her life, her mother bowed her head to her.

"Lady Maddalena!" cheered Sir Warrek.

The queen had stood and she clapped her hands slowly, out of time with the crowd. The prince still smiled, and Lena wondered if she was right to think it more appreciative than amused; there was something hot in it, something illicit. She dared not look long, feeling it too much in her hyperaware body, along her lips and neck, her breasts. Yes, better to look away.

Lena's heart beat and fluttered in her chest, as if it could escape and fly away to be with Matella herself, yet the pit of her stomach clenched in trepidation, for how could anything ever feel like this again? She held the king's hand, in the heart of the king's palace, the center of the kingdom, with her mother smiling, her father cheering, the crowd chanting her name. What could ever compare?

7

Sweat pooled in the hollow between Bel's collar bones before slicking down his bare chest. It was hot in the kitchen, hotter than usual, the hearth fire roaring and seemingly every candle in Finhöln gathered close. Pol had even lit the several lanterns he kept in case Malthus left for home in the dark—or a nighttime run. He sat on a stool in the center of the kitchen, feeling like a goose pie crisping in the oven. All he needed was a celery stalk and some butter.

Bel sucked down another mouthful of rum; he was drunk but not drunk enough.

He watched Pol's profile as the man flipped between two pages of the book Bel brought from his library. Pol liked detail—from precisely chopped carrots, to neatly resewn buttons, to the tidy lines of the garden, Pol liked to get things right. He didn't begrudge him that, Bel certainly wanted this done right, but he was starting to see double. Pol had been studying the same two diagrams for over ten minutes, and Bel, having nothing else to do, had drowned his nerves in half a bottle of rum. Malthus wouldn't be happy.

Bel lifted his wing, almost hitting his mark and brushing Pol's leg.

Just do it, he signed. Probably. His fingers weren't feeling articulate.

Pol's gaze flitted back to the diagrams, giving them one last look before coming to stand in front of Bel. Pol had become something of an anatomy expert on avians in Bel's time here. Bel had found the old medical text years ago and it'd helped Pol in more than one reset.

They'd done this often enough that there was something ritualistic about it. Candles and alcohol, an old book to preside over, initiation through pain. The ceremonial resetting.

This could be the rum talking.

I'm ready, he gestured.

Pol cocked an eyebrow. *I can see that.* He deftly plucked the bottle from Bel's grip, steadying him as he swayed.

Just do it, he repeated. *Don't want to be found out.*

Don't worry about the knight. Worry about the headache you'll have tomorrow.

Bel shot him a sour look as Pol eased behind him. Gently the man took hold of Bel's right wing. Pol's hands were warm as he slowly extended the wing as far as it could reach with its two breaks.

Bel gritted his teeth; even soused this would hurt like hell.

Pol gently probed the area, getting a feel for the two pieces of bone. A knot of blood and scar tissue had formed around the new break, and Bel could feel the heat of it pulsing against Pol's hands.

His good wing wrapped around his shoulder and side, and Bel breathed a little easier cocooned in feathers. He closed his eyes, seeking the serene stupor the rum promised.

There was the sound of Pol shuffling around, looking for a good angle. The fire crackled. Bel tracked a rivulet of sweat as it ran from behind his left ear, down his neck, over his clavicle, and across his chest. It soaked into the band of his trousers and still Pol poked and prodded.

Another pat, Pol's hands on either side of the break, and then, for a moment, nothing, sweet nothing that tasted like fresh snow, a cold bite. Then, pinpricks of pain, almost nothing, a flicker though, and he was aware of the heavy breaths he took, in, out.

Then pain. Hot, red. It rushed through him, a thunderclap, sparking from his back to his chest, his arms, down to his toes. It rang in his ears, an avalanche, a concussion that sounded of nothing but pure noise.

Bit by bit, Bel came back to himself through the pain. He fought it every step, wanting to go back to the nothingness. He hated this part, hated all of it. Bile burned the back of his throat, tasting like sharp, sour rum, and he almost heaved.

As Bel sat slumped on that stool, he wondered what his radial bone looked like. He had a vision of Pol sliding it out like a steel pipe, the flesh and cartilage left behind to collapse, and peering at him with one blinking eye through the hollow center, marrow dripping off the end. The pipe would have cracks, serrations where it had knit back together again and again. Would there be drips, places where it hadn't knit quite right? Bel heaved onto his hands and knees and vomited to the sound of a slow, steady drip. *Plink, plink, plink.*

His throat burned, but it was nothing to his right wing and shoulder. He slammed a fist into the ground, making it flare with pain too. How could the wing still feel pain? How were there any nerve endings left to shudder with the sensation?

A cool cloth ran up his back to hang around his neck. Bel shivered.

Hands drew him up off the floor, balanced him on the stool again. His hair was pushed off his face, and all Bel could see were Pol's eyes. Deep lines fanned out from the delicate skin around his eyes, little canyons of flesh.

Maybe not rum next time.

He shuddered—no, there wouldn't be a next time. He couldn't—he wouldn't go through this again. How long before his bone gave up and dissolved to dust?

Pol patted his face, not quite a slap, until Bel's eyes focused.

He fisted Pol's shirt, keeping him there when the man would have moved away. "Thank you, my friend," he said, no strength left for signing.

He didn't know if Pol managed to read the clumsy words spilling from a sluggish mouth, but he nodded, gave him another pat, and then shoved a tankard of water into Bel's hands, tipping it into his mouth. He made the sign for *Drink*—or maybe it was *Swish*—and went to fetch bandages to splint the newly set wing.

The water was bliss itself, but he could taste his own acrid breath on each swallow. He slowed to swish water around before swallowing.

Pol replaced his empty tankard with a small mug of his willow bark and lavender tea. This time, Bel didn't mind the bitter poppy milk, could barely taste it. He lost himself to the slow sips and rhythm of Pol winding the splint round, round, round his chest.

Life was easy in this state, eroded to only the essentials. There were his breaths, long and deep, expanding a chest and back that ached. There was the contraction of his throat as he swallowed, the intermittent brush of Pol's hands as he tied off the splint.

When he finished, Pol leaned back, hands on hips, and let out a gusty breath.

Stay still.

"Where would I go?" Bel laughed, but the words were lost; Pol had already moved to start snuffing candles.

Once again left with nothing else to do, Bel nursed his drink. It slid down his throat like water over rock, cool and milky.

From behind his closed eyes, he could tell the room was steadily growing darker with the death of each candle. When light only came from his right, where the main kitchen fire still crackled away, he slit an eye open to watch Pol moving around the cooking area. A knife tapped the cutting board, *tap tap*, then a sucking sound as it moved through something soft.

Where would I go? The question hung over Bel like a fog, drawing him back to a time when it was Pol, not him, asking. Bel had asked Pol once why he stayed, why he and Malthus didn't just leave. Yes, they received funds and supplies to keep Finhöln running, but neither of the brothers had any deep love for the castle. Malthus spent most of his nights in Longbourne, and there were places within the castle Pol refused to go.

You could go, Bel had once signed to Pol, back when his gestures were clumsy with newness. *Why stay?*

Pol had turned a deep frown on Bel, as if the answer should be obvious. *Where would I go?* He'd gestured at his ears that did not hear a sound, not able to keep Bel's gaze. The answer had resonated with Bel, sitting in his heart as a reassuring weight. He'd understood Pol then, perhaps more than he wanted, and while some of him pitied Pol that he thought his deafness should limit him to this mountain, a larger part welcomed the knowledge that at least he wouldn't be alone with a warden and squire. That he'd always have Pol. He knew it was an ugly thought, and so it remained unsaid between them.

It felt like he'd just closed his eyes when Pol was beside him again, urging him into one of the stools along the table. He went slowly, trying not to move his upper body, and wasn't too proud to lean on Pol. When he was situated to Pol's liking, the man brought over a tray of bread, cheese, and stew.

Eat. Fill your stomach.

Bel made a begrudging sound but dutifully picked up the spoon. He had no appetite, but experience had taught him that having a full stomach was best for the coming long night of sleep. He didn't intend to leave his room for at least a day—he needed the rest, and he couldn't afford to let the warden see him like this. Those hawk eyes of hers saw everything.

He chewed mechanically, still reduced to essentials. He focused on the clench and release of his jaw, the grind of his teeth.

He spooned the stew into his mouth until he hit the bottom then began ripping bread and cheese into chunks. Pol watched him from the hearth, arms across his chest, slowly drinking from a pewter mug.

With most of the rum purged, food in his belly, and a wing that pulsed more rapidly than his heart, the drunkenness had faded for the most part, but Bel still felt fuzzy around the edges. His vision was blurry and a nice buzzing warmed the base of his skull. Something moved his arms and hands, definitely not him. The poppy milk did its work, separating him from his body; the pain was still there but it wasn't his and he didn't care about it anymore.

He blamed the tea for not hearing the steps on the stairs. He only noticed someone standing on the landing when Pol pushed off from the counter, eyebrows nearing his hairline.

Bel raised his head to behold the warden standing in the threshold, taking him in. His body tensed, heart beating fast and brutal. But Bel, in his poppy milk haze, only chewed a hunk of cheese, eyelids heavy and slumberous. Somewhere in the back of his mind, he knew he must look insolent. But Bel, in his poppy milk haze, didn't care.

The warden cleared her throat. "You're both burning the midnight oil."

He was about to say that they'd been burning candles, not oil, but that part of him that wanted to survive kept his mouth shut.

"I wonder, Master Pol," she said, keeping her gaze on Bel, "if I could put the kettle on." She made a few rudimentary hand signs, *drink tea kettle heat.*

Bel's mouth tightened to see her communicating, however clumsily, with Pol. If he'd been sharper, less poppy milk, more stew, he might even have thought himself resentful, maybe even jealous. It didn't sit well in his gut; but then, nothing was sitting well tonight.

It looks like the warden needs something to help her sleep, he signed to Pol. Because he could.

Pol shot him an unhappy look before nodding at the warden.

"Something to help sleep," she said. *Tea sleep.*

I have the thing, Pol replied. *It will put you right to sleep.*

Make it strong, Bel added when Pol gave him a wide-eyed look.

Pol huffed.

With Pol filling the kettle and otherwise occupied, he and the warden had little choice but to look at each other. They both attempted not to—Bel looked to the corners of the ceiling, deciding he'd need to help Pol clear the cobwebs one afternoon when he wasn't one large throbbing nerve ending.

From the corner of his eye he watched the warden fold her hands behind her back and infinitesimally widen her stance. It was something of a subdued battle stance, but she looked too tired to be threatening. She'd shoved her feet into boots, but otherwise she had no leathers, no armor, only a loose sleeping tunic hastily stuffed into her trousers. Even the knot of braids she usually had was tamed into one thick, loose plait swinging from the back of her skull. She didn't look soft, per se, more like her edges had been dulled. A little. Though, the poppy milk made everything hazy, so it could've been that too.

He'd heard her and the squire hammering away all day today, trying to patch the great hall's roof before the first snows came. It'd been annoying, and for a while all Bel could do was count their hammer strokes rather than work—he'd stopped at two-hundred fifty-seven. But the hammering was to his advantage; he expected they'd both be exhausted, falling into bed after dinner not to awake again until past dawn, when his wing would be reset and he'd be safely holed up in his chambers out of sight.

Clearly, he kept forgetting all his plans went to hell nowadays.

He sensed she was looking at him again, the down at the base of his wings twitching, so he returned the favor. The woman was always assessing him, eyes searching. Bel never knew if he wanted her to find what she looked for, whatever it was.

"Are you all right?" she said.

He blinked, his addled brain fighting to make sense of what she'd said. He nodded, the move turning into more of a loll by the end.

Her gaze roved over his face, down his neck and arms. She looked at his loose fist holding the mangled cheese when she said, "You're drunk."

"Was," he agreed. A smile that had nothing to do with self-preservation crept onto his mouth. "Not a rule against it."

It was probably for the best that Pol was turned away and couldn't see Bel's stupidity, but damn it all, Bel was in pain, didn't want curious eyes on his healing flesh. Doing what was best for his body, for himself, shouldn't feel illicit, but under that gaze of hers, he almost felt guilty for what he and Pol had done. That seemed her way, looking for wrongdoing. Perhaps that's what she searched for when she looked at him.

Wasn't his fault she couldn't see what she looked directly at.

"No." She nodded at his bad wing, bound to his side. "Does it still pain you?"

"It always pains me."

He thought he heard her grinding her back teeth and held his tongue. But then there was something in her face. He almost missed it, but there, there it was, a flash, a twinge of guilt, or if not guilt then shame, or if not shame then unease.

Pol blocked it with his stocky shoulders and well-meaning smile.

She took the mug of tea from him, *thank you tea.* Pol beamed like she'd just thanked him with a damn sonnet.

After taking a sip of her tea and giving Pol a pleased smile, she gazed deep into her cup as if it would answer an unspoken question. She couldn't have been divining the leaves; she hadn't drunk enough.

"I suppose that's what I'd do too, if it were me," she said. "Get drunk until I didn't remember anything."

She gave a start, as if coming awake, before throwing another nod at Pol and turning on her heel to leave. Her boots echoed lightly on the stone until even that, too, was gone.

Pol faced him, a beatific smile on his face, and Bel grumped at his smugness.

I told you she seemed different. Honorable.

Because she gets drunk like us peasants? Bel began to mutilate the cheese again.

Pol shook his head, vehement, reminding Bel of a stallion who'd been bothered by a pesky fly one too many times.

Bel, listen. It had taken a year, but Pol had made Bel his own hand sign. It started with the wings or avian sign, thumbs intertwined, fingers together and straight, but instead of flapping his hands, Pol drew them together until the fingers of one hand wrapped around the other. Bel's heart always lurched to see his name, and now was no different. He gave Pol his gaze, dropping the lump of cheese.

I have watched her, her and the squire. They are different. I do not think they intend to hurt you.

Bel's good wing drew around him again. *They have all intended to hurt me, one way or another. The only question is how. And when.*

8

Usually, Lena didn't mind mucking out stables; there was something calming about being in the warm nest of hay and horseflesh, but today she counted the minutes and strokes of the pitchfork. Winter invaded the mountains, soon to lay siege to Finhöln and Longbourne far below. Just this morning, Pol had warned her that the season's first snow would be coming soon.

Bloody fantastic, to quote Alix.

It was already cold enough to leave frostbite on unattended fingertips, making her usually meditative task of mucking out the stables a real chore. It kept her body warm, but Lena had to wonder, if this was just the cold harbinger, would her hands start to freeze to the staff of the pitchfork when winter truly came. Even now her fur-lined gloves stuck to the frigid wood.

Thin morning light crept into the stables. Matella shone down on the mountains, big and full, and while Lena was the closest she'd ever been to the goddess here, at least physically, somehow Matella was far away. Little of her warmth made it to them here, even when the noon sun was high in the sky with not a cloud to be seen.

Lena knew now why King Artemian sent the new wardens in autumn. There was just enough time to get to the northern reaches before the mountain passes became unnavigable; the guilty knight would soon feel the bite of the king's justice with winter nipping at their heels. She'd thought her own guilt a heavy burden, a yoke that surpassed any other punishment.

Not so. Winter had yet to turn her full face on the mountains, and still the cold seeped into Lena's flesh, deep down to the bone, where it froze her anger, her resentment into an icy ball of despair. She kept to her chores and her tasks, from training Alix, to mucking the stables, to repairing the great hall's roof, so she could keep herself warm, could melt that frozen core of misery. She worried that if she didn't, it would lodge there forever, freezing her from the inside.

As she finished making one large pile of the horses' manure, Lena wondered which one of the Seven Hells was an arctic wasteland. At least if she ended up there when it was her time, she'd know what to expect.

"It's *freezing*!" Alix announced in a cloud of her own breath. The squire tromped into the stables, knocking frost off her boots.

"You say that every day," Lena said.

"Doesn't make it any less true. So, where are we off to?" she asked.

"Down into Longbourne. Master Malthus said a shipment of supplies is coming in and agreed to take me with him."

"Should I stay behind? Keep an eye on the prisoner?"

Lena turned to fetch riding blankets so that Alix wouldn't see her smile. Alix, scrappy as she was, was no match for the avian. He outweighed her by at least four stones. The image of him splitting Alix down the middle like firewood erased the smile from her face.

She'd seen little of the prisoner since that awkward encounter in the kitchen, three days past. He'd made himself scarce, which relieved Lena. His eyes were too watchful, and she didn't trust leaving Alix long in his company.

From what she'd surmised about past wardens, the state of Finhöln, and a few comments muttered by Malthus and signed by Pol, Lena assumed the prisoner didn't need to be kept under heavy watch to stay put. He could easily march through the massive hole in the curtain wall in the night while they all slept. Something kept him here, possibly the crippled wing, and Lena was curious to see what he'd do if she left.

Lena handed Alix one of the saddle blankets in answer, and the girl's eyes lit up.

"You think they'll let us in the pub? I remember something about ale when we got here…"

Lena rolled her eyes. Of course, Alix remembered that. Alix liked to squirrel away promises, digging them out again when opportune.

"If there's time…"

Alix whooped and began saddling her horse in earnest. Lena smiled to see her enthusiasm. Despite the cold that made them both irritable, Alix always sought the pleasures in life, small as they came.

"D'you suppose they've got meat pies there? Or beef? Master Pol's a good cook and all, but I've never liked venison."

"Since when are you a picky eater?"

Alix sniffed, making Lena laugh.

They walked the horses out into the bailey, a cold surge of air hitting Lena in the face like a physical thing. She gave a long shiver before turning to close the stable door. The two packhorses they left inside seemed happy to keep indoors. Yvain, who loved nothing more than a good trot, hating to be cooped up, made a chuffing noise and looked longingly at the stables.

"No such luck," Lena said, giving him a pat.

She and Alix mounted up, waiting for Malthus.

He came from the south tower to meet them. Lena thought he scurried everywhere more than walked; with his shoulders hunched and his strides quick, it made him look like he was in a hurry to commit a crime—or leave the scene of one.

He had everything covered save his face, as rocky and unforgiving as the mountainside. He'd never been a handsome man, Lena thought, and wondered if joy or pleasure had ever warmed his face. His scowl had chiseled a long, deep crease in his forehead and dug heavy lines to frame his mouth. His eyes were the only slow-moving part of him, taking their time to watch and assess. Lena could respect the thoughtfulness glinting there, but it made her wary too. This was a competent man, yes, but one not to be crossed.

"Good morning, Master Malthus," she greeted.

"Morning."

Lena waited, but he said nothing more. She couldn't help noticing he didn't have a mount and realized she'd never seen one stabled for Malthus or Pol's use.

"We've an extra saddle if you'd like," Lena offered. "All the horses could do with some exercise before the snow sets in."

He eyed the two of them atop their horses. "More trouble than it's worth, taking them down the slope."

"Is it not safe for them?"

Malthus shrugged. "Safe enough. Just makes a mess of the path when the frost melts."

"Melts? I don't think it'll get warm enough to melt today."

"That right."

She shifted in her saddle, feeling fidgety as Malthus stayed stock still, waiting. Her fingers itched to pick at her thumb. Clearing her throat, she dismounted. "If it's all the same, I'd like to bring them along. They could use the fresh air."

"Suit yourself," he said and turned on his heel to march out the barbican gate.

Lena glanced back at Alix in time to see her making an imitation of Malthus's scowl. A snort of laughter escaped her before she could smother it in her glove.

Alix stayed put in her saddle as their little party headed down the path to Longbourne. Lena's cheeks burned to think how ridiculous it was for her to be walking just because of Malthus. Why was it that she was warden, yet she never won these little exchanges?

The trek down to Longbourne took a little less than a half-hour on foot. Lena had her eyes trained on the ground, at once watching her footfalls and then Yvain's, her concentration so acute she didn't notice at first when they made it into town. The sharp tang of smoke teased her nose, and she looked up in time to see Malthus take a sharp left turn around the corner of a building.

She glanced over her shoulder to find Alix peering with marked interest at everything, head swiveling, eyes ricocheting from one face to another. Alix was used to the hustle and bustle of the city, and Lena wondered sometimes how the girl managed to keep her boredom at bay. Lena often itched for something to do, and they'd been here only a short time.

They followed Malthus around the back of a large log building. A wide porch stood sentry around the building's backdoor, and a small group of men worked to unload a caravan of carts onto the almost-empty porch. Malthus mounted the four steps to shake hands with a man presiding over the activity.

Lena watched with interest as canvases were thrown off with a satisfying snap, revealing more crates and barrels to be unloaded. She caught a glimpse of apples and pears in unlidded crates, and the smell of cider wafted from a small barrel, already cracked open on the porch. Malthus took an offered cup from the man and the two started to chat amiably like two birds on a branch.

She felt the warm, musky wave of horseflesh on her right and looked up to see Alix beside her. The girl had a gleam in her eye that Lena had become well acquainted with. She was starting to doubt she'd ever cure Alix of it.

She pointed a finger at her and said, "No."

Alix huffed. "You never let me have any fun."

"And where would you hide one of those barrels? Under your tunic?"

"You know you don't like it when I explain my talents," she said with a feline smile.

"Knights don't steal."

"Sure they do. And I'm not a knight."

"No, but a knight-in-training." She cocked an eyebrow, keeping the girl's gaze until finally Alix nodded with an exasperated huff.

Lena turned to the wide porch. The man and Malthus fell silent before she'd even reached the first step.

"Good day," Lena said.

The man nodded but said nothing. She looked to Malthus expectantly.

He sighed. "This here's the new warden."

"Suspected as much," said the man.

"Lady Maddalena," she said, since no one else was about to do it. "Pleased to meet you, Master...?"

"Vidar."

She inclined her head. One of her mother's favorite sayings was that manners would get you far. That didn't seem to be the case in Longbourne.

"Is this the shipment for Castle Finhöln?"

"That and more," Vidar said. He was carefully not looking at her. His broad face was ruddy in the cold, his bulbous nose almost purple. Though his nose was big, it fit his face, as did the graying blond hair that peeked out from the fur cap he wore.

"She wanted to see where the caravans came to," supplied Malthus.

"Run the trading post," Vidar said with a nod, jabbing a thumb over his shoulder at the building behind him. Even from her spot below him

Lena could see he was missing a chunk of flesh from the tip to the pad, making his thumb almost crescent-shaped. "Most everything that comes into Longbourne goes through here."

"Excellent. And what's bound for Finhöln? Is everything accounted for?"

"Haven't looked it over yet," Malthus said.

Right. "Did you need help loading up the carts headed to Finhöln? I've two horses with me, both strong enough to pull a load up that slope."

Vidar stood straighter, shoulders squared, as if to make himself bigger and block her view of the goods already unloaded.

"Not necessary, lady. The boys are used to their work. Spirits are always high when the caravan comes."

"Oh." Lena clenched her jaw to keep from offering more aid that wasn't wanted.

She met Malthus's gaze. He kept his face neutral, but his attention kept flicking to the goods being unloaded, a hungry gleam warming his eyes. She waited until he was looking at her again before swinging up into her saddle.

"You'll let me know when we're ready to head back?"

"If you want."

"I do. Either of you know where the mayor might be today?"

Vidar shrugged his blocky shoulders. "Saw her go to the pub earlier."

"Very well. Which building is the pub?"

"Straight across the town square," Vidar said. "My wife, Bryn, mans the taps. She'll take care of you."

That sounded more like a warning than neighborly advice.

Lena gave them a brusque nod and a short "Gentlemen," then urged Yvain back around the porch.

She had to make an effort to smooth her pursed lips. For the last six years, whenever she'd entered a town, people had opened their arms and homes to her. Knights were a symbol of justice throughout the kingdom, a person to trust. Thanks to her sentence, she was a disgrace, a person to scorn; she might as well have been a leper for all the kindness this town showed her. Not even a little politeness. And she had to take it. Lena ground her back teeth, the thought melting a bit of the frozen core of despair tucked away in her chest, drips of anger suffusing her body. She wanted to prove herself to these people, to show them she wasn't someone to scorn or mistrust, that she wasn't like Sir Ollander or the other wardens. She needed to prove she was a knight who had and would defend the innocent and abused.

A knot worked its way through her gut, making her feel squeezed and sullen. Her face was tight, her shoulders stiff when she dismounted Yvain before the stables built on the side of the pub.

Alix gave a gusty sigh. "You're the only person I know who's disappointed at getting out of work."

"It's the principle, Alix. We need to show them that we aren't like the other wardens."

"Well, sniffing around the caravan isn't the way to go about it."

"What do you mean?"

The girl snickered. "The postmaster probably takes a cut of everything that comes in. Doesn't need a *knight* looking at the books or taking a tally."

"But Malthus was perfectly open to showing me where the shipments come in."

"It'd look suspicious if he didn't. Besides, you wouldn't get anything for helping. Not their thanks. In fact, they'd thank you for ignoring them."

Wonderful. Runners and cons were judging *her*.

"Well, come on then. Let's try the pub. Perhaps the mayor will be more receptive."

"Doubt it," Alix chirped as she tied up her horse.

"You know, you're not acting like someone who wants free ale."

That feline smile of hers made a reappearance. "I can talk myself into anything."

"Yes, but can you talk yourself *out* of anything?"

Alix opened her mouth and closed it twice, making her look like a fish. Lena nodded decisively.

"We'll try it my way."

Alix gave a long sigh, holding it longer than necessary. "Lena, what's the point? They don't want our help. You won't get anything for trying."

"It isn't about getting anything."

Alix gave her a pinched look that said how much she believed Lena, but she dutifully followed her in without another word. Well, there might've been a mumbled, "Gratitude is something," but she chose to ignore it.

Lena mounted the steps to the pub and pushed one of the two doors open. She had to put her back into it, the doors a solid five inches of oak to keep the cold out.

A welcome wave of warmth washed over Lena as she and Alix stepped into the pub. It was a wide, square space filled with mismatched chairs and tables of various sizes, broken up in the back by a long L-shaped bar. A mighty hearth took up half the north wall, the inlaid stones sheltering a tidy fire. The crackling flames gave the space a warm ambiance, making the polished woods glow. It was all golds and ambers and burgundies. A few forest green cushions and one purple armchair gave a burst of color. Lena immediately liked this place. It reminded her of the great room of the chambers she shared with her father at the academy.

There was an overwhelming smell, not unpleasant, of the apple cider they brewed in Longbourne. Over half a dozen large casks of local and faraway brews were open, presided over by a tall woman with ringlets of red hair. Bryn, Vidar's wife, she presumed.

Lena headed for the bar, winding around the many unoccupied tables and chairs. She made for the barkeep, leaning her hands on the glossy wood of the bar to get her attention. Alix plopped onto a stool beside her.

"You must be the new warden," said the barkeep as way of greeting.

"Yes. I'm Lady Maddalena, pleased to meet you."

"Haven't had a lady knight before." Her hand wound round a pewter goblet, drying it with a rag. The motion was strangely hypnotic.

"So I've heard. Are you Bryn, Vidar's wife?"

"That's me. Been to see him, have you?"

"I came with Malthus to see the supplies shipment. Figured my squire and I could wait for them to load the carts here."

"You recommend anything?" Alix piped up from her seat.

Bryn graced Alix with the first real smile Lena had seen on the woman's face. Alix could have that way about her, putting common folk at ease. Alix liked to say it was to put *marks* at ease, making it easier to pick their pockets, but Lena didn't think she meant it. At least not completely.

"Everything here's the finest. Can't go wrong."

"Hm. Heard that before."

Bryn laughed. "Got a daughter with a mouth like yours, about your age," Bryn said, shifting her willowy body towards Alix, giving Lena her profile.

"Yeah? She around? Haven't seen anyone my age in a while."

In answer, Bryn called, "Violet!" at a threshold leading presumably to the back room.

A girl indeed around Alix's age came out from the back to the bar, wiping her hands on an apron. The girl had her mother's red ringlets, but where Bryn was dotted with freckles like a leopard's spots, Violet's skin was like cream.

"Take care of them, Vi. I'll finish in back."

But before Bryn could disappear, Lena reached across the bar to her. "Is Tilda Yarlsson here, by any chance? I was hoping to talk with her."

One of Bryn's brows arched as she slowly blinked at Lena. It was a long moment before she said, "Over there, in front of the fire. Her day to listen to complaints and claims and she comes here to do it."

"Thank you."

Rather than moving off as she'd seemed keen to do before, Bryn looked Lena up and down before leaning close, her gaze flickering to Alix. "It's not right, you dragging a nice girl like that into exile with you."

Lena felt the color drain from her face. She didn't even open her mouth to retort, since she agreed. A small part of her rallied, wanting to argue that she hadn't wanted Alix to come, had begged her not to, but what difference would it make?

At her hesitation, Bryn left for the back, leaving a stunned Lena in her wake. She stood there for another moment, only half-listening to Alix and Violet's giggling conversation.

"What's your favorite?" Alix asked.

"Cider. The house makes the best cider in town."

Alix leaned forward conspiratorially. "It really better than ale? I'm partial to ale."

"This'll be your new favorite." Violet winked. "Promise."

Lena put a few coins down on the bar then left them to it, pleased for Alix to find companionship. The girl liked to talk and sometimes her loquaciousness was wasted on Lena. If Violet provided distraction, Lena was grateful. She could give Alix this.

Bryn's words left a bad taste in Lena's mouth, and she didn't appreciate a resurgence of another of her guilts. She had enough to be sorry for.

She hadn't noticed the mayor when they'd first come into the pub because of the high, winged back of the armchair she occupied. A weathered old man with a battered homespun flat cap sat across from her, and they talked over something in hushed voices. Lena respected their privacy by hanging back and looking about the inn. Mounted heads of big game hung about, mostly elk, caribou, and moose. There were a few wolves, bears, and lynxes caught mid-snarl. She glanced away quickly. She'd never been one for hunting.

When the old man stood up creakily and bid the mayor farewell, Lena waited a moment and then took his place.

The mayor sent her a mild look over the rim of her mug as she took a drink. "I didn't expect to see you in town so soon," she said.

"I came with Malthus to see the supplies shipments."

"I see. I assume everything is to your liking."

Lena shrugged. "Everything seems in order. Malthus is the expert. I was just curious to see where it was received. I wanted to see more of Longbourne, too."

"Oh?"

Lena ran her tongue over the roof of her dry mouth. Why did all of her conversations in this town have to feel like a fencing match?

Perched on the edge of her armchair, Lena ran her palms up and down her thighs. "Mayor, I wanted to speak with you. I don't know how the previous wardens behaved, but from my one day with Sir Ollander, I can guess. I'm not like them—at least, I intend to be different. I want to help, if I can, but I'm not here to step on any toes."

The mayor chuckled. "Lady, I think you're the type who steps on toes anywhere you go."

It was Lena's turn to open and close her mouth. A hot flicker of indignation crackled through her chest.

"I'm sorry you feel that way, mayor. It wasn't my intention."

But the mayor waved her hand, as if to bat away Lena's words. "You like things a certain way. I can see that. Well, so do I. Longbourne is running just as it should and does best when it has little to do with that castle."

"I mean you no harm, and Finhöln's prisoner doesn't seem the violent type," she said, perhaps exaggerating. "I doubt you need to worry about him."

"Haven't worried about that one in years. It's the castle itself we're wary of. It's one thing to live in the shadow of a crumbling castle. Nothing wrong with that, lots of folk around Vagora live so. But in the shadow of a prison?" The mayor shook her head and took another sip from her mug. "Finhöln's a prison because of where it is, so high up, so far away. The king sent that avian and all the wardens up here to be forgotten. What does that say about Longbourne?"

Lena could only blink in surprise—that the mayor knew about the avian and that Lena hadn't thought of how the town would feel about Finhöln and its warden.

"The king forgets about us up here. Always has. He forgets a lot of things."

"The king has much on his mind," Lena argued, albeit halfheartedly.

"Oh yes, indeed. Got wars to wage from his cushioned throne."

It's solid gold and looks uncomfortable.

"It isn't safe for the king to be at the front," Lena said. "We need him safe and ready to make decisions."

"Any decision worth making would need to be a quick one. How far is it from the front to Highclere? You should know, lady. Five years' active service on the front, returned within the last year. Yes, I've read your papers."

"Five weeks' hard ride," was all Lena said.

"For a knight who's been banished, you've still a lot of love for the king."

"I made vows to king and country. That means something to me."

"Vows you broke."

"Only once. And it wasn't the one I made to king, country, or the people of Vagora, you can be sure."

Silence fell between them, filled only by the hissing crack of the fire. After a moment, she could hear Alix and Violet laughing about something.

The mayor took a drink from her mug, and Lena wondered if there was really anything in it or she just needed something to do. She watched as Tilda ran a finger around the rim.

"I think we've reached an impasse, Lady Maddalena."

It was the first time anyone had addressed her fully since Sir Ollander. It placated her, perhaps more than it should.

"I didn't come to argue politics, mayor. I enjoy a good joust as much as anyone, but I only wanted to make what amends I could for the wardens of Finhöln. I understand you didn't choose this for your town. I propose we make the best of it."

"How so?"

"I'm still a knight of the realm," Lena said, as much to herself as Tilda. "I hope you might call on me if there's ever a need. I may have been sent here, but I haven't been dismissed from service and I still have all the training and skills required of knights. If you ever have need of them, you know where to find me."

Determined to have the last word, Lena stood and gave a stiff bow from the waist. The mayor looked her up and down for a moment before giving a nod.

She wound back through the tables to the bar. The girls' laughter floated through the air, giving off as much warmth as the fire. Lena slowed her stride, giving them a few more moments.

When she cleared her throat, Alix swung around in her stool. "You done?"

"Seems that way," Lena said.

Alix drained her mug and then smacked her lips together. "You make a fine case," she told Violet. "But I think I'll need to come in and try again. Make sure it wasn't a fluke."

"The door's always open to you."

Alix threw a wink her way before hopping off the stool to follow Lena. Before they were even outside, she was whistling a ditty.

"I think you had a much pleasanter conversation than I did," Lena said.

"Probably. Not surprising, though. Better company."

Lena couldn't help but agree.

—◆—

Behind the trading post, they found Malthus and Vidar strapping a heavy canvas over the cart bound for Finhöln. They declined her offer of help, this time more congenially—perhaps because Finhöln's was the only cart left, not a spare crate or barrel in sight.

Lena and Alix trailed behind Malthus and the cart on the way back up the slope. She said it was to watch out for the goods, but they were, as Malthus pointed out, securely strapped down. Mostly she didn't want Malthus to watch her help Yvain pick his way around in the muddy mess of the path. She watched the cartwheels make two deep, oozing ruts through their footprints from this morning with dismay.

After the climb back to Finhöln, she and Alix followed Malthus around to the kitchen. Again, Lena offered to help with the load, ignoring Alix's exasperation. Malthus was about to refuse, probably thinking she'd want to stack the barrels and crates in a different way, when Pol came outside to see.

With a few gestures at the cart and the kitchen door, Lena explained her proposal, which Pol accepted graciously. Lena smiled before waving Alix down from her horse to help. The four of them made quick work of it, and soon the storage room was bursting with foods, spices, three barrels of cider, and paper stuffs.

Before Pol could lead Alix off to an early dinner, Lena pulled him aside. Using one of the hand signs she'd learned from him, she asked if the avian was inside.

Pol smiled, repeating her first sign—intertwined thumbs and flapping hands, an imitation of wings—with an affirmative nod.

Lena thanked him but went to check on the avian anyway.

She left behind the warmth of the kitchen for the drafty corridors. When she reached the door to the avian's chambers, she hesitated. Should she knock or just go in? Her fist hung in the air as she debated with herself.

Finally, she knocked twice before slowly opening the door.

The room blazed with candle- and firelight. It was almost steamy, wax dripping from the candles on the mantle, the window panes fogged and crying little streams of condensation. At the worktable, surrounded by ink, parchment, and ancient-looking tomes, sat the avian.

A loose linen tunic hung from his shoulders. There were buttons, but from the way the fabric gathered at his sides, she suspected he tied it in the back somehow too. One wing draped across his shoulder and upper arm, almost like a cloak. The other was still bound to his side.

She didn't like to see the broken wing. The sight of Sir Ollander breaking the radial bone still stung in her mind. Lena understood the need to defeat an enemy, but she never condoned torture, and that's what it was, if only from the pleasure Sir Ollander took in doing it.

How long would it take to heal? Well, not *heal*. Not properly. He'd had it splinted ever since her coming, some three weeks now. Lena had never watched an unset bone heal, not this long. Did it take longer, knitting together two pieces that didn't fit right? Her mind conjured up a twisted tree branch, growing in one direction until nature dictated otherwise, sending it in another, a gnarled knot to mark where things had gone awry. The image made her queasy.

He shifted, hiding the wing from her view, and she realized she'd been staring. Returning her gaze to his face, she watched his pupils dilate, focusing on her.

He held perfectly still, the quill in his hand held in a loose grip, as if he thought he'd need to abandon it for a better weapon quickly. It saddened Lena, seeing him always expecting the worst from her, preparing for abuse. He had the same look as he did that night in the kitchen, though his eyes were markedly clearer—like violence was imminent, expected, scripted. She had a part to play and he waited for her to take her cue.

"A shipment of supplies has come in," she found herself saying. "Malthus says some of it is for you. You can collect it when you're ready."

"Yes, warden."

"I believe Pol has made an early dinner. Should be ready soon."

His brow lowered in a slight frown, and she could understand—she was confused by her half-invitation too. She still didn't want him near Alix.

She cleared her throat, resisting the urge to scuff the toe of her boot against the floor. She'd run countless laps around the academy thanks to that little nervous habit.

"I'll leave you, then."

She made her retreat, not stopping to think until she was at the landing of the kitchen stairs. She rubbed a hand across her forehead. She was baffled that the avian had apparently taken no notice of her absence, content to play his part as prisoner.

But why? Why not leave?

Matella knew, if she had a choice, Lena certainly would.

9

Lena did as her mother always told her to do: survey the battlefield before formulating a plan, get a feel for the land, for the opposition. She did as her father told her to do as well: she took in the air—this time not so much to taste the land, but to fortify her spirits.

Four other cadets from the academy played a kick game with a soft ball, made from two cured pig's bladders and cotton. From her observations, Lena thought there were multiple forms of the game, and the other cadets rarely stuck to one set of rules—usually choosing the ones that favored the team already in the lead. It never struck Lena as fair, but then, the more she watched, the more she thought perhaps that wasn't the point of the game.

She watched from her place along the south steps as the four cadets, ranging in age from nine to twelve, raced around the south lawn, the two teams trying to keep the ball away from the other.

Lena wanted to be on a team. Wanted it with a fierceness that sometimes scared her.

Whenever she watched the cadets play the kicking game, something tugged at her, a yearning that made her chest ache. She'd felt it before, whenever Da gave her a quick embrace or Mama bestowed a pat on her head—a deep, tugging longing for *more*. To have arms thrown around her in a tight embrace that didn't end. To sit in the saddle before her Da like she'd done before they'd moved to the academy. To lie in the grass laughing in a pile of sweaty limbs and dirty faces with her kick team-mates.

Lena wrung her hands once, twice, before she realized what she was doing and stopped. Mama always said fidgeting would be the death of Lena. But Lena could never seem to stop; when she'd first come to the academy with Da, she'd started biting her nails to the quick, then the skin around them, until her fingers were a bloody, gnawed mess. Mama put an end to that by dipping her fingers in sour linseed oil. But then came the hair twirling—Mama cut her hair to her ears, making Lena look more like a boy than she already did. Then plucking at her eyelashes—Mama strapped oven mitts to her hands with two small belts. Then scuffing her boots, toe to heel, wearing out the premium leather—Mama had made her run laps around the academy for hours barefoot until she appreciated the quality of the boots. Mama had asked her before why she felt the need to do these things. *"It just needs to come out,"* Lena had answered, but that only seemed to aggravate Mama more.

A soft *thwack* brought Lena's gaze back to the kickers. The ball had gone wide, bounding towards her.

Lena's heart leapt into her throat as the ball rolled closer, closer.

She stood on shaky legs until her knees locked. She took the steps two at a time, scooping up the ball.

The other four cadets still stood out on the lawn, watching her. Lena felt too warm under their gaze, and for a moment, she hadn't any clue what to do. Nothing in the knight's code covered kicking game etiquette.

"Oi! Kick it back!" called the tallest of the three boys.

Lena looked down at the ball. How hard could it be? Similar to a leg sweep, only upright.

Da had always taught Lena to envision what she wanted to happen and then make it so. She imagined dropping the ball, and in its descent, wind back the leg and—

The ball shot straight up into the air, managing a narrow arc, before bouncing back onto the ground a few feet in front of Lena.

Her cheeks glowed red and she had to stop herself from reaching for an eyelash to pluck.

The other cadets looked amongst themselves before giving Lena a collective unimpressed look.

Lena bent and retrieved the ball before carrying it to them out on the lawn. She repeated to herself what Da always told her, that failure was often better than success when it came to learning, but it was a cold comfort under the cadets' stares.

She handed the ball over to the smallest boy. He seemed safest.

"Sorry." She cleared her throat. "What are you playing?"

"Two-Kicks," said the oldest boy, Derric. He was taller than Lena but only just, and despite being a year younger, he was in the same grouping as Lena. He always seemed to have people around him, always had a shoulder to clap and someone to laugh at his jokes. Her stomach fluttered around him sometimes, and she wasn't sure she liked it.

"What're the rules?"

"Not many," said the middle boy. She thought his name was Hans.

"Well, why not?"

"Gets in the way of the game," said the girl, Beatrice. Her scowl reminded Lena of those territorial female wolves in spring.

"Do you maybe need an extra player...?"

Lena's question hung there like a lame bird, doddering in the wind.

The cadets looked amongst themselves again, talking with their eyes, and Lena wished she knew how to do that with someone. Mama and Da could do it too.

"It's called *Two*-Kicks for a reason," said Beatrice.

"Two teams, two players," Derric added.

"Oh." Lena scuffed the toe of her boot. She wanted to ask if there were other games they knew, games that could have five players. Surely there had to be one—if not, surely they could make one up. Lena had watched and knew they made up half the games they played, only to forget them the next day and make a new one.

She was about to forge ahead, despite the looks the others kept tossing between them, when someone called her name.

Lena turned her head to see Kerry, the head cook's young son, loping towards them.

If it was possible, Lena flushed an even deeper red. Kerry was a year younger than her, but they'd often played together when they were little. He was the only other child who lived in the academy's main house, the other cadets' rooms in the two barrack wings. It'd been a relief to find a friend, especially one as hapless as Kerry. With floppy flaxen curls that inevitably ended up in his eyes and legs that were weak and knobby from an early childhood fever, Kerry was always on the verge of tripping. It'd endeared him to Lena, letting her save him from falls and guiding him around obstacles, but now, as she watched him approach with his ungainly stride, Lena only felt ashamed.

He managed to get to them without tripping. Lena stiffened as he stood beside her panting, trying to avoid Derric's blue, apathetic gaze.

"What, Kerry?" she whispered, almost in a hiss.

"Lady and Sir want to see you," he wheezed, hands on knees.

Lena looked up to make her excuses to the others, but the cadets had already moved away at the mention of her parents, the imposing founders and overseers of the academy. Da always advised her to learn when a battle was lost, and she thought perhaps this was what he had been talking about. Lena swallowed, nodded at the cadets who weren't even looking, and marched back across the lawn towards the main house.

She kept a pace that she knew Kerry would have a hard time matching, but he tried, nonetheless.

"Want me to walk with you?" he huffed.

"No." And she put on a burst of speed to outpace him. She made the south steps and was into the house before Kerry could ask her to wait up.

She took the servants' stairwell up to the second floor, heading for her Da's office. Whenever 'Lady and Sir' wanted to speak with her, it was always in her Da's office. She'd always been in slight awe of the room; it was where her Da held a sort of court, where people came sometimes to seek his and Mama's help, sometimes to get a child into the academy. Letters were always flowing into the office, bearing many magnificent seals from across Vagora.

The office sat at the end of a long, carpeted corridor. The hall was dim, the windows only partially visible behind the heavy burgundy drapes. The wood paneling was dark, soaking up the meager light and creating dark, pooling shadows in the corners.

She heard voices from the end of the hall, Da and Mama, and it made her stomach flop. For a moment, she wondered if she'd lose her breakfast.

She walked slowly, heel to toe, practicing. Mama always said she had the loudest feet, that if her fidgeting didn't get her killed, her feet would. So Lena tried to sneak up on Mama whenever she was home.

The voices reached Lena before she reached them.

"She's doing well, Margot. Extremely well." Da's voice was tired, heavy, his voice when a conversation had already gone on too long.

"Doing *well*," Mama spat, as if the words tasted foul. "Is that all?"

"I just don't understand what more you want from her. She's giving everything to this."

"I want her to be *more*, Warrek. Don't pretend like you don't want to see your daughter become the greatest knight Vagora has ever seen. You've wanted it too, ever since we put her first practice sword in her hand."

"She's twelve. She's got time yet."

"Warrek, what were you doing at twelve?"

A pause. "Fighting with Sir Yoric in the south."

"Earning distinction. Becoming his head squire. You'd already been with him for two years. You were already a head taller than all the others and a cut above the rest. I was serving alongside Ilona in the army ranks, halfway to earning my spurs. Lena hasn't even been squired out yet."

"She's been ready for awhile now," Da argued, though Lena thought some of the fight had left his voice. "You want to take her to squire. So take her. That's not Lena's fault, Margot. Stop waiting. Let her prove to you she's ready for this."

"If I thought she was ready, I would've taken her a year ago. But no. A year ago she was doing *well*. Today, she's still doing *well*. I need her to exceed, Warrek. She should be exceeding—look at everything we've done. Put a sword in her hand at four. Built this academy for her. She has double the opportunities the two of us had put together and still she's only doing *well*. I need her to be better."

Lena's eyes stung with hot tears, catching her off guard. She blinked quickly and backtracked, toe to heel, until she was back by the staircase.

She gripped the cool wood of the banister so that her hand would have something to do. Lena always needed something to do, especially with her hands—Mama thought if she had her hands always full, she wouldn't fidget.

A hot, dark feeling rose in Lena, a feeling she'd only had late at night, when she was supposed to be sleeping. It was like being in a rowboat without an oar, in the middle of a wide sea that ended only where the sky began; floating but adrift, safe but stranded, alive but impossibly small.

She straightened her spine, as she'd seen Mama do countless times when someone important walked into a room—or someone she needed to intimidate. She walked like that down the corridor again, making sure her footfalls were heavy and announced her.

Mama opened the office door wide, looking at Lena's feet. She shook her head and waved Lena into the room.

Da was seated at his desk, a small mountain of correspondence littering the right side. Lena always liked seeing the stack, liked knowing that her Da was so important that he got scores of letters. Lena had received seven letters in her whole life, mostly from her grandma, Da's mother, before she'd died, and Lena still had all of them, tucked away in a book of old Vagoran poetry at the bottom of her trunk.

When he nodded at one of the empty chairs before his desk, Lena took a seat. Mama remained standing, and Lena widened her eyes, trying to enlarge her peripheral—Mama always said not to let anyone get in her blind spot.

"Your mother and I have some good news, Lena," said Da, a wide grin overcoming his face. Lena always liked the small fan of lines that rippled from the corners, liked how they pointed the way to the soft brown of his irises.

A warm hand cupped the back of her head, running down the length of her short plait. "You're ready, Lena," said Mama. "It's time you squired out."

Little soap bubbles of excitement fizzled in Lena's chest.

"You really think so?"

Da nodded. "We've all been looking forward to this for a long time now. You've earned it." His gazed snapped to Mama when he said, "You're ready."

"Who will I squire with?"

"You'll come with me," said Mama. "Won't that be good?"

Pop, pop went the bubbles.

Lena nodded, knowing she should, and tried not to look at Da's throat. She'd hoped, really hoped, that Da would decide to go into service again, to take her with him on his journeys. She'd even hoped that she would maybe even go with Sir Yoric, the knight who squired Da; he might've been an old curmudgeon, as Mama put it, but he held great influence in the capital as King Artemian's head advisor.

"Yes, Mama."

Her Mama's arm wrapped around her shoulders, bringing Lena in close to her body. For a moment she was caught there, her face cradled in the crook of Mama's neck, feeling the strong arm that had defended Vagora for over twenty years at her back. She had just enough time to smell Mama's soap, light and earthy, before the arm disappeared.

That longing rose in Lena again, making her stomach churn as it mixed with the disappointment of not squiring with Da.

"We'll draft all the papers, and the day after tomorrow, you'll leave with me to Highclere. There are some people who I want to meet you. But you'll start your new training tomorrow morning, bright and early. Understand, young lady?"

"Yes, Mama," she said again. Maybe things wouldn't be so bad with Mama—she wasn't Da, and Lena would miss Da fiercely. He'd made the academy feel like home over the past seven years, had always managed to find time for Lena even though he had five hundred other youngsters under his wing. Still, right then, Lena didn't think she'd mind getting away from the academy.

Lena knew she wasn't Mama's first squire and she wouldn't be her last, but she could be her best. She smiled up at Mama, and for the fourth time in Lena's life, Mama smiled back. She leaned down and kissed Lena's forehead.

"You'll see—I know you'll prove to be a great knight, Lady Maddalena."

10

Noise echoed from the bailey, wafting in through the windows despite the latch locked tight. Bel buried his head in his hands as the squire's ballad reached a pitched crescendo, her voice holding on an impossibly high octave.

This wasn't singing. It wasn't. This was caterwauling.

Groaning, Bel dipped his quill in the inkwell, trying for a fourth time to get through the same sentence. Concentration had eluded him almost entirely since the new warden arrived. If it wasn't singing, it was the clatter of wooden swords in training; if not training, then hammering shingles to the new stable roof; if not hammering, then shouting, laughing, sweeping, running, washing, riding…Just constant, incessant noise!

Ten years Bel had lived almost alone on this mountain. Ten years Bel surrounded himself with the rustle of treetops, the trill of birds, the scuff of paper on wood. Ten years of forced solitude and silence. Broken in only a score of days.

Were all people as noisy as this squire? Was he just too sensitive? Did the birds' and deer's and badgers' ears ring with all the noise, too?

He abandoned the quill in favor of tunneling his fingers through his hair, tugging where he found tangles. There were a lot of tangles. He hadn't left his chambers in four days, not for anything, not even a bath. It went with the ritual, the ceremonial sequestering, but it always reminded Bel of those dark first months in Finhöln, when he'd been scared, in pain, unable and unwilling to care for himself. Bel swallowed down the sudden sour taste in his mouth.

The caterwauling annoyed him to the very core of his being, but he was annoyed with himself as well. If he was honest, he welcomed the distraction.

A thick volume sat open before him, a heavy presence in his little library. The yellowed pages followed him wherever he went, to tend the fire, to rest in his nest of blankets. He carried it on his shoulders, felt the weight of it push on his back and knees.

He rifled through the pages again, rethinking where he'd start.

This wasn't the first time Bel had pieced together a pattern for the human king's thinking. What texts King Artemian wanted translated spoke in their own ways, telling silent stories. If Bel had learned anything from his imprisonment, it was to listen for what made no noise, to wait for what didn't want to be found.

In some ways, he'd been expecting the demand for translations on the fortress of Hadria for a long time now—the campaign had ground to a halt at the foot of the mountain. Before his messages from Eamon stopped, Bel knew the humans had swept through the Grass Sea like wildfire. They burned further east, consuming Aeriand, but, as all fires eventually did, the campaign ran out of fuel when it reached the craggy Gogona Mountains, all but snuffed.

Still, looking through the volume on Hadria's history made Bel uneasy. Much of the text centered around the legendary past of the fortress and its almost mythical beginnings as a mine, where avians were enslaved underground, denied sun and sky. The slaves had eventually freed themselves—from humans or rival avians, the text didn't elaborate; old runic could be both epic and vague—and taken over the mountain, building it up into the fortress of today.

Bel remembered his one visit to Hadria, on a royal tour with Maddok. It'd been a dark, damp place, a warren of snaking corridors that sometimes went nowhere. Bel, flushed with boyish curiosity and dread, had followed one to a deep pool of black water. It'd looked like oil, inky and slick, gobbling up the light from his torch. He hadn't needed Eamon's admonishment to stay away from pools like that, already suspected old things from the deep lurked there, waiting.

King Artemian was convinced the way into Hadria was through these old mine shafts; he'd thrown away enough time, supplies, and human life trying to scale the high, sheer rock walls—he needed another way in. Artemian might be on to something; Bel didn't think even his people knew where all the tunnels led.

The volume by itself didn't worry Bel—it was all pomp and no circumstance. He'd be happy to translate the avian slaves' struggle for freedom, seizing the mountain and leaping into the sky, to freedom. It was one of the better avian legends.

But King Artemian didn't just want this volume. With the shipment of supplies the warden and squire had brought back with them had been a leather-clad sheaf of old maps. Pol had delivered them yesterday with Bel's dinner. Where the human king had obtained copies of Hadria's layout, from the fortress at the top to the tiers of tunnels, cisterns, and caverns beneath, Bel couldn't fathom.

But King Artemian didn't just want the volume and maps translated—he wanted them done with due haste, to be sent back the instant the ink dried. His dictate was quite literally spelled out for Bel in thick, harsh scrawl, the runic almost illegible in places. But Bel understood.

Never had Bel been on a deadline; the translations always went with the old warden and new instructions came with the replacement. Once, the king had sent a message to abandon a project and start on another. But this? This worried Bel, kept him up late into the night.

He looked from the first page of the volume to the top map, a detailed cross-section of the mountain. What chambers it showed had hasty labels, written in Vagoran, postulating possible names and functions for the various rooms. Heat crept up Bel's neck when his gaze snagged on *King Dartegn's bedchamber?*

They wanted him to fill out a map showing how to conquer the mountain and re-enslave his people. Bel dragged his fingers through his hair again, hoping for tangles. The tugging somehow made him feel better.

Bel had mistranslated before, had made it his mission to sabotage what he could of the king's secret intelligence on the avians. It was always small, a wrong word here or a north instead of east here, a little rebellion Bel could get away with since so few humans could read runic, let alone old runic—fewer still who would understand how he had mistranslated. It fueled him, the slightly altered words rushing through him, a drug, an aphrodisiac—it was boyish curiosity and dread, yet more, so much more, a deep yearning to push and find nothing, a success that always demanded more in return.

But this...this would be different. He hadn't a choice, he couldn't give them what they wanted. If King Artemian indeed found an abandoned tunnel the humans could dig into, or worse, a cave leading into the mountain, the humans could flood the fortress from the inside, flush the avians out into the steel-spiked nets they so loved to use.

Bel grabbed the map and was across the room before he could blink, holding the parchment over the crackling fire. He could smell the parchment heating, like sunburnt skin, the flames reaching for but not quite grasping it. It would be nothing to toss it into the flames, to wait until the king demanded the documents and claim they never reached him.

It would be nothing to do it, but it could cost him everything. The damned warden was sharp; he wouldn't put it past her to have inventoried the shipment. She knew there had been things for him, had told him so herself.

"Damn," Bel growled, pulling the map away from the fire.

He held it in shaking hands, trying hard to swallow the urge to at least crumple it, rip it to pieces. It was thick, would require force, maybe even teeth. A dark lick of longing curled through him, thinking of ripping the map apart with his teeth, chewing up all the labels, swallowing the words.

As quick as he'd jumped from his seat, he took it again, smoothing down the map.

He had to do this.

There was no other choice.

The human king couldn't know the whole of it.

Bel always began his projects deciding where he'd mistranslate, to make sure it fit with all around it, drew no attention, part of the whole. He knew already what he would change about the volume—he knew already what the king would want from it. The volume detailed the avian slaves' march through the mines, where they turned, where they found the overseer and strangled him with his own entrails, where they overpowered the door guards and rushed to freedom. The king would want to know their upward movements, where they began and how they made their ascent. He would couple that with the maps, using the slaves' journey and the maps to guide the humans.

The irony tasted like a mouthful of salt.

The map would be tricky. The size of each room lent obvious clues to the humans. He couldn't call the main hall a broom cupboard. But say a cistern was a storeroom...? Bel smiled viciously.

Two knocks hit his door, and Bel felt them inside his head. His thoughts popped like soap bubbles, turning to empty nothing once again. He came back to his library, in time to see the warden enter the room.

He didn't like how often she'd caught him unawares.

Adrenaline flushed through him as her eyes took him in, barely looking at his workspace. His face burned and his limbs grew hot, ready to move. If she looked, if she found out what he planned to do, it would be the end. He'd have to run. He would. This time, he would run. The snows would be thick soon, but his wings would counterbalance his weight, she'd never catch him, he could—

"Are we on schedule?" she said, snapping him to attention.

"Schedule?"

Her eyes gave him a once-over. "Yes, schedule. The king has given you instructions, I presume. Are you working at a proper pace to make sure everything is done in time?"

He opened his mouth to repeat her words as a question again but quickly shut it with a *click*. He made an effort to get his thoughts sorted, to push down his surprise and nervousness at having her burst into his library. Wardens before her had come in unannounced, no doubt a tactic to make him wary and paranoid, but he wasn't convinced that was her strategy.

Could she really be here to give him a work schedule?

"It will be done in time," he said carefully.

"You're sure?"

"I've done this enough times to know."

She raised one eyebrow at him, their gazes battling in a war of attrition, before finally she looked away to his shelves.

"What are you working on?"

His pulse beat so loudly in his ears he knew it had to be throbbing at the base of his neck.

"This one for now, these later," he said, keeping the maps angled away from her.

She gave the masses of parchment only a cursory glance before returning her gaze to him.

"And this will keep you busy for two years?"

"Thereabouts." She didn't need to know about his new assignment, or that a schedule would be precisely what her king wanted.

Her mouth thinned into a line. It made her look older.

"Do you think you could do more?"

He gave a noncommittal shrug.

Her lips completely disappeared into her mouth now. "Well?"

"It would depend."

"On?"

"Several things."

"Like?"

"Length of the book. The book's contents."

She made an unhappy noise deep in her throat. "Well, a schedule would help, yes?"

Bel caught himself before he could grind his back teeth. "Not necessarily."

"Still, I think it's something to consider. We must prove industrious. The king needs this information and we are the king's servants. We—"

"Prisoner."

"What?" she said, startled out of her diatribe.

"I'm King Artemian's prisoner. Not his servant. Lady," he added.

Stupid, he thought. His heart gave a sharp pang, readying again to move, to dodge a blow.

Their gazes clashed again, but there was no attrition this time, instead something else, something dark but inquisitive. She cocked her head infinitesimally to the side, as if to gain a new angle. Her eyes searched his—she was always searching, looking for something. Bel didn't know for what, but body and mind rebelled against letting her find it. He felt his chest tighten, as if whatever she looked for was there, and he had to curl around it, hide it away under flesh and bone and viscera.

"I should think they're quite similar, really," she said, almost too quietly for him to hear.

Bel's throat worked to swallow.

"Still, it never hurts to please a king," she continued, louder now.

"I only appease."

"In my experience, appeasement only gets you so far, and often it isn't much."

He sucked on his teeth, wondering if this was advice or a threat. "What I want isn't much," he said.

"You don't think your life is much?" She seemed surprised; her gaze became unfocused, pointed inward when she said, "It's the least you can ask for."

"The least and the most," he replied.

He didn't want for clothes on his back or food to eat or firewood to keep the fire alive. He didn't want for purpose or enterprise. He didn't even want for company—he had Pol and Pol, he'd learned over the years, was enough. What he truly wanted the human king would never give; it had taken him time, but Bel now knew he'd only have his freedom if he took it, reclaimed what was his and what only he would fight for. That was his lot—there was no older brother and hero, no Maddok to save him now.

"I will do this," he said slowly, "I'll appease the king and keep my life. That's all I'll do and that's all I'll get. To expect or attempt more is pointless."

He could see his words pulled at her, watched something painful and tumultuous burn in her gaze as the words came tumbling from him. It pulled him in return, a clench in his chest, as if a string had been sewn to his beating heart and she held the other end tight.

"Yes," she said, again barely loud enough for him to hear. Her arms wrapped around her middle, making her shoulders hunch in a way that made Bel flush with both pity and wariness. That string tugged him again, gave a lurch, and he waited for her to say something else, that he was wrong, to get back to work, something.

But what she did say, mouth barely moving to form the words, was, "I'll leave you now," and she did.

She shut the door with a soft *snick*, taking all the air with her.

He heard the distant slap of her boots along the corridor, but that quickly faded. Silence overtook the chamber, painful and absolute; the force of it pushed on his ears, making them feel hot and full.

His hand shifted along the maps, the crinkling of parchment finally breaking the spell. He worked to swallow the knot in his throat, his tongue dry and his mouth filmy.

With the sun dipping behind the mountain to cast long shadows over the pines and aspens and castle, Bel ended where he began, with his hands in his hair, fingers boring. He rested his head in his hands, the heels of his palms pressing into his eye sockets; it created a warm, pleasant pressure.

This afternoon had been yet another in a string of odd, inexplicable encounters with the warden. Bel didn't like odd or inexplicable; he liked to know what he was dealing with. One day she was a bear, direct and unyielding, willing to challenge to have her way. Others she was the fox, canny eyes watching, movements small, cards held close. Before taking her leave today, she had been the deer, skittish, flight her first instinct.

Bel's survival depended greatly on a warden's established pattern. In the first weeks of a new warden, Bel had to be watchful, careful, wary; learn everything but give nothing away.

He'd had many days now, yet there was always something new, something unexpected. He thought a pattern might be taking form, but it was too much to hope for. It was too much to think Pol might be right about her.

Bel sighed. His eyelids weighed heavy as he took in the volume, maps, and blank scraps of parchment that would eventually outline his mistranslations. Bel wondered if this was what the humans meant when they talked about signs of the divine. The timing of it all made suspicion burn low in his belly.

First an enigmatic new warden, and now these translations. Translations that, more than any before, could not find their way back to the human king without alterations.

The siege festering around Hadria would depend on these maps. Bel could only guess at how his former translations had been used—he knew without a doubt what these were for. These would be used, implemented, put to the test. And Bel had to be gone before the humans used or discovered the bad intelligence.

Weariness hung over Bel, descending like night now did over the mountain, gradual, hazy. A dark cloak to wrap himself up in.

His choice that wasn't a choice, not really, had consequences. He would have to run. He couldn't be here when he was discovered—and he would be discovered.

He knew what they'd do then.

There was something he wanted as much as his freedom and that was his healthy wing left unharmed, wanted one part of his avianness left unbroken, wanted it with a feral ferociousness that made him tremble, made him scared to even think about it.

He would escape, he would run to keep what was left of himself.

It didn't matter if Lady Maddalena was still his warden, didn't matter that she seemed different, didn't intend to harm him—he would sever that string that had connected them for one horrible, breathtaking moment, and he would run. She would chase him, oh yes, those hawk eyes of hers would scour the mountain, the entire kingdom to find him. She would make him regret what he'd done, would prove just how like her predecessors she could be. He would run and she would chase, but Bel swore, to himself, to his brother's ghost, even to the human's goddess in case she was listening, that she wouldn't catch him.

Resolve settled as a leaden weight deep in his gut. It didn't energize or galvanize him, there was no flush of excitement or rush of determination. He sank further in his chair, shoulders slumping. His face disappeared into his hands again, a warm, dark cavern.

He drew his wing around his left side, took comfort in the slick softness brushing across him. He didn't think of his escape but of Lady Maddalena's eyes in that moment. Bel thought that perhaps he understood her then, knew the look that crossed over her face. Truths could do that to you, could make you buckle. Sometimes truths were the worst things of all.

II

The worst part of the lashes scoring Bel's back wasn't the pain. It wasn't the lingering sting that cut down to the bone, wasn't the thought that the whip had struck so hard it'd left narrow gouges in his shoulder blades. It wasn't the blood running in rivulets along his skin, pooling at the small of his back, soaking his trousers and blankets and feathers. It wasn't even the pain that came in waves, steady waves, keeping time with a tormentor who wasn't there anymore, waves that made him remember standing there in the bailey, naked, chained to a post, exposed and vulnerable and trembling, waiting to take the next lash, for there was always the next lash.

No, the worst part of the lashes scoring Bel's back was the cold. It seeped into the opened flesh, licking along the red mess of it, making Bel imagine he could feel every severed blood vessel, every muscle fiber ripped apart. He was wrapped in the cold everywhere except his back, where hot blood still oozed, a counterpoint.

He buried his face in his pillows, burrowing. He breathed in his own stale breath, but at least it was warm. The cold kept up his trembling, and every quake and shudder sent little starbursts of agony up and down his body.

All this because he'd been hopeful. All this because he'd been stupid. Bel had woken this morning free; cold, hungry, but free. This time yesterday, he'd been outside, running, running, running as fast as he could from Finhöln, from Hallan. And what he had to show for it were angry, oozing lines up and down his back, lines that would scar into gnarled, silver stripes.

He groped for the hate that had filled him before, that had got him through that long afternoon of agony. It'd kept him warm while his body steamed in the frigid mountain air, his every pained gasp a dewy puff. Now it seemed too much effort, mind and body too exhausted for anything other than breath and cold and pain. Now nothing kept out the cold.

Moving slowly, Bel dug beneath his pillows for his treasure.

The inky feather looked worse for wear, barbs missing, the black dulled to an almost dark gray. But the words were still there, painstakingly etched along the shaft.

Bel drew it close, let the soft edges brush across his face, taking comfort in the feathery touch. Slow and steady, unwilling to miss anything— sure he must have, desperate that he must have—he ran his thumb down the shaft.

TAKEN LONG TO FIND YOU BUT GEESE SWANS AND DOVES HAVE ALL SEEN YOU ON MIGRATION NORTH. KEEP SAFE AND I WILL SEND WORD WHEN I CAN. BE BRAVE LITTLE HAWK. DARTEGN IS NOW KING. EAMON.

Bel read the message three more times, twice with his thumb and once with his eyes, though the last was hazy with tears. He hadn't missed anything, knew every letter, every word by heart now. He'd gone over the message again and again, combing through it as the whip cracked, searching for more.

But that was all. A handful of words, disappointing and precious.

Nothing about coming for him, nothing about Dartegn vowing to find him so they could seek vengeance together for Maddok.

He had to take hope from Eamon finding him at all—and he did, a little, let it buoy him just enough to stop from sinking into the dark sludge of misery that pooled around him. But those words made Bel hunger. They were dear but not enough. He wanted more, wanted to know where Eamon was, what he was doing, when he would come for Bel.

The hunger was the dark side of the message, but there was also hope. Small and fragile, Bel gripped it with both hands, unwilling to give it up, unwilling to see if he'd broken it in his clumsy grasp. That hope had made Bel stupid. That hope got him dragged behind Warden Hallan's horse for miles in the snow, got him strung up on a post, naked. It got him whipped and welcomed the cold into the warm gush of his flesh.

Bel hated the message for that.

An eagle had come two nights ago, nearly invisible in the hazy dusk. But Bel had seen. At first, he hadn't trusted his eyes, but as the eagle swooped down to him, the embers of his heart burst into flame.

As the eagle had perched on his windowsill, the bird bowed its head to him in a sign of respect Bel hadn't seen since that awful night. It'd been a balm to wounds that ran far deeper than Bel would admit, soothing over the jagged edges of his anger and grief. For a moment, he had been Prince Arubel Adiiron again, son of King Skandar IV, brother of King Maddok V, heir to the avian throne.

Bel hadn't realized, until that moment, that he was no longer any of those things. He'd forfeited all of them when he failed his king, his brother. The humans that ambushed them that night had not just taken Maddok's life, they'd taken Bel's as well.

Bel never knew that hope could be such a dangerous thing. In his life before, hope had been the sight of his brother, tall and strong, armed for war. It was Eamon's hand on his back, guiding him through the *ari-ant* forms. It was watching the persimmon trees that ringed the palace at Aeriand bloom in the autumn and the apple trees in the spring. Bel saw these things and knew he was safe, knew avians would be safe.

Now, Maddok was dead, Eamon somewhere east. The persimmon

trees had long ago bloomed and faded again, dormant for the winter.

Bel couldn't remember making the decision to do it—his head had been full of apple blossoms, the delicate white petals and growing fruits, and the overwhelming need to see them in spring. He remembered unlatching his window. Then nothing, not until the cold bite of snow sank through his old, ratty boots.

He'd run.

There was no turning back.

For one day and one night, Bel had been free. He'd scared rabbits and foxes back into their dens as he ran, his lungs full to bursting with air and joy and fear. He'd gorged on blackberries and mountain streams, kept himself warm with pine needles and the thrill of running, always running.

Bel liked to think that if his wing had only been healthy, he'd be gone from here, somewhere east, somewhere closer to Eamon and Dartegn and Aeriand. Maddok would be in Aeriand, his ashes spread toward the east orchards. He remembered thinking that as he stopped for a drink, that Maddok and apple blossoms and east lay ahead of him. If only he could—

And then the terrible trembling had come, the earth quaking beneath his feet. The stream had rippled, little tidal waves splashing against the gray pebbles. A horse screamed in the distance, the dense trees cutting the sound so it came in all directions.

Fear, dark and slick, coated Bel's insides. Even as he ran, blood and arms pumping, his fingers had been cold with it.

If his wing had been healthy, or if not healthy than useable, Bel would have flown. Flown high and away, stopping for only a moment to look back at Warden Hallan's face. The look of rage and defeat would've fed Bel's soul for years.

But the human king was crafty. He'd known exactly how to keep Bel close.

His right wing base throbbed, as if it knew he blamed it. He could feel his pulse there, and slowly, radiating from that old, unhealed wound, Bel found his hate again.

For this place, cold and damp all months of the year. Its stones gray and lifeless. The library the humans had made for him, full of avian secrets, secrets that weren't theirs to know or have.

For his wing, broken. Flightless. The ultimate avian shame, the punishment inflicted by his people on traitors and murderers.

But mostly for Warden Hallan, with his narrow dark eyes and chipped front tooth and full mouth that was always ready to stretch into a cruel smile for Bel. The man lurked around every corner, was in every dark niche. Bel could feel Hallan's breath slicking down the back of his neck, even when he was in another part of the castle.

Bel swallowed the bile creeping up his throat. It was one thing to feel the wounds Hallan inflicted—it was another to know the man liked it, craved it even.

A creaking sound interrupted the swirl of Bel's dark thoughts.

It was an effort to lift and turn his head, a trial to crack his eyes open. It probably should have worried him, but aside from the hate he felt, already dissipating, too much to sustain, he was tired, just too tired.

It took him a moment to realize the sound was his door opening. Despite his exhaustion, he tensed. It wasn't like Hallan to come after punishment—he'd rather keep Bel isolated, alone in his pain. It *was* like his squire, however, to come and look, poke and prod the avian prisoner.

He sucked in a deep breath, readying.

But it was neither of them. The figure standing in his library, at the threshold of his bedchamber, was too short to be either warden or squire. The figure shuffled closer, ungainly as they maneuvered a heavy tray.

A lantern glowed on the far corner of the tray, adding light to the dark cave of Bel's room. The yellow glow dimmed the blue moonlight slanting in from the windows. Bel caught the two points of colored light reflected in the wide eyes of the cook.

Pol. That was his name.

"What do you want?"

Pol came closer, slow and careful, nothing sudden. He made to lay the tray on the nightstand but stopped at all the clutter. Balancing the tray in one arm, he lifted the lantern to get a better look at Bel's nest.

Bel knew what he saw. More light only made it worse. The nightstand was a casualty in the war raging throughout the room. Dirty dishes sat strewn across the room, what had once been food caked onto the pewter in brown and gray and green crusts. Film coated half-full goblets, and something grew from a cluster of jars in the corner. Heaps of linen and blankets lay knotted together like a breeding ball of snakes, twisted and gory. This wasn't the first time Bel had bled. Clothes and blankets had been used, bled upon, used again. Wrinkles, rips, stains didn't matter.

Sometimes, when night came but the sky was still smoky with the remnants of day, Bel gloried in the filth. And that's what this room was, heaps and piles of filth. Grime had replaced the grout between flagstones, the windows were opaque with smoke and handprints.

Sometimes, Bel gloried in the filth. But not tonight.

The urge to curl up into a ball, spread his wings over himself and hide was overwhelming.

He waited, watched as Pol set the lantern down and began clearing space for the tray. Bel could see two bowls and a neat pile of bandages, could smell rabbit stew and yeasty bread.

It was all for him.

The thought slammed into him with the force of a charging warhorse. Pol had come to take care of him.

His next thought was, *Why bother?*

Bel snarled, swiped at the tray when Pol would've set it down. "Get *out*!"

Pol took a step back, startled. Stared at Bel.

A hot wash of something ugly and sour assaulted Bel, making him choke. He'd felt this before, that night, watching the humans swarm Maddok's guards, listening to the sucking sound of a sword gutting his brother. Bel didn't know he could ever feel this again, didn't think it was worth living with shame this strong.

He knew what he must look like to Pol, a cornered animal, scared and violent. He felt like an animal then, wanting the intruder out of his territory, his nest. This was supposed to be a safe place, only for him, but Bel didn't feel safe, only shame.

"Get. Out," he growled again.

But Pol only blinked.

Then Bel remembered; the man was deaf. Couldn't hear a thing. Bel thought he'd been stupid too when he'd first seen him—eyes downcast, shoulders hunched in an obsequious slump. He didn't look stupid now. And that made Bel feel worse.

When Pol made to put the tray down again, Bel swiped, catching the corner. The tray flipped, spilling its contents, bowls clattering, soup splashing. Rolls of gauzy bandage bounced and unwound. The bread hit stone with a crunch, the crust cracking and flaking.

"*Out!*" He punctuated with a jab of his finger, towards the door.

He held his regret inside but not the grimace of pain as his skin stretched, new, wet scabs opening to ooze again.

Pol took in the mess with slow eyes. He gathered the bandages first, making a neat pile of them before retrieving the bread and upended bowls. The soup was a lumpy mess, reminiscent of animal sick. The other bowl had had water, sweet smelling, infused with rose or lavender perhaps.

The man cleaned up the soup, gathered everything but the bandages onto the tray, and left.

The door closed behind him, and so did Bel's throat.

He buried his face in the pillows again, holding in a howl. He was an animal now, gave in to it.

He reached for sleep but couldn't find it, the dirty, unkept blankets and pillows not as comforting as they had been a moment before. He imagined he could feel the layers of his own sweat and blood on them, felt the old rubbing along the new.

Bel groaned. He hated Warden Hallan. He hated Eamon and his message. He hated this place and this room and this bed. And he hated Pol, for making him hate the few things he hadn't hated before.

He didn't need to look around the room to know what it was. Filth. He'd made himself filth by living in it. *But,* Bel thought, *but...*He had been Prince Arubel Adiiron, heir to the avian throne—Prince Arubel didn't *know* how to clean up after himself; he didn't know how to sew rips in his clothes; he didn't know how to wash his soiled linens and blankets; he didn't know how to build a fire in a fireplace or bake bread or wash dishes or even make a bed. Prince Arubel didn't have to know these things.

But Prince Arubel Adiiron is dead.

Yes. And so was King Maddok.

And it was all his fault. That was the worst bit, the portion he just couldn't swallow. If he'd only looked harder, if he'd only taken more time—but he'd wanted to get back to Maddok, to prove he'd be a good soldier, a good heir, a good brother. This was all his fault, and now he quite literally wallowed in it.

Bel drew in a wet, wobbly breath, feeling it shudder in his chest. Maddok and Arubel were dead. But Bel was here, and he'd need to learn. He didn't want to be an animal. He would have to learn, probably teach himself, because he couldn't...he couldn't run away again. He couldn't escape. The lashes began to sting again in earnest, as if to agree. He couldn't run, he couldn't go through this again—something withered inside him at the mere thought of being shackled to that pole again. So he'd learn, because he...he had to *live* with this. Because of him, there was no Maddok to save him now. Eamon wasn't coming. And Dartegn... Dartegn was king now.

But for tonight, he just wanted not to be anything at all.

He was drifting in that murky place between sleep and wakefulness, night and dawn, when his door creaked again. A familiar shuffle pattered around the library.

Bel watched from his dark hiding place as Pol set down a fresh tray on his worktable. In his other hand he held a heavy, lumpy sack, which he set down before the cold hearth. Pol began stacking coals into a cone, and then from the lifeless black heap slowly coaxed a fire.

With the fire crackling away, Pol stood and came through to Bel.

He carried more than a tray this time. He set down his first burden in the space he'd made on the nightstand before, then unfurled a clean wool blanket, dyed a rich, deep green. The blanket absorbed the light in the way wool does, dulling it, spreading it. Pol gave it a snap, working out the folds, and draped it over Bel's legs.

A strangled choke worked up Bel's throat, but Pol didn't hear.

He dipped a clean rag in the lavender water, held it up to Bel's face to show him, and then methodically began to dab at the edges of the wounds, careful not to reopen any.

Bel lay there in silence and let the man work. His limbs wouldn't move, too heavy to lift. Everything sank into a sort of comfortable numbness, the amber warmth of the fire seeping into the room, the wool blanket cocooning him in scratchy softness, the gentle lavender dabs cooling and soothing his fevered skin. Bel let out a long breath, felt his chest deflate as the air and some of the sting left him.

Another sound came up Bel's throat, something pained and re-lieved. It wracked his whole body, drawing Pol's gaze.

Bel shook his head, told the man to get on with it. He buried his face again, hiding it away from Pol.

Pol soothed a hand over Bel's hair, matted with sweat and blood. He made a sound in his throat, a sort of hum, a shush shush, as if he somehow knew the sound people used to comfort. It didn't sound quite right, though, more of a cluck than a shush.

Sshhkh. Sshhkh.

It was garbled, clumsy. And it broke Bel.

He felt it, deep inside of himself, down in the very dregs of his gut and soul, something shift and shatter. It wrenched a gasp from his throat, squeezed tears from his eyes.

Bel wasn't cold anymore, but hot, too hot. He sobbed, felt the wet gush of tears coming, tasted the saltiness along his upper lip. He sobbed and sobbed and sobbed, and it hurt, oh it hurt, deep down *there*. It felt as if deep down wanted to come up, out of his mouth and eyes, the tears pulled from the very core of him, unstoppable.

His teethed bared. Everything was leaking out of him from everywhere. *This is what it is to come apart.* He was dissolving.

But hands were there, warm and dry, that smelled of yeast and bread and other warm things. They stroked over Bel's hair again. Then an arm cradled his head to the crook of an elbow, took the weight. Bel filled a fist with Pol's shirt, hanging on.

Sshhkh washed over him, and Bel fell into the sound. *Sshhkh, sshhkh.*

12

Winter came to the mountains in a tempest, besieging Finhöln and burying Longbourne. The force of it had taken Lena's breath away as she listened to the heavy sheets of sleet batter the old castle. How could this heap of stone bear it every year? She saw evidence of winter everywhere in the castle, eating away at the stone, rotting the wood, freezing the windows and pipes—it was a slow consumption, and Lena wondered when Finhöln would simply give. It seemed inevitable under the growing white weight.

Lena had experienced winter before, but never had she *lived* it. This was winter in its purest, most complete form; it shaped the landscape, and the mountain had been preparing. Pines grew many needles, ready for the weight to mat them down, insulating the barky flesh beneath. Predators had hunted relentlessly, filling their bellies to prepare for a time of thin meals. Squirrels had buried away their treasures; birds found mates to keep them warm in the nest.

Longbourne too had been ready; after enough snow accumulated, its own weight made it slide off the steep rooves. The town may have been buried, but dozens of smoke columns rose into the sky, hearths stocked.

Winter came and the only one surprised by it was Lena.

And she *hated* it.

She hated the colorless world, the white ground and gray sky. She hated the blanket of dreariness that swathed the castle, dug in as they were so deep into the snow. And she especially hated the cold. People said you stopped feeling it after a while, that numbness set in. Those people were liars. She knew numbness, knew the lack of sensation when the field medic prepared an area for the needle or knife. It wasn't numbness if you could feel something, and Lena *felt* cold. It chased away the blood, cooling flesh until only the sharp bite of it was left.

Lena huffed, the steam making her nose run and lips tingle. The spade she wielded was a cold weight in her arms, heavier than it should have been. It wasn't strength driving her anymore but mere muscle memory and a dogged determination that this had to be done. Down, scoop, lift, toss. Again.

She hated it.

The cold was beginning to have a taste, a little metallic. She imagined biting into a hunk of rock tasted similar, grainy, hard, tooth-shattering.

When she reached the stable door, she discarded the spade and fisted her hands on her hips, surveying her work. A tidy, nearly straight canyon led from the great hall doors right to the stables. It was a vital, thankless task that had to be redone each time snow fell. Which was almost every other day now.

Lena struggled with the stable door, the hinges frozen and squealing in protest. She squeezed herself through the sliver of space she made and shut out the cold.

The stable was a refuge of hay and warmth, musky and humid with horseflesh. Yvain and the others didn't lift their heads, only blinked at her drowsily. They were roosting like content chickens, the heavy snow at least insulating them. Lena had tried exercising Yvain after the first flurry hit, but the warhorse had been apathetic at best, more than happy to quit early and return to the others in their straw haven.

She made the rounds, inspecting stalls and patting velvet muzzles. Yvain gave an affectionate nicker as she scratched his forelock.

"I'm glad some of us are enjoying ourselves," she grumbled. It was a blessing that the horses were content and warm, but that didn't mean she wasn't jealous of their comfort.

To her, the cold was restless nights, trying to find a warm spot for her feet in the blankets. It was wearing two pairs of socks to bed, and Lena had always hated wearing socks to bed. It was confinement inside clothes, blankets, stuffy rooms, the dark shelter of the castle. It was cold sweat and soaked boots and running nose and broken eyelashes. It was a sore body and an achy spirit.

"I should get back," Lena told Yvain, running a hand down his heavy neck. "Matella knows that girl stops the instant I can't see her."

That girl being Alix. With the bailey filled with snow, Lena had had to make do with the great hall and find new ways to continue Alix's training. Lena had set her the task of mastering woodcutting. At first Lena worried Alix wouldn't even be able to lift the axe Pol had given them, but as the girl set to chopping, she wielded the weapon with an unnerving gusto.

"If the worst should come, at least we'll be able to feed ourselves when this is over. I can find a job shoveling and Alix can chop." Yvain nickered again, finding as much humor in her poor joke as Lena did. Rather than lightening her mood, her words sat sour on her tongue.

With a final pat, Lena did battle with the stable door again. The cold hit her like a lance, dead center. Her whole body quaked in one long shiver, and she gritted her teeth.

She watched her footfalls in her little canyon, the snow compacted into the cobblestones from her tread. She'd found out the hard way that she made her own slippery ice this way.

As she opened the door to the great hall, scrabbling caught her ear and she looked in time to see Alix heft the axe for another swing. Except there wasn't a log lined up to split.

Lena had found it mildly amusing the first time she'd caught Alix pretending to still be at work. On the fifth, with her tunic plastered to her back from cold sweat, her frozen toes, and her soggy gloves, she only snapped, "You aren't fooling anyone, Alix."

Her squire didn't have the decency to look ashamed, instead going for wide-eyed innocence. "I was just—"

"That wood needs to be chopped or else the fires will die. A castle can't keep itself warm."

Even though Lena desperately wished it could.

Three fireplaces had sat unused for who knew how long in the great hall, two smaller ones along the east and west walls and the great hearth behind the dais to the south. It had taken a full day just to get them ready to function again, cleaning out old soot and debris. No amount of cajoling or threats could get Alix to shimmy into the chimney, so when they'd laid the fires, the hall hissed and popped with burning spiderwebs. Thick as cloth, the layers of thread burnt like fuses, the flames licking holes until the webs looked like an orange-rimmed mouth, sucking up smoke. The webs had smelled of burning hair.

Now all three fires roared with crackling flames. A stack of wood taller than Alix and as long as Yvain sat in the northwest corner, ready to feed the fires. They demanded Lena's weight in wood each day; yet another thankless task to keep them hearty.

But the great hall was warm. Shucking her two layers of gloves, Lena flexed her fingers and shook them out, relieved to have feeling trickling back.

Yes, the fires required almost constant maintenance to sustain. Yes, they were running out of available wood to chop and would soon have to go looking for trees to fell, something neither she nor Alix had any experience in. Yes, they hadn't managed to patch the roof fully and so some of the heat escaped out into the cold, requiring that much more fuel. Yes, it was trying, yes, it was enough work to keep two people busy almost all day.

That was the point.

With the snows here, claiming the entire landscape, there was little else to do other than maintain what they could. Lena had chosen her snow tunnel to the stables and keeping the great hall useable. It wasn't much, but it was hers to do. In defiance of the cold and snow, she would keep the tunnel dug and the great hall warm; *she* was the warden of Finhöln and she would have her way in something.

She heard Alix grumbling and turned to cock an eyebrow at her. Usually, after a few moments of unblinking stares, it was enough to get Alix going again on whatever it was Lena wanted her to do.

Instead, Alix dropped the axe and crossed her arms over her chest.

"This is pointless," she said.

"No, it's not."

"We don't even have to be *in* the great hall. We—"

"I offered to do lessons in the kitchen today, but you said, and I quote, 'Reading two days in a row is asking to go cross-eyed.'"

"We don't have to do reading lessons."

"We *should*, with the progress you're making."

Alix opened her mouth but said nothing. Lena felt her own words slap across her face; she too opened her mouth, to say something, to apologize, but Alix was already turning away.

Lena swallowed. "Alix..."

Alix shook her head, as if to bat Lena's words away. She drew her bulky wool scarf around her head and stomped away to the kitchen.

"I didn't say you were done," Lena called halfheartedly.

But Alix didn't stop, and soon even the sound of her angry stomps disappeared.

Lena drew in a long, humid breath. The fires warmed her from the inside out, but they had nothing to do with the heat radiating from her face. She knew she could be ill-tempered, but that had been uncalled for. To suggest Alix was stupid...it picked at a scab that had only just started to heal over.

"Damn it all." This cold was making them both irritable and sensitive, a dangerous combination.

Peeling away her outer layers, Lena laid them near the east fire, where they'd set up a makeshift rack for that very purpose. When she had complete feeling back in her hands, she took up the axe Alix had dropped and began chopping.

She handled the axe with less gleeful abandon than Alix had at the beginning, but there was still something satisfying in the downward thrust, the heavy *thunk* of steel meeting timber, of cracking a log down the center. It had a pleasant rhythm to it, and in the warmth of the great hall, it was infinitely preferable to shoveling snow. There was nothing beyond the swing, nothing to make her think about the walls of snow trapping her inside the belly of this old stone beast.

On the first day of snow, she and Alix had nested in one of the big bay windows of the north tower with a mass of blankets and a pitcher of warm cider to share. From their perch they watched the world turn white, watched as the land settled into a long, frozen sleep. They'd sat there the whole morning and most of the afternoon, just watching. Alix had lounged, sometimes chatting, sometimes drawing shapes on the frosted windowpanes. She luxuriated in the day of nothing to do, content as a cat to lie around and watch.

As for Lena, she'd hated that too. She hated sitting around, and she especially hated sitting around knowing there was nothing she could do.

The snow came like an encroaching army, taking all in its path. Lena watched as passes became impassable, the mountain cut off from the rest of the world. In that moment, Lena truly understood what it meant to be alone in the world, to know that no one would, *could*, come for her. The mountain had claimed them and wouldn't free them for months. Even with Alix sitting on the other side of the window seat, she felt the weight of that loneliness; she was a daughter of knights, used to the military lifestyle. She was used the noise of that life, the bustle of hundreds of cadets at the academy, the clatter and hum of being on the road, the rhythmic drum of marching on campaign. Even with Alix, it was so quiet.

She was alone up here, banished from king and country, from her parents, from the crown prince, from all she'd known, and it had only just begun. Winter was the longest season here on the mountain, the truest landscape for these rocky peaks. She would do all this again come next year. Yet in just a few weeks, Lena had already seen as much of the castle, the mountain as she could ever want to. A few weeks, and the familiarity made her heart sick.

But the worst thing, Lena had realized, sitting with Alix on that lofty window seat, was that it wouldn't end. They would serve Lena's two-year term and escape the mountain, but the shadow of it would always follow her. As much as her family name told a story of bravery and service, her sentence would cast a bigger specter over anything she had done or would do.

The thought had almost had her jumping from her seat, anxious to show herself it wasn't true. She'd needed to make it not be so with a desperation; she'd needed to prove to herself, to the whole world that she wouldn't just sit here and let this be. She wanted to race into Long-bourne, to demand they give her a way to prove herself a good warden, a good *knight*. But Lena knew, as quickly as she'd had the thought, that that wouldn't happen. She was trapped here in the snow without a way out.

Lena wiped away sweat and perhaps a few tears—from exertion, surely—with the back of her hand. Her next swing went wide, the axe catching on a knot in the wood she'd wanted to avoid. The blade stuck fast, not going with Lena's momentum, and she dropped the shaft before her wrists could overextend.

"Hells," Lena growled, shaking out her hands.

She stepped away from the block to catch her breath. As pleasingly numbing as the chopping was, it'd begun to aggravate an old mass of knotted, scarred flesh stretching from her left inner thigh over her knee. To make it worse, the cold made her ache. Never before had she felt so impotent, her joints rickety from the chill, her eyes heavy, and her movements sluggish. She knew she only exacerbated it by pushing when she should rest, but she feared rest more.

Lena pulled her outer tunic over her head, grimacing at the wet crescent stains from the undersides of her breasts. Then she pulled and stretched her muscles, alleviating some of the tightness before she set to chopping again.

If she was just a swing, a body in motion, then she couldn't think about the snow or the castle or how the days, short as they were, seemed to draw out into a long haze of white. If she worked herself to exhaustion, the long dark nights passed quickly, leaving no time to think about how winter had only just begun or despair that she'd do this all again a year from now.

⸻ •◆•• ⸻

She didn't know how long she stayed there swinging the axe, but eventually Alix crept back into the hall. She carried a plate laden with stew, a hard wedge of cheese, and a hunk of the dark bread Pol was fond of making. Lena took it from her when she offered it up with a nod of thanks.

Alix retreated to the other side of the hall as Lena broke to eat her midday meal. The stew was hearty, the bread savory, and the cheese had a pleasant, creamy tang to it, but it may as well have been porridge for all Lena tasted it. She ate it knowing she needed the strength, and though Pol's cooking was excellent, it didn't change the fact she'd been eating this meal twice a day for a fortnight, with no end in sight. Sometimes the stew had carrots, sometimes turnips, sometimes lentils or peas. Sometimes all four. Lena didn't check this time, just gave it a perfunctory stir and swallowed it down.

"Alix," she said, gazing deep into the dregs of her stew, "I didn't mean it like that."

The squire's gaze flitted towards her without directly landing. She gave a jerky nod before turning to the east fire again.

Part of her knew she could, should make a better attempt; the other part, the part that felt like frayed, broken threads, resented giving even this much.

"We can't just sit around and do nothing. We have to occupy ourselves."

"Didn't say I didn't want to do anything."

"No, but you've complained about everything I've suggested. If you didn't want to work or train or learn to read, then you shouldn't have come with me." There, she said it, it was out. Alix should've done as Lena asked all those weeks ago, when the world was still livable and Lena's heart was not so heavy, and stayed in the south.

"Oh," Alix laughed without humor. "Here's why you're mad. We're going to do this again, are we?"

"We aren't doing anything again, I'm just saying—"

"Look, I get it, we're supposed to be proactive and better ourselves and whatever. I just don't see the point in this." Alix waved a hand at one of the crackling fires.

"First, it's rude to interrupt. Second, the point is that it's useful."

"Why? This place was probably hard to keep warm when it was a nice castle with a full staff, but now...it's pointless, Lena. You just want to do it to show that you can."

"That's not..." It was. It *was* why she did this, it just made her grimace to know Alix knew that too.

"Lena, we've done what we could for the place. If you want, we can continue repairs in the spring, but there's really nothing to do now but hunker down and wait out winter."

"Then we should just sit around?"

Alix snorted. "Didn't say that. You're terrible at sitting around anyway."

"So let's do something to keep ourselves occupied. It keeps us warm, gives us a purpose. If you don't have any suggestions for something else as worthwhile, then let's get back to work."

Alix's apathetic face, mouth drawn to one side, nose scrunched, told Lena plainly that they had different definitions of *worthwhile*, but after a moment the girl got up to start stacking the wood Lena had chopped into a neat pile against the west wall. Alix sighed long and with feeling the entire way.

It was a hollow victory, but when Lena had finished her meal and threw herself back into chopping, she was thankful, as she always was, for the quiet, if prickly, company.

•◆•

They passed the next four days like that, quiet, taking turns chopping and stacking wood. For four days they did little else, and even though they spent almost all their time in the warm great hall, the aches in Lena's body grew. She became just the swing of axe, so much that her body didn't want to swing a sword or go through the forms. Morning training dwindled from two hours to one, to half, and finally, to nothing.

The cold made her want to give up something she'd done every day since the age of five. It wasn't a chore or even really training, it was something her body needed to do. The forms centered her, let Lena feel the stretch of her tendons and the strength of her bones. But she woke up each morning more tired than when she'd closed her eyes for the night, not wanting to do her forms, not wanting to spar with Alix, not wanting to rise from bed at all.

Lena hated it. She hated that her body ached, hated that her mind was weak enough to let it rule her. She hated that her knee throbbed, that every movement reminded her of the old wound from a time when she was useful, a wound she received defending king and country, a wound she didn't feel at all on warmer days. She felt like one of those old soldiers who complained about their aches and pains, who could tell when it would rain because their crooked big toe ached or a battle would go a certain way because their right shoulder hurt more than their left. She was twenty-seven, still in the prime of her life, and what was she to do with it? Waste it here, in this dreary place. She would be nearing thirty when she finally left, would be competing for rank and position against much younger knights, knights who didn't have the looming specter of Finhöln hanging over them.

On the fifth day, Lena rose creakily from bed, determined to put a stop to all this. It was enough. It was time to reclaim her routine, her way of life.

She rubbed the back of her neck as she climbed the stairs from the kitchen to the great hall. Her back was a series of knots, the muscles and ligaments a pile of tangled thread. She moved on to circle firm fingers down the back of her arm.

The flesh gave. Not much, barely at all really, but there was a softness there, a small yielding that somehow felt like a battle already lost.

Lena worked her fingers lower, feeling the same give in her forearm.

The chopping had only worked her into knots.

This softening body wasn't hers. Her whole adult life her body had been a hard pack of muscle, lean and strong; arms and shoulders for wielding sword and shield, a core to take the impact of blows, thighs that supported her fighting stance and could direct Yvain with just a flex, calves that could run for miles in full armor.

Lena hadn't looked at her own flesh in over a fortnight, too cold to spend any time uncovered. Now, she feared what she'd find.

This body wasn't hers; this snappish person wasn't her.

She took the stairs two at a time just to feel a familiar flex in her legs.

She found Alix already chopping—there'd been a war of attrition between them these past days; Alix hated to stack the wood and Lena much preferred to chop it.

"Leave it for now," Lena said, fetching their training equipment from its makeshift place on the dais. "We've put this off too long."

Alix seemed eager enough, abandoning the axe for her practice sword.

They stood opposite each other, feet wide apart, weight centered in a fighting stance. Lena cracked her wooden sword on Alix's, forcing the girl back, leaving her no time to do anything but go on the defensive.

They chased each other around the great hall that way, Alix managing a few theatrics, bouncing off steps and dancing around logs. If Lena had told her once she'd told her a hundred times—such things took up energy she needed to conserve, especially in a drawn-out fight. But Lena had no breath to spare to lecture Alix.

They fought so long the fires were in danger of dying, but still Lena pushed. She demanded everything from Alix and more, perhaps too much.

Lena smacked her sword into Alix's side, perhaps too hard, ending the round.

Alix huffed, grimacing, and Lena apologized between pants.

"Again," she said.

But Alix shook her head, sweat dripping from her chin. She unceremoniously dropped to the floor, as if her bones had turned to liquid, and laid like that on the floor, spread eagle.

"Do you yield?"

"Mmph," Alix groaned, pulling her practice sword up to her chest. She laid like a sarcophagus, hands folded around the hilt of her sword, legs straight together, eyes closed and face serene. Lena would've believed it, if sweat hadn't been running down her face and neck, or if she hadn't been cracking a wily grin.

Lena barked a laugh, conceding.

When she went to toss her practice sword on the dais, she noticed a form standing in the threshold to the kitchen stairs.

The avian—Bel—stood silently, and Lena realized she hadn't noticed him watching. If she wasn't so exhausted, she might've been slightly unnerved.

She found herself engaged in yet another one of their bouts of staring. It was always this way with him, silent, unmoving, waiting to see what she'd do, planning how he'd then respond. Lena had had times where she thought of herself as a weapon, as an extension of her blade swiftly bringing about death, but there was something slightly different about how Bel regarded her. It was like she was weapon, yes, but one without a steady hand to wield it, something just waiting to lash out, to cause indiscriminate pain.

Her nerves bled out of her pores, replaced by a sort of grudging annoyance. She'd better things to do than threaten him.

She lifted a brow expectantly. She swore she could hear a gauntlet hitting the ground.

He shifted his weight from one leg to the other.

"You leave your left side unguarded after striking," he said finally.

Lena almost scoffed in surprise. When had he seen this? It gave her pause; had he found a weakness, a possible point of exploitation in her laxed form and softening body? That didn't sit well with her; if he had to view her as a weapon, let it not be a dull one.

Bel gave her no time for a comeback, instead looking quickly around the great hall, dimmer than it had been in days thanks to the dying fires.

"It's very hot in here," he said, before disappearing down the steps.

That it was.

Lena blinked. Alix snickered.

The avian could be very...odd. She would try not to see his first comment as a threat.

Lena passed a still-prone Alix on her way to the wood pile. "Just going to lie here," Alix mumbled, and Lena waved her on.

She meant to get the fires going once again, but the stack's height drew her attention. It was already dwindling. She looked to where Alix had sunk the axe into their chopping block and found no new logs to split.

They'd hauled the last of the available wood in yesterday morning.

The pleasant hum of her blood from the mock fight quickly ebbed, replaced by a slick dread that made Lena's stomach clench.

They were out of wood. There was nothing left to chop, and the stack would last them two, perhaps three days with all three fires going.

She'd exhausted Alix, herself, and their wood stores. Pol had enough wood and some coal in the kitchen to last a few days, but Lena couldn't take that. The kitchen had to have fuel.

Lena's shaking legs gave out from under her, and she sat ungracefully on the ground. She stared at the wood pile, her achievement from days and days of toil. Soon to burn into nothing. She'd wasted all the firewood for what? To chop more firewood? All that time and effort and sweat—for nothing. All she'd done, all she'd worked for, used up, everything to go up in smoke.

Lena let out a humorless laugh. Oh yes, this was hell, and worse, a hell of her very own making.

13

It came early this year, the restlessness that overtook Bel once the snows arrived. He wished he could be like many of the forest creatures who found warm dens and slept through the worst of winter. As much as sleeping for so long terrified him, wasting so much of one's life in sleep, he had to admit he was wasting his anyways, sleep or no.

Bel struck through his last sentence, ink running in sloppy lines and pooling in puddles. A growl worked up his throat and while he didn't cast this page into the fire, it was close. It would've been his third discard of the day.

He was losing himself in a maze of his own making, the twisting tunnels of Hadria switchbacking until even he couldn't tell which were the true tunnels and which were dead ends. At this rate, he'd probably get the humans into the fortress with utmost efficiency.

Disgusted, Bel pushed away from his desk and took to pacing. But eating up the room in three strides and turning to do it again didn't soothe him, only made him feel like a caged animal.

Out. He needed out.

Bel set about the routine he always did before leaving his rooms; he strategically hid all incriminating pages, laid out correct duplicates, rearranged the mess of his desk a bit, and banked the fire. He'd had to filch firewood from the knight's pile at night for a while there, so thorough was she at finding all available wood.

Next, he pulled on the thick cloak Pol had made him several winters past. It was a patchwork of blue cloth slit up the sides to accommodate his wings. As he stepped into the drafty corridor, Bel sank his nose into the bearskin collar. He still didn't know where Pol had managed to find all the materials, or the time, to make the cloak, but then again, the cook was a sprite like that, full of tricky ingenuity.

He quieted his footsteps on the stairs as he approached the great hall. The knight and squire had abandoned their quest to keep the great hall warm at all hours of the day, instead making do with one hearth whenever they used the large empty room. It'd been a relief when they finally quit; it'd felt like walking through hellfire to get down to the kitchen. Though, it had been nice to know where the two of them were, predictable, so hard at work they barely noticed him, even when he walked through the room.

There was no one in the great hall, the one fire banked and glowing sleepily. He heard voices down in the kitchen and so made his way through unscathed.

The sky was clear for the first time in days, almost painfully blue above a world covered in white. Bel couldn't help the shiver that ran up his spine as he stepped from the lukewarm hall into the frozen daylight.

He navigated the snow tunnel the warden dutifully kept shoveled, careful to put his feet where existing prints and ruts already compressed the snow. He paid his footfalls and then the creak of the door so much attention that he didn't notice the squire already in the warm stables.

She sat on a bale of hay, chewing a piece of straw as she and one of the horses made faces at each other.

He hovered in the doorway for a long moment, tempted inside by the warmth and sweet tanginess of the hay, warned back outside when the squire's eyes took him in with avid interest.

Her gaze flicked over his shoulder before she said, "You're letting all the warm air out."

Bel sucked in a breath and came inside. He tried not to wince as the latch caught. The squire was a wisp of a thing, nothing to be afraid of, more curly black hair than anything else.

"What're you doing out here?" asked the squire.

"Same as you, I expect."

A spark of devilish delight lit her eyes. "Oh? So you're hiding from Lena too?"

Bel recognized a trap when he saw it, so he didn't answer. If there was one thing Bel still did well from his time as a prince, it was ignoring people. He busied himself with taking off his cloak and hanging it from a peg just inside the door. He felt exposed without it, the trace of the squire's eyes up his wings like a physical touch, but it was too warm to keep it on.

Rummaging through the supply cabinet, he found the brush he liked and a clean rag.

He hesitated only a moment, then went to his favorite of the four horses quartered here. He called him Gray for obvious reasons. The gray turned to silver on his flanks, so deep in some places that it seemed blue. When he moved in the right light, the dappled gray spots looked like sunlight glimmering over water.

Gray had the most attitude Bel had ever found in the horses stabled at Finhöln. He sometimes imagined it was Gray who was doing Bel the favor by letting him groom the horse's coat. The gelding stood two hands taller than the other horses, his thick legs and flank made for working, his broad chest stretched wide over heavy muscle. Most of the wardens' horses Bel had seen were sorry animals, overworked. The winter was the worst, left in the stable to stand in stalls for days at a time.

Bel had always made a habit of looking in on the horses. He liked the beasts, liked how gentle they could be. He liked being in their warm realm, liked the comfort of their soft breaths and muzzles. At first, they were usually wary of his wings and the rustling sounds they made but grew accustomed to him, especially when his presence meant a long, thorough brush down.

Gray had only blinked at him the first time Bel came, nickering once as if to say, *Well, get on with it*. He struck Bel as a warrior at ease, content to laze about, feasting on hay and idleness. But the warhorse was meant for action, and Bel longed to see him at work.

As an avian, he'd never had a need for a horse—travelling overland was much slower and more arduous than just catching an updraft. He still didn't know how to ride, knew that trying to learn would cross a line he wasn't willing to test. However much past wardens had neglected their animals and may have turned a blind eye to the free care he provided, they would've seen learning to ride as preparation for escape. Not to mention, horse theft, especially warhorse theft, was a high crime in Vagora.

Bel held out his palm for Gray, letting the horse snuffle and nuzzle at him. When he didn't find any treats, Gray dropped his head to give Bel a horse nod. He was free to proceed.

He could still feel the squire watching him, but she'd stayed curiously quiet. The other horses were at attention, looking forward to their turn under his brush. The horse she'd been playing with now ignored her, instead watching Bel's progress with Gray impatiently.

"That's Lena's horse," the squire finally said, her voice neutral. Not quite a warning.

"Yes." He'd certainly think so, given Gray was much too big for the squire and he was a born, bred, and trained warhorse. Not to mention he'd observed Lady Maddalena riding him.

When she saw that he didn't mean to move away, the squire said, "His name's Yvain."

Bel met Gray's eyes and smiled. "Yvain. A hero's name. I'm not surprised."

"Yeah?" The squire shifted on the haybale, crossing her legs and getting comfortable. "What hero?"

"She hasn't told you the legend of Sir Yvain and the Green Dragon?"

She shook her head, eyes big.

"Shame."

"Oh, come on," she huffed. "Don't be a tease. *Bel*."

He glanced at her, eyebrows lifting. She was looking mischievous, feline eyes daring him.

Bel was just bored enough to play along. "What will you give me in return? *Alixandre*."

She shot him a sour look. "Ugh. It's *Alix*."

"Well?"

"How about a story in return?"

"Hm. It would have to be a good one, to match Sir Yvain. And a dragon."

"What if it's a true story? True stories are always more valuable."

"You think so? Well, what makes you think Sir Yvain and the Green Dragon isn't true?"

She gave him that put upon look, the one only young females could perfect; equal parts exasperation and disdain. "Because," she said slowly, drawing it out as if he was simple and this was painfully obvious, "dragons aren't real."

"Who says?"

She opened her mouth, but he gave a quick rustle of his good wing. Her gaze snapped to it, and her expression turned pensive.

Humans had a way of doing that, relegating other intelligent beings to myths and legends. In a time before, give or take an eon, humans hadn't been so alone in the world. Avians had shared the sky with dragons, griffins, faeries, sprites, and harpies. The seas had churned with serpents and sirens. Ogres, centaurs, and manticores had been as plentiful as trees in the vast forests. The world had teemed with the magical and the dangerous, all manner of intelligent creatures at once living together and fighting each other. There were still a few stories, the oldest tales of all, that recounted the epic battles waged between ogres and dragons, harpies and centaurs. Yes, eons ago, the world had been a fuller place.

The stories couldn't quite say when the tide had turned, when those creatures impervious to magic had tipped the scales in their favor. Humans lacked the ethereal powers of the others, but they made up for it in cunning and immunity to magic. The faeries and sprites had gone first, lacking other defenses. The griffins, harpies, sea serpents, ogres, and manticores had fought tooth and claw, but even their immense power couldn't stop the onslaught of humans, who hunted them to the corners of the earth. The dragons holed up deep underground with their hoards, kept warm in deep volcanic vents—they had lasted longer, but many, too many had fallen asleep, claimed by the volcanoes that sheltered them. The centaurs, the shiest of all, had disappeared into the highland mists. Bel had found stories that they still existed, deep in the hilly forests of the east, but nothing more. The sirens too had slipped away, sinking beneath the waves, never to be seen again.

After all the death, only two intelligent creatures remained, humans and avians. Here, in a bit more modern time of history, Bel could pinpoint where the scales had tipped. That night, when Maddok was murdered, a king slain, the tide had turned against the avians yet again.

He pulled himself away from those thoughts, concentrating on the soothing repetition of brushstrokes over Gray's back.

Alix stuck another piece of straw in her mouth and twirled it around with her tongue. She cocked an eyebrow at him and said, "Well, have at it, then. Let's see if you can make a believer out of me."

Bel laughed despite himself.

He told her his favorite version of the tale, the one Eamon had told when they gathered around the hearth in his room, the north winds howling against the windowpanes.

"Once, there was a brave man named Yvain. Sir Yvain was a great knight—"

"They always are," said Alix.

"—his arm strong enough to lift mountains, some said; his face so ferocious that armies surrendered at the mere sight of it, said others. He was undefeated. Many fearsome beasts' heads lined his castle walls, and he carried dozens of maidens' tokens tied to his lance—"

Alix snickered.

"—A time came when Sir Yvain felt the eastern wind in his hair. It always came, a restlessness that had him looking for a new horizon. The denizens of the kingdom begged Sir Yvain to stay, but the world called to him, and who was he to deny it?

"Sir Yvain mounted his trusty steed, riding east, towards the rising sun. Many a court rode out to meet him, begging for his presence at feast, but Sir Yvain declined, always moved towards the rising sun. Eventually, he came to the eastern sea. Far out on the horizon, he could see a mighty black cloud smudging the skyline. When he asked the fishermen what the cloud meant, they spoke of an island just out of sight with a mighty volcano at its heart. 'The folk there say it's a dragon making the mountain shake,' said one fisherman. 'Haven't been able to sail far because of the waves the rumbling makes,' said another.

"A brave crew agreed to sail Sir Yvain to the island in the hope that he could stop the dragon and make the seas navigable again. The waves crashed against the boat, tossing them about. The fishermen were frightened, for the sea had never been so angry. But Sir Yvain gave them courage and urged them on to the island.

"Villagers came rushing from their homes to the beach where Sir Yvain's boat came ashore. They saw he was a knight, with his strong sword arm and his fierce visage, and pleaded with him to slay the dragon that terrorized them.

"'The dragon has demanded tribute,' said the village chief. 'He has demanded a virgin sacrifice and we—'"

"Why is it always a *virgin* sacrifice?"

"For the same reason things always go wrong at midnight," said Bel. "Now hush."

"Sir Yvain headed into the mountain, with the villagers' hopes and the east wind at his back. He ventured into the heart of the mountain, where the air was hot with the earth's molten lifeblood. Steam rose around him, and he could feel the heat of the volcano through the soles of his boots. The air hissed and cracked with the smell of sulfur.

"Sir Yvain found a central magma chamber, the ceiling high and chandeliered with stalactites. The lake of lava swirled, and from its depths rose a mighty dragon. The great serpent climbed from the lake, its green scales glowing from the heat. Its slitted eyes glared at Sir Yvain.

"'Ah, so they have sent a knight to kill me, then,' grumbled the dragon—" Here Bel did his best draconian grumble.

"The dragon lunged for Sir Yvain, but the knight was too quick for the massive jaws that tried to gobble him up. They danced around the chamber, steel and fangs flashing.

"'You shall pay for terrorizing the villagers,' said Yvain.

"The dragon rumbled and laughed. 'This is only a taste of my fury. The villagers have reneged on our bargain. I have every right to claim what is mine!'

"'And what bargain is this? They promised you a virgin sacrifice?'

"The dragon laughed again. 'What need have I for a virgin human? No, the village has promised me two rams every new moon so that I may sleep without venturing into danger. In return, I keep the lava flows away from the village.'

"'If this is so, then why are you threatening them?'

"The dragon snuffed, smoke billowing from its nostrils. It told Sir Yvain that it had not received a ram in over four moons, that it was hungry, that the village chief had gone mad with power. He thought they could live without the dragon, that they themselves could divert the volcano. He had sent men to try, and many had lost their lives in the flows.

"Yvain sheathed his sword and said, 'If what you say is true, dragon, I cannot slay you.'"

"Wait, what now?" Alix spat out her piece of straw in surprise.

"—Sir Yvain climbed from the volcano with the dragon's promise to hold off new flows until he could uncover the truth. In the village, he questioned the people. He found those men who had returned from the flows, hands and feet often burned away from their limbs. He found those wives and children who had lost husbands and fathers to the volcano. He found many willing to send rams in to the dragon, if only he would stop the flows.

"When he heard of Sir Yvain's questions, the village chief drew his sword and bared it at Yvain. 'You side with a dragon against your own people? What kind of knight are you?' Sir Yvain bested the chief easily but spared his life, leaving it to the village to decide what to do with him. The people cried with relief and gave Sir Yvain many sheep to take to the waiting dragon.

"Sir Yvain returned, and the dragon ate his fill. Licking his chops, the dragon said, 'You are a curious one, human knight. It took much courage to leave the volcano without my head.'

"'I do not slay the innocent,' said Yvain.

"Wishing to reward Yvain, the dragon took him into another chamber that held his giant hoard. Jewels and armor and coins littered the ground, sparkling in the amber light of the fiery mountain. From the pile the dragon plucked a shining sword, its steel so sharp, so polished, that it shone white. It was an enchanted sword that would never break or tarnish, would never need to be oiled or sharpened, and its aim would always be true.

"Sir Yvain thanked the dragon. He gave the beast his own sword, which he had had since his days as a squire, to add to its hoard.

"And so Sir Yvain sailed from the island, the smoke cloud already fading on a gentle eastern breeze. He sailed back to the mainland, where a north wind stirred his heart. He turned his eye north and mounted his steed, ready to ride where the wind would take him." Bel finished, patting Gray. The horse tapped his chin with his muzzle, as if wondering why Bel didn't go on.

Alix too seemed confused by the end. "But why didn't he just slay the dragon? An enchanted sword is good and all, but what if the peace didn't last?"

"Because the dragon was innocent," said a voice from the stable door that almost made Bel jump. Lady Maddalena had entered without either of them noticing.

Bel's brows rose in surprise. Is that what she thought the story was about? Could she have heard the same version as him? He doubted it could still be a popular story—it was very old and, as Alix's response showed, most humans probably wondered why the dragon wasn't just slain, for expediency.

The knight took him in, hand on her horse's back, her squire easily within his reach. Her gaze flicked between him and Alix, her mouth pursed and expression taut.

"Off with you, Alix. There are things still to do today."

The squire made an unhappy *humph*.

"Didn't you want to accompany Malthus down to Longbourne?" she said to Alix, though her eyes were still on Bel. "He'll be leaving soon."

That got Alix moving. She hopped off the haybale, brushing away straw. "That I did. Going to see Violet again." She waggled her eyebrows. "Got a crown? Just borrowing it, of course."

Bel thought a small blush overtook Lady Maddalena's face, but she quickly ducked her head to fish in her pocket. When she flicked Alix the coin, her face was carefully expressionless.

Alix pocketed the coin, but rather than leaving, she said, "Oh, but I promised Bel a story in return. You're always going on about knights keeping their promises, Lena."

Now Bel knew for certain she blushed. Without reason to duck her head this time, Lady Maddalena gave her squire a long stare, as if imagining strangling the girl.

"Perhaps later. On with you."

Alix shrugged. "All right. I'll see you later, Bel."

Lady Maddalena grimaced, but Bel gave the squire a quick nod.

Alix wrapped herself up in layers of wool, topping off with a voluminous scarf that hid everything but her eyes and cloud of black curls. She waved at them both before leaving with a blast of cold air to greet her.

All the cheeriness went with her. He'd always found the stables warm and comforting, but right now, it felt too warm. A slick of sweat trailed down from behind his right ear, down his neck, down into the collar of his shirt.

He and the knight stood there in silence once again, and Bel almost sighed with the weariness of it. Always it was this way with her, circling each other, looking for an advantage. Except today, after a soothing rub down of Gray and watching Alix's amusement at his tale, Bel didn't feel like fighting.

"He's a fine horse," he said, giving Gray a pat before carefully moving away from the warhorse on to one of the packhorses. He called the brown mare Nippy, as she tended to nip.

"Yes," said Lady Maddalena. "I trained him up from a colt."

He waited for more, but nothing came. He dared a glance at her and found that same taut expression on her face.

With a sigh, he stopped brushing. "I won't hurt her, warden. Alix is a child. Even villains like me have boundaries."

"Alix can be...aggravating at times," she said, though it wasn't an accusation of Alix but of him.

"She could be a demon sent personally to torment me and I still wouldn't hurt her." Bel placed his hand over his heart and bowed his head, a sign he knew meant sincerity and respect to Vagorans. "I swear it."

Lady Maddalena blinked, as if she didn't quite believe it. Then she cleared her throat and nodded, hopefully accepting his promise.

She turned her back to him, stroking a hand down Gray's neck, and Bel set to work on Nippy. The mare nickered happily and tried to give his wing an affectionate bite.

"Oh, she does that," said Lady Maddalena. "Here." She rubbed a circle around the white splotch on Nippy's forehead before scratching behind her ear. "She wants her ears rubbed."

Bel contained his surprise to a simple nod of thanks. A third blush overtook her, and she moved back to Gray.

Silence ensued again, but this time it wasn't so uncomfortable. He didn't feel like whistling a ditty, but his skin didn't crawl with it either.

"Why Sir Yvain and the Green Dragon?"

Bel glanced over his shoulder at her, gauging. Lady Maddalena was carefully avoiding his eyes as she mucked Gray's stall.

"Alix wanted to know where you got the name Yvain. Why..." He cleared his throat. "Why Yvain?"

She didn't answer right away, and for a moment, Bel didn't think she'd answer at all.

"Because Sir Yvain went on many quests, saw all corners of the earth. He defended the innocent and symbolized justice."

"So you like the reminder."

"I like the name."

Bel shut his mouth.

"Did you...did you fight? In the war?" She said it so quietly, with a face so tense and eyes so full of dread, that he thought perhaps she didn't truly want an answer.

"Barely. I'd just finished training and moved up to the army when I was...captured." He swallowed the last word, feeling it move down his throat in a knotted lump. "Did you?" he asked, though he knew the answer.

If possible, she looked even more uncomfortable now, her whole lean face pinched. She wouldn't meet his eyes when she said, "Yes."

"You were at Aeriand?"

"Yes. That was three years ago."

"Yes."

"You weren't...?"

"They took me ten years ago."

"Ten years ago. Then you must have been just..."

He looked up when her words petered out. Did she not know he'd been here so long, that Finhöln had been made a prison specially for him?

Her gaze, heavy with pity, took in his right wing. She traced its sagging angle, comparing it to his healthy wing that arched well above his head. The old, unset break didn't allow Bel to hold his damaged wing properly, made the primary feathers drag on the ground when it wasn't splinted to his side. He hated that the wing swept over dirt and stone, hated that it was a battle to keep the wing clean. He hated what a sight it must make, drooping, obviously damaged.

Bel turned his back again. He knew these words were dangerous to speak, knew he walked a knife's edge, but he wanted to know. And wanted her piteous gaze off his wing.

"At Aeriand...many died there?" He needed more than Eamon's feather had given him. In all his time here, Lady Maddalena seemed the only source able, perhaps even willing to give him what he wanted.

"For both of us. It was...in many ways a waste."

"Then why do it?"

The silence grew thick, and for a horrible moment Bel was the anvil, waiting for the hammer's strike.

"We're at war, Bel."

He almost laughed. "I know that. Of course, I know that." Maddok's face came to him, ghostly and taut, his golden wings rendered a sickly yellow in the pale moonlight. That sound, that awful sucking sound of the sword being pulled out of Maddok's chest, Bel could hear even now; it woke him in the night, to a bed filled with his own cold sweat, ringing in his ears. "But why take Aeriand? Why invade? Your king took what he wanted—you have the Hollenheim Mountains, you have the Grass Sea. Why?"

He watched her face hardened like setting steel. "Why?" she repeated. "Why attack from the sky? Why set villages alight? Why attack at night like cowards?"

The words bit into him and he winced. It wasn't a proud memory, that avian tactics included setting fire to enemy targets from the air. Maddok had used the age-old tactic when he felt they needed to send a message to the humans or when they needed to divert the main army. From the whispers he'd heard over the years, the strategy had become a favorite of Dartegn's, human villages his favorite targets.

"As you say, we're at war." It was a useless and rather pathetic thing to say, but Bel had nothing else to give her.

"And all's fair, is that it?"

"I didn't say that."

"But it's what you meant."

"I don't take pride from it. But sometimes there are things you feel you have to do."

"So, you set rooves on fire? You attacked civilians?"

"How many innocent avians were killed at Aeriand?" he shot back. "Did it matter to you if it was a soldier or a civilian killed? Or did it only matter if it had wings?"

"You didn't answer my question."

"And you refuse to answer mine."

Lady Maddalena huffed. She turned to face him fully, fists planted on her hips. Little suns blazed in her eyes, but he didn't think she was truly angry, at least not with him. Her warrior's body was still somewhat loose, ready but not wary, a possible threat but not an immediate one.

She considered him for a long moment, those green eyes of hers as bright as new grass shoots, before she said, "Many were killed in the siege of Aeriand. I can't say our campaign was overly discriminate, but the crown prince did keep the main attack objectives on army sites of operation. Civilians were killed, but none by my hand."

Bel swallowed. "I carried out orders once to attack a village from the air. We usually aim for town centers, pubs, places of governing, rather than homes if we can. It's an old tactic—we've used it on ourselves before, when we were only separate flocks rather than one kingdom."

She accepted his answer with a nod, and they both turned back to what they had been doing. It felt like a truce of sorts, a parley.

"Can I ask, warden." She looked up. "Why Aeriand? The borders between our people have existed for a long time—they may favor one side over the other for a while, but they've been more or less the same. Why now?"

"It's to be the final war," she said.

"Final war?"

"Our people have been at war a very long time."

"Forever, it seems," he agreed. The humans and avians had long been warring over the eastern Hollenheim Mountains, where avian creation myth said a human man and a harpy mated to create the first avian. It was the cradle of avian life, the first aerie, sacred. It was also a veritable trove of riches, precious and semiprecious stones abounding. Humans had wanted the gems, uncaring if it was a sacred site. The two species had warred over it for generations, taking and surrendering. The campaigns had eventually spread south, to the Grass Plains, where the iron and marble and gold were plentiful. By then the avians had learned to covet what the humans wished to take from them. By then they were willing to die for shiny rocks in the dirt, if only so a human couldn't have them.

"King Artemian wants this to be the last war, no matter how long it may take. He wants—" She bit off her words, suddenly turning from him, as if realizing how much she'd said.

"To eradicate avians, yes, I understand." He scratched Nippy behind her ear when she made to bite him again. "So, it'll be genocide, never peace."

"Peace treaties have never lasted," she said, though without malice.

The weight of her words settled over Bel like water over river stones, heavy and turbulent. She was right of course, all the treaties signed between humans and avians had only lasted perhaps fifty years. It seemed they were doomed to fight until only one remained, and Bel mourned that it wouldn't be his people who survived.

Lady Maddalena too looked like her words weighed heavy. She found no enjoyment from them, he thought; she said a truth rather than a belief. She had the same look on her face as she had when she'd interacted with Sir Ollander. Resignation.

"And what will happen when you've finally rid the world of us, when you're finally alone in the world? Who will you fight then?"

She didn't even open her mouth to reply, just stared as if she didn't see him. She didn't try to give him an answer, for she didn't have one. Bel doubted any human did.

There was a silence so long that Bel began to think they'd come to their end.

"Sometimes you have to fight," she said quietly. "As you say, sometimes there are things we have to do."

"Fight until there's nothing left to fight?"

"Fight until we're safe."

"Safe from what?"

"From the threat. From *you*."

"And why are we such a threat?"

"I think all the broken treaties answer that."

"And we broke *all* of them, did we? Is that what they tell you?"

He felt the sting of her frown prickle along the back of his neck. "Excuse me?"

"Is that all they need to tell you, to make you commit a whole species to the sword? You actually believe it's always our fault?" He gave a humorless laugh. "We're all just unfeeling monsters with no honor. That's why I'm kept here, so far away from everything, isn't it? So no precious humans see how *monstrous* I am."

She turned the full power of her angry glare on him, a righteous fire burning there.

"What would you know about the war? Why weren't you at the front? If you feel so strongly, why have you been here for *ten years*? Only a coward would hide away like that."

Coward. The word, the accusation struck him in the gut. It punched the air from his lungs, not leaving enough to find a retort, a rebuttal.

She took his silence to mean something, her lips thinning into a displeased—disappointed?—line. He didn't like the look she gave him then, as if he was less, as if he had been something a moment before that he wasn't anymore. It felt like the moment he'd realized he was no longer Prince Arubel, that that part of himself had died. He didn't appreciate the memory.

Her boots shifted in the hay, almost drowning her muttered, "Good day, Bel," and then she was pulling on coat, cloak, scarf, gloves. She disappeared beneath the layers and without a second glance, she left him in a gust of frigid air.

He watched the space where she'd been for longer than he should, buffeted by regret and guilt and anger, a new emotion for every beat of his heart. He ran a hot gamut before settling on indignation. It steeled his spine, soothed his ruffled feathers, but left a bitter taste in his mouth.

A nicker had him looking at Gray, the warhorse regarding him with those big equine eyes that understood everything. Gray snorted, shaking his mane.

Bel snorted back. Of course, the warhorse would be on *her* side.

14

If Lena closed her eyes and imagined, imagined hard, she could pretend the scrape of metal around her wrists was just overtight gauntlets. Just ill-fitting armor. There was no shame in thinking armor uncomfortable —it was a necessary evil. There was no shame in cringing every time the metal chafed against her raw skin, no shame in counting the blisters lining the delicate undersides of her wrists.

A great hush fell over the basilica, whispers of silk and brocade rustling as the good nobles of Vagora anticipated the king's entrance.

Lena cracked open her weary eyes, the lids heavy. Her eyes felt grainy, each blink bringing an unpleasant pinch. She took in a breath, as her father had told her. The land, the basilica, was full of enemies this day, too many for Lena to contend with. But she might have an ally; she had to hold onto that hope, or else she had nothing at all. Nothing had gone right since the start, but she would stand before her king, she would tell her side. It had to be enough.

The king swept into the hall on a tide of ornamental gold armor. Shafts of light streamed in from the strategically angled windows high above, gilding King Artemian in Matella's warm gaze. He shimmered like sunlight on water, his rich waves of brown hair parted down the middle and flowing behind him. His face, though.

Lena shuddered.

She didn't want to look at his face, more thundercloud than eyes or nose or mouth. A sun god displeased.

She felt the weight of those amber eyes, felt the heat of the noonday sun slanted down on her back from yet another strategically angled orifice of the great basilica. A bead of sweat travelled from her head, down her neck, into her collar. A sheen of sweat and coat of grime were Lena's armor today. No cuirass adorned with her family's crest, no tall shoulder guards to frame her face, no golden pins in her hair. No shield against the many eyes that bore into Lena, undressed her, flayed her.

She had an itch between her shoulder blades; it'd been there since she was thrown into Lord Merle's dungeon ten days ago. It was the least of her current torments, but if Lena could wish for one thing, it would be for someone to ease it. She didn't dare wish for more.

King Artemian came to the center of the royal dais. Forgoing his throne, he towered over Lena and the restless crowd behind her. Queen Ilona sat to the king's right in her throne. She carried nothing, not the ceremonial sword that had graced Lena's shoulders six years ago, making her a knight. She had nothing but censure in her gaze and distaste on her lips.

The king took in a long breath, the plates of his armor clinking. He sucked in air and Lena felt all hers leave, lungs conflating, chest caving.

A sound of indignation sliced through the silence, followed by a grunt and scuffling. From the group arranged on the steps to the dais on Lena's right—a place where her peers, other knights, stood, a place Lena would not, could not look—barreled Alix.

The girl shoved bodies out of her way unceremoniously, throwing a baleful look at anyone brave enough to meet her eyes. Lena's mother grabbed for her, but Alix danced out of the way, making it to Lena in five quick, powerful strides. Her thin body vibrated with rage, and for a moment, all Lena wanted to do was throw her arms around the girl.

"Who is this child?" the king demanded.

"No one," Lady Margot said, stepping forward.

A palace guard stepped forward, too.

But Alix widened her stance, shoulders square. "I'm Alixandre of Highclere, squire to Lady Maddalena Montcaer." Her voice boomed, moving like a physical thing through the basilica. Lena rocked from the impact, and the crowd behind them chittered.

"This doesn't concern you," Lady Margot hissed.

"Margot, just let—" Margot turned her glare on Sir Warrek, and he closed his mouth. His eyes skittered towards Lena without meeting hers, and they both looked at each other's chins, knowing the other grimaced without having to look higher. They both withered under Margot's glare; there was nothing for it.

Lena shifted her weight, angling her body to shield Alix from her mother's flinty glare. Lady Margot had never liked Alix, had demanded Lena make a better choice for her first squire. Squiring Alix had been Lena's first major defiance of her mother.

"Article Five of the knight's code," Alix said with all the poise of a lawyer, her gleaming eyes and slight snarl aimed at Margot. "Section one, 'a squire is to stand with their knight.' Section thirteen, 'a squire may stand with their knight through trials, arraignments, and sentencing to offer moral comfort.'" Alix looked to the king then, having the sense to temper the fire in her glare. "I'm standing with my knight. And no one can or will move me from this spot." And, as an afterthought, "Your Majesty."

Lena made a helpless noise. "Alix—"

"Let the girl stay." A dark figure moved to Lena's left, and she shuddered instinctively. If King Artemian was the day, then Lord Balderak was the night, clad in black leathers and cloak. He moved like something from a dark nightmare, wide shoulders hulking, long, tapered fingers steady on the hilt of his sword. Black hair threaded with gray swept around a face that looked too young, a face that was like smooth wax, with rounded, sensuous lips, the upper slightly fuller than the lower.

Those lips were pulled back into something like a smile, dark eyes glittering as they moved over Lena and Alix. Many a court lady found Balderak exquisitely handsome. "This concerns her too, after all."

With a flourish, Balderak swept the right side of his cloak away, the cloth landing in a crisp fold over his shoulder. He held the stump of his wrist at chest height, enough for the king, for all on the dais, to clearly see the bloodied bandages that had replaced his sword hand.

His smile was too triumphant for a man who'd been maimed only a fortnight ago.

The tips of Lena's fingers went cold, her hands itching for a weapon. For one awful moment, she wished she could cut off his other hand, hear the wet splash of his blood painting the floor.

She snapped her gaze back to the king, pushing away such thoughts. They would only make it worse.

The unhappy mutterings of the noble crowd at her back filled Lena's ears as Lord Balderak held his mutilated arm higher, for all to see. One of their own had been hurt, his station violated. "*Blood for blood,*" she thought they said. "*Hers for his, an uneven trade.*"

King Artemian seemed to hear the whispers too. He looked out over his nobles, taking their measure, before returning to Lena. The lines around his eyes deepened, his mouth a mere lipless slash of shadow. Her eyes widened, and she felt her head shake, silently begging him to wait, to ignore the whispers.

Alix slipped her hand into the crook of Lena's elbow.

King Artemian inclined his head to Balderak. "The throne will hear your claim, Lord Balderak."

He bowed low, ceremoniously, from the waist, maimed arm held high. He turned slightly on his heel and threw a smile Lena's way.

Her stomach flipped, saliva flooding her mouth. She swallowed back the sudden sick.

"Your Majesty, ten days ago, this woman attacked me without warning, in cold blood."

No. It hadn't been nearly so sudden. The list of accusations had taken almost a half-hour to get through, but Lena wanted to be thorough, to make sure he understood. *"I know everything,"* she'd told him, *"and soon the whole kingdom will, too."*

"I was unarmed."

No. The ring of a blade being drawn had cut through Lena's words. Balderak had bared his teeth and sword at her, his eyes dark, those of an animal cornered and desperate. Those eyes had flicked to Alix, standing quietly in the corner, and he'd seen his way out. Lena only had enough time to draw her own blade, to choose between Alix and him.

"I barely escaped with my life!"

"That's a lie!" The voice was Lena's, even though she didn't remember speaking, or even wanting to speak. The words came up her throat, torn from her lips. The manacles bit into her wrists, the chains securing her to an iron loop in the floor clanging as she strained.

"Lady, you will—"

"He drew first!" Alix yelled above the king. "I was there. I saw what happened. He was armed and he attacked us!"

"She's lying, Your Majesty," said Lord Balderak.

"The only one lying is you, you fucking filthy son of a—"

"I'll restrain that wretch myself, Your Majesty," Lady Margot cried, even as Sir Warrek held her back by her shoulder.

The king looked down at their drama with an impassive face. To Alix he said, "Your testimony is biased, squire. You'd say anything to help your lady, that much is clear."

"And *his* isn't?" Alix jabbed an accusing finger at Balderak. "*He* should be the one in chains. He's an animal! What he did to those women—"

"You aren't the one making claims today, squire. Besides, what evidence do you have against Lord Balderak? The evidence of Lady Maddalena's crime he will carry for all his days. Where is yours?"

Color flushed Alix's face, and her eyes dropped like stones to the floor. Lena heard an incriminating sniff, and her chest ached when she saw Alix holding back tears. She lifted her bound hands to lay them on Alix's shoulder, the best she could do right now.

"It's not your fault," she murmured. She'd told the girl this many times now, assured her it was Lena's own fault for asking such a thing of her, of trusting that the documents were going to the right hands. But Alix only shook her head, as she always did, and Lena ached to think she would carry this burden of guilt for any longer.

They'd spent months gathering statements, written testimonies of Lord Balderak's abuses. Lena had caught wind of it when she'd walked into the castle kitchens late one night to find the cook cleaning up a battered scullery maid. The women had been cagey, first saying the girl had fallen down a few stairs, then that the head hostler was drunk. It hadn't stopped with the maid, and Lena had worked to earn the castle women's trust. Sometimes, it took Alix to bring them round, the girl's buoyant spirit infectious, endearing. Weeks went by before the women's suspicion eased, weeks Lena spent proving she wasn't a goon for Balderak, that she knew and upheld the knight's code. That she would see justice done.

She'd gone to Balderak with what she knew, gave him the opportunity to say his piece, as she was required to. But Lena hadn't been stupid enough to show the documents to Balderak, hadn't given them up when he'd demanded, threatened—*"They're out of your reach,"* she'd told him, *"just like all the women you've hurt."* In desperation, he'd attacked. She cut off the hand that went for Alix, her vision nearly blinded with red.

In that state of rage, she'd gloried in Balderak's howl of pain, loved watching the horror on his face as he looked at his severed hand, still warm, drowning in a pool of arterial blood.

She hadn't waited. She'd taken Alix and the documents and fled Balderak's manor, riding hard through the night for Lord Merle's holdings to the east. She had to bring the evidence to one of Balderak's peers, had to have their backing for her accusations.

Somehow, Balderak had sent word ahead of them, and rather than gaining an audience with Merle, Lena had been ushered into his dungeon. Desperate, she'd given Alix the documents, told her to take them to Merle, to make him see, to understand.

Alix had come back soon after dawn, emptyhanded and black-eyed.

Another helpless noise crawled up Lena's throat, and she blinked away her own tears.

Goddess, what a mess this had become. Months of taking statements, of gathering evidence as she was supposed to. Going to Balderak first, to see if he'd confess his guilt, as she was supposed to. Taking the evidence to one of his peers, a protector of the realm, as *she was supposed to*.

That scullery maid's battered face came to Lena then and she swallowed bile. She'd wanted to help those women with a fire, a purpose, she'd never felt before, not even when she'd fought beside the crown prince and slept beside the crown prince. She'd known the knight's code, could recite most of it by heart, but looking at that girl's face, Lena had *understood* it, had known what all her life had been leading her to, what she'd been training for. This was her purpose; this was what her parents had raised her to be.

And for what?

She looked to the king again, pleading with her eyes since another outburst seemed ill-advised. If he knew anything of her, he'd know she had good reason, good intention. If he knew anything of her, he'd know she wanted to protect those women, to carry out her duty as a knight of *his* realm.

King Artemian's gaze skittered away, as if he couldn't hold hers, couldn't look at her anymore.

As if he could smell Lena's defeat, Lord Balderak smiled again. "She has no evidence because there isn't any. If I'd committed these crimes, especially as many as Lady Maddalena claims, why has no one come forward? Surely, someone would have said something by now."

"They say nothing because they fear retribution." This for the king, for there was no reasoning with the likes of Balderak. "They fear losing their positions, their livelihoods. They fear their families will be punished by the very man who is supposed to *protect* them."

The king wore a considering frown. "That doesn't stop them from going to someone else. Another knight. A neighboring lord or magistrate."

"We've all seen what Lord Merle's willing to do about this," hissed Alix, though some of her fire had been doused.

"And miss a day of work? Your Majesty, Lord Merle is the closest to Balderak's holdings and it's a day's hard ride. Two if you're walking. These women cannot afford to miss such work. And what if the magistrate keeps them? Who will work? And what if they do all this, and Lord Merle doesn't even believe them?"

For a long moment, the king said nothing, that pensive expression still on his face. For one horrible, wonderful moment, it swelled the sliver of hope in Lena; her heart gave a tentative flutter in her chest.

"While this matter deserves investigation, you have no evidence, Lady Maddalena. None of the women you claim gave testimony are here."

"Most of them are peasant women—how were they supposed to get here in time?" Alix demanded.

Did they even know I went to trial? Did it matter if they did? What they would know for certain was that the knight who'd wanted to help them, who promised them justice, had been arrested, taken away in infamy.

"All of this is needless. I am not the accused," said Balderak. He held up his stump again, and Lena thought he was perhaps overplaying his hand. *Oh.* She didn't know whether to smile or weep. "Here is your evidence, Your Majesty. That woman has betrayed the knight's code by attacking a superior and I am within my right to demand justice."

"And what is your justice, Lord Balderak?" asked the king.

Lena already knew what he would demand before he said, "Both her hands. I will have to learn how to swing a sword again, how to write once more. But it doesn't mean anything if she's allowed to walk amongst us—she's a threat."

Relearn how to fight and write, perhaps. He would find it much more difficult to abuse those he was supposed to protect, too. Lena had to remember that. If not, she feared finally succumbing to the sucking despair that had lingered in her mind the past fortnight, always there, waiting for her to stumble, to give in.

"And what do you have to say to that, Lady Maddalena?" asked the king, though his pointed look was for Alix.

Lena lifted her hands from her squire's shoulder and took a half-step forward.

"I have served as a knight of the realm for almost six years now, Your Majesty. I spent most of them serving beside your son, protecting him. What I did, I did to protect the women of Vagora. I did everything as I was supposed to do, I gathered testimonies and gave Lord Balderak a chance to confess. He attacked my squire and in the moment, I chose her life over his title. I regret that it came to that, but his pain is *nothing* compared to what he's done to the women of his holdings. If you must cut off my hands, then do it—only, don't let Lord Balderak leave here. Don't let him punish others too. Do what I couldn't and protect those women from that animal."

Lena wasn't too proud to admit practicing that speech. She'd had little else to do during her imprisonment, had spent those dark days preparing. She didn't think it was too much to ask of the king, of Matella, to watch out for the people.

The king nodded slowly before turning his attention to the side of the dais where her parents and other high-ranking knights stood. There were always a group of peers present at a royal trial—whether that was a blessing or curse for the accused was subjective.

"Will any of you speak for Lady Maddalena before I pass judgement?"

The knights, with their gleaming armor and clean-cut faces, looked anywhere but at her. Eyes flinty and hard, they bore her shame in silence. They saw an end that did not justify its means, and Lena knew which part of the knight's code they held dearer.

The basilica held its breath as the knights shifted their great weight from foot to foot until finally, Lady Margot stepped forward.

"I will speak for her, Your Majesty. Maddalena is my daughter. I trained her myself. Whatever she did, it was in a moment of madness. It doesn't represent her, her service, or Sir Warrek and I. She is a good knight. She has her whole life yet to serve, to make this right."

Alix made a sound of disgust at the same moment Lena thought, *Is that it?*

She looked to her father, but his gaze went everywhere but near her. He stood by. Silent.

The king sighed, his golden armor clinking again. Lena remembered being entranced by that sound, thinking it the sound of victory. She had thought there was nothing to compare to standing before her king, nothing that could be better. His gold gauntlets glittered as the king slowly clasped his hands behind his back. He stood firm, like an adorned statue, solid, unmovable. Condemning.

Lena's eyes slid closed again. Partly because she didn't want to see her king pass judgment, partly to keep the well of tears from escaping.

"The claims made today are serious and no matter what I say, the kingdom loses a valuable warrior."

Alix's hand clutched her arm like a vice, cold and bony, nearly cutting off blood to her forearm. She held on so hard, Lena could feel Alix's racing pulse. It matched her own.

"Due to available evidence and testimony, I have no choice but to condemn Lady Maddalena. She attacked her superior, permanently disabling a peer of the realm. The kingdom is under attack from the outside and cannot afford threats from within. Lady Maddalena must prove to me that she isn't a danger to the kingdom; she must prove to me that she will keep the vows she made when I knighted her. I therefore banish her to the north, where she will carry out a two-year sentence. Lady Maddalena." His voice tugged at her, demanding her eyes, but for the first time, Lena was reluctant to give her king what he asked for.

North? Why north? Why couldn't she face punishment now and be down with it? Lena was tired of this.

She opened her eyes, beholding a man encased in ornate but impractical armor, ready to condemn her for staying true to her vows and doing what was right.

"Use your time in the north wisely. Decide where your loyalties lie. I give you this one chance to prove to me that you are still the loyal knight I saw six years ago. That you are still a worthy protector of this kingdom."

Prove myself. Always, to prove myself. And for what?

If she could, Lena would've wrapped her arms around herself. There was too little shielding her; clothing wasn't enough. She thought of her practical, familiar suit that Alix begrudgingly maintained. She longed for the weight of it, to feel the cinch of the buckles and *snick* of the joints snapping into place. She wanted to hold herself, to keep herself together, for she feared she might splinter, never to fit back together again.

Despair crashed like a towering wave around her, and she couldn't breathe. It was everywhere, it knew she was buckling. It swirled inside her, twisting her insides, squeezing her heart, filling, consuming and—

And just as quickly, it relented. She drew in a shallow breath and focused on the feeling of her feet under her. They were steady; her knees had locked to keep her upright. She would not fall, not in front of the king, Balderak, her mother.

The storm ebbed, drawing back behind the breakwater of her resolve. She'd worked her whole life to prove herself once. She could do it again, even if weariness dogged her at the thought. There was nothing else for it.

"Yes, Your Majesty," she said, looking him in the eye. "I won't fail."

15

Lena had had her suspicions over the last fortnight, but after her argument with Bel in the stables, when she'd stood so close to him trading barbs, she could say it for certain now—his wing had been reset.

She couldn't say when or how he'd done it, but she had her suspicions about that too.

The question now was, what would she do about it?

The directive, a battered leather volume stuffed full of scraps of notes written by at least eight different hands that sat in the unused warden's office in the east tower, had very explicit instructions: the wing must be rebroken.

Lena had stared at the words for a long time one afternoon while fat snowflakes wandered through the gray sky.

The directive was a jumbled document at best, a waste of good parchment at worst. It'd started out as a neat set of papers sewn into a stiff leather binding, the king's instructions for Finhöln, the warden, and the prisoner outlined over twenty pages, split into five sections. Over the years, margins were filled in with notes about Bel and the avian species; with wardens' complaints about the castle, the food, the weather; with veritable diary entries from one warden who fancied himself a poet; and even with—and here Lena suspected a bored squire—anatomically incorrect doodles of penises.

Lena hadn't consulted the directive since deciding that there wasn't a rule against Bel training. On top of the twenty pages laid out by the king and his advisers, other wardens had penned in their own rules for the castle and its lone prisoner, ranging from practical to ridiculous, but none specified or even mentioned Bel's training.

There were a few notes, meticulously penned in small, straight letters on the inside cover, that chronicled the punishments meted out on Bel's body. The ink was brownest, the most faded here and the handwriting matched other notes that took up prime margin space elsewhere in the directive.

From the oldest additions, Lena pieced together Bel's first years here. The first warden, Hallan, had thoroughly documented his encounters with Bel and how he made this place a living hell for him. Lena's stomach had threatened to heave at Hallan's detailed planning and description of how he'd damaged Bel's right wing base, crippling him as no other break could.

Lena thought uneasily of that break as she stuck her twice-socked feet into her stiff boots. The bed warmer of coals she used for warmth during the night had long ago burned out, and Lena dressed hastily, everything tugged on, buckled, and tied through muscle memory. She'd gotten her routine down to a minute and a half, so within two minutes of peeling back the blankets, Lena was taking the steps down into the kitchen two at a time.

She submerged in the smell of yeasty brown bread the further down she descended. She had long ago stopped tasting the bread, but the smell still pleased her. It reminded her of Pol, of warmth, of conversation. Though the cook spoke with his hands, he was quite eloquent, and between she, Alix, and Pol, they often had lively conversations that broke up the harsh monotony of winter.

Pol was busy at work chopping vegetables for the day's soup, and so Lena left him alone to collect her own breakfast. She portioned her plate and then ate at the heavy carving table methodically; while the food beat army rations any day, there was something about it all tasting good that chafed. She should like it, yet Lena was starting to resent the warm crackle of the brown bread and melting square of salty butter. She sometimes wondered if she'd prefer rations, because at least then she'd be allowed to hate what she filled her mouth and belly with.

Since eating took little thought, Lena turned her mind back to the problem at hand.

Well, problems.

She was, on paper, expected to rebreak the wing of her prisoner, the prisoner she was actively avoiding.

Lena wasn't proud of it, but since their argument, she'd tried not to lay eyes on the avian. Just the thought of the words they'd volleyed at each other was enough to ignite a fire in Lena's blood. So far, she'd channeled it into her training with Alix, determined to make up the ground they'd lost over what Alix was calling The Great Conflagration, but Alix could only spar so long. Eventually, the squire would give up, protesting by becoming boneless, dead weight and refusing to move until Lena agreed they were done for the day.

Lena had thought it'd be easy to avoid the avian; they'd danced around each other with ease up until recently. Yet, the avian now seemed to be everywhere. When she and Alix were climbing up the kitchen stairs, he was descending. She passed him in the corridors, caught glimpses of him finishing his training in the great hall, saw signs of his work in the stables. He was everywhere now.

Lena gnashed her teeth, wondering if he was doing it on purpose.

She wouldn't put it past that wily son of a—

"Good morning!" Alix chirped as she skipped down the steps.

Lena grumbled a hello, but Alix's attention was on Pol and her breakfast.

"I suppose I don't need to ask why you're so bright this morning," said Lena as Alix settled across from her with a plate piled high with food.

Alix's appetite always made Lena question the dimensions of the human stomach. "Violet's working the bar today?"

"I wouldn't know," Alix said with all the sincerity of a politician.

Lena snorted. "So we can skip the pub and go to the east orchards and order the apples Pol asked for?"

"Didn't say that."

"Mm."

As Alix finished her meal, Malthus came in through the kitchen door, caked in frosted layers of ice. He shook away the snow from his oilskin cloak and brushed it off his grizzled beard. Without a word he lumbered to the fire to let its heat melt the frost from his eyelashes and brows before they could break off.

"We're ready when you are," Lena told the man.

"Better sooner than later," he said. He splayed his hands wide, as close to the flames as they could be without catching fire. "Don't like the look of the sky today." Said with the wisdom of a soothsayer; weather wasn't just an idle topic for pleasantries here in the mountains. Lena had learned the weather made for lasting conversation here, the upcoming days' possible threat of snow always a topic of debate.

By the time Malthus had warmed himself enough, all his frozen bits melted just in time to freeze again, Lena and Alix had donned their layers. After bidding Pol farewell, they followed Malthus down to Longbourne. Lena hadn't bothered with the horses since her disastrous first supply run.

They picked their way down the mountain, and with the snows up to their thighs in places, it took over an hour of trudging to make it into Longbourne. Lena hated every minute of the trek, but at least it proved an easy way to avoid Bel. He'd find it hard to intercept her confined to the castle.

For some reason, the thought only made her gloomier.

They passed through the east gate of Longbourne's snow wall, built up after every storm when the dutiful townsfolk came with their shovels to clear away the new accumulation. If Lena found keeping her little snow tunnel to the stables hard, she could only imagine the amount of work it took to keep the town's pathways useable.

"Want help?" Lena asked, as she did every time they accompanied Malthus to fetch supplies.

And, keeping with tradition, Malthus huffed, "No need. See you in an hour."

Knowing already what Malthus's answer would be, Alix was a few paces ahead, making for the pub. Lena buried her nose further into her collar and followed.

The few townsfolk she came across gave her a wide berth, and when, thanks to her furs cutting off much of her peripherals, she nearly collided with a man he only growled, "Warden," less an apology and more an insult.

Lena tried to shrug it off as she did with the snow on her cloak, but that *Warden* stuck to her like mud.

She hung her outer layers on a peg next to Alix's in the mudroom of the pub. Stepping further into the building, the tangy sweet smell of ale assaulted Lena's nose, bringing her out of her cold stupor.

Alix was weaving between tables, aiming for the bar, but Lena's eye caught on a rather large group of townsfolk near the great hearth. Mayor Yarlsson stood at its center, her muscled forearms crossed over her chest. Lena thought she looked flushed, and not just from the heat of the room.

"I won't stand for it!" spat a man with dark hair and a beard that was two shades lighter, almost ginger. His freckled face glowered at the mayor, his lips a snarling white slash within the tangle of his beard.

"What do you want me to do, Karel? It's the middle of winter and there looks to be a storm on the horizon. Let the bastard freeze to death."

"He knows this mountain as well as the rest of us. Who's to say he'd die?"

"The man has the shirt on his back and that's it."

"There are homesteads to the south. He could rob them. Or worse. You want to take that chance?"

The mayor grimaced. Her eyes and voice became softer when she said, "How is Sigrid?"

It was the wrong thing to say, and Lena winced as the man nearly foamed at the mouth with rage. "Terrified! She won't feel safe again until I cut the cock off that bastard!"

Something in Lena stirred, something deep in her chest that got her heart pumping. Her back straightened and her hands steadied, no longer cold. She stepped forward.

"Mayor, what seems to be the trouble?"

A dozen pairs of eyes whipped to Lena as she slowly approached the small crowd. She kept her gaze on the mayor, and after an initial moment of hesitation, the crowd parted to let her into the circle.

The man with the ginger beard and feral gaze hissed at her, "This doesn't concern you, warden."

There it was again, that *warden*. But Lena was the boulder and his words were the river, flowing around her. They could eventually wear her down, but not now, not today.

"A convict has escaped," the mayor said finally.

"I see. What has the man done?"

Another growl from the man, Karel.

The mayor looked between him and Lena before finally admitting, "Attacked a woman."

Lena's stance widened out of habit. "Then he's right," she said, nodding at Karel. "The man should be apprehended as soon as possible."

"In case you hadn't noticed, warden, it's the middle of winter out there." Tilda sighed, as if she'd been saying this over and over again. "He'll freeze before we ever find him. The snows will bring Sigrid justice."

Lena took another step forwards, palming the hilt of her sheathed sword. "If there's one thing I've learned about this world, it's to never assume justice will find those who deserve it. You must do it yourself."

"And what would you do, Lady Maddalena?" asked Tilda, her eyes closed now, looking wearier by the minute. "Send a search party after him? Risk good men? Go yourself?"

"Yes."

That earned her Tilda's gaze. "What?"

"I'd go." Another step forward. "I told you before, I'm still a knight of the realm. With all that entails."

"And does being a knight of the realm come with tracking experience through feet of snow?"

"I'll make do."

"So, no."

"Why are you arguing with her?" demanded Karel. "You won't let us go, so send *her*!"

Lena decided to overlook the implied insult, for it played in her favor. Tilda seemed to be considering, a shrewd glint in her eyes.

She felt a tug on the back of her jerkin. Alix had come up beside her silently, a wariness about her narrow shoulders.

"Lena, don't..." she whispered.

"It's my duty to protect the people of Vagora. *Our* duty," she said, loud enough for the dozen rapt eavesdroppers to hear.

"Very well," the mayor said, watching Alix now. "Bring him in and take him to the magistrate, lady."

"What should I be looking for?"

"Tall, thin man. Short brown beard. Club ear. He was wearing a blue tunic last anyone saw him."

"Name?"

Tilda opened her mouth, but for a moment nothing came out. "Uther Yarlsson."

Murmurs swelled around Lena, and Karel shot the mayor another baleful look, but she tried to school her face, tried not to let them see her surprise. It didn't matter if the man had the mayor's name, he'd be brought in all the same.

"It's a start."

Alix had her hand buried in the back of her jerkin, but Lena still managed to turn to Karel. The man glared at her, but his snarl had been tucked away for now.

"I'll see justice done for your wife," she told him.

Karel swallowed whatever he might've said, throat bobbing. When Lena realized he wasn't going to say anything, not even acknowledge her vow with a nod, she turned on her heel and made for the door.

Alix was close behind, clumsily pulling on layers in her haste to keep up with her as Lena cut across Longbourne.

"Wait!" Alix rushed to get in front of her. "Lena, they're just using you."

She snorted. "Hardly. I volunteered. Besides, this is what knights do, Alix. I thought I'd taught you that by now."

She tried walking around the squire, but Alix scuttled to the side, blocking her path.

"So, what's the plan? We go riding off into the snow—"

"*I* will come back down to Longbourne and follow his trail from there. You will stay in Finhöln where it's safe."

A high, indignant sound erupted from Alix's throat. "You can't leave me behind!"

"I can't take you with me. This man is dangerous, Alix. He's already harmed one woman, and out there, with nothing to lose, he'll be desperate. I won't let him hurt you too."

"And what if he hurts *you*? Lena, it isn't Balderak. You aren't—"

"Get out of my way, Alix," she said through pursed lips.

"No."

"I said—"

"No! You're going to get yourself killed!"

"Just because I haven't taught you to track yet doesn't mean that I can't. Now get out of my way. I won't ask again."

She made to brush past, trying to keep her anger coiled tightly inside. She'd need it for the hunt, to keep her warm as she followed the frozen trail.

But Alix grabbed at her shoulder, trying to hold her back. Muscles moved out memory, and in two motions, Lena broke the hold on her and sent the attacker stumbling away.

If it weren't for Alix's nimbleness, she would've gone down face-first into the frozen mud. She took three stumbling steps before getting her feet under her again, then whirled to glare at Lena.

Lena glared right back, the heat in her face doubling when she saw the mayor and Karel scrutinizing them from the pub door. Other townsfolk had stopped to watch the spat, curious stares and smirks taking in Lena's angry blush and Alix's furious, unshed tears.

Lena turned away from Alix, from the stares, and made for the path back up to Finhöln. She barely saw or remembered the trek, her anger, her embarrassment, fueling her steady steps. She would see this done. This was what she'd trained for, to have the civilians of Vagora trust in her to see justice done, to protect them. Now, she could do this for Longbourne, could prove she wasn't like the wardens before her.

When she made one of the switchbacks in the path, she saw the wispy form of Alix trudging up the path behind her.

Lena kept walking.

⁂

Yvain was fast asleep and rather cranky when Lena woke him from his nap by struggling into the stables. His coat gleamed, no doubt from another thorough brush down from Bel. The thought annoyed her.

She could take care of her own horse.

Yvain huffed as Lena threw quilted layers over his back, but by the time he'd been equipped, he looked resigned and followed Lena out of the stables with little grumbling. She brought him round to the kitchen door, only to find it cracked open, a harried Pol trying to do several things at once, including watching Alix. She still huffed from the hike up to the castle, but that didn't stop her as she ranted and gesticulated.

It took her only a moment to realize the gist of it was that Alix thought she was an idiot.

When Pol caught sight of Lena in the doorway, he looked relieved.

Going out? he signed.

Yes. Need food, rope, and tinder kit.

Pol nodded and quickly set about gathering supplies. As he began packing a satchel of food, he pointed Lena towards the storeroom for the rope.

Alix followed her inside.

"I don't like this."

"You've made that plain enough," said Lena. She weighed two knots of rope, deciding on the lighter coil.

"What if you need help out there? What if—?"

"Do you really have no faith in me?"

Her cheeks burned at that, and Alix's gaze dropped to her chin. "It isn't that."

With a huff Lena fisted her hands on her hips. "Well?"

"What if something happens to you? And you don't have...and I won't be there to..."

"Alix, I'm a knight. This is—"

"Stop saying that! Being a knight doesn't make you invincible."

"I know that."

"Do you?"

"Yes. I'm here, aren't I?"

"That's not..." Alix crossed her arms over her chest, a thing she sometimes did to make herself look bigger, but now she just hugged herself, as if she needed the comfort. It made a knot form in Lena's throat. "Not everything is about Balderak."

"Then why do you keep bringing it up?"

"Lena, they don't care if you bring back the convict or not, especially not the mayor—hells, she probably *wants* him to get away. They just feel like they have to do something."

"*I* care."

"But they don't! They won't thank you for it. They won't invite you for a drink or—"

"I'm not doing it for that. I'm doing it because it's right. Not everything is an exchange," Lena sighed. "I thought I'd taught you that by now."

Alix made a frustrated noise, still not looking higher than Lena's chin. "Just promise me you'll come back."

Lena shouldered the rope turned to look for the tinder kit. "I was planning on it."

"No." Alix moved in close, which would've negated Lena's arms in a fight. "*Promise* me."

Lena looked down into that fierce face, reminded of the day she'd first seen it. It'd been warmer, much warmer, and Alix had been in dirt and tatters. The demand she'd made of Lena that day had been much different but no less powerful, and just like on that day, the words snagged in Lena's gut, giving it a wrench.

"I promise," she said.

Alix nodded, silently watching as Lena finished gathering supplies.

They walked back into the kitchen to find Pol trying to fit a whole cheese wedge into an already-bulging satchel.

Lena waved to get his attention and then signed, *That is good. Thank you, Pol.*

Suddenly, Alix grasped her forearm. "I have something—don't leave 'til I get back!" And with a screech of leather on stone, Alix bolted from the kitchen, up the stairs.

Lena only had time to share a bemused look with Pol before another pair of feet appeared on the stairs. Bel came down into the kitchen, looking around curiously. He took in the satchel and supplies, the saddled horse just outside, and said, "Going somewhere?"

Lena sniffed. "Just an errand."

To her chagrin, Bel stationed himself near the hearth, leaning against the countertop. He crossed his arms, looking for all the world comfortable and at ease.

She didn't believe it for a second.

The urge to leave, to get the hunt underway, ate at her, but she ground her teeth and helped Pol load her supplies into two saddlebags as they waited for Alix.

The squire didn't keep them waiting long, barreling into the kitchen at top speed. She pounced on Lena and wound her voluminous scarf around her head and neck. It turned into a sort of cowl, hooding her head and ears, before wrapping around her jaw and nose.

"So you won't be so cold," said Alix when she stepped back to survey her work.

Lena was thankful the scarf hid the pained smile that broke across her face.

"Stay safe," Lena told Alix, "and stay out of trouble."

Alix scoffed then threw her arms around Lena's waist and hugged her tight, making Lena's ribs groan in protest. She hesitated a moment, unused to this sort of thing from Alix, unused to this sort of thing from anyone. But then, as if they knew what to do, her arms slipped around the girl and returned her embrace. It touched Lena deep down in her heart of hearts, that soft, warm place where she'd once hoped for her mother's approval, where she'd dreamed of being the greatest knight in

Vagora. Lena wasn't sure she liked feeling that heart of hearts.

But she wouldn't begrudge Alix this, even if it felt like her squire was bidding her farewell to the battlefield.

Over Alix's head, Bel's gaze caught hers. She narrowed her eyes, searching for calculation. She had his word, but she still didn't like leaving Alix alone near him. Could she trust being gone so long from Finhöln?

Bel hadn't run yet, she contented herself. And he wouldn't. A coward wouldn't.

When Alix finally unwound herself, Lena stepped back. She thanked Pol, shot Bel another cautious glance, and then she was on Yvain, headed back down the mountain. She pushed the thoughts of Bel away; she had to focus now. The mountain would be as much an adversary as her quarry, and she needed her wits about her.

—•◆•—

In Longbourne, Lena inspected where the convict had been kept, in the basement of Vidar's trading post. He'd somehow cut away and broken the brittle, frozen wood to create a hole just big enough to wriggle out of and run north, out of town.

With a heading, Lena turned Yvain out the north gate and into the wilderness.

It grew colder the further Yvain trudged. They headed deeper and higher up the mountain, where the snow was even thicker and trees denser. It came up to Yvain's chest in places, and Lena had to lead him away from the higher drifts and onto easier paths.

When the trees allowed it, Lena looked to the sky. There was no sun today, only a heavy bank of steel gray clouds shrouding the horizon. Judging by the light and crispness of the air, she only had a few hours before she'd have to make camp.

Yvain and the cold were her companions here, this far up the mountain. The forest creatures had wisely holed up long ago; not even the twitter of birds or rustling of tree branches broke the heavy silence. Only Yvain's crunching steps and hot breaths did that.

Her only guide was the deep divots in the snow, the convict's footprints like shallow, sapphire pools of water in the dimming light. He'd made little secret of his path, but then, what choice did he have, unprepared for the cold? Sometimes the footprints came with a deep handprint or violent upturn of snow, as if the man had stumbled and just caught himself before falling into the white berms.

Lena supposed it'd be too much to ask for to come upon him like that, sunken in and ready to be dragged behind Yvain back to Longbourne.

16

Bel took the stairs to the kitchen gingerly, listening. There were voices down there. He should turn around. He'd had the bad luck of continually running into the warden now that he was trying to avoid her, finding her in stairwells and ducking out of the great hall after training just in time. But he was hungry, and if she was going to throw more insults at him, so be it. He'd started their ill-fated chat in the stables but gotten in a few jabs of his own, so there was that.

Halfway down, he heard scrabbling and then Alix barreled up the steps. When she got to Bel she flailed her arms to get him to move.

He couldn't help the grin that cracked across his face as he edged out of her way, as slowly as possible.

"Gah!" She shouldered him out of the way and then took the steps two at a time.

"Something on fire?" he called after her. An undignified snort echoed back down the stairwell, aimed at him.

Bel came to the landing to a sight he didn't expect. Lady Maddalena and Pol were stuffing saddlebags with food and other supplies. Through the widely cracked doorway he spotted Gray outfitted for the cold, little more than his ears exposed to the wintry chill.

He could feel her gaze on him, making his skin prickle. He made sure to keep his expression serene when he looked at Lady Maddalena and asked, "Going somewhere?"

"Just an errand," she sniffed.

Like hell. Bel almost gave his own undignified snort. She was most certainly going on a journey of some sort, saddlebags heavy, knight and horse armed and outfitted.

Bel situated himself near the hearth, leaning back against the thick countertop. He observed from his perch, knowing the warden watched him from the corner of her eye. In between rearranging a saddlebag to make room for a wedge of cheese, Pol nodded at him then a steaming mug near the hearth. He took the drink and hummed with happiness as the lavender tea eased down his throat.

Alix came back in as quickly as she'd left, breath puffing from her haste. She looped a familiar knit scarf around Lady Maddalena's head, nearly drowning her in it, and Bel had to bite back his laugh.

The squire then threw herself into her knight's arms. Lady Maddalena looked around helplessly for a moment, but then returned the embrace. Bel stared unabashedly, curious at this display. Alix was acting like she'd never see her again.

The knight met his interested gaze over Alix's head, her eyes narrowing. Bel's spine stiffened under her suspicion. There it was again, that look of hers, searching him for something. Expecting the worst of him. He'd thought, perhaps, maybe, they'd gotten past this.

But she would always expect the worst of a *coward*.

The word rang through his mind, had become a constant litany in his head these past days. She thought so little of him, and he couldn't blame her for it. He *was* a coward, had given in to his life here. In the dark of night, when it was safe to think such thoughts, Bel could admit to himself that he didn't even hate Finhöln. It wasn't the castle keeping him here, and he didn't hate or resent his life—he hadn't been born to the life of a scholar or recluse, but he took to them well enough. He was fed, clothed, kept warm. He had a good friend in Pol and a commanding landscape outside his window. He was left alone, for the most part. It wasn't a hard life most of the time, and Bel had stopped hating it a long time ago. What he did hate was who he was within these walls, a prisoner, a cripple, and...a traitor.

How many secrets had the human king eked from him over the years? How many secrets had Bel haplessly given away in his early days, before he'd learned to mistranslate? How many avian lives lost were his fault?

He hated who he was here, prisoner, cripple, traitor, and now, coward. He'd kept himself from the word, the most painful of them all, for there was no prisoner, cripple, traitor without the coward first, earning his safety, his half-life, with that of others'.

It made his stomach roil, that she'd been so right, and the lavender tea didn't taste good in his mouth anymore, just hot and acidic. How many days had he spent, belly full of Pol's good cooking, idling his time away? Even with the restlessness of winter settling over him, even with the mistranslations looming over him, it was a comfortable life. It scared him that he didn't know what was beyond the tree line he could see outside his window. What kind of world was out there? What was left of the world he'd been stolen away from ten years ago?

Movement drew his attention back to the scene before him. Lady Maddalena said farewell to Alix and Pol, mounted up, and then was out of sight. "I'll see her off," Alix said, presumably to herself, and then scampered back up the steps to watch Lady Maddalena make her way down the mountainside.

Once the echo of her footsteps faded away, plus another minute, Pol turned to Bel, a sort of fevered excitement making his eyes wide and glassy.

Pol made a flapping move so that Bel would look when he signed, *It's your chance, Bel.*

For what? he replied with slow fingers.

To escape! Follow me.

The man began hurriedly gathering more supplies, moving so quickly that it took three tries before Bel got a good grasp on Pol's tunic and pulled him to a stop.

Bel asked him to explain.

The warden is hunting an escaped fugitive, Pol signed quickly, his movements jerky with excitement. *She could be gone for days. This is your chance. With her away, nothing is keeping you here.*

Pol moved towards the storeroom, but Bel stayed him again.

It's the middle of winter. What chance would I have out there?

But his words only made Pol smile a mischievous smile. With a crook of his finger, he bid Bel follow him into the storeroom. Bemused, he did. The space was dark and cavernous, musky with just a hint of spice from the drying herbs hung from the rafters. Pol hunkered down, moving crates around until he could pull out two worn leather satchels. He ushered them to the door but waited in the threshold. He pointed at his ear, then looked at the stairwell.

No one is coming, Bel confirmed.

Pleased, Pol began unloading his hidden treasures. A heavy fur-lined leather coat was first, a wool cloak with oilskin lining next, thick gloves, a pick axe, rope, compass, a canvas tarp, three tinder kits with flint strikers, tightly wound spools of gauze, wooden pots of balm and ointment, a sheathed dagger, and, most surprising of all, a small pouch of gold coins. They made a happy *clink* when Pol proudly bestowed them in Bel's palm.

You've been planning this, he signed with unsteady hands.

Pol's gaze searched his for a long moment before replying, *One of us had to. Bel, I will not let you rot away here forever.*

He followed Pol back into the kitchen numbly, carrying all of the treasures. Everything he might need was either in the satchels or in the kitchen. Everything he could need to trek through the wilderness, through the Hollenheim Mountains, through the Grass Sea, to Hadria.

Bel's heart constricted, too full to beat properly. Feelings battered him, at once profound gratitude, the kind that could never be repaid. Disbelief, that Pol could scheme, could gather such supplies unnoticed. Most dangerous of all, hope, hope that lit a little flame in his chest, just enough to keep a steady thrum going through him. But mostly he felt fear, fear that numbed his hands, made his legs feel leaden, frozen to the floor. How could Pol expect—Bel couldn't really—there wasn't—

Pol gave his shoulder a friendly shove. *Are you a statue? Get moving! You are wasting daylight.*

So much could go wrong. It's too—

Pol caught Bel's hands in one of his. *This is your chance, Bel. Don't you want to be free?*

Yes, Bel replied immediately. But then, *I don't know if I can.*

Of course, you can. You couldn't ask for a better chance.

A-l-i-x—

I will keep the girl busy.

The warden—

Deep into the snows by now. It may take her days to find and bring back the man.

She will come after me. Hallan did.

Pol made a garbled growl at the old name. *She is not Hallan. Maybe she will come after you, maybe she won't. But you will be far ahead. And I do not think she will harm you.*

Why wouldn't she? She's expected to. She thinks little of me.

You must trust me. This is your chance. You cannot squander your life away.

With a jolt, Bel met Pol's eyes, glassy again, but now with tears. Pol waved between them and then pawed at his eyes with the heels of his palms.

Please, Bel. You were never meant for these crumbling walls. One of us deserves to really live. I am too old, but you, you are young and strong yet. You can make it.

Bel swallowed around the growing knot in his throat, relieved that he didn't have to speak to talk to Pol. He didn't know if his voice would work properly.

It was all so sudden, so unexpected. The little flicker of hope continued to burn, but he kept it from conflagrating. He hated himself for holding back, for not seizing this chance, this *gift* Pol gave him. He hated his hesitation but couldn't make himself take what Pol offered.

So much could go wrong. It was the middle of winter. He was crippled, and with the reset bone healed but tender, he couldn't even glide. He didn't know which direction the warden or the convict were headed. There were other people on the mountain. When he didn't send the translations, someone would come looking.

And on the heels of all these worries, one word. *Coward.*

He was a coward for not taking his chance. He was a coward for not escaping, for not returning to his people with all that he knew. He was a coward to hide away, to cling to this half-life.

He saw Lady Maddalena in his mind's eye then, saw the look she'd cast him. *Why are you here?* she'd demanded to know, and Bel had only had uncomfortable answers for her, ones only he and the night knew. *Because I am a coward.*

But I don't have to be. I am better than she thinks I am.

A sigh shuddered through him as Bel released his held breath, and he gripped Pol's shoulder to steady himself.

All right, he signed, and Pol smiled.

Later, Bel couldn't say he remembered the particulars of readying for his escape. He knew he went to his room to gather clothes and blankets, his one sturdy pair of snow boots. He knew he ran his hands over the spines of the old tomes in his library, those companions who had seen him through many long days. He knew he returned to the kitchen for Pol to outfit him piece by piece, first thinner layers, jerkin, jacket, wool leggings, then leather trousers, oilskin chaps, coat, cloak, and finally the satchels, one over each shoulder with a bedroll strapped on top.

Pol stood before him, cinching the straps of the satchels. Bel wished he too had something to do with his hands, but all he could do now was watch Pol, watch that dear face as it scrunched and grimaced and finally eased as tears slipped from his eyes.

Bel held still as Pol drew the cloak's hood over his head. Pol smoothed out the wrinkles for a long moment before taking Bel's face between his hands. He didn't have his hands to speak, but he didn't need them as he held Bel's gaze.

Be safe, said his eyes, demanding a promise. *Be free.*

Hot tears spilled from Bel's eyes and then he was pulling Pol into an embrace. Pol gripped him hard, stronger than he looked, and Bel wrapped his good wing around them, embracing in the avian way.

Pol made a gulping sound and ran a hand over the downy feathers. It was a long time before they pulled away from each other. It was Pol who stepped back first, halfheartedly signing that they were wasting time.

Bel dried his eyes, trying to contain the swell in his chest, the ache he already had from missing Pol, from knowing he'd never be able to repay his friend, from knowing he may never see him again.

Pol waved a hand between them. *Go, while you still can.*

Thank you, my friend, Bel signed, then placed his hand over his heart.

Bel fled the kitchen before he could think anything else, before he could convince himself to stay. He ran through the garden, to the crumbling east wall, and lifted himself over the granite blocks.

His feet landed with a soft crunch in the snow. For the first time in nine years, Bel was outside the curtain wall, and for a moment his body couldn't move from that spot, the wall at his back, the choice to stay still there, still viable. It tugged at his chest, a chain that bound him to the castle, pulling taut now that he was outside.

Bel took one step, then two, three, and he was running, running without really seeing, charging through the snow until his thighs ached with the work and his lungs heaved like bellows and his breaths came in heavy clouds of hot mist. He ran until he couldn't, until the forest swallowed the castle, swallowed him too, and then he fell to his knees in the snow.

He'd done it. He'd run.

17

Lena lost the light sooner than she'd hoped. She could tell when the sun disappeared behind the mountain face, as if a cold shudder went through the land with its loss. The white snow took on a bluish tint, and she lost the few hints of green peeking through the snow, all of them turning so dark that she couldn't tell the difference between a downed or low branch and a hole.

She dismounted to lead Yvain. His legs and ankles turned so much more easily and were much more important.

She was considering lighting one of the torches stowed away in the saddlebags when the white landscape broke, a blocky shadow disturbing the serene horizon. Her eye caught, she tried to make sense of the hazy shape. It was far too wide to be a tree.

Drawing closer, Lena left Yvain behind at the line of trees, knowing his dappled gray would fade into the snow. She watched her footfalls, wincing every time the snow crackled underfoot. As she drew closer, her eyes traced angles too straight for nature to make.

Lena touched a gentle hand to the structure's side and felt the rough grain of old timbers through the leather. It was a small building of some sort—a hunting outpost? It had a threshold with no door and was just big enough for a horse and rider to huddle inside, away from the worst of the weather.

She quietly pulled a dagger from the sheath strapped to her right thigh as she crept up to the threshold. She held her breath for three counts, listening, heard nothing, one, two, three and—

The solitary room was empty of life. Lena took a cautious step inside, checking the deeper pools of shadow at the far corner. A few old, rickety chairs were stacked in one corner, a makeshift pallet in another. A battered trunk with a rusting iron latch sat between them, its lid flung open.

She crept further in, peeking over the lip of the trunk. Blankets and clothing lay inside, or at least, once had. There were only scraps left, strewn about the trunk.

Her quarry had been here but hadn't stayed. Why? Was this a well-known waystation?

Why not tell her about it? Why not give her all the places a man with nothing but the clothes on his back was likely to go to?

A growl worked up Lena's throat, but she bit it back, instead hurrying Yvain into the shelter. A little searching yielded a hearty pile of peat near the doorway, next to a makeshift firepit. She'd never cared for the smell of burning peat, preferring spicy wood smoke, but beggars couldn't be choosers, not in weather like this.

With a fire crackling, Lena pulled off Yvain's barding but left the quilted sleeve and cape. The horse nickered, twitched his ears back and forth, and then settled in for the night. After watching the inky shadows play tricks on the pearlescent snow outside for a while, Lena too settled in, though she kept on her leathers and laid her sword and daggers within easy reach.

Lena allowed herself to rest, allowed her eyes to close, but she didn't truly sleep, instead falling into a doze that all soldiers perfected. It was a light sleep that anything could break, but rather than listening for the sentries' horns, or shout of a commander to rise, or the crack of her mother's voice, Lena listened to Yvain's steady breathing. The horse would know sooner than she if someone else approached.

Nothing disturbed them through the silent night, not even an owl. When she rose with the dawn and stepped outside to relieve herself, however, she saw the wide pawprints of a lynx pacing around the perimeter of the outpost. It made her uneasy, thinking the cat had been so close without she or Yvain noticing. She didn't care to be the hunted.

The fire was doused, Yvain was saddled again, and Lena left the outpost before the sun had crested the mountain peak. The storm Malthus and Alix and Tilda Yarlsson had worried so much about hadn't come yet, and Lena sent a silent prayer up to Matella for small favors.

The convict's prints had iced over, deep crevices in the otherwise virgin snow. The footfalls were steadier now, she noticed. Less stumbling, less catching himself on branches and berms, leaving behind broken needles.

His northward path had made sense to her; from what she knew of the area, there were few mountain passes still open this far into winter. Northern towns were nearly cut off from the rest of Vagora; the well-used roads to the south would be fifty feet under snow. One narrow pass remained open to the northeast, a dangerous, craggy route if the maps Lena had skimmed were anything to go by.

His heading made sense—so she was surprised when the footprints turned sharply south. Was he headed for another waystation? He had to have stopped for the night sometime, even with supplies. Did he know of other shelter, to the south? It was more than two days' walk to Whitewater, the fortress that lay south, down the mountain. He couldn't have made it that far yet. So where was he going?

Lena puzzled over this as Yvain trudged on, dutifully following the neat trail of footprints. She began to wonder if the man was going to lead her right to him, when a second pair of footprints crossed the first. These were older, filled in somewhat with fresher snow. But once they crossed, both pairs looked fresh, the snow compacted to the same depth.

Lena sat on Yvain for a long moment, deciding. She tried the northeast trail first, thinking it made sense for him to head for the useable pass. Eventually, the trail became old footprints again.

She turned Yvain around and went back to the cross-section of prints, following the southeast trail instead. Was there a pass she didn't know about? Another local secret townsfolk would know intimately but the hapless Warden of Finhöln wouldn't? She couldn't help the exasperated huff that erupted from her throat.

A sound caught Lena's ear, and she pulled on the reins. Yvain nickered softly but then fell silent, ears swiveling.

Lena slowly dismounted, aiming her boots for the footprints to avoid crunching new snow. She crept up to a berm, laying herself flat, teeth clenching as snow found its way under Alix's scarf and between her glove and sleeve.

Below the rise, the snow had been cleared to make a hole deep into the snow. Finger-shaped divots raked the snow, and Lena's breath caught in her throat when she realized she had to be nearly on top of the convict, holed up in a snow den.

She slowed her breathing, a deep in out, in out, as she listened. It was faint, but there it was, the scrape of cloth over snow, the distinctive crunch of snow compacting.

Slowly, moving one muscle at a time, Lena raised herself to her hands and knees. She peered over the edge, hoping for a better angle, but only caught the bottom lip of the snow den. There was a chance she could backtrack, come at it from another angle, but from the silence within, she suspected he already knew she was here. From any other side, he'd see her coming.

First one leg then the other, Lena edged down the slope of the berm, putting her weight on exposed piles of pine needles and scrub roots. It was slow going but quieter. Before reaching the bottom, Lena palmed a dagger in each hand, throwing dagger and long dirk.

She put her right foot down on a leafless shrub, ready for the last step to the ground. She thought she heard a sharp intake of breath, the crunch of a body shifting ever so slightly.

It drew her gaze to the snow den, where she could just see a booted foot peeking out. Her heart jumped then beat a rapid staccato.

Lena watched that foot move, and she moved in kind, stepping down—

She saw the cold glint of metal in the weak morning sunlight too late. The hunting trap gave a terrible *snick* before biting down into her right calf, and Lena couldn't help it, a pained cry escaped her lips as the den erupted, snow flying everywhere as the convict ran for the trees.

18

The crisp mountain air burned Bel's lungs and he loved it. The world was a quiet white around him; a few intrepid birds flitted about, but otherwise the world slept, turned a blind eye to his escape. Somehow the world was wider than he remembered, the borders reaching far past his sight. The openness of it, the sheer scale, sent a shiver of fearful delight through him. The trees seemed taller, grander, and the snow whiter, crisper. The air had a cold, sweet tang to it.

He picked his way through the snow, using his wings to balance and distribute weight so he could walk atop it in places. He headed southeast. The mountain that shadowed Finhöln was the head of a long, curving spine of mountain ranges that hooked in a crescent all the way to the Southlands. He knew he had to go east, past these north mountains that sheltered humans and mountain goats and lynxes, through the mountain valleys that sparkled like emeralds and diamonds with their dense aspens and pines and crystal lakes, finally to the high stretch of the Hollenheim Mountains, the ancestral home of avians. There was nothing there for him save a path unknown to humans, a path that would lead him deeper into avian land.

Well, former avian land. A vast swathe of land lay between him and avian-controlled territory. The journey would be long, longer than if he'd escaped nine years ago. But it was already underfoot, and there was nowhere to go but forward.

Bel repeated that to himself as the afternoon waned, *nowhere to go but forward.* It was just comfort enough as he followed the mountain range, headed for the little-known pass to the southeast. Pol had told him about it before, signed, *Only local townsfolk are mad enough to use it. Them and mountain goats. Barely a pass at all.* But Lady Maddalena knew nothing of it, so he had to hope her chase of the convict led both humans toward the nearer, more navigable northeastern pass.

The further away from Finhöln he went, the heavier Bel's chest felt. The initial exhilaration of freedom had worn down to shivers of unease that slivered up his spine whenever he stopped to take a quick break. What if the warden found the convict quickly and was back to Finhöln by nightfall? What if she was as good a tracker as Hallan? He wasn't exactly covering his trail. What if she blamed Pol? What if Pol was punished for Bel's escape? What if his freedom cost Pol his own?

Bel swallowed the bile trying to surge up his throat.

He found welcome distraction in the effort it took putting one foot in front of the other. Even with the counterbalance of his wings, his feet still sunk in the snow, some sticking to his boots, compacting into an icy weight. Each footfall was more work than the last, and Bel shivered as little rivulets of sweat ran down his neck, steaming in the cold air.

Sooner than he'd like, he lost the sun. Bel trudged on, using what little light remained. When the moon replaced the sun, he used the incandescent, pearly light of moon and snow to work further into the forest, his eyesight better than a human's.

The moon was high in the crystalline sky when Bel finally stopped to make camp. His body ached; while strong, it was used to the *ariant* forms, the strike and parry of the sword, not slogging through snow. His thighs burned and it took long minutes for him to catch his breath.

Though tired and achy, he had little appetite. He gnawed on a small hunk of bread and chunk of cheese only because he could imagine Pol wagging his finger at him to eat.

Meal finished, Bel looked around the little clearing he'd stopped in. Near him was a snow berm that would do. Setting down his satchels, he began making a snow den, carving a little cave for himself within the hill of snow. When he thought he had a good enough hole that wouldn't cave in on him during the night, Bel dragged in his treasures, laid out bedroll and cloak, and collapsed.

Sleep wouldn't come. Though the mountain slept, little noises tickled Bel's straining ears, reminders that he wasn't safe in his bedchamber in Finhöln. Every crackle of snow, every gust blowing the snow-laden branches, every shift and twitch of his own body, he came awake.

The world was blue and dark, the shadows long and deep. Bel kept his front to the entrance of his den. Each time a shadow moved, he thought it would be the warden. He thought he heard movement once, the soft padding of feet. He told himself it was too light to be human or horse, but he held his breath, heart beating furiously, until the footsteps passed.

He must have fallen asleep sometime in the night, for though he kept thinking the warden had found him, it wasn't Lady Maddalena he saw over the lip of his den. Hallan, with that cruel, twisted mouth, searched for him with a rabid intensity that burned bright in his dark eyes. Bel shuddered and huddled deeper into his den.

When he opened his eyes again, it was to a bright, glittering morning. Fractals of sunlight danced off the snow, slanting in through the heavy pine limbs.

Bel took a deep, cold breath, not quite ready to venture from his den. Dread from his hazy half-dreams still clung to him, making him distrust the bright world beyond the den. He lay there, silent and unmoving, straining his ears for the slightest sound. The sun had eased half a hand's width through the sky before finally, Bel emerged.

He stretched each limb, one at a time, shaking out his feathers and cracking his spine.

Bel broke camp as quickly and quietly as possible, chewing a few bites of cheese as he did. It was hard, nearly frozen, but after thawing in his hot mouth, Bel took comfort from the creamy tang of it. It was the taste of breakfast, of Pol's care and cooking, and Bel sucked on the cheese until it nearly went liquid in his mouth.

He inspected the area around his den, finding only the prints of a few snow hares and a lynx probably in pursuit. No human foot or horse hoof anywhere that he could see.

Pushing down his dread, Bel struck out into the snow again. He paced himself this time, pushing only to a bearable ache in his legs. Bel kept his ears alert and his head up as he walked, taking no comfort from the silent world around him today. It felt false, this silence, a façade somehow, as if the snow swallowed everything but the closest noises. The sound of his footfalls was like a thunderclap, echoing and alarming.

He saw nothing but snow and trees and rocks as he walked, no hares or birds. But things saw him; little eyes watched him from nests and dens, tracking the lumbering intruder that disturbed their quiet woods.

Bel had worked himself into a rhythm—left foot, right foot, look left, left foot, right foot, look right—when he heard a soft nicker.

Heart in his throat, Bel dove behind the nearest tree, pressing his back into the frozen bark. His eyes swiveled, but he saw nothing before him, nothing but snow and trees and rocks. Slowly, he looked over his right shoulder.

Gray, Lady Maddalena's warhorse, stood there looking at him from across a small clearing. He was just as Bel remembered from yesterday, cape and leather chamfron and saddle. But where was—

There, a figure slid down a big snow berm. With her brown leathers and agile grace, Lady Maddalena looked like a wood nymph. Her attention was on the ground below her, allowing Bel to take a breath. She hadn't seen him yet.

He eased himself to his side, letting the width of the tree conceal him. Leaning slowly, inch by inch, he peered around to see Lady Madda-lena creeping down the slight slope.

What was she doing? From this angle, Bel couldn't see anything but her and the side of the berm. Had she cornered the convict here? Had he made a snow den too, in the berm she was easing down? Why else would she leave her horse?

She continued to move, catlike in her quietness, and Bel's heart pounded in his ears. She hadn't seen him, only Gray had, and the horse wasn't moving towards him or drawing attention to him. He should get moving, she was too close, she had only to look up and to her left and she'd—

A *snick* broke the echoing silence of the clearing, and then every-thing happened at once.

A wet sound made Bel wince as a hunting trap sank its teeth into Lady Maddalena's left calf.

Her cry tore through the frigid air, her pained scream a hot puff from her cracked, red mouth.

The berm exploded in a rain of snow, another human bursting from their hiding spot.

Bel got the impression of a man under all the layers and hood. His heart jumped into his throat as the convict raced through the clearing, unknowingly straight toward Bel. He instinctively huddled back into the cover of the tree.

Then there were two feet pounding through the snow. Grunts, a shout, the sound of upturned snow.

Bel rolled his head to get a look, unable to move anything else.

The two humans wrestled around in the snow, each trying to get atop the other. Somehow Lady Maddalena had pulled the trap from the ground and leapt on the convict, taking him down to the snow where she could use the rest of her body to overpower him.

Once he'd looked, Bel couldn't look away, entranced by the scene before him. Despite her wound, Lady Maddalena fought like a hellcat; whenever the convict managed to buck her off, she was right there again, subduing him. When he pulled a knife, she knocked it from his hand, sending it flying towards Bel. He noted where it fell, the hilt glinting in the sunlight.

Bel didn't know how, but as they wrestled each other deeper into the snow, Lady Maddalena managed to shout between strikes and blocks, "Uther Yarlsson—in the name of Vagora, King Artemian—and Sigrid—I arrest you for the crimes—of assault, evading capture, and—"

"Fuck you!" he growled. "You got no right—"

"I have *every* right!" she roared. A shiver of something went through Bel at the fierceness in her voice, in her eyes—not quite fear, not dread, something more like...awe?

She fumbled for a length of rope on her belt, and the convict used her move to land a hit to her face, cracking her lip. But she only grunted and struck back, harder, dazing the man. Using her won moment, she unsheathed a dagger and hit the man's temple with the metal hilt.

The convict slumped unconscious into the snow.

A feral noise erupted from the knight at her victory, and Bel thought she was going to kill the man, or at least spit in his unconscious face. After a long moment of glaring contemptuously at the still body beneath her, she did neither, instead using her rope to tie the man's arms behind his back, then his ankles.

With the last knot tied, Maddalena swayed on her hands and knees, almost crashing to the ground, but she bared her teeth in a grimace and crawled towards a tree on the opposite side of the clearing from Bel. She dragged the untethered trap behind her, a trail of blood seeping from the bitten flesh.

Bel kept absolutely still as he watched her slump back against a tree. Her breaths came in shallow pants, the fight and blood loss showing on her drawn, haggard features. Her normally golden skin was leached of color, her lips only a blue-tinged grimace.

She sat still for a long moment, just catching her breath, then with a groan stripped off her gloves and eased up to inspect her leg. She probed the broken flesh, and even from his hiding spot, Bel could see the blood oozing out around the iron teeth of the trap. She made a little whimper but quickly buried it in a growl.

He watched in morbid fascination as she worked her fingers beneath the teeth and began prying, trying to free herself. She pulled once, twice, three times, her blood-slicked hands losing their grip, letting the teeth sink further in with each slip. She bled more and more, puddles of it painfully red against the white snow. She bled, and Bel felt himself bleeding with her.

He didn't like seeing her like this, shivering and in pain. He knew she was strong, wholly believed she'd eventually get herself and her captive back on Gray and back to Finhöln. It might kill her, but she'd do it.

The thought stayed Bel when he should've looked for a route to escape.

She could die here, bleeding, in the snow. If the blood loss didn't kill her, the cold might.

Bel gritted his teeth. It wasn't his duty nor in his interest to help her. He owed her nothing.

But he couldn't help but watch her struggle, trying again to pull out the trap. She made it further this time, but again her wet, shaking fingers couldn't hold on long enough. The trap sank back in, pulling another ragged grunt of pain from her.

Her whole body slumped before she clenched her fists, turned her face to the sky, and screamed.

It wasn't the sound a victor made. It was the cry of the defeated, the condemned, the worn-down. She screamed and screamed and screamed, and something inside Bel screamed with her. He recognized this beaten, feral part of Maddalena, this person stripped down to only survival. He saw her pale, tear-soaked face, and he saw someone he knew, someone whose soul cried out just as loudly as his own, for relief, for a chance.

Her lungs gave out finally, the sudden end of her scream leaving an aching echo in the clearing. Her scream cut off in a sob, a noise that struck Bel even deeper, but only two escaped before she bit her cheek and was silent.

Bel leaned his head back against his tree, unable to bear the sight of her pain anymore.

What now?

He had to leave her.

Pol was right, this was his chance. Not only was the warden of Finhöln stranded in the wilderness, ignorant of his flight, she was wounded, incapable of bringing him back. He'd never had a chance like this, doubted he ever would again. To go back was to stay. He knew that. He would ease back into his habitable life at Finhöln, continue to train for a day that he knew would never come again. She would always be suspicious of him, always watch every move he made with scrutiny. Any semblance of freedom, of independence, would evaporate. And after another winter, a new warden would come, a new unknown.

Her life, for his.

Bel couldn't swallow, could barely breathe around the knot tangling his throat. *Coward, coward, coward* beat his head in time with his rapid pulse.

He'd run to prove to himself, to *her*, that he wasn't a coward, but now, he thought perhaps running would only make him more a coward.

Her life, for his. His half-life, for hers.

Bel drew in a breath, feeling it shudder in his chest. He sent a silent apology to Pol, to Maddok too, for what he had to do now.

He pushed away from the tree and slowly walked across the clearing to Maddalena.

She didn't notice him until he was nearly upon her. Her eyes were closed, and for a moment Bel worried she'd lost consciousness. But then her eyes flickered, and he looked into a green so vivid it burned.

He picked up the knife she'd knocked from the convict's hand as he came, and he watched her stiffen. That was her only response to seeing him, her whole body going rigid. She didn't scoff or shout or demand what he was doing, only stared as he came near, then hunkered down by her wounded leg.

She held perfectly still, except for her eyes, which darted from the knife to his face to her leg and back again. He watched her from under his hood, not quite ready yet to peel it away.

"What are you doing here?" she finally said. There was no censure in her voice, only weary, mild curiosity.

"I saw what happened."

"Come to finish it?" She looked pointedly at the knife.

"No. Could've let the mountain do that. Now let me look."

The fight seemed to go out of her, and if it was possible, she slumped even further against the tree, as if her bones and muscle and sinews hadn't the strength left to support her.

"The release is broken," she informed him without inflection to her voice.

Bel used the knife to cut away bits of her trouser leg and boot so that he could get a good look. The wounds were clean punctures without any jagged edges, but they were deep and needed stitching. She'd been lucky, though; the iron teeth had found the meaty part of her calf, missing her shin bone.

He set his packs down and dug through one for a roll of gauze. He set it within easy reach before readjusting slightly, taking off his gloves, and finding a good handhold.

He heard Maddalena take a long, deep breath, and then she closed her eyes. "Do it."

He pulled, ignored the pained sounds she made, pulled until he felt the teeth slipping free. He paused only long enough to adjust his hold, then pulled until the teeth were free of her flesh. In one quick move he slid the trap free and threw it before it could clamp on his fingers.

Round, round went the roll of gauze, and he tied it off near her knee in a makeshift tourniquet. When it was done, he pulled out his extra blanket and covered her with it.

She was looking at him now, her gaze faraway. He reached a hand out to help her up, but she only stared at it. They stayed like that for a long time, and Bel thought she wanted to say something, but whatever it was, she eased it back down her throat and took his hand.

Once he had her standing, balanced against the tree, he went to fetch Gray, but she told him not to bother. Putting two fingers in her mouth, she made a sharp whistle that sent nearby birds flying.

Gray appeared from the other side of the berm, his gait easy and steady. Bel helped her into the saddle, and then to rearrange her leg so that less blood would flow down into it.

Maddalena kept Gray in place as Bel dragged the convict over to them, hefted him across the horse's flanks behind her saddle, and tied the man's wrists and ankles together.

All this he did in silence, knowing she watched him. She said nothing when he retrieved the daggers she'd dropped in the scuffle and handed them to her, nothing when he took Gray's bridle in hand and began to lead him into the trees.

He thought they'd make the whole journey back to Finhöln like that, and he couldn't decide if that was for the best or not, when she said, "Why, Bel? Why do you not run?"

Bel glanced at her over his shoulder. "You need help. And I'm not so much a coward to refuse it."

She said nothing more, her mouth thinning to a troubled line the only acknowledgement of his words, and they journeyed the rest of the way in silence.

19

Lena kept stealing glances at the baffling avian as he led them down the mountain slope to Finhöln. Whenever she looked at his oilskin hood, with little wisps of golden hair escaping around the brim, she thought, *Yes, surely this is a dreamworld.* Nothing felt real anymore, not since she'd waded into the snows yesterday, leaving behind Finhöln, Longbourne, and all other human presence. She'd thought she'd understood the world she entered, thought it would be her against all obstacles, mountain, man, or otherwise.

But this...

What he'd done...

When she could overcome her dazed astonishment long enough to look inward, she shifted in the saddle to realize she felt none of the things she should. There was no fury, no indignation. When she'd seen him striding towards her through that clearing, the first thing, after shock of course, that had run through her was relief. Relief that someone had come, relief that she wouldn't fail, relief that she wouldn't die alone on this goddess-forsaken mountain.

Lena turned her attention outward again, not quite comfortable or reassured by the swirl of feelings she did and did not have.

They made good time down the mountain, Bel taking care to lead Yvain around suspect patches of snow. She couldn't bring herself to say anything, instead resigned to shivering in the saddle, letting herself be led back to the safety of Finhöln. She should take her reins back, should tie Bel's hands together and drag him behind Yvain like the fugitive he was, but she didn't want to do either of those things.

She was too tired, too cold, too relieved.

She watched his back as the decrepit castle walls began to peek through the trees. It was hard to tell, but she thought his back straightened, shoulders stiff under all those layers. Her heart gave a lurch, and she bit back the *Everything will be all right* that clambered up her throat. She couldn't promise him it would be. She shouldn't promise him anything.

They rounded the barbican gate to the stunned audience of Malthus, coming up from town. The older man's jaw hung loose, the red of his mouth hot and stark against the frozen castle around them. Lena met his wide-eyed gaze and lifted her chin.

They left Malthus standing there, Bel leading Yvain through the bailey, down the north steps, to the kitchen door. Lena pulled her feet from the stirrups, gritting her teeth in preparation for dismounting.

A gloved hand touched her knee. "Here." And then she was sliding down not to the ground, but into Bel's arms.

"I can—" But it was too late, he'd taken her weight, supporting her beneath the knees and across the back. Lena didn't know what to do with herself as Bel took two long strides to the door.

They stayed like that, not looking at one another, for a long moment before Lena realized she was the only one with hands free. She undid the latch and Bel kicked the door open.

It took a moment for Lena's eyes to adjust to the kitchen, dim compared to the harsh white outside. Alix jumped from her stool at the carving table with a yelp. She rushed to Bel and Lena, her sudden movement drawing Pol's attention. He looked perhaps even more shocked than Malthus had, and Lena noted a flush overcome Pol's face.

"What happened?" Alix demanded as she hovered around Lena.

"Hunting snare," Lena said.

"Here, set her here." Alix pulled the stool she'd just vacated away from the table.

Bel carefully set Lena on the stool, not pulling back until he seemed sure she could sit on her own. She sought his gaze, trying to snag his eyes with hers, but he was determined to look anywhere but at her, instead pulling up another stool for her leg.

Alix gave a low whistle at the sight of Lena's bandaged calf. "Holy hells, it got you good."

"I hate those things," Lena grumbled. "No wonder animals chew off their own limbs to escape."

Alix made a face at her morbid remark. "Well, thank Matella and all the Maidens it didn't come to that."

"Yes." She looked for Bel again, uneasy at his silence. He was signing with Pol, the two of them gesturing at the same time, and she had the rather distant thought that this was what an argument of the hands looked like. Somehow, she doubted they were arguing over the particulars of freeing her from the snare.

"Did you get the fucker?"

"Yes," she said, no energy for an added *of course*, or even *Alix, language.*

"Should bring him in, I suppose. I'll do it."

"No—"

"I'll go," said Bel, detaching himself from the grip Pol had on his shoulder. He strode out the kitchen door into the cold, leaving the three humans to look amongst themselves.

Pol blinked at her before his gaze—guiltily?—fell to the ground. He made himself busy collecting supplies and putting on a kettle of water to boil. Alix helped Lena out of a few of the more cumbersome layers she wore, her thick gloves, Alix's knit scarf, the top three buttons of her overcoat.

When she was done, Alix stepped back and frowned at the large satchels Bel had set down near the hearth. "Did he help you into the castle?"

"He found me." Alix's head whipped around so fast, her black curls fell across her eyes, and she had to shove them back. "I'd gotten the convict subdued but the trap's release was broken and I couldn't get it off. He came out of the trees, got it off, helped me onto Yvain, and then we came back here."

"You mean he...ran away?"

Lena nodded slowly, watching Pol's back as he poured boiling water from the kettle into a clay pitcher. "It looks that way, yes."

A troubled look crossed Alix's young face, all downturned eyebrows and big, hurt eyes, but Lena didn't know what else to tell her, not when her own feelings about Bel's escape roiled around in her gut.

Bel came back into the kitchen hauling the convict. The man was awake now, his bloodshot eyes panicked as they skittered throughout the room. When they landed on Lena, he growled and began fighting Bel, but the avian only tightened his hold, making the man wheeze.

Between Bel and Alix, they got the man tied down onto a chair as Pol carefully unwounded the bloody bandage from Lena's leg. Pol made an unhappy humming sound at the sight of all the seeping punctures, deaf to the man's ranting.

"Get your hands off me, filth," spat the convict at Bel. "You got no right to hold me! I'm innocent, Karel's just jealous I—"

"Gag him," Lena snapped, tired of him.

Alix smiled evilly, fetching two dirty dish rags. She stuffed one into the man's mouth as Bel held his head and tied the other around his mouth.

The man was wild-eyed, his raving now a muffled *hmph mmmf mmmm*, but he persisted even as Bel and Alix abandoned him to the corner of the kitchen. They came to watch Pol gingerly work Lena's boot off her leg and roll her trousers up to her knee. Wordlessly, Alix came to her other side and gave her a hand to grip.

As Pol gently prodded and peered at the punctures, he made a few quick signs at Bel, who nodded and set about pulling ingredients out of the cupboards. Lena chose to watch him rather than Pol cleaning her wounds with the hot water. Bel moved efficiently, though he still seemed stiff, measuring out milk and other liquids. When he was finished, he brought her a pewter mug full to the brim with a sweet-smelling concoction.

"Should help the pain," he said quietly.

"What's in it?"

"Lavender and chamomile, poppy milk, and some rum."

Alix made an appreciative noise while Lena grimaced.

"Could be worse," she supposed, and tipped the mug back. The concoction slipped down her throat like a caress, and almost immediately, the poppy milk made the world a creamy haze full of soft edges. Even the needle Pol began to weave through her skin didn't look sharp.

It wasn't the first time Lena had shoved something questionable down her throat before a medic went to work with needle and knife somewhere on her body. It wouldn't be the last. Her first time had been the worst, a deep gash to the side; Lena had seen her own insides, had stared in morbid fascination at just how pink those vital bags of tissue and fluid were. She remembered little else but the pinkness of her organs and the red, sucking mouth of the wound itself, drooling blood all over her and the medic. Her strategy afterwards was always to remember that things could be worse, she could be looking at pink organs.

The biggest of the punctures only required two or three stitches, as the wounds were deep rather than wide. Pol sutured the muscle where he could, the wounds not big enough for his fingers to work. Each time he began a new stitch he glanced up at her, his worried, crinkled brow making his forehead look like folded cloth. She waved him on each time; once she offered a smile, but it must have looked like a grimace because it made Pol stop and gesture for Bel to give her more poppy milk. Lena refused and didn't try to smile again.

It was done soon enough, Pol quick and precise when he wasn't clucking over Lena's discomfort. At Lena's request, he rearranged her trouser leg, bandaged everything up, and helped her navigate back into her boot. She gritted her teeth at the tight fit.

"Let me go get another pair of trous for you," said Alix.

"No, it's just blood and everything's wrapped. Help me up."

But Alix put a hand on her shoulder and kept her down instead. "Why?"

Lena nodded at the convict, who'd quieted, letting his black glare do the work his mouth couldn't. "I have to get him back to Longbourne."

"That can wait! Your leg—"

"Alix, I've had much worse. And I don't want him spending the night under this roof. It's best to see this done and have it over with."

"You need to rest. We can just keep him tied up."

"No, I'll see this done. Go and saddle the palfrey for me. We'll get him tied to a horse and then I'll take him down to Longbourne.

"No, Lena, that's—"

"Alix. I wasn't asking," she said as gently as possible.

Alix looked to the others, seeking support, but Pol had his back turned, cleaning his needle and pitcher, and Bel was again avoiding eye contact. Seeing she fought alone, Alix frowned at her, looking for weakness, but Lena stood—well, sat—firm. Finally, the girl huffed, grabbed her coat, and stomped out of the kitchen.

She left a quiet kitchen in her wake, the only sounds now the crackle of the fire and the convict scuffling in his seat. Lena slowly buttoned up her coat again, waiting. She wanted Bel to speak though she didn't know what she'd say in return. She only knew she had a ball of tangled feelings swelling in her chest, and she wanted them to either go away or be released.

Finally, almost too quietly to hear, Bel said, "Are you sure about this?"

"Yes. I don't want him near Alix. The sooner he's in a secure cell the better I'll feel."

"But your leg…"

Lena nodded. "I won't pretend I don't need help getting in the saddle. But that's where I'll stay. I just need to take him down to Longbourne."

He seemed about as convinced as Alix, but he said nothing more.

"Bel, I…" She what? She had his gaze now, had him talking, but now what?

She watched the ball of his throat bob as he swallowed.

Pol bustled between them, putting a plate of bread and cheese within easy reach of Lena. She busied herself with eating, trying to find the words she wanted to say. There were so many and too few; she had enough for her gratitude but not for her confusion, couldn't articulate her regret or her resentment.

Soon Alix came through the kitchen door, announcing sulkily that the horse was ready for the convict. Without being asked, Bel untied the man from the chair and led him outside.

Alix and Pol hovered like mother hens as she slowly stood, putting just a little weight on her wounded leg. A stab went up her leg, but soon eased into a manageable ache. The shot of pain cleared away the last of the poppy milk haze, and she was thankful for it. She needed her wits about her.

Bel was tying the man's hands to the saddle horn when she and her custodians made it outside. He'd tied the man's boots to the stirrups and left the gag in his mouth. Fine with Lena.

Again, without being asked, he came to her and Yvain, helping her up into the saddle. His ungloved hands closed around her waist, helping her climb atop the warhorse. His ungloved hands clasped her knee, moving it around in the stirrup so that less blood could flow down.

She reached out and grasped his ungloved hand in her own, catching his gaze. A shudder went through her when his hot skin met hers; it was a surprise, but not unpleasant. Not unpleasant at all. The tangled mess of emotions throbbed, and she swallowed hard to keep some of them down.

"You will be here when I return," she said softly. "I would like to speak with you."

She watched him swallow again, and he took a step back from her. She released his hand but not his eyes. Shoulders stiff, he nodded.

"I have your word?" She wanted to hear it.

"Yes."

"Good." She cleared her throat, feeling overwarm with so many eyes watching her as she pulled on her gloves. "Thank you, Bel, for what you did."

He only nodded again, but Lena supposed this would do, for now. She wanted to speak with him, wanted to give him more than her thanks, but she still hadn't the words. She hoped the trek down the mountain would give her time to think of something.

She gave Yvain a soft kick, and the warhorse started climbing the wide, shallow steps up into the bailey. Alix followed on foot with the palfrey.

When they neared the gate, Lena stopped and took the palfrey's lead rope from Alix.

Leaning down, she told Alix quietly, "I want you to watch him."

The girl's lips pursed, and she stole a glance over her shoulder. They were alone in the bailey, but still she whispered. "What if he leaves again?" There was something in Alix's voice, a low thrum Lena thought might be hurt, but she didn't have the time to consider.

"Don't confront him, just keep your eyes open. I don't...I don't think he'll run again."

Alix gave a disbelieving snort. "You didn't think he'd run in the first place."

"Maybe not. But can we really blame him for trying?"

"Humph," she grumbled, sort of an agreement, sort of a dismissal.

Lena left Alix at the gate, the palfrey trotting contentedly behind her into the snow. She turned her own words around in her head as they descended—*can we really blame him for trying?*

And what a disloyal, treasonous thought that was. It sat heavy in her gut like slag pooling beneath purer metal.

He was her prisoner, the king's prisoner, the humans' enemy. She should be furious, livid at what Bel had done, and part of her was, but not because he was a prisoner. She was angry that she'd needed him, that it took another's help for her to bring in one convict. It'd been her mission, her chance to prove to herself and Longbourne that she could be relied upon. That even just one knight could make a difference. Instead, she needed the help of her own prisoner.

What had he been thinking, running away? Didn't he know she'd be forced to hunt him? Didn't he know it was the middle of winter? Didn't he understand how much human territory stood between him and other avians? How could he have thought to escape?

But can I blame him for trying?

She should blame him, should resent how close she'd come to losing everything without even knowing, without even having any control of her plunge. But underneath her tightly coiled anger and resentment, she knew she didn't, not truly. She couldn't blame him for wanting to be free. She knew what it was to be buried beneath the snow.

She'd stood in the stables with him not long ago, calling him a coward for not running. Could she blame him for doing the very thing she would do in his place?

There were no easy answers, always a *yes, but*...or a *no, but*...It made her all the wearier, her eyes so tired they stung with every blink.

A tug on the palfrey's lead rope drew her attention, and she heard the soft *thump* of the convict trying to get the horse to move away from Yvain.

"There's no point," she called over her shoulder. "She's trained to follow. She won't move from the trail."

The convict made a garbled growl, his attempts to get the horse to run away growing more frantic as they neared Longbourne.

Lena felt as if she passed through some opaque veil when she entered Longbourne through the snow gate. She'd done this very thing only yesterday, but already it felt so long ago. Her leg throbbed in reminder, but it was more than that—today, she had two prisoners, one she'd happily wash her hands of, and the other...the other didn't feel like a prisoner anymore.

She and the convict drew the rapt attention of everyone they passed, but she stopped for no one, not until she and Yvain nearly climbed the steps to Tilda Yarlsson's house.

The woman hurried to intercept them, her skirts swirling as she came to look over the convict. The man turned pleading eyes on Tilda, his manner suddenly obsequious, shoulders slumped, expression pathetic. It turned Lena's stomach.

"Is the gag really necessary?" asked Tilda.

"I wasn't interested in anything he had to say."

Tilda put her hands on her hips while she looked up at the man. Lena thought there was some resemblance, but she was too young to be the man's mother. Behind them, a small crowd of townsfolk gathered, whispering to each other.

"Look at you, Uther," Tilda whispered. "Trussed up like a hunted deer."

The man's face turned red and his teeth gnashed against the gag, trying to spit out words. He only let spittle fly.

"I found him not too far from what I assume is a hunting waystation. He took many of the supplies there. I suppose you know the place I mean?"

"Yes," said Tilda without looking at Lena.

"And you didn't think to tell me of the place? You didn't think to tell me anything."

"I gave you my brother's description. Seems you did fine." But her words weren't praise, far from it. If anything, she seemed disappointed.

"If I didn't know better, I'd say you didn't want me to find him, mayor."

That earned her Tilda's attention. The woman's icy blue glare tried to burn her words away, but Lena only stared back.

"Your brother has hurt a woman grievously. He tried to evade capture and justice. He attacked a knight of the realm. Is this really a man you want to keep in your community, mayor? Do your blood ties mean more than the safety of your people?"

The crowd at their backs grumbled.

Tilda pressed her lips together so tightly they disappeared into her mouth. "I believe you were asked to bring him in *and* take him to the magistrate," she said. "You'll find the trail clear enough. Lady Berengia is the nearest, down the mountain. A day's ride, if you hurry."

Lena's temper throbbed as surely as her leg, and despite the cold, she felt it splay across her cheeks in an angry blush. "It's already midday. And..." she bit down on her pride, "I've been wounded."

Tilda only raised her eyebrows. "It's what a knight would do, see the criminal to the magistrate, see the job done."

"Yes." Lena straightened in her saddle, sitting as tall as she could over the other woman. "It might be best. I wouldn't want him escaping again."

Tilda's mouth puckered into a moue of anger, but Lena ground her heels into Yvain's flanks, leaving her behind. Why had she ever wanted anything from that woman?

The crowd parted just enough to let them pass, uneasy glances bouncing between Lena and the convict. Lena set her jaw and tried to ignore the looks, as if one convict followed another and the only difference was who led whom by a lead rope.

The man whose wife had been attacked, Karel, stood on his porch as they passed. His glare was only for the convict, as if his hate alone could strangle the man in the saddle. He didn't even look at Lena, let alone acknowledge what she'd done, and as she and the convict headed out of town, down the mountain path, Lena supposed she shouldn't have expected him to. She shouldn't have expected gratitude or thanks or respect. She shouldn't expect what others would never give. Hadn't she told Alix just yesterday that not everything was an exchange?

But doing the right thing for nothing wasn't always much comfort.

The thought ate at her almost as much as the cold. Lena shrugged further into her layers and tried to let her stiff, cold body move with Yvain's easy stride.

⸻ •◆• ⸻

The trek down the mountain was lonely, the landscape stark and harsh compared to the vibrant greens and blues she remembered from when she and Alix had first come. She thought of that day with a heavy, saturated sort of bitterness that made her jaw ache and the purple crescents under her eyes throb.

Lena ascended the mountain that day thinking she had little to lose but much to prove. She remembered feeling so alone in the world, even with Alix beside her. She remembered the banked fire in her that day, the need to prove herself simmering in her chest.

Winter had buried her deep beneath the snows, snuffing that fire.

The knotted ball of emotions that'd lodged in her throat the moment the hunting trap sank into her leg began to roil, writhing beneath her skin in hot waves. It pulsed along with her leg, pushing against her throat, her chest, her skin. It wanted out.

The sensation wasn't a new one, had been Lena's companion for days as she awaited her trial for maiming Balderak. The writhing mass wanted out, through sobs, through tears. Lena didn't give in to it today, not when the tears would freeze her cheeks and break off her lashes. But it was tempting.

She'd come to this mountain to prove herself. She'd gone after this damn convict to prove herself, too. And for what? Did she think Tilda would thank her, write a grateful letter to King Artemian, commending her?

No, that'd be a naïve, foolish thing to think or expect, but she'd hoped...

And where had her hopes ever gotten her? What had they ever amounted to?

Her whole life she'd hoped for honor, distinction, respect. She had none of those things. Not when she'd headed out yesterday, not when she returned with her quarry. She'd even lost the one prisoner she was supposed to be warden of. In her quest to prove herself, Bel had nearly slipped through her fingers.

Horror replaced her need for tears, sucking everything down into the cold pit of her stomach. Bel had nearly escaped. She'd been on the knife's edge of telling her king that she'd failed to contain a prisoner that no fewer than five other wardens had managed to keep locked away. Even Sir Ollander had managed two years of it. Lena hadn't lasted the winter.

He'd run and she'd nearly been ruined without even knowing.

Yet, he'd come to her aid when she'd needed it most, much as she hated needing it at all. He owed her nothing. She'd called him a coward. And still he'd come to her aid.

She couldn't say the same of Longbourne. What she'd done, she'd done for them, and for what? That sucking feeling sank lower, deep into her gut. She'd done it for nothing. Yes, she'd rest easier knowing such a man wasn't anywhere near innocents, but the townsfolk would forget the part she played in this drama soon. They wouldn't thank her. They certainly hadn't helped her.

And what if she needed help again? The thought made her frown, but she couldn't dismiss it just because she disliked it. Living this high in the mountains was treacherous. What if something happened to Alix or Pol? To her again? The townspeople wouldn't help. Would Bel?

He'd proven an ally in the most unlikely of times, when she'd needed one most. And Lena needed allies. She had Alix, but Alix was her charge, still just a girl. But Bel...

He was her prisoner, one who'd escaped, one who'd reset his wing. Was he really someone she could ever trust?

•••◆••

Lena hated how much time she had with her own gloomy thoughts on their way down the mountain. It was late into the evening before she spotted the fortress and town surrounding it from above. She could see little of Fort Whitewater in the growing dark, just outlines and silhouettes against the amber glow of many fires, and remembered even less from when she and Alix had passed through on their way up to Finhöln.

The houses were neat but smaller than those up in Longbourne, their rooves not so sloped, and their rafters unadorned. The paths were wide, deep ruts indicating the town saw many wagons passing through. The mountain path she'd been following quickly widened into something of a promenade, leading up to the fortress walls.

Little moving flames told Lena sentries walked the perimeter of the catwalk above. As they neared, she tightened her grip on the lead rope. The convict had grown quiet as they approached Whitewater, perhaps resigned, perhaps plotting. She'd take no chances.

As expected, a sentry called for her to halt before the lowered portcullis.

"State your business."

"Prisoner for the magistrate."

"At this hour?"

"I didn't want to waste any more time. He's already made one run for it."

The sentry made a *humph* before he asked, "And who're you?"

"Lady Maddalena. Warden of Castle Finhöln."

She couldn't hear the surprised whispers of the sentries, but she knew they did it, could feel the prickling weight of their stares squinting through the dim firelight.

"Better come in, then," one of them said, and Lena almost laughed. *Better come in, then,* yes that sounded right for the day she was having.

The portcullis made a heinous groan before it began to steadily rise to the *clink-clank* of chain links winding together. Lena urged Yvain beneath the iron teeth when they were high enough to pass under.

They walked through a second portcullis before coming into a dark courtyard. A wide square of snow-covered lawn was bisected by a cross of cobblestone pathways. The old stone walls seemed to have a gentle curve to their shadows, making it feel as if she'd just led her little party into a great stone bowl.

From narrow stone steps to her right came a pair of sentries, torches held high to illuminate the newcomer. Lena stared down at them, letting them take a good look at her face. They wouldn't know it for certain, but she hoped her look, the set of her shoulders, conveyed her knighthood. And her bone-deep need for a bed.

The taller, older man with a grizzled gray stripe running through his beard gave a sideways nod to a young woman. She pivoted and made for the tall doors on the other side of the courtyard, to the great hall, Lena figured.

The man waved a hand, and he led Lena across the courtyard more slowly. She knew it was rude to stay mounted, to look down at the sentry from her perch, but Lena no longer cared. She was too tired, her heart too sore to care for manners now. Somewhere south, Lady Margot no doubt gasped in outrage—if it was even possible to still outrage her mother, that was.

Lena stayed in the saddle even when the sentry began looking over her prisoner. The convict squinted into the torchlight, shying away from the sentry's curious perusal.

"I'll be damned," said the sentry. "It's Yarlsson."

"The mayor's brother, yes."

The sentry indulged in a hearty chuckle, slapping his thigh and everything. "Now what'd he do?"

Lena fixed the man with a glare. "Raped a woman."

The laughing died, and the sentry shot her prisoner a withering look. Lena was just thankful for the quiet.

The young woman who'd run off soon returned with an older woman behind her. Lena could recognize a fortress's master on sight. Lady Berengia strode towards them with a calm, easy gate, her leather boots making crisp *clicks* on the cobblestone, her heavy wool skirts swishing. They were slit up the sides, revealing leather trous beneath. In the dark, Lena couldn't distinguish the color of her skirts, just that they seemed to absorb the warm glow of the torchlight as she neared.

Even in her advanced years, the woman's face was all sharp lines and angles. Her eyebrows arched in an uncompromising line, her eyes glittered black in the low light. A nearly lipless mouth angled downwards towards a pointed chin. Shallow wrinkles fanned over her face, but rather than softening it, the lines only drew attention to the severe cut of her nose and intelligent sparkle of her eyes.

All this sharpness meant that when her mouth cracked into a wide, vicious smile, Lena almost shivered from the impact. She was glad it wasn't aimed at her, but the convict.

"Well, Uther," said Lady Berengia in the way a cat would speak to a mouse it had between its claws. "What's happened now?"

The older sentry repeated everything Lena had told him, Lady Berengia nodding along as if the source of the information weren't right in front of her. When the man finished, the noblewoman looked the convict over head to foot and smiled again.

"What a mess. Tilda won't be able to save you, boy. You've gone too far this time."

Lena frowned at the implied politics between the two leaders. Had she stumbled into a regional rivalry? She almost laughed again. Of course she had.

"Lady Berengia?"

The older woman finally pulled her avaricious gaze from the squirming convict and turned it towards Lena. She almost wished she hadn't.

"Lady Maddalena, I'm told. The new warden?"

Lena inclined her head. "Yes, my lady."

"Did he give you much trouble?"

Lena's mouth twisted, lips unsure what words to form. But Lady Berengia just laughed, drawing what she wanted from her silence.

"Come on then, lady. Let's see you fed for your troubles."

Steeling herself for the dismount, Lena slid off Yvain with as few movements as possible and hobbled over to Lady Berengia. The lady took in her uneven stride with a raised eyebrow.

"Perhaps a visit from the healer as well," she said.

Lena only nodded, suspecting this generosity came more from her pleasure at getting to throw Tilda Yarlsson's brother into a cell than from actual concern for Lena's comfort or wellbeing. Did it bother her? Not as much as it would have yesterday. Did she let it stop her from accepting? Of course not. She didn't care what stewing pot of regional politics this stirred; she was happy to wash her hands of Uther Yarlsson and this whole situation. And she was starved.

She followed Lady Berengia through to the great hall after asking the sentries to take good care of her horses. The great room was rather narrow but tall, its arched ceiling like the timbered bowels of a warship. The architecture had a whisper of familiarity, and Lena wondered if this was what Finhöln would have looked like in its better days.

Tables were arranged in the old style, a long table with chairs along one side sitting atop a dais at the far end, three long tables spanning the length of the hall below. A few people sat ranged about in groups, what looked like off-duty sentries, perhaps a knight or two, and several officials. All eyes fell on her as Lady Berengia led her to an empty section of the furthest table, near the dais.

She sat where the lady bid her, not looking at or acknowledging any of the curious glances aimed her way. She'd be gone soon enough, and she hadn't the patience to deal with the disgust on their faces when *Finhöln* and *warden* were finally mentioned.

"You've saved my messenger a trip, Lady Maddalena. If you'll wait a moment..." And the lady of the fortress was gone with a swish of skirts.

Lena busied herself with taking off her gloves, unbuttoning her coat, and propping her leg up on the opposite bench. She sighed in pleasure as the pressure eased off her wounded leg.

Soon a bowl of stew and loaf of bread were deposited in front of her by a sleepy-eyed serving maid. Lena had eyes only for her food as she tucked in and filled her belly. She was scooping out the dregs before Lady Berengia reappeared.

"Here we are. Both bound for Finhöln." She placed two missives before Lena, one thick and encased in a leather jacket. She'd seen similar packages and suspected it was for Bel. The other was thin, with the royal crossed-swords engraved across the letter face. "This one," the lady indicated the thin, yellow-papered letter, "is a kingdom-wide announcement. One was sent to every fortress throughout Vagora."

She had just enough surprise left in her to raise an eyebrow. "Oh?"

"The crown prince is returning to us from the front."

Lena's face heated at the mention of Arion. It'd been almost a year since she'd seen him, longer since she'd shared his bed. Her face reddened further, and she dropped it, making a show of opening the missive.

She could barely concentrate between Lady Berengia's stare and her memories of Arion, but she got the impression of more losses at the foot of Hadria, of the prince being recalled for his own safety. A flutter of relief cooled the burn in her face; Arion was safe, was headed home.

Perhaps, when he knows what's happened…

She squashed that thought ruthlessly. She'd been Arion's cause once and promised herself never again.

"I suppose you wish to stay the night?" said Lady Berengia, drawing Lena's wandering attention.

"If it could be arranged."

"Of course. I'll leave you to your meal and have someone show you to your room once it's been made. Healer Bjorn will see you in the morning."

"Thank you, my lady."

Once she was alone again, Lena let everything not immediately holding her upright relax; fingers, arms, thighs, calves. She just barely caught herself before letting her head slump onto the table, instead eased it into her hands, hiding away from the lingering stares of Whitewater.

Ironic as it was, she longed for Finhöln, for her icebox of a chamber. She'd light a modest fire, slip beneath her familiar bedding, shove her toes as close to her bed warmer as she dared, and close her eyes. It would be quiet, peaceful, and isolated. No stares. No politics.

Alix would be just a door away.

Bel would be two flights of stairs and three corridors away.

She was too tired to consider why she drew comfort from the thought, just held onto it.

20

Hells, Pol! What were you thinking? Letting him go, giving him—*hells*, Pol, you gave him supplies, *my* supplies, and you—what if that warden finds out what you did? What if she reports to the crown? Hells, do you want the law up here?"

Bel edged further into his corner, avoiding a livid Malthus who, once he'd started, didn't seem capable or inclined to stop. Along with his angry words came spittle and a few jerky hand-signs; *madness* and *my supplies* and *the law* and *fuck-fuck-fuck* again and again. He seemed too agitated for clear signs, but Pol got his point well enough.

Arms crossed, Pol kept hold of his heavy rolling pin. The brothers had never been violent; Pol was the only recipient of the few tender looks Bel had ever seen grace Malthus's face. Yet Pol kept an aggressive stance, eyes wary. Whenever Malthus spun or looked away, Pol checked on Bel, making sure he stayed well out of the way.

Bel didn't need to be told.

"And *you*!"

His gaze snapped up from the floor in time to watch Malthus stalk towards him like an incensed boar, all fury and snorting breaths. Bel widened his stance and tucked his bad wing further behind him.

He nearly went cross-eyed watching the finger Malthus shoved in his face.

"You stay away from my brother. Don't know why he's so keen to take pity on you, but you've taken advantage for the last time. You're a prisoner here, so get used to it."

"I didn't ask him to do this," Bel said quietly.

"That doesn't matter! You were caught! And you won't take my brother down with you."

He didn't think it worth the effort to correct Malthus. The man wouldn't listen, didn't care about the particulars. Much as he disliked the finger still waving too close to his face, Bel could admit he shared Malthus's sentiment.

"Pol won't suffer for me."

"Damn right he won't!"

Malthus jabbed his finger into Bel's chest once, twice, but seeing that Bel wasn't going to retaliate, he rounded on Pol again.

"Stay away from the avian," Malthus growled and signed. "He's only trouble."

Pol's lips thinned into an unhappy line, and Bel almost groaned at the determined lift of his chin. *He's my friend,* Pol signed with deliberately slow movements.

Malthus made a hot, angry sound somewhere between exasperation and disgust, slammed his fist on the carving table, and then stormed from the kitchen.

He left an aching sort of silence in his wake, an emptiness that Bel was loath to fill. For all his anger and bluster, Malthus was right, much as it rankled.

Bel sighed, raised his hand to tell Pol this, but Pol sliced the air with a hand.

Ignore Malthus. He is always angry.

He is also right.

Pol gave a violent shake of his head. *No! Do not say that. He just worries over his illegal trading.*

He worries for you. The warden will suspect I had help.

She will not hurt me, Pol signed with conviction.

Bel sighed. *This argument is old.*

Because you will not listen to me. But Pol waved his hand, erasing his words from the very air. *This is not important now. Not when you should be going, while the warden is away.*

Bel was too surprised to sign back, only blinked at Pol.

Pol nodded, hands flying. *If Malthus is right, then the warden took the man down the mountain to Fort Whitewater. She will not be back until tomorrow afternoon. She is hurt, tired. You will have a lead. Bel, you must take your chance. And do it right this time.*

He winced at Pol's admonishment. All his friend's hard work was now for nothing, just because Bel decided to have a conscience out in the wilderness.

I promised I would be here when she returned.

Pol leveled an incredulous look at him. *You do not have to honor your word to her. Your freedom is more important.*

She would come after me. You know she would.

Perhaps. But—

It is the middle of winter. What is the point of running if I will only die out there?

Pol looked like he wanted to argue, but they were interrupted by the quiet patter of Alix's footsteps on the stairs. When he saw the girl standing there on the landing, Pol moved away to the hearth, leaving Bel to come out from the corner.

Despite Bel's slow, wary movements and avoiding her eyes, Alix marched into the kitchen, her anger plain. A frown transformed her whole face, banishing the usual amused glint that brightened her eyes. Instead the jade green of her eyes seemed to swim in the shadow of her brow, trained as they were on him.

Bel deposited himself onto one of the stools and waited. She'd been throwing him these looks all evening, as if he'd insulted her mother or kicked her dog. Between her glares and Pol's insistence and Malthus's warnings, he felt like an exposed nerve, a sore tooth that kept getting prodded. He'd had a long enough day, a day that started with him being free, and didn't see the point in fighting off Alix. He'd take whatever it was she came to lob at him and then go sleep for days, mourning what could've been.

The squire didn't waste time with preamble. "You ran away," she said, all accusation and hands on hips and jutting elbows.

"Yes."

"Why?"

He nearly fell off his stool. "You understand the concept of prisons, yes?"

She shot him a look he'd only seen human girls perfect, part eye roll, part upturned lip. "I mean, why did you run without saying anything?"

"To who? You?"

Somehow this seemed to tip the argument in Bel's favor, but he didn't understand why Alix suddenly shuffled her feet.

"It was a stupid thing to do." She waved vaguely in the direction of outside and all the snow there.

"If you want something enough, a few feet of snow won't stop you."

"It was still stupid. What if something had happened to you?"

"You mean like something happened to your knight?"

"Don't try it again," she warned, neatly sidestepping his distraction.

"Oh, so you're warden now?"

"Stop responding in questions!"

"Why?"

"Argh!" She marched up to the table and smacked her hands flat on the wood surface, but it was less impressive than Malthus's similar display, given only Alix's chest reached the table.

"Do you know what you've done? You could've been hurt. You could've *died*. And Lena—"

"What, it's my fault Lady Maddalena could've been hurt recapturing me? Sorry if I don't feel too bad about that."

"I *was saying*, you would've put Lena in an impossible position."

Bel dignified that statement with a snort. "Oh yes, the impossible question of whether to give the runaway a head start, give him a little hope before recapturing him, or set out immediately."

"Stop it," she growled. Alix climbed up onto the stool opposite him, sitting on her knees so she was slightly taller than him and could plant her hands on the table and lean toward him. It was less threatening than she perhaps thought, but it still got Bel's attention and he had to force himself not to lean back as she inched forward.

"Lena wouldn't do all that. She isn't cruel. You just would've made her choose between her duty and her conscience."

His curiosity flared, but Bel had had enough, enough of today, enough of others shaming him for wanting to be free. Was the deer, the eagle, the wolf blamed for roaming the wilderness? Was the river shamed for cutting through the land, or the mountain for reaching to the sky? He'd decided to not be a coward, to take what should always have been his, and here he was, sitting across from a slip of a girl who thought she occupied the moral high ground, who thought she had the right to criticize, to condemn him.

"And what were my choices? You seem to think I did this because of your knight. That I should've asked my *prison warden's* opinion on escaping. I won't apologize for not taking her conscience into account. I won't apologize to her as she takes me to the whipping post!"

A shudder went through Bel, his back prickling with the memory of those old lashes. Alix stared at him with wide eyes, and Pol too had stopped to give him a concerned look.

The kitchen's silence sucked all the fight out of Bel, doused his fire. The remnants of it hissed through him, making him itch, but then it was gone in a puff of white smoke. He buried his head in his hands and waited for someone else to speak. He was done.

"Lena wouldn't do that," Alix repeated, much quieter this time. There was another beat of silence, weighing heavier than the last; she sounded like she wanted to reach out and touch him. Instead, she sighed. "Do you know why Lena's here, in exile?"

*Does it matter? She'll leave after her sentence, while I...*But Bel remained quiet. He was done.

Alix didn't need an answer, pushed on. "After her service on the front, she was pulled back for leisure time. She was assigned to Lord Balderak, in the south. After she took me on, we went to his holdings where Lena was just supposed to serve an easy post, keep the peace. But Lord Balderak was hurting the women of his demesne, making them..." Alix cleared her throat. "He hurt a lot of them. They were terrified. Lena found out about it and tried to help. We gathered statements and evidence, got the women to all trust us. Lena went to Balderak with the evidence, but he tried to attack me. She cut off his hand."

Here Bel looked up in surprise. He grimaced at showing his interest, quickly burying his face again, but Alix had seen and continued.

"We went to a neighboring lord, to give him the evidence, but Lena got thrown in the dungeon and I...a couple guards got the papers off me. I put up a fight, honest! Gave one a black eye and got the other good in the—" she spat the words but quickly bit them off, her cheeks coloring. "Lena got hauled in front of the king. All our evidence was gone and Balderak accused Lena of attacking him for no reason. Nobody believed Lena. The king made her come here, to prove herself. Her own parents stood by and watched her get fucking exiled." Alix's face turned dark, darker than Bel had ever seen, and he realized he'd never truly seen her angry before. When she'd come down to the kitchen, that'd been nothing compared to the black rage that peeked out from behind her eyes now. The insubstantial, writhing mass of it filled the kitchen, making even Pol twitch. Alix looked like a she-wolf, snarling, the last line of defense for the den behind.

Bel scrubbed his face with his chapped hands. It was a nice story. It fit what he'd seen of Lady Maddalena, how she treated others, Pol's belief that she was different from the other wardens. Her five predecessors had deserved to be here, deserved to be the prisoners, and Bel was sure that was part of his ongoing punishment by the human king. But Lady Maddalena...

But did any of it matter? Bel didn't see how it did. She was still the warden, still—

Alix did reach out then, grasping as much of his forearm as she could with her small hand. Bel gave a start, the touch soft and warm and unexpected. The second such touch today. He remembered Lady Maddalena gripping his hand, how strong her fingers were, how soft, even with the rasp of callouses. That touch had been different than Alix's, something more in it. It wasn't unpleasant, something closer to nice. And confusing.

"Bel," she said, pulling his thoughts away from the feel of Maddalena's skin against his. "Lena's a good knight. She believes in right and wrong. She defends the innocent, stands up for the abused. She sure as hells doesn't tie them to a whipping post."

His mouth opened, whether in surprise or to ask if she thought *he* was innocent and abused, he wasn't sure. But nothing came out, nothing feeling right.

Alix gave him a long look, a look that said she understood the weight of the words she'd laid down before him. "You can't run again, Bel. Please. It's dangerous for you and...for Lena. If you ran and escaped, it'd be one too many strikes against Lena. She'd never be taken back, never trusted again. They might even...kill her."

Bel shook his head at the idea of humans killing their own. He knew they did it often enough, as avians did, in anger or calculation or retribution. But for the king to kill Lena for being a good knight? The thought churned inside him, making his gut spasm.

"Please, Bel. Vagora needs knights like Lena. Ones who actually believe in the code. Ones who stand up for what's right. She's done right by so many. She could do right by you, too."

The loyalty shone in Alix's eyes, her conviction nearly coming out in passionate tears. It made him wonder how knight and squire had met, for Alix to make such a plea for Maddalena.

"Do you know what you're asking for?" His voice sounded off, as if he hadn't used it in days. Everything felt raw.

"Yes. At least...at least talk to Lena when she gets back. You said you'd be here when she came back."

"Talk to her about what?"

Alix shrugged. "Just talk to her. She won't hurt you, Bel. Neither of us will. I...you're my friend."

Bel held back the scoff that wanted to escape his throat. She looked at him so earnestly, her eyes so big and pleading. Sincerity and perhaps a sliver of desperation glittered in her eyes as she returned his stare, as if she could convince him through strength of will alone.

He sighed. "I'm not going anywhere tonight."

Alix nodded, accepting his meager capitulation. The girl looked as tired as he felt, the shadows beneath her eyes long and deep, and even her curls seemed deflated.

Pol came over, offering mugs of chamomile tea. He and Alix accepted them without a word, sipping through the dregs in silence.

The squire's blinks were long and languorous when she bid them good night on the tail of a yawn. He and Pol watched her go, still nursing their tea.

Did you see what she said? At Pol's slow nod, Bel asked, *Do you believe her?*

Pol nodded again, though it seemed begrudging. *I still think you should run.*

Bel filled his lungs with a deep breath, feeling his chest expand, his ribs creak. *I'm tired,* he signed, and got off his stool.

He left the kitchen without another word, and Pol didn't try to stop him. There wasn't anything left to say. And Bel was done.

Bel's chambers didn't feel quite right when he returned to them, as if they were a mold to be filled but Bel was not quite the right shape, not anymore. But the bed, at least, didn't feel too strange as he settled, arranging blankets into a suitable nest. He stayed like that, sometimes dozing, sometimes watching the shadows dance with the moon's descent, until dawn eked into his room, the gray light making his chambers look like little more than cluttered stone boxes. An uneasiness gathered in his throat, and, waiting only long enough to change out of his layers into more familiar clothes, he abandoned the rooms, not even laying coals out for a new fire.

Despite the tiredness that weighted down his spirit and stung his eyes with each blink, Bel silently descended into the kitchen. Sore as he was in heart and body, he didn't want to be alone in that cold stone box he'd called home for ten years.

The thought made him pause on one of the middle steps. The idea of living again in those rooms chafed against an already agitated wound. He didn't know if he could do it. Bel tugged a hand through his hair and pressed the sleep from his eyes with the heel of his palm. He didn't want to stay, knew he didn't have to stay, but he was too tired to do anything but stay.

He supposed he didn't have to solve this problem that very moment on the kitchen stairs, but the frayed ends of this tangled knot vexed him.

Both Pol and Alix were already awake and about. Pol stood near his hearth, chopping what looked like a handful of root vegetables, while Alix pressed her nose to a book, surrounded by the eviscerated remains of her breakfast.

Bel accepted his own breakfast from a tired Pol. He caught the man's eyes and tried to give him a conciliatory smile but thought it might've looked more like a grimace. Pol's lips twitched and he nodded, waving for Bel to eat.

He set himself across from Alix. As he twirled his spoon in his oats, he realized he'd never seen the squire read, or sit still for so long. A deep frown creased her forehead, and Bel wasn't sure if this was her look of concentration or she was trying to set the page on fire with her glare.

"Good book?" he asked.

"Humph," she said without looking at him.

"So not a good book."

"It's the history of Vagora. Volume *three*," she sneered.

"If you don't like it, then why are you reading it?" Though *reading* was a strong word; from observing her over his bowl, he thought she was mostly glowering at it.

Alix humphed again before grudgingly admitting, "Lena's been teaching me to read. She's big on knights using their minds as much as their sword arms."

"Seems a sound idea."

"She always asks what I did to improve myself today," Alix grumbled. "I didn't train yesterday, and I don't feel like it now. So I thought..." She gave a mighty sigh that sounded heavy with frustration. "I hate this thing, though."

"So read something else."

"We didn't bring much else. I've already read volumes one and two." She was more aggravated than proud of that fact.

Bel considered as he chewed his oats. He appreciated this lighter subject; the kitchen didn't have the heaviness of last night, no shouting or pleas or writhing anger. Alix seemed happy enough to take today as a new day, and even Pol hadn't brought up yesterday. It was altogether a relief to Bel, uncertain as he still was, sore as he still felt.

"Wait a moment," he told her, standing from his spot at the table and taking the kitchen stairs two at a time.

He retrieved one his favorite volumes, one he'd never needed for translating but had found its way to him in a shipment of texts. He placed the volume of knight tales before the squire, pleased when her lips arched into a grin. The tales were written in a slightly old style, but it was one of the few books he had in low Vagoran.

"Would this be better?"

"Oh, yes!"

Alix flipped through the pages, eagerly seeking the illuminations, as Bel settled again across from her. When she finished with the illustrations, she asked if this had the tale of Sir Yvain and the Green Dragon. Bel pointed her to the page.

"Let's see how good you told it," she teased.

Alix began reading, sounding out the longer words and asking for help when she needed it. Bel watched in fascination as she used her finger to keep track of her progress, her lips moving as she read the words she knew. The first few times she struggled her cheeks turned into ripe apples, and she asked for help without looking him in the eye. Bel would turn the book around, find the word or phrase, and sound it out with her. She seemed to like this minimal help, liked that when he wasn't looking at the book, he was eating or washing dishes or chopping food—Pol told him with a twinkle in his eye that if he was going to stick around the kitchen, he might as well be helpful.

They passed the morning like that, Alix reading, Pol cooking, and Bel being a mildly helpful nuisance. Bel could feel them falling into a rhythm, a pleasant one. He even liked the silences that stretched because they weren't the true silence of his little library; there was always the fire crackling and Pol chopping and Alix turning pages. If he wanted noise, he talked. It was...comfortable.

The warmth of the kitchen and the ease of the company lulled the three of them so much that when Maddalena came in through the kitchen door on a gust of cold air, it was only a slight surprise.

Alix jumped off her stool as Maddalena knocked the snow off her shoulders and boots. The squire hovered near, hands anxious to help. Sodden layers were peeled off, slowly revealing Maddalena's rather haggard form beneath.

She hobbled to the table and took Alix's stool with a nod of thanks.

"I'll see to the horses!" said Alix, bounding to the door and throwing on her own layers. She was out the door quick as that, and Maddalena's eyebrows rose at her eagerness.

She turned that surprised look onto Bel, still perched on his stool with piles of different vegetables stacked around him. They gazed at each other for a long moment, and Bel waited as she searched for something to say.

Pol came with a mug of one of his concoctions, huffing and cooing over Maddalena's leg. He insisted she put it up on another stool so he could look at it. She let him fuss, taking off her boot to show him the fresh bandages.

Maddalena made a few hand signs, stopped in frustration, and turned to Bel to ask, "Can you tell him a healer down in Whitewater looked at me this morning? He complimented the stitch work."

Bel dutifully relayed the message, and Pol nearly glowed with pleasure—if he'd been avian, his wings would've given a little happy flap. He graciously signed that the bandages were well placed and tied, and that she'd been taken good care of. Once Lena assured him she'd stay off her leg a while and saw her sipping her drink, Pol moved back to his cooking, satisfied.

The rhythm Bel had found so comforting now became the beat of his heart, pulsing in his ears. The silence of the kitchen wasn't so companionable anymore, yet he didn't feel under threat. Perhaps it was the tired rings beneath Maddalena's eyes or the steady presence of Pol only a few paces away, but Bel was content to sit there and wait. He did, however, draw his bad wing behind himself. Habit.

Maddalena took one then two long draws from her mug before carefully replacing it on the table, running a fingernail along the rim, looking at Pol from the corner of her eye, then finally, cleared her throat.

"I'd like to talk now, since it seems I'm forbidden from moving for a while."

Bel nodded. "The man is locked up?"

"In a cell in Whitewater," she agreed. Maddalena put an elbow on the table and leaned forward slightly. It was barely anything, nothing compared to Alix's aggressive show last night, and Bel found himself leaning forward too, closer to her, watching her face as she quietly considered something. "I wanted to thank you," she finally said.

"You already did," he reminded her.

She shook her head. "Maybe, but it was in haste. I wanted to do it properly. Thank you, Bel, for helping me when I needed it most. Thank you for getting both me and Yarlsson back here safely. I know what it cost you."

Bel nodded, not knowing what to say. He wasn't sorry for running, wouldn't apologize for wanting to be free, but he knew it'd be too much to think her sorry that he'd been caught. It was an impasse he didn't think surmountable, but then, he reminded himself again that not everything had to be solved today.

Maddalena drew in a long breath, filling her lungs completely. "I also wanted to...to offer a—truce, I suppose."

It was Bel's turn to lift his brows in surprise. "All right," he said quietly. He'd never made a deal with a warden before. His curiosity piqued; what sort of deal could the upright Lady Maddalena make him?

He watched with interest as her face flushed and her gaze skittered away. "I'd like your promise not to run away again. If word got back to

King Artemian, I'd be...well, it wouldn't be good. I'd like your word to stay through my wardenship. In exchange, I won't report your escape." Her gaze flicked to his bad wing, and he instinctively drew it closer. "Nor will I rebreak the wing you've reset."

She knows, his heart thrummed, *she knows, she knows, she knows.* Over and over it drummed in his ears, his chest, his fingertips. A shudder went through both wings, making his feathers flutter. He had to stop himself from looking at Pol, from implicating his friend.

He pulled in air when he realized he wasn't breathing, and with each gulp, he tried to stop his racing heart. She was watching him now, waiting for his response. He focused on his breathing, one, two count, used the *ariant* exercises to get his heart back under control.

When he could hear his own thoughts finally over his heartbeat, her words skipped through him like a flat stone over water, hopping, skating, before finally sinking in. No report, no punishment. No whipping post, no crushed radial bone.

For a glorious moment, something surged inside Bel, something warm and comforting. Hope, security, relief. *No broken wing!* But then he realized...

"So I stay put, locked away in return for not being harmed, is that it?"

"Bel—"

He shot her a smile that was more teeth than anything else. "How is that any different from what I already do?"

"Because you wouldn't be a prisoner!" she snapped back.

He stared at her, his retort melting back into his mouth. Wouldn't be a prisoner? How could that be, when the castle itself was a prison? When she herself was its warden?

Maddalena took another sip from her mug, seemingly for something to do, and Bel almost started chopping vegetables again for something to do himself, for something to slice through, to control.

"You helped me when you didn't have to. When it wasn't in your interest to help me."

"So you're doing the same? Doing something not in your interest?"

"It's in my interest to finish this wardenship without incident. But, Bel," she said, making sure she had his eyes, "what you do after, that's your business."

His fingers were going numb, he clenched his fists so hard. He dug his nails into the fleshy part of his palm, waiting for the bite of pain to get his mind going again, but no, he couldn't think, couldn't move. The shock of it sat heavy between them, almost as heavy as the words she left unsaid.

"Why?" he managed to push through his throat.

"Because," she said slowly, "this doesn't feel right. None of this," she swirled her finger around in a vague circle, "feels right. Finhöln is a joke. This castle is coming down slowly and barely fit to live in. It's cruel to keep Pol and Malthus here. It's cruel to have a prison so close to the people of Longbourne without any real oversight. But most of all, it's cruel to you. Why keep you here for so long? Why not do a prisoner exchange? It makes little sense to me. It's pointlessly cruel. And I don't believe in such things. I know injustice when I see it."

Her last declaration snapped Bel out of the awed stupor her speech had woven around him. It wasn't that he didn't believe her; indeed, in a voice so steeped in righteousness and feeling, Bel begrudgingly admitted he had a difficult time not believing her. But if Alix's story of how Maddalena found herself at Finhöln was true, then either she was exaggerating, lying, or truly blind to the injustice done to her.

The thought crept through him, warming him from inside out. Sympathy was a disused feeling for him, and it took a moment to identify it. With such a selfless attitude, Bel could see how Alix got so exasperated with her, but he found it...noble. Maddalena was noble, if perhaps a little blind.

Bel had loved someone dearly for their nobility, had worshipped the ground his brother Maddok walked on for his inherent goodness. His brother had seen the world in much the same way Maddalena seemed to, wanted to right injustice, wanted to protect others. A memory of that night came to him, of the hot scorch of Maddok's big hand on the back of his neck as he shoved Bel to the side, taking the blade that would've skewered Bel.

"We've both found ourselves victims of circumstance," said Maddalena, apparently thinking he wasn't going to speak. He clung to the sound of her voice, let it pull him out of his memories. "I don't think either of us were meant to be here, but that doesn't mean we can't make the best of it. I know you have little reason to trust humans, but I'm serious when I say I mean you no harm. I think humans have done enough to you."

"Yes," he said, his voice raw-edged as it worked around the lump in his throat. "But we aren't victims of circumstance."

One of her brows ticked up. *And?*

"Your king did this. He chose this place for me, for all the wardens. He doesn't care about me or Longbourne or avians. He doesn't care about..." *You.* But Bel didn't have to say it. She took his meaning with a surprisingly mild nod. Her tight, downturned mouth hinted that she didn't agree, but it seemed they wouldn't be trading barbs again as they had in the stables.

Her easy, if begrudging, acceptance gave him hope that perhaps she meant what she said; that they could now be two beings sharing a space, rather than warden and prisoner.

Maddalena rubbed her thumb up and down the curve of her mug's handle. Bel watched, entranced by the repetitive move. Their silence wasn't as comfortable as the one he'd shared with Pol and Alix earlier, but it was easier to be around her than it had ever been.

"You can join us tomorrow, if you want, for training."

He looked at her in surprise.

She nodded. "I can already guess Alix hasn't trained while I was away, and I'll need a few days of rest. I'd like her to keep on schedule. And when my leg has healed, the two of us could train. Together."

She said all this as if it were a simple thing, but her gaze said something different; she took his measure, not as a threat, but as one warrior to another. He felt himself sit straighter, a little thrill of pride zinging through him. He hadn't felt anything like this since he'd sparred with Maddok that last time, before leaving for their mission. His brother had smiled while wiping sweat from his brow, had saluted him in the warrior's way, fist to heart. Bel had felt like his wings could stretch out to each horizon line, he was so proud.

"I'd like that," he said.

"Excellent. We keep to a regular schedule."

"I've noticed."

One side of her mouth kicked up into a rueful grin and Bel nearly fell off his stool.

"I..." Bel cleared his throat and nodded at the two books Alix had left on the table. "I can help Alix with her reading. If you like."

Maddalena followed the line of his gaze and reached for the books. She flipped his knightly tales closed to look at the cover.

"You got her to read this?"

"Yes."

"Willingly?"

"Yes. She didn't like the history, so I got her this."

"Then by all means. I haven't been able to get her interested in books, but if you could convince her, I'd be grateful."

"Of course. Sometimes it just takes the right book."

"Mm," she agreed. She sat straight in a jolt then reached for the pack she'd dropped at her feet. "That reminds me. Lady Berengia said this was bound for Finhöln. I suspect it's for you."

She placed the leather-bound sheaf of papers before him, and Bel felt all the warm feelings of the day drain away from him into the crumbling grout of the floor. All this talk of cohabitation, of cooperation, and here was proof that outside Finhöln, all it ever would or could be was talk.

She saw his reluctance, saw how slowly his hands reached for the missive, how hesitatingly his fingers drew out the papers. Maddalena splayed her hands on the table and pushed herself up, balancing most of her weight on her good foot. With a small, benign smile she told both Bel and Pol she would rest upstairs for a while.

Bel was grateful to be left alone with the missive, the reminder of his captivity. It was a nice lie Maddalena offered him, and he knew he would grab onto it with both hands. But he would still be the human king's prisoner, if not Maddalena's.

He read the new instructions without any real feeling or surprise. The translations for the tunnel systems under Hadria were imperative, and his deadline had been moved forward to spring. Bel held the weight of his head in his hands, hovering over the missive. He could read what wasn't said; the humans must have suffered another loss, the tunnels had become their only hope of victory.

He would have to send off the translations, with all his careful mistranslations, in spring. How soon would they use the intelligence? How soon would they realize Bel had misled them?

Bel closed his eyes and retreated into the warm cave of his hands. Barely afternoon and he was already making a liar of himself, for how could he keep his promise to Maddalena now? Her wardenship still had more than a year. Could he hope it'd take the humans that long to realize what he'd done? Would his luck hold?

He huffed. What luck?

You don't have to solve it today. He was comforting himself with that mantra a lot today, perhaps too much. There was so much to solve, so many questions he didn't have answers for.

For the first time in a long while, Bel didn't feel the crush of needing or wanting to escape. His presence here was a favor to Maddalena, nothing more. Yes, he quite liked thinking about it that way. Untrue as it was outside Finhöln. For the first time in a long while, he had something to work toward. He would train with her, would learn to fight another being again rather than an imaginary foe made of air. Perhaps he could even convince her to teach him to ride a horse. For the first time in a long time, Bel had a reason, a palatable reason, to stay.

But there was something he could do. Bel stared down at the missive again, calculating his time. A bird strong enough to fly to Hadria, and one who was willing to go at all, would be hard to come by here, this deep into winter. He had to try, though. He had to write to his cousin, Dartegn, tell him of the mistranslations.

It was small but something. It was something to ease his conscience, something that meant he wasn't a liar, not yet anyway. And Bel could content himself with that.

21

Come back here, little hawk! I mean it now!"

Instead of heeding Eamon, Bel put on a burst of speed, using his little wings to push himself through the air in great hops and bounds. He could hear Eamon's feet slapping on the blond sandstone somewhere behind him.

How did Eamon keep finding him? He'd snuck away from training to find everything he needed, including the helmet all of his brother Maddok's soldiers wore. How could Eamon tell it was him every time?

"*A-ru-bel*!"

Oh, his full name—Eamon was getting serious now. Bel pumped his arms, skidding around a corner. He startled two scholars, robes and parchment went flying, and Bel lost himself in the chaos. His helmet slipped down his face, and he felt himself go head over wings into a purple-leafed shrub.

Bel's foot snagged in someone's hem, and for a moment he couldn't figure out which was his right wing and which was his left. From the darkness of the helmet, he could hear the others trying to right themselves while hissing *Disgraceful* and *I never* and *Thank the skies he's the spare.*

He'd never admit it, but he might have sniffed away tears under his helmet. He too was happy Maddok was king and himself the spare, but it didn't feel good to have others say it.

Big, callused hands wrapped around Bel, plucking him from the ground. Bel squirmed, knowing Eamon's hold anywhere, but his tutor had a firm, if gentle grip. He hefted Bel up his chest and tipped the helmet back.

"And just where do you think you're going?" huffed Eamon. His face was red, gleaming with a sheen of sweat. Bel had heard rumors that Eamon had once been one of the handsomest avians in all the kingdom, but with the red and purple scar bisecting his scowling face, Bel had a hard time believing it.

Bel wriggled in earnest. "I gotta go see him! Lemme go, Eamon! Gah!" He kicked his little legs, hoping to strike something painful, but Eamon just adjusted his grip.

Eamon gave the sour-looking scholars a glare that had them scurrying away. Bel was always in awe of Eamon's glare—he wished he could get people to do what he wanted with his own face. Eamon might have been handsome once, but Bel thought this older face of his was better. Better to have people do what you want than be handsome.

When the scholars were out of sight, Eamon went to lift the helmet off Bel's head, but he wouldn't suffer the indignity. A soldier only took his helmet off when his commander allowed, and Bel hadn't made it to his commander yet. "No!" he squealed, giving up pushing at Eamon's chest to hold the helmet to his head.

Eamon's soft chuckle was a muted echo within the steel helmet, but Bel felt it through his whole body, pressed up to the older avian's chest.

"You look like a proper avian warrior now."

"I *know*," Bel groaned. That much was obvious. It was the helmet. "But warriors aren't carried around—put me down!"

He felt himself sway as Eamon eased forward, moving along the terrace at a more moderate pace than Bel had been. He lifted the brim of the helmet to see that Eamon was taking him in the right direction, just slower.

He started squirming again. "Faster, Eamon! Maddok's leaving!"

"He wouldn't leave without seeing you, little hawk. Be calm."

Be calm, Eamon always said. *Be calm,* because Bel really never was. Calmness wouldn't get Bel assigned to his brother's side, and he *had* to go with Maddok. He'd heard his brother's advisors, those old, stuffy men with their belts always cinched too tight, say that Maddok could be gone for a year. A whole year! And that was if the campaign against the horrible humans went well!

A year was too long. Bel already saw little of his brother now that Maddok had become king. In fact, Bel could hardly remember a time before Maddok was king. Their father had died almost three years ago now, when Bel was just barely three himself and Maddok fifteen. Since then, his brother was always surrounded by people; advisors, councilors, soldiers, allies, diplomats, and others with official sounding names that Bel didn't understand. Eamon did his best to explain royal functions to Bel, but Eamon himself was a soldier and always said he wasn't and never would be a courtier. But that was all right with Bel; the only part of a royal function he cared about was when it'd be over and he could talk to Maddok.

Bel tapped his hands on Eamon's broad shoulders, and finally the soldier picked up the pace. A breeze lifted Bel's hair and made Eamon's gray feathers rustle. Aeriand was high above the ground and set against the wind, and here in the upper levels, where the palace was carved, the sun seemed closer, the sky bigger. The terraces weaving around the palace were wide and uncovered, ready for an avian to take off or land, exposed on the windward side.

Bel had always been told Aeriand was carved from the very mountain it'd been named for, but he hadn't understood what that meant until he went with Maddok on a royal visit to the stronghold of Hadria last spring. It was the first time Bel had left Aeriand. Perched on Eamon's broad back, between the downy wing bases, Bel had looked over his shoulder at his home. It'd looked like some giant beast's tooth, wide at the base but narrowing to a spear point at the tip. The wide terraces and open gardens made little sloping pockmarks and patterns on the surface, making him think no, not a tooth, but a shell, like the ones Maddok once brought him from the eastern sea, the ones Eamon said little crabs lived in until it was time to move on.

The image had always stuck with Bel, his first glimpse of Aeriand from a distance. His home was beautiful, with its blond sandstone and amber-veined marble and flapping golden banners. It made him proud to be prince of such a place, prouder still that Maddok was king of it and more.

Eamon ducked into a corridor, taking narrow, steep steps down to the base level of the palace. The further they descended, the more avians they came across. The kitchen staff clambered for a look at the king's guard and a glimpse of Maddok. Councilors, scholars, and other courtiers made another ring, their colorful tunics bright in the midday sun. Eamon used his elbows to make them part.

Finally, finally Bel saw the glitter and gleam of armor. Yes, at the far side of the palace courtyard, where the polished stone railings fell away to a sheer drop off, stood the hundred avians who made up Maddok's elite guard. Their armor shone so bright in the sun it was a silvery blue, incandescent and impossible to look at for long. Gossamer banners flapped in the wind, announcing units and ranks. Maddok's standard, golden eagle alighting, stood above them all.

Bel eagerly began rearranging his helmet, wanting it to look as fierce as it did on the soldiers. It covered their foreheads and pointed ears, the curved surface polished to a high shine. Hard, steely eyes blazed beneath the brims, and the thin, bronze nose guards made sharp lines of their grim faces. Bel's body hummed in eagerness, but he hid his smile, trying to look as serious as the soldiers.

They broke from the lines of courtiers to face the vanguard. Bel recognized the man at the front, a tall, rangy avian with black wings who served as the Head of Maddok's guard. Ophir. Eamon and Ophir were friends, but Ophir always terrified Bel in a way Eamon never had. It was the uncompromising line of his mouth, how it barely moved, even when he spoke.

Eamon hefted Bel higher on his chest, so that Bel's head was above everyone else's. A few rows back, talking with several avians, Bel spotted the golden head of his brother.

Bel made an excited squeak. "Eamon, there he is!"

"Prince Arubel, to see his brother, the king," said Eamon to Ophir, one side of his mouth kicked up in a grin.

He nodded. "Make it quick." No side of his mouth grinned.

The soldiers parted, allowing Eamon to carry Bel into their midst, to Maddok.

One of his brother's commanders was there with him, along with their cousin, Dartegn. Bel frowned to see Dar in armor too, armor like Maddok's guards'. He even had the royal crest stamped onto two rondels on his shoulders, like them.

Dar saw them first, turning his dark head. His brown curls had been shorn in a soldier's style, and a broadsword was buckled to his waist. Dar caught him staring, and one eyebrow inched up, along with his lips into a smirk. Bel didn't like the look but stopped himself from pouting.

It didn't matter, because then Maddok saw them, and he reached for Bel. He squirmed in Eamon's arms, reaching out for Maddok too.

"I was wondering where you were," said Maddok, shooting Eamon a look over Bel's head. His deeply set eyes danced with mirth, looking to Bel like the clearest of skies.

"Led me on a merry chase, my king."

Once he was settled in Maddok's arms, Bel tipped his helmet back far enough to glare at Eamon.

"And where'd you pilfer this, hm?" Maddok flicked Bel's helmet, making it ring in his ears. Now he glared at his brother, too.

"I *found* it. In the armory." He sat taller, putting his hands on Maddok's soldiers. "Soldiers know where the armory is. That's where they get their helmets."

Maddok leaned backwards, eyes skimming up and down Bel. He sat straighter in his brother's arms, shoulders back. When he felt the helmet slipping down his forehead, he raised his brows, trying to catch it, but the brim sank ever downwards. The pout he'd been holding in puckered his lips, but Bel kept his shoulders square. Soldiers had dignity, even if their helmets didn't quite fit.

Tilting the helmet back into place, Maddok nodded. "Yes, you do look fierce."

Bel puffed out his chest and his wings gave a happy flap. "So I can come with you?"

Maddok's smile slipped—just a little, almost not at all, but Bel knew his brother's face, had watched it during those long, never-ending royal functions. Maddok was good at smiling, when he was happy and when he wasn't. Bel couldn't remember if their father smiled so much as king, but Bel preferred Maddok's way. Avians were at ease when he smiled— it filled the room with comfort and ease, making his brother's broad face crease with dimples and his blue eyes shimmer and dance. Maddok's smile always made something grow and shine in Bel's chest, expanding his heart until sometimes it felt like it would surely burst.

But Maddok's smile wasn't a real smile now, and his eyes no longer danced.

Bel took hold of his brother's face between his little hands. "I'm coming with you, Mad."

"No, Bel. Not this time."

Something expanded his chest, but it wasn't that golden feeling from his brother's smile. It was dark and roiling and felt red. It made his heart beat loud and furious and urged tears from his eyes.

"I'm coming with you!" he said again, louder, so Maddok would understand he wasn't asking.

Bel dug his fingers into Maddok's armor, under the shoulder guards to find the leather buckles beneath. He wouldn't let him go, would hold on like those lizards that scaled the sheer walls of Aeriand, their toes like little suckers that held fast to the weathered stone.

Eamon stepped closer at the tone of Bel's voice, but Maddok shook his head.

"I'm a soldier now—I want to be a soldier and go with you—I have to go with you," Bel said between hiccupping sobs. His face went red, knowing it wasn't dignified; soldiers, *princes* didn't cry in courtyards where the kingdom could see them. But it couldn't be contained, and he held onto his brother harder.

Dartegn came to them, giving Bel a little pat on his back. But Bel didn't want his comfort, just wanted him to go away.

"Give him back to Eamon," said Dar quietly so that only Maddok could hear. And Bel. "We have to go."

Maddok took a long, deep breath, making his armor clink as his chest expanded, and looked down at Bel's weepy face. Bel shook his head furiously, the helmet slipping down his face again, but he didn't care, just clung with his arms and legs to Maddok's chest.

Bel felt Maddok turn, body easing forward, then heard Dartegn grumble, "Mad..."

But then it was silent except for Maddok's boots scraping against the flagstones, and Bel felt himself being carried away from the others. The fleeting feel of other bodies whispered past, and Bel used one hand to lift the helmet off his head to see them retreating from the soldiers and Eamon and Dartegn. His cousin had a sour look on his face, but Bel didn't care. He stuck his tongue out at Dar.

They broke from the circle of guards near the railing of the courtyard. Maddok hitched him higher on his chest and Bel wrapped his arms around his neck.

His brother wasn't smiling now, real or fake. He looked out over Aeriand with a quietness that made Bel want to fidget and look away. But he didn't, needing to memorize his brother's face. He didn't understand why he had to look nowhere but Maddok, commit everything to his memory, but the need to do so sat heavy in his chest.

A gust reached up the wall to lift their hair and ruffle their feathers. They had the same golden hair that tended to curl at the ends when grown too long. Bel had been told it was their mother's hair, that hers had fallen to her waist in a glowing waterfall of gold curls. He had one of those curls, tied with ribbon and stowed in a little bronze box. He would touch that curl sometimes, wondering what it must have looked like on his mother's head. He'd seen her face in the stained-glass windows and mosaic tiles decorating the palace, but it wasn't the same. The gold curl was the only part of her he could touch that had once been alive, not cold glass or stone. She had died bringing him into the world, trading her life for his. He'd heard that it was no wonder his father hadn't been long for this world after her death, so heartbroken was he at the loss of his beloved mate. Bel couldn't remember ever seeing his father smile or laugh. His face, with its dark hair streaked with silver, seemed more stone than flesh. Bel wondered if love could really do that, could turn flesh to stone when it was lost. How terrifying love could be.

But he had her curl, and sometimes that felt like enough. He had his brother too, another part of his mother that still lived. And she lived through Maddok's stories of her that he told Bel on those dark, cold nights when he couldn't sleep.

He wanted his mother's curl now, to clutch to his chest as he watched Maddok look out over the city. Sometimes he imagined the curl still held the faintest smell of her, and he'd breathe it in, dreaming of a faceless comfort that would hold him close and sing to him. He wanted that feeling now, for even though he was held in his brother's arms, it felt like Maddok had already left him behind.

"I have to come with you," he said again, more to break the somber spell over Maddok than to convince him.

Finally, his brother turned away from the city below. For a moment, when the full force of that grim, serious look fell upon him instead, Bel wished he hadn't.

"It isn't safe for you, little hawk," said Maddok. "Where we're going...It may be very dangerous."

"Then you shouldn't go either."

"I have to. I'm the king, Bel. I must fight for the kingdom. How could I ask others to do it if I won't?"

"But...but you need to be here." The kingdom needed him—he might be small, but Bel could see what Maddok meant to the avians of Aeriand, saw their love and devotion to him shine through their eyes. But mostly Bel wanted Maddok to be here with him, even if it meant royal functions. Just as long as Maddok stayed, away from those wingless demons to the south.

"I'm needed in the west. Our people, our sacred sites in the Hollenheim are threatened. I have to protect them, and I can't do that from here. And I can't take you with me. If I did, I'd be scared all the time."

His helmet went tumbling to the flagstones, Bel's head jerked up so quickly to stare at his brother, his mouth gaping open. The wind blew inside, whistling between his teeth and drying his tongue.

"You're never scared," Bel said.

"Is that what you think?" Maddok smiled again, but it was sad, full of things that Bel didn't like. "Bel, I'm scared all the time."

Bel shook his head, unwilling to believe it, but his brother wasn't looking at him anymore. Instead he gazed, unseeing, out over the warm stone of Aeriand.

Another long, deep breath expanded Maddok's chest, and Bel felt himself holding his own, as if Maddok needed all the air. There were lines in his face, but not the dimples from smiling. Those lines were hidden away. In their place, creases made shadows flicker over Maddok's face He looked old. Bel knew Maddok really was young, compared to others like Eamon and Ophir and the councilors, but to Bel, who was so much younger than Maddok, his brother looked like one of those old avians, lined and weathered.

Bel didn't like it, and rubbed his hands over Maddok's face to make the lines go away.

"Everyone gets scared sometimes," Maddok said. "Even kings. Especially kings. There's so much..." He glanced at Bel as his words trailed off, but Bel remained quiet. Sometimes Maddok did this, spoke to him even though the words weren't all meant for him. He didn't care that he didn't understand half the things Maddok said, just cared that they were said *to him*. So he stayed silent, waiting for Maddok to start again.

"The humans want to take the Hollenheim from us again. Father wouldn't have lost it. The council says—well, everyone says if we can stop them there, the kingdom should be safe. We have to show the human king that I won't stand for invasion even though I'm young." The words didn't sound like his own, something more like when Eamon made Bel parrot phrases of old avian poetry or war tactics back to him. "Everyone's watching, Bel. I have to do something now. I can't worry about you too. You have to stay safe."

Bel swallowed around a lumpy throat. He eased his head onto Maddok's shoulder, not caring that the metal plates dug into his neck and scalp. Maddok held him closer, leaning his head against Bel's for a time.

"I didn't mean to burden you with this," he whispered into Bel's hair.

"Don't be scared," Bel whispered back.

Maddok inched back so he could see him, brows arched in surprise. Bel nodded.

"Don't be scared," he said again. "You're good and brave and strong and you'll beat that evil human king. You don't have to be scared. I know you'll win." He gave Maddok the warrior's salute, his little fist clenched over his heart.

Maddok smiled then, a real smile, though his eyes still seemed sad. "One day, you'll be all grown up and we'll defend the kingdom together. The humans won't stand a chance against two Adiirons."

"And I'll come with you then? When I'm grown?"

"Yes. Always. I'll need my fiercest protector by my side."

Bel couldn't help it, his wings, still covered in gray fledgling down, gave another happy flap, and he grinned a wide grin, making Maddok smile even bigger.

"You promise?"

"I promise."

Bel flung his arms around Maddok's neck again, hugging him tight, and Maddok returned the embrace. He buried his face in Maddok's throat when he felt them turn, felt Eamon's calloused hands rasp against his tunic.

"Bel, I have to go."

"When will you be back?"

"I don't know, but…"

"For my first flight?"

"Bel…"

"Mad, you—you *have* to be here for first flight!"

"I'll try, little hawk. I promise."

Bel could only nod, for that's all his brother could give him, promises. A king's promise meant a great deal, Eamon always said. But he didn't want a king's promises, he wanted Maddok's. And even then, sometimes promises felt like nothing, or if not nothing, then not quite enough. Never filling, never satisfying; always sweet on the tongue but bitter in the stomach.

When he was in Eamon's arms again, Maddok plucked Bel's helmet from the ground and set it on his head before donning his own, handed to him by one of the guards. Maddok's was gold, a crown of feathers etched along the brim and sides, the primary feathers arching up and away from the rounded back. It was their father's helmet, a king's helmet, and that's who gave him a soft smile before moving back into the circle of guards, the avian king.

Bel plopped his head against Eamon's, the older avian not even grunting when the steel of Bel's helmet smacked against his skull. He hitched Bel higher so he could watch Maddok say a few words to the crowd that had them cheering. Then, as one, the circle of guards turned toward the drop off. One, two, and more ran to the sheer drop, legs and arms pumping, wings unfurling.

He watched Maddok's golden head and wings disappear, Dartegn right behind him, and a second passed, two, and then there he was, soaring over the city, the guards swooping and diving into formation around him.

"Now that's a sight to see," said Eamon, watching as more than a hundred pairs of wings cut through the sky, gold and white and black and gray wings banking and flapping and swooping. "He'll make us proud, little hawk. Just you wait."

But Bel was already proud, prouder than he could say. Sometimes that pride was enough, but other times, like now, as he watched his brother disappear into the horizon, it was as satisfying as promises and pieces of a mother he'd never known.

It made him want to grow, be grown, all the faster. When he was grown, he wouldn't need promises. He'd see for himself that Maddok always came back to Aeriand. And he wouldn't just be the spare but an Adiiron prince who stood beside his king and made his brother proud of *him*.

22

For all that it was her idea, Lena found herself picking at her thumb as she and Alix set out equipment in preparation for Alix's first training session with Bel. When she'd made the offer, it'd sounded like a good idea, and it still did—even if her nerves made her jittery. But when she'd offered, in her mind, it had been *her* training with him. When her leg healed up a little more, she would be a match for the hard-bodied avian.

Alix was...well, Lena could lift her easily, even soaking wet. She'd joked once that a third of Alix's weight came from her big, untamable black curls while another third was her ego.

But she'd held her tongue during breakfast. Bel had come down from his chambers to eat with them, and while little conversation flowed between them, Alix had made up for it with her happy chatter and boasting. She'd even tried to get Pol to place bets.

Now, as they waited for Bel to come up from the kitchen to join them in the great hall, Lena wanted to pace, to work out her nerves, but the sharp twinge in her healing leg kept her frustratingly in place.

As Alix threw herself into her forms with gusto and exaggerated battle cries, Lena did what she could to stretch out her leg. It didn't pain her per se, but she was aware of each puncture every time she took a step. When she put weight on it, a phantom sensation of tendon and muscle flexing and releasing made her think of fraying rope pulled to its limit. The longer she stood, the more she felt blood sloshing in the fleshy holes.

Not that anyone let her stand for very long. Since returning from Fort Whitewater, Alix had kept close, always ready to shove her down on the nearest chair or a bowl of stew under her nose. Lena could admit she'd never been a good patient, and Alix's clumsy caregiving grated on her. It touched her that the girl cared so much, it really did, but she was already anxious to stop being Alix's charge and instead be her knight again.

Soft tread sounded from the stairs, and then Bel stood at the landing, looking on at them with a carefully neutral expression. After a pause, he came forward, and Lena's brows rose nearly to her hairline when he set one of the kitchen stools in front of her.

"For..." He gestured at her leg and swallowed audibly.

She felt just as articulate as a blush swept across her face. "Thank you," she mumbled, too abashed to feel any grumpiness at being taken care of. If Alix had done this, she would have sighed and grumbled before giving in, but Lena quickly slipped onto the stool without a word.

Bel looked her over once before nodding and walking woodenly out to meet Alix in the middle of the great hall. Even beneath the feathery curtain of his wings, Lena could see how stiff his shoulders were, barely moving as he walked.

Lena felt the heat of her face under the pretense of scrubbing her hands over her cheeks. Bel had asked after her leg during breakfast and seemed satisfied with her offhanded, "As good as can be expected." She didn't quite know what to do with the gesture, small as it might have seemed. Did he see her as weak now? Exploitable?

Mustn't think like that, she reminded herself. They had a truce now, they were to be allies, perhaps even uneasy friends. She couldn't think like a warden, not if she didn't want him to think like a prisoner.

Lena watched as Alix hopped out of her last form, brandishing her practice sword in wide swings. If Alix was the picture of eagerness and excitement, then Bel was the epitome of hesitance. His stance grew stiffer by the moment, and though Alix laughed and joked, Bel only mustered a creaky grin that made Lena wince.

Seeing Bel nervous only made her more so—did he worry about hurting Alix too?

Having the two of them squaring off only put their differences in sharper relief. Even with the fluff of her curls, Alix's head barely came to the bottom of his chest. At ease, arms held at his sides, he was easily three times as wide across as her squire, and though he was covered from neck to wrist in a linen tunic, the dips and shadows of his muscled limbs made Alix look positively twiggy.

Yet, of the two of them, Bel was the one who looked nervous. Alix had begun hopping from foot to foot, her practice sword held loose in her hand but ready. A sly little fox goading and baiting a reluctant bear.

Lena hid her smile, knowing neither of them would like the picture.

When it became clear that Bel wouldn't be the one to begin, Lena clapped her hands once, the sound making a ringing echo in the hall. "If you're both ready, form one."

Bel swallowed again. Alix only grinned.

"You're blocking while I attack," Alix explained before she became a frenzy of jabs and flying curls.

Lena watched, heart hammering in her mouth, as their two practice swords came together in a wooden slap. The sound reverberated in her head, stirring her unease.

Despite Alix's quickness, Bel deflected her initial attack and then her second, third, fourth...Alix's sword never touched him, yet his movements were stiff, jerky, lacking the fluid grace Lena had seen in her many battles with avians. He was only a little better than a new squire, a sword still new to the hand and relying almost entirely on instinct. There was no finesse, no strategy. It was like watching someone dance for the first time—she thought Bel might start looking at his feet if only Alix gave him a moment's reprieve.

Bel sidestepped to the left, completely avoiding Alix, and the squire went stumbling before using her practice sword to catch herself.

"Humph!" she cried. "Lucky dodge!"

The fire crackled in the east hearth behind her, casting the two combatants in warm tones. Lena could already see little tracks of sweat beading down Bel and Alix's foreheads, and she wondered how long to let this go on, if Bel was breaking a sweat at essentially swatting Alix away every few moments. Lena knew Alix's panting was mostly due to all her taunts and banter.

"Fight me like a man—er, avian!" she'd shout. "My grandmother fights better!"

"So big with those wings of yours, you think you can outmaneuver me? Can you dodge this—or this—or—?"

"Bet you've never seen *that* before. Invented it myself."

Here Bel shot Lena a look over Alix's head, part question, part plea. Lena only smiled and shrugged. Alix's fighting style was unique in that she talked through most of it.

If Lena hadn't been watching so closely, she wouldn't have immediately noticed the gradual easing of Bel's shoulders or bend in his knees. Slowly, as Alix's boasting moved from loud to outrageous, Lena beheld a transformation in Bel. Slowly, she began to recognize an avian warrior within this quiet man.

He began to move in a way she recognized as distinctly avian, using all six of his limbs; his wings might seem ungainly on land, and one might be crippled, but they gave him balance no human could rival. She'd known the avians must have some form of martial arts, something that made up the basis of their fighting technique, and the more she watched Bel, the more she thought she understood. Where she'd been taught to use her legs and core for support, the avian fighting style relied on the wings and back.

While not as flexible or maneuverable as an arm, he used his good wing to full effect, parrying and blocking and distracting with the gleaming feathers. It was effective against Alix, who was easily dazzled by his displays. Lena had seen similar techniques on the battlefield, but she'd never been able to truly admire the style.

She too was dazzled by the demonstration. In the warm glow of the fire, his wings gleamed almost gold, the white base yellow-tinged while the dappled tips flashed like worked bronze. She watched those wings deftly work in tandem with his arms, even at one point shrouding Alix in a feathery veil and disarming her with a sweep of his wing.

She gasped, not recognizing the trap for what it was until too late, and neither did Alix. Lena was torn between wanting to clap for the maneuver and to check on Alix.

Alix barked a laugh and lunged for her sword.

The battle started again, but rather than worry over her squire, Lena watched in astonishment as Bel gradually began using his crippled wing. He had less range of motion than with the other, couldn't sweep it in the elegant arc he'd used to distract and disarm Alix, but he used it how he could. She was so used to seeing Bel pull it behind him, hide it away, try and make her and others forget he even had it, that to see him brandish it made a warm swell of...pride expand her chest.

Alix launched herself at him while Bel twirled away as deftly as a dancer.

"Is that all you can manage, bird man?" Alix joked, panting.

"Big words from a pint like you," Bel laughed.

It took Lena a while to understand what was happening, and her cheeks reddened with the realization and how long it took her to come to. They were having *fun*. This had ceased to be training and instead became a game. They were *playing*.

She watched in amazement for another half-hour as they flew around the great hall, parrying and blocking and goading each other. When focused, Alix was always a scrappy fighter, eager to learn and improve and impress Lena. But she'd never seen such enthusiasm in Alix's fighting. She'd never seen her train this long, especially not without complaint. Alix's whole face was drenched in sweat, her cheeks rosy, and she glowed with happiness. She was having fun, fun training, fun with Bel.

And it was then Lena knew that this hadn't been a mistake. That, even though she wasn't one to gamble, this had been worth the risk, if only to see Alix's wide, cocky smile. Lena hadn't the heart the correct Alix's form or the courage to make suggestions to Bel, so she eased the weight off her bad leg and just enjoyed the show.

⸻ ◆ ⸻

I think we'll call it a draw," Lena said, ending several minutes of arguing about who had won their sparring session. Both Alix and Bel guffawed at the suggestion but didn't refute it. Pleased, Lena carefully stood from her stool before stooping to grab the pewter pitcher at her feet. As she poured a cup of water, she nodded at Alix.

"Take care of the equipment and then we'll stretch."

Alix held her hand out to Bel. "I'll put yours away too."

Bel blinked before looking down at his hand, holding his weighted practice sword in a loose grip. Lena waited quietly to see what he'd do, if he'd allow Alix to touch it. She didn't know if it could be more personal than touching his wings, but everything with Bel felt momentous. He could be so reserved, so enigmatic, and Lena was starting to learn she had to carefully watch for the little glimpses he allowed into his deeper self. Playing with Alix, wearing his own smile, had been Bel at his purest. Lena had seen nothing like it from him before, and she wanted to see it again.

Bel gave a jerky nod and handed the practice sword over. Alix made a show of hefting the weighted wood, making Bel and Lena roll their eyes as she pranced off to put the swords with the other equipment in a battered old trunk Alix had found.

Lena offered Bel the water and he took it with a nod, avoiding her eyes.

He drank, his gaze trained on the opposite side of the great hall, and Lena had to stop herself from watching the bob of his throat as he swallowed. She didn't know why she found the simple movement so mesmerizing; perhaps because until a few days ago, she'd never been so close to him, had never really gotten to just look at him. Now, she noticed things about him like the cut of his jaw and the fine shape of his lips—things she wasn't sure she should be noticing.

The sound of Alix dropping the equipment into the trunk pulled Lena out of her thoughts. Instead, she watched Alix rummage around in a trunk almost as big as her and looked like it could have swallowed her whole.

Without letting herself overthink it, Lena reached out and gripped Bel's forearm. His surprised gaze cut to her, and she watched his wide birdlike pupils dilate, nearly taking over the liquid turquoise of the iris.

"Thank you, for today." She nodded at Alix, only the girl's legs visible as she fished around inside the trunk. "Sometimes I forget she's so young and needs to have fun."

She held still as Bel's eyes flicked between hers. She kept her hand on his forearm, pressure light, and felt the muscle and tendons flex and release, flex and release.

Finally, a small smile broke across his face, like the sun breaking through a clouded sky.

"We all need to, from time to time I suppose," he said, though Lena had a hard time imaging him having fun, even if she'd just seen it for herself. He was always so serious, so guarded. But then, Lena had a hard time imaging herself having fun either. It was a new and somewhat troubling realization.

"Yes." She realized she was still holding onto him and let go, folding both hands behind her.

"Ready!" Alix announced, taking up one of the first stretches of their regimen in the middle of the great hall.

"Would you like to join us?" she asked Bel.

"I have *ariant* forms waiting to beat me into submission," he replied, angling a ways away from where Alix had taken up position.

"Ah. Best of luck then. Will you come to training tomorrow, or did Alix scare you off?"

He glanced at Alix for a moment, and another warm smile overtook his face. "Yes, I'll come tomorrow."

"Perhaps we have things to teach each other," she said.

"Perhaps," he replied, grinning again before he moved away to put himself through those mysterious *ariant* forms.

The pleasant flush from the promise of tomorrow kept Lena warm throughout her stretches, her afternoon chores, and well into the evening. Whatever this was, whatever easiness was blooming between them, Lena welcomed it.

23

For two days, Bel agonized over his message to Dartegn. As he oscill-ated and prevaricated over each word, each rune, he fought the memories that edged into his mind at the thought of his cousin. It felt as if Dartegn inhabited a different world, had been his blood kin in another life.

Bel tugged a hand through his tangled hair, tracing the message in his mind as surely as he'd traced it with his fingers over and over again, agonizing over the runes that would be his first words to his cousin in ten years.

COUSIN. HAVE BEEN TRANSLATING FOR HUMAN KING ABOUT HADRIA. GIVING WRONG INFORMATION ABOUT TUNNELS ETC. AWAITING YOUR INSTRUCTIONS. BEL.

He'd written a dozen different messages before finally deciding to scratch the final one into the shaft of one of his own secondary feathers. Somehow, none of the messages, not even the one he'd finally settled on, felt right. What did he say to a man whose life he'd ruined? And ruined it he had. Bel knew how much Dar had hated royal functions, only atten-ding to be a comfort to Maddok. Bel knew how much Dar loved to fly fast and free, how much he hated being subordinate to anyone, even custom. But most of all, he knew how much Dar had loved Maddok, and not for the first time or with any less bitterness, he thought the world would be a very different place if Dar had been Maddok's true brother.

As he considered his message, he felt a tug of sour dissatisfaction in his gut about it. He'd settled on formality, efficiency. The only familiarity he'd included was *cousin* at the beginning, a reminder of their kinship that was, admittedly, a gamble; and *Bel*, his calling name, at the end. He thought these emotionless words would stand the best chance of being read all the way through before Dar destroyed the feather.

And he would destroy it.

Even from a thousand leagues away, Bel thought he could sometimes feel the fiery lick of Dar's temper. It was an awful thing to behold, both powerful and frightening, and Bel suspected that he'd know when the feather reached Hadria, would feel the rage sizzling through the air to him on his mountain.

Bel was supposed to be dead. The blade had been meant for him that night, a mere glint of steel in the moonlight to his eye. Maybe it was because he was king that Maddok thought he could thwart fate; that he, not it, would have the final say over Bel's life. Maybe he'd merely acted on some deep instinct to protect Bel—but Bel didn't like to consider that. Whatever Maddok's reasons, he'd put himself between Bel and that blade. Bel was supposed to be dead, wasn't supposed to live beyond that night, and he knew he hadn't in Dartegn's heart.

He could only hope his message was read at least once, maybe even found its way to Eamon somehow. Eamon would know what to do once Dar's rage had settled. He would know what to tell Dar, what to tell *Bel*.

He'd done what he could and for now could only wait in the hope that word was sent back, word that would help him decide what to do. Tumbling and indistinct, his mind tied itself in knots thinking about the message and what it meant for his pact with Maddalena.

The thought of her didn't come with the dread it had before.

He knew he'd be a fool to let his guard down completely, to put all his trust in this truce of theirs. But if he was honest, this had been one of the few good gambles he'd ever made in his life. For the first time in ten years, he didn't feel scrutinized. Sometimes, when he laughed at something ridiculous Alix had said, it didn't feel like he had a warden at all. And even if it was only true within the walls of Finhöln, Bel saw no reason to wake from the delusion.

For the first time in ten years, Bel had begun to welcome a knight and squire's presence in his crumbling castle. His few moments of reprieve from Dartegn's message came when he was training with Alix, a watchful but good-humored Maddalena nearby. Even now, his muscles ached in that delicious, satisfying way after a long bout of training. It buoyed him, giving him the courage to face down the note yet again.

It was time to act, find a bird to bear his message east.

Bel dreaded this part.

Pushing himself up from his chair, Bel stoked the crackling fire before easing one of the casement windows open. A blast of frigid air kissed his face and slipped beneath his collar. His first shiver was pleasant, his second less so as the chill began to spread across his face and chest.

Bel remained in the casement for a long time, his back warm from the fire and his front slowly turning blue. He waited, listening to the castle. It was late in the afternoon; everyone else should have been in the kitchen. If he stayed much longer in the open window, they'd wonder where he was—a new sensation for Bel. Even before coming to Finhöln, he'd rarely ever been expected. Only Eamon, and sometimes Maddok, had needed him somewhere at a certain time; otherwise, Bel had always kept his own time. It was odd, and a little pleasing, to know that someone would note his absence, perhaps even *miss* him.

Finally, when he'd heard nothing, not from the bailey, or the snowed-in walkway directly below his window, or from the corridor beyond his unlockable door, Bel opened the window wider and leaned his head out.

He put two fingers in his mouth and whistled, the unpracticed sound sputtering before finally ringing out into the trees. He cupped his other hand around his mouth, opening and closing the pocket he'd made with his hands and mouth. The whistle undulated, becoming a warbling chirp.

He practiced his call, repeating it again and again until it was a continuous trill, echoing up and down the mountainside. *Need a strong flyer to bear message east,* he called. *Need a strong flyer...*

He hadn't called for a bird in over three years, since his last message from Eamon had come. His throat gave out sooner than he liked, but he was mollified that he'd done it.

Bel quickly shut the casement and rubbed his face as he stalked to the fire, working feeling back into his flesh. His heart raced at what he'd put into motion, but there wasn't the slight sickness he'd felt in his gut before his few escape attempts. He wasn't trying to escape now. Maddalena would never know what he'd done, if he did this right.

Still, to betray her trust so quickly...

Bel sank down into his chair again, unsure if he should go down like this. He thought perhaps she might see the guilt on his face. Her hawk eyes missed little.

He tugged his hand through his hair again, leaning his head on the back of the chair to watch the shadows dance across the timbered roof. The birds would pass his message on until one came to volunteer. Many were buried beneath the snow in their nests, but birds liked to chatter. The call would go out. He had, at most, a handful of days to wait, he thought.

Bel let out a long breath as warmth began to seep into him again. It was out of his hands now. A bird would come soon, and he'd hand over the message, and the responsibility, to them. After, all he could do was wait.

Bel stood and stretched, then patted down his clothes to get the creases out of the linen and wool. He'd found his rooms less sanctuary than stifling the past few days, and he didn't relish waiting here for a bird to come. None would until morning at least.

He slipped from his chambers into the cold castle, seeking the warmth and company of the kitchen. He'd done some small thing for his cousin—his king—and his people. For now, it was all he could do, and it was little reassurance. So Bel went down to where he knew he could find a little more, even if no one knew they gave it.

24

Lena made her escape after breakfast, dumping Pol's latest tonic out in the snow. She kicked a pile of powder on top, hiding the evidence. She liked the man, she did, but there was such a thing as too much care. Every morning and each afternoon for a fortnight, he had a new potion for her, clucking his tongue and signing that he wished to see her heal faster. Despite Pol's concern, her leg was nearly good as new; very soon, she'd be able to train with Alix again. And start training with Bel.

The thought sent a little thrill through her; it clenched in her gut, not unpleasant. She hadn't had a decent sparring partner since she was begrudgingly sent home from the front and the crown prince. And Bel was more than decent.

Yes, there was a grace to the way Bel moved, and Lena looked forward to testing herself against him.

Slipping the now empty bottle of tonic back into her coat pocket, Lena hiked up the south steps into the bailey. The sky was a uniform, steely gray above, a color she'd learned to dread. Dark, bluish clouds brought rain, clouds the color of bruises meant thunder, but it was the light, steel gray that harkened snow. Best to see to the horses now before she had to shovel herself to and from.

In the bailey, a movement had Lena stopping. She planted her feet, finding familiar tread in her little path, and looked to the east wall. At first she squinted, not quite sure what she saw, only that something moved. Then, mottled brown caught the meager light, and Lena recognized the great pair of avian wings.

Bel had his gray oilskin hood up, concealing the gold of his hair, and though he kept his wings close, stray feathers fluttered in the wind and escaped the confines of the cloak. She watched the broad expanse of his shoulders move about, as if he reached for something. Easing closer to the wall, Lena leaned back into the cold, hard stones. Not hiding, just... quietly observing.

She'd never seen anyone up there on the east ramparts, had told Alix to stay away from the crumbling catwalk and questionable stairs. The east wall had that gaping hole Lena first noticed on their ascent up to Finhöln, the one that ate at her every time she saw it. Why would he climb up there?

Something else moved, and Lena squinted harder. A tree limb, heavy with snow, rocked up and down, dislodging snow. The pine needles were a stark green against the white, as was the glimmer of gold and bronze that emerged from the tree. A beautiful golden eagle hopped from the limb onto the crumbling parapet.

The eagle ruffled its feathers and adjusted its wings before, with one talon-tipped foot extended, bowing low to Bel, beak nearly scraping the snow and rocks.

Lena blinked, hardly believing what she saw. Had Bel trained the bird? Who trained a bird to bow? She hadn't seen him use any falconry equipment, but then, she hadn't seen much of Bel before they'd made their truce.

The thought of their deal had Lena's stomach sinking, this time unpleasantly. It was still so new, so untested. Had she made a mistake in offering peace?

She was fairly far away and couldn't hear much, but she thought the bird chirped at Bel, and that Bel chirped back. At least, that's what it sounded like. It seemed as though Bel spoke; he gesticulated and a few noises reached Lena's ears, but like with Pol's hand signs when she'd first arrived, it was nothing Lena understood or ever encountered before.

Can he really speak with birds? The thought darted around her mind, at once improbable and incredible. Did others know avians could do this? *Could* all avians do this?

Bel's conversation with the eagle lasted a while longer, and Lena wondered what they discussed. Was this how he dealt with the loneliness, talked to the only creatures who could understand his need to fly? Compassion swelled in Lena's chest, and though the cold pit of dread and suspicion remained in her stomach, she tempered it as she watched the two feathered creatures speak.

The eagle opened its beak and made a little croak before bobbing its head. Bel's shoulders seemed to sag just a little—in relief? Resignation? She couldn't tell, couldn't see much of him besides his cloaked back as he drew something out of a pocket.

Lena was too far away to see much, but whatever he held was long, white at one end and mottled brown at the other tip. *A feather,* she realized. *One of his own feathers.*

The eagle seemed to coo, and with another head bob it reached out to clasp Bel's feather in its beak. The great yellow orbs of its eyes gazed unblinking up at Bel, and Bel must have gazed back. A few more gestures and chirps were exchanged before the eagle turned on the parapet, shook out its tail feathers, opened its great gold wings, and took to the skies.

The force of the eagle's wide wings beating threw Bel's hood back, his gold curls bright against the colorless landscape. He turned slightly to keep the eagle in his view, watching as the bird climbed higher into the sky.

Lena's legs tensed, ready to leap back around the corner of the wall, but Bel didn't turn. He stood there, unmoving, watching as the eagle spiraled upwards on a draft. Soon, the world settled back into sleep as the eagle became a mere dot in the gray sky; but still Bel stood watching.

Lena didn't know how long she stood there, only that he did not move, and so she did not either. It felt like a spell, or how she imagined one would, as if she couldn't move until he did. He stood vigil over the craggy horizon and Lena stood vigil over him.

Though she couldn't see it from her vantage point down in the bailey, Lena thought the eagle must have soared over the mountains by now. Yet Bel would not move. If it weren't for the occasional breeze sneaking over the curtain wall, lifting his hair, he would've seemed more statue than flesh. The snow Lena had dreaded began in soft, drifting flakes, accumulating on Bel's shoulders.

Why did he remain out in the cold?

And why did *she* remain out in the cold, watching him?

Part of her wondered why he'd given the eagle one of his own feathers. It didn't seem random or like a gift. Could it be a message of some sort?

He shifted, finally proving that he was real and not a figment of Lena's frost-crusted imagination, but it was only to draw his wings out of the cloak and drape them about his shoulders in a second layer of warmth. She envied him that.

Even in the paltry light, his wings glimmered like the sea at sunset, a mirror that shone with fractals of gold and blades of white, and Lena couldn't help but think how beautiful he was. She'd thought for a long time that avians weren't beautiful—yes, their wings were otherworldly, sometimes frightening or dazzling, but otherwise they resembled humans enough that Lena could see past their wings. But Bel wasn't otherworldly to her then, just beautiful.

Sad, but beautiful.

That niggling of compassion pulled at her heart again, as if a thread had been stitched there and he held the other end, tugging lightly.

She should be suspicious of that feather, and part of her was. But they had made a deal, she had made a promise, and she wouldn't be the one to renege now. The feather could mean nothing. It could be a message—and then what? Would avians come to retrieve him? Lena somehow doubted it. It was a long way to avian-controlled territory. And in the ten years Bel had been here, no avian had come for him. Why would they now?

At that thought, the thread pulled at her, not a mere tug but something stronger, something that had her legs moving of their own accord. Carefully, she ascended the east steps, picking her way up then across the catwalk.

He must have heard her approach—she didn't try sneaking up on him. The snow and stones beneath her feet crunched, announcing her long before she reached him. Yet Bel didn't move, nor did he turn towards her. His gaze was only for the slate of the sky, his mouth a down-turned line as he looked out, unseeing.

A great sadness seemed to envelope him, a nearly tangible thing that pushed back against Lena drawing closer. She came anyway, her steps slow and careful. Perhaps he too was under some sort of spell. Perhaps he wouldn't welcome her company now. But Lena came anyway, not stopping until her shoulder nearly brushed his left wing.

They gazed out at the world beyond together, snow falling in quiet whispers around them. Lena no longer found the quiet of winter so disturbing, rather imagined the world slept under this white blanket, waiting. Or at least, held its breath.

She thought, at the moment, it was the latter. She could feel the tension in the air, as if the world waited, held its breath in anticipation. Her lips tingled with it and the cold.

"The snow is coming again," she said, hating every word as it left her mouth. They were trite and pathetic and made her cringe. She was grateful Bel wouldn't look at her, wouldn't see the grimace she wore as she tried to find something more substantial to say.

The sadness that engulfed him caressed her too, and she felt his melancholy suck at her. These past days, she had seen a Bel who smiled, who was patient with Alix and teasing with Pol. Just this morning, she had watched his face brighten with laughter as he sparred with Alix. He had become a man to her rather than an enigma, a being rather than a prisoner, and Lena didn't like to see him so downtrodden. It felt like a step back, and deep inside herself, Lena knew she only wanted to go forward. After their deal, they couldn't go back.

"It'd be best to go inside," she tried again, only marginally more satisfied with her second attempt. "It'd be a shame if you froze."

"Would it?"

She glanced at him, tracing the sharp lines of his profile. "Yes, of course it would."

But he said nothing to her reply, and they lapsed back into the silent stillness. It was beginning to unnerve Lena, how still he could be; she imagined he didn't even blink but knew he must be.

"It'll come in the night," he said finally, and she thought he must mean the brunt of the storm. "And after there will be another, then another. It's never-ending here."

"Mm," she agreed. "But we'll dig ourselves out tomorrow."

"Just to do it again the next day."

"Yes. Until spring comes. Winter must end, even here."

He looked at her then, snow sifting through his hair and spilling from his shoulders. He said nothing as his eyes moved over her face, and Lena felt that gaze as if it had been his hand instead. It was slow, tentative, not quite caressing, but not analytical either. She held her breath along with the world, waiting.

"Spring is very short here," was what he finally said.

"It's better than more winter, and summer always follows."

He made a noncommittal noise and resumed his vigil. With a lingering look, Lena finally turned back to the mountain too.

The eagle was long gone, leaving a barren sky and mountainside.

The trees, with their snow-matted limbs, had long ago stopped looking frosted with confectioner's sugar, but instead, with the heavy layers of snow, resembled rotting teeth.

What a morbid thought, Lena mused to herself, but it was true. She wasn't the person to find much beauty in winter.

The snow began in earnest, dusting their shoulders. Lena pulled her scarf up her face to protect her mouth and nose, but she didn't move from Bel's side. Something inside worried that, in his mood, if she left him now, he'd stay here through the night and surely freeze. His thoughts were heavy and sad, taking up too much of his mind to leave room for anything else.

Despite herself, a shiver ran through Lena. She'd dressed warm but only thought she'd be going to the stables. Spending the afternoon outside required more layers, but she was loath to leave now.

She heard Bel shift, snow crunching with the transfer of weight from foot to foot, and then something exquisitely soft brushed over her shoulders and back, the tip of her nose and her brows. The scent of warmth and down surrounded her, and she looked up in surprise to see Bel's left wing extended over her, sheltering her from the thickening snow.

He rested the wing just the barest amount on the top of her head, providing shelter and insulation. He eased a little closer to her side, making their shoulders brush, so that his wing could completely cover her.

Lena opened her mouth to say something, but nothing came. She felt the tugging in her chest again, and she offered a small smile in thanks, though he was still in profile and didn't see. It didn't matter. She abandoned words and instead stayed with him, standing in silence as the day waned and the snow continued to fall.

The sun disappeared, the world quickly darkening before Lena coaxed Bel inside. They were both stiff from the cold and welcomed Pol's clucking and warm stew. They ate in relative silence, letting Alix's cheery chatter fill the void, and Bel soon retired upstairs.

But though he left, the smell and warmth of his wing stayed with Lena through the night, a comforting weight as she slipped into bed. It kindled a longing in her, a familiar one, that yearned for more. More of what, she couldn't quite say, as her chamber's fire was stoked and she was warm and drowsy and already half-asleep.

$$25$$

Bel didn't go down to training the next morning. He hadn't gone to sleep the night before, either. Just laid on his back, watching the shadows lengthen and distort with the changing light. Warmth slowly seeped back into him through the night, though he'd recognized it in a distant, apathetic sort of way. He supposed it was the price paid for standing out in the snow all afternoon like a ghost.

He stayed there, prone and unmoving, long after the sun rose. Well, he assumed it rose, behind the bank of clouds muting the sky. He wondered if Maddalena and Alix would train without him. He wanted to avoid their eyes, especially Maddalena's—despite his flesh warming again, there was still a soreness to him, a raw feeling that wouldn't go away. He thought her gaze would chafe him too much to bear.

He hadn't asked her to stay with him yesterday; at first, he hadn't wanted her to either. But as the day had passed like a sluggish river, winding and fluid, Bel had grown used to her shoulder pressed to his, even started to...like it.

He hadn't planned on putting his wing over her either, just felt her shivering with the cold and acted. He'd held perfectly still as the radial bone met her head, delicately balanced along the crown. She'd done nothing, just exhaled a long breath and moved a little closer, a little deeper into the down.

Even now, buried in his nest of blankets, Bel could still feel her nestled beside him, a phantom presence that he didn't quite know what to do with. He thought it was a comfort, but it was new, and new often meant dangerous to Bel. New and possibly dangerous—but still...pleasant. Something he might want again. Maybe.

He was brooding again—he could feel it, and in the light of day, it felt a little ridiculous to lay there doing nothing but thinking the same thoughts again and again.

Bel pushed himself up and made himself presentable—meaning his cleanest pair of breeches and the least wrinkled shirt he currently had. As he tied off the knots on either of his flanks, modifications he'd made himself to accommodate his wings, Bel thought of the finery he'd worn in his life before.

There'd been silks and finely woven cotton, gold-threaded tunics and leather worked so well it felt like butter that would melt under the heat of a hand. He hadn't given much thought to his clothes, only considered them as Eamon or someone else dressed him in them or suggested them to him or were throwing them at him—the last one was only Eamon. He supposed part of being a prince, an Adiiron, was the clothes. He didn't have a memory of Maddok being unkempt. Sweaty, a little dirty perhaps, but the lines of his clothes still crisp.

Maddalena was always dressed crisply too. Not in the same way as Maddok—she hadn't the army of workers to wash her clothes after only one wear—but still, she was almost always clean, and more often than not buckled into that boiled leather cuirass that molded to the womanly form underneath. Did she think him sloppy?

The thought didn't necessarily trouble him as he emerged from his room, descending to the kitchen. But it did perplex him.

Bel heard them before he'd even made it into the kitchen; Pol was chopping something with his favorite knife while Alix chattered and Maddalena made soft noises of agreement. Somehow, Bel was starting to associate these sounds with warmth, coziness, companionship.

The scene he came upon was different from the one he'd imagined.

Pol was indeed chopping, but his focus was on Alix and Maddalena, a chess board scattered with pieces sitting between them. Maddalena had her chin resting on her folded hands, a smug smile adorning her lips. It was the closest thing Bel had ever seen to evil on her face, and he stared.

Alix was levered over the game on splayed palms, as if a higher angle would help. She made little mouse squeaks of frustration. Bel pried his gaze from Maddalena's smirk and glanced at the board, seeing Alix's predicament almost immediately.

From the hearth came Pol's huffing laugh. Bel looked up to see him sign, *She has had the girl on the run all morning. A-l-i-x wanted to place bets, but it is good now she didn't.*

Bel laughed at that, glad to take a mug of warm tea and no questions about his lateness from Pol. The cook was used to his odd hours; it was more unusual for him to keep a schedule than to be absent for days at a time.

This is the fifth day in a row I've seen you at the same time for break-fast, Pol had told him only a few mornings ago. *I don't know if I've ever seen you this much so close together. Not sure I like it.*

As Pol plied him with the morning's baked goods—dark bread, berry tarts, and sticky buns, the cinnamon sticking to his fingers in a buttery bronze gloss—Bel watched the game between knight and squire with interest.

Maddalena stole quick little looks at him but said nothing about yes-terday, for which he was grateful. She hadn't said anything as she stood with him either, and he appreciated her not asking. He couldn't tell her why sending a message to his cousin had him so tied up in knots—he couldn't tell her about any of it. He was happy to preserve the façade of their truce and didn't intend to betray it again. That had to be enough.

Maddalena waited patiently for her squire to fall into her trap. A feline smile overcame Maddalena's face, and Bel was lured to the table to get a closer look. He'd never imagined she could look devious, never mind even *be* devious.

"Where've you been?" barked Alix without looking up from the board.

"Upstairs..."

Alix grumbled, a good impression of a bear. "Could use your help here. She's been toying with me since breakfast."

Maddalena's smile grew, eyes twinkling in wicked delight. "You're the one who wanted to play."

"That was two hours ago. And before I remembered how...*competitive* you are."

Alix touched several pieces without moving them, each time stealing a look at Maddalena to see if she'd give anything away. It was like watching a cat toy with a mouse between its paws; Maddalena would cock her eyebrow or smirk or shrug, and Alix would huff and take her finger off the piece, searching for a new move.

"Be-e-el," Alix whined.

He winced at her high pitch and cocked his own eyebrow. "Yes?"

"Help me! You can't let her win!"

"I don't know that it's fair to do two against one—"

"Then I'll quit! You finish her!"

Bel looked to Maddalena, thinking she might have qualms about playing against the two of them or him taking over for Alix, but her smile only grew more beatific.

"By all means," she said. "Alix has been sulking the past half hour and makes a move every ten minutes. It'd be nice to have a challenge."

Alix made a show of rolling her eyes before slipping off her stool, in search of food. Bel took her place.

He stopped Maddalena when she reached to clear off the board. Their hands met for a moment, something warm and a little electric in the touch. She met his gaze, lifting her brow again, but this time there was something cocky in it.

She was playing with him.

And it delighted him.

"Wanted to set them up yourself, did you?"

"No," he said, "just wanted to save you the trouble. You don't need to reset it."

"No? You don't want a fresh board?"

"I don't need one to win, if that's what you're concerned about."

Alix snickered from the hearth, but Bel kept his gaze on Maddalena, watching the surprise and amusement and finally the challenge spark in her eyes. It was like a fire coming to life, first little embers that burned bright and fast, until the kindling took. It warmed Bel's center and radiated out, filling up all the dark niches and loosening the knotted mess of his conscience.

Maddalena conceded with an overly gracious wave of her hand. Bel accepted with an overdone bow of his head.

He took a moment to survey the board before moving one of the eight pieces Alix had left. Maddalena made a pleased noise deep in her throat and leaned forward to make her next move.

He couldn't help but trace the curve of her neck as she considered, her eyes hooded. It was sometimes hard to tell under all the winter clothes and her serious braids, but Maddalena had a graceful neck, not too long, not too wide, a perfect column of warm, golden skin. Her skin was always this color, no matter how long she spent inside, making Bel think of warmer climes and the smooth marble and sandstone that adorned Aeriand.

He snapped his gaze away before she could catch him, telling himself to pay attention. He'd made a boast and the only reasonable thing to do was win and prove himself right.

He got Alix out of Maddalena's trap in four moves, making her sigh. "All that beautiful planning, for nothing."

"Not for nothing," he laughed. "Would've doomed a lesser warrior."

"Hey!" Alix cried.

"Where did you learn to play?" Maddalena asked, shifting one of her knights forward.

"We have a similar game," he explained, waffling over which pawn to sacrifice. "It has a bigger board and there are three players, though."

"Are you saying this is easy in comparison?"

He shrugged, making her laugh. The noise was a little foreign to Bel, but he liked it.

Alix eventually moseyed back to them, sitting at the end of the table with her head cradled on her folded arms. "Teach her a lesson, Bel," she goaded.

"All in good time."

"Ha!" Maddalena scoffed. "We'll see. I think this avian is all feathers and no bite."

Bel smiled serenely as he took one of her rooks two moves later.

"I don't know if I believe you're this good just from having a similar game," Maddalena said with suspicion as she eyed whether to take the easy bait of his unguarded bishop.

Bel shrugged again. "Pol taught me one winter. Lots of time for it, as you've discovered."

Maddalena waved to get Pol's attention. He looked up from carving a roast.

Teach Bel c-h-e-s-s? she signed.

Yes, everything he knows. But not everything I know. Pol winked.

Bel joined in Maddalena's laughter, not minding so much that she was determined to learn Pol's signing. He'd always liked that he was one of only a handful who could fully communicate with Pol, but it was nice to know Pol had others to talk with, as Bel wasn't always good company. Perhaps it was that Maddalena felt...if not safe now, then at least not dangerous. It wasn't dangerous to let her near.

Their game eased into a fluctuating rhythm; sometimes it was rapid, pieces tumbling over one another, while others it was slow, methodical, pieces moving forward and back again. Pol put a lunch of sliced meat, bread, and cheese near their elbows, but Bel didn't remember eating it, just moving a plate of crumbs out of his way once it was eaten. Over an hour had to have gone by, but he didn't feel its passing.

They overtook each other's territory like generals, claiming each other's pieces and reclaiming lost soldiers. For a few harrying moves, she chased his king around the board, nearly trapping him twice. She was a bloodhound with the scent of prey in her lungs, persistent and hungry.

He made a trap, setting up his few remaining soldiers to draw her in. It was risky but could mean victory. He had nothing to lose.

And she nearly fell for it. He watched her eyes dance across the board, tried to contain his excitement when he saw her see his feigned weakness. She even picked up her bishop to move it in for the kill—but stopped. Twisted the wooden piece in her fingers. And replaced it. She moved her queen two spaces over instead, negating his trap.

Alix hooted, crumbs from her half-eaten biscuit flying.

They moved across the board again, Bel trying to set another trap, before realizing she'd been coaxing him into one of her own. It was too late when he realized it, though he put up a valiant effort for three more moves.

Gently, Lena used her queen to topple his king. "Checkmate," she said.

Bel blinked, his heart still racing. His stomach growled, reminding him that it had been a while since Pol deftly inserted lunch, and his gaze took a moment to focus on the surrounding kitchen. Emerging from his competitive daze felt like breaking the surface of water, smooth, everything suddenly louder.

Alix was munching noisily on another biscuit, the apples of her cheeks round and red with mirth. Pol was pretending to stir the cauldron boiling over the hearth fire, but really snuck looks at Bel. And Maddalena watched him quietly from across the board, her fire banked.

Bel blinked again and realized he'd lost. That she'd beaten him, despite his boasting, despite his earnest desire to win. That she hadn't *let* him win.

She was competitive, as Alix said. She was clever and merciless and teasing. But most of all, she hadn't let him win. And he realized then, it was because she didn't pity him.

His mouth stretched wide in a delighted smile. He watched its impact as Alix chuckled and Maddalena returned it with a tentative one of her own.

Bel picked up his king and replaced it in its starting square.

"Again?"

26

Lena's heart beat like a fluttering bird caught in the cage of her ribs. She'd woken with a swell of excitement in her chest this morning, had thrown both legs over the side of the bed and stood. Just stood. Her leg had finally healed, no trembling or phantom sensations.

And she knew then that today, today she would spar with Bel.

He stood now about ten paces away ruffling his wings a bit and rotating the wrist of his sword arm. She wondered if he felt it too, this thrum of anticipation than ran warm and viscous through her like honey. She watched his eyes as they darted from her to Alix to the fire and back, the way he kept rotating his wrist, how his wings fluttered and dipped.

Lena found that the wings were his biggest tell. Though he kept them as hidden away as physically possible, they still shivered and fluttered and even flapped when he felt something strongly enough. During their chess game two days ago, she'd figured out when he meant to trap her, read his mischievous excitement in the shudders that went through his wings, making the feathers flutter and shimmer like a slant of dawn light.

There was something exciting and relieving about being able to read him, even a little. Now she had clues to follow, and her longing to know more only grew.

Bel cracked his neck for the third time, and his wings twitched, the strong left wing arching back and brushing the ground.

He feels it too, she thought. A ferocious smile broke across her face.

Bel blinked at it, and Lena's brows nearly arched off her face when he countered with a cocky little grin.

"Is this sparring or a staring contest?" Alix complained from her place sitting on the equipment trunk.

"You should always take the measure of your opponent," Lena said in her primmest schoolmarm voice.

Bel's grin grew, and he angled himself completely toward her. She thought his chest might have even puffed out.

"You should always know what you're getting into," Bel agreed. "Knowledge is an advantage."

His gaze swept over her, from head to toe and back again, and Lena felt it as if it was a physical touch. Her cheeks threatened to redden, so Lena returned the favor, making sure her perusal was too slow to be strictly sizing up an opponent.

"You're doing it again!" Alix called through her snickering. "On with it!"

Lena held her sword in front of her, bowing slightly at the waist in a swordsman's salute. Bel replied by holding his sword at his side and tucking his other arm across his abdomen as he bowed. They both laughed when Alix groaned long and with feeling.

Lena took the offensive, darting forward and bringing her sword down in a wide arc. It clattered against Bel's as he parried, scraped as he threw her off. She danced back a few paces, feeling almost giddy with the easy stretch and flex of her leg. A sense of rightness overtook her, and it made her limbs feel like flexible iron, strong and invincible. This was what she was good at, and it felt like coming home to finally be sparring again.

Bel took his turn driving her back a few paces, and they fought for a time like that, back and forth, testing each other's range and agility.

He wasn't as stiff as he'd been his first time sparring with Alix, but

Lena sensed a hesitancy in him, even pulling his strikes at the last moment. They got her attention but didn't debilitate her. As they pressed each other, Lena struck harder, waiting for his answer. She wanted him to *fight*, to challenge her. She wanted to see all he could do.

Lena took the offensive again, driving him back, further and further. She caught his eyes flashing in frustration, and finally his wings gave a flap and she was ducking away from the feathery club.

A laugh escaped her as she escaped him, dodging his second blow. He followed her, keeping close quarters, making both their sword work quick and jerky. She was at a disadvantage like this, his broad chest filling her vision and his arched wings her periphery. He was trying to overwhelm her, but all Lena felt was the thrill of a good fight, of testing him and being tested in return.

Fighting so close to an avian in the field would've meant almost certain harm, probably death. Usually bigger and with a second pair of limbs, they could overwhelm a human soldier, as Bel was trying to do now—but the battlefield had taught Lena many things.

She caught his sword with hers, twisting them in a tight circle before flinging his away from her. His arm went with the momentum, and she spun away from him, gripping his shoulder as she went. She heard Bel grunt as her fingers filled with feathers, and then her practice sword laid against the wing base, ready to take away the advantage.

Bel went completely still.

For a moment, Lena could hear nothing but the blood rushing through her ears, but slowly sound—or lack thereof came to her. Somehow Bel was both panting and keeping absolutely silent, barely moving except for a slight tremble in his muscles. Even Alix sat frozen, watching from her perch.

Lena backpedaled, moving so that both she and her sword were easily within Bel's sight.

He stared at her, and she stared back, watching, as their lungs worked in time to take in great mouthfuls of air. Lena felt the sweat beading along the crown of her head, felt how it stuck to the underside of her braid and the small of her back. She didn't move to wipe any of it away, could only watch Bel.

The cockiness had drained from him, and he'd angled himself again so that both wings were strictly behind him, his body between her and them.

From somewhere behind and to the right, Alix cleared her throat. "Match," she said tonelessly.

Lena swallowed hard, feeling as if a spell had broken when Bel glanced away from her, at Alix instead. She watched him gather himself, shoulders squaring again. He tightened his grip on his practice sword and began rotating his wrist again.

And his wings gave a flap, another, coming to rest slightly away from his body. It made him look larger, taking up almost too much space.

"Again?" he said.

A smile spread across her lips. "Again," she agreed.

Alix clapped her hands. "Go!"

It was Bel who charged this time, and Lena hurried to back away and give herself room to maneuver. He chased her around the great hall, their practice swords slapping and clattering, and Lena laughed again.

She raced for the dais, using one of Alix's favorite tricks; she jumped, used the dais and her left foot to push off and spin away from Bel, going on the attack when he wasn't completely ready. He parried and lunged; she parried and struck.

They resumed their dance. Lena had never been one for dancing, had hated the two years of dance instruction her mother insisted on during her squiring, but there was something about sparring with a partner as good as Bel that felt like dancing. It was fluid; sometimes Bel was the rock, steady and immovable, and she the river, flowing around him, trying to get him to budge. There was a grace to it, an excitement that

Lena had rarely ever felt. Though they moved in tandem, she didn't always know what he would do, when he would feint or strike true. She thrilled with the mystery, relishing when she read his tells, longing for his next surprise.

She didn't know how long she and Bel sparred; after the first, they didn't call match again, just moved back and forth across the hall, following the other's lead. By the end, they were striking only to watch and admire the other's parry. By the end, Lena knew she wanted to do this again, to feel this way again. The thrill of it beat in her blood, and it wasn't until they finally decided to call it a draw and quit the field that Lena recognized the feeling for what it was.

It was small, a spark in her chest that was there and gone again, but she couldn't deny that in the heat of their faux battle, Lena had felt lust for Bel.

27

Bel dipped his quill into the inkwell for the fourth time. Little speckles and droplets of ink sat drying on the page rather than any actual words. He'd been at this for the better part of the morning, trying to find a way to begin the next section of his translations.

This was the part of the project that usually took the least time; he worked himself into a rhythm, and the translations—and his mistakes—began to flow so seamlessly Bel could barely discern fact from fiction anymore. But Bel's mind was elsewhere, dancing from one thought to the next, and none of them were about his work.

One thing, one person occupied the majority of those thoughts. Bel had felt the mood of the castle shifting of late—it was still a gray, somber place, yet he hadn't thought to check over his shoulder or stop on a landing and listen for over two fortnights. The castle felt safe in a way it never had before. Since his truce with Maddalena, he'd stopped having to watch for attack or abuse, had even stopped anticipating it. Bel had long since stopped thinking of the castle as strictly a prison, knew that the biggest prison was his own hesitance to take his chances for escape, but as winter peaked in the mountains and the world began to think of spring, Bel didn't find the perimeter of his existence so small anymore. Though he knew his and Maddalena's truce meant nothing anywhere else, within the walls of Finhöln, he was free.

Blinking, Bel realized he'd been staring into the fire again, and all the ink in his quill had either dripped out or dried up. He put the quill down, deciding it was time for an official break; all he was really doing now was wasting ink.

He laced his fingers together and cracked his knuckles. The crackle and pop brought a soothing reprieve from the slight ache in his hands and wrists. For three years he'd trained in the *ariant* forms and with his practice sword, but now that he had two willing sparring partners, Bel's body finally understood again what it was to *train*. There was no substitute for a live partner, one who met each strike and gave as good as they got, one whose eyes flashed with challenge and mirth every time he spun away from her ploy or nearly trapped her in one of his own.

He massaged the wrist of his sword arm, relishing the ache in his muscles. Maddalena had declared today a rest day; she and Alix, as far as he knew, were still in the great hall doing their stretches. Bel had declined to join them or even do his *ariant* forms; his project had been falling to the wayside and he needed to catch up.

He hadn't, but at least he'd tried.

Bel stood, stretched out his neck, and began his new little routine. He straightened his hair and clothes. Wiped excess ink off his hands and from beneath his nails. Fluffed his wings. Made himself presentable. And didn't think too hard about why he was doing it, either.

Down in the kitchen, he found all three humans in various stages of pulling on winter gear. Alix, only her eyes visible above her bulky knit scarf, saw him first.

"'Ere he 's," came through the little holes of the scarf.

Maddalena looked up as she slipped on a lambskin coat. "Oh, good, Bel. I was coming to find you. Pol needs help today bringing in wood."

Bel looked in surprise over at the cook, who, after he finished tying down the ear flaps of his cap, signed, *We have enough wood to last a few more days, but we need to collect at least one tree. Malthus is sick and cannot help, so I asked L-e-n-a and A-l-i-x.*

Malthus is sick and you're here?

Pol rolled his eyes. *Already brought him soup. You know how he is when he's sick.* Pol hunched his shoulders and made few garbled growls—an imitation of a grumpy bear, Bel thought.

"Did you need me to watch the fires?" he asked and signed.

Pol frowned, but there was also a little smirk poking at his lips. His gaze cut to Maddalena, and Bel's followed.

She was shaking her head. "I thought you could come with us. Pol's the only one who knows what he's doing, so we could use all the help we can get."

He just blinked at her, blinked for so long that Alix laughed and said, "You break something in there?"

"You want me to come with you?" he choked. "*Outside* the castle?"

She had to understand the gravity of what she'd said, and he thought he recognized the weight of her decision gleam in her hard-set eyes, but she didn't miss a beat when replying, "That's what I said. Unless you know of any trees to fell inside Finhöln?"

"But it's..." He made a vague gesture at the outdoors.

Maddalena quirked one brow, and though she tried to look amused, Bel thought she was a little nervous at her proposition. Not as much as him, but still.

"Do you not want to come?"

"No! I—I do. I'll go get—" And he raced back upstairs to get his own gear, realizing how silly it was of him to deny or question such a chance. *Outside.* He would go beyond the castle walls without fear of capture, of punishment. He would be like anyone else who was free and walk beyond the curtain wall. His heart swelled, as if it could feel the borders of his life expanding.

He tore apart his bedchamber, looking for everything he needed. It wasn't until he'd put his coat on backwards that he stopped, took a breath, took the time to do it all properly. Jerkin, jacket, wool leggings, leather trousers, coat, oilskin cloak. They were the same clothes he'd donned for his escape, but this time, he was free of the thrum of dread that'd accompanied him. Then, it had felt like putting on armor, piece by piece. And not against the cold.

Mittens, gloves, scarf, and cap in his hands, Bel descended to the kitchen again. Pol and Maddalena were filling satchels with what looked like an easy lunch.

Maddalena glanced at him when he stepped onto the landing, looked him over from head to foot, and nodded in approval. Pol handed him one of the satchels.

Outside, Alix had pulled out and prepared two sleds. Wrapped in an oilskin bundle were all manner of saws, wedges, and axes, the old metal gleaming but not shining in the thin daylight. With a wave, Pol led the way to the garden gate.

Bel swallowed the lump in his throat. Not ten steps away was the crumbling wall that he'd pulled himself over in his escape. A creaky groan pulled him back from the memory, and Bel watched as Pol wrestled the gate wide enough to get the sleds out.

Then, they were outside the castle. Snow-frosted trees stood sentry into the sleeping forest, their bark dark and rigid. They lined Bel's vision, like a gate to slip through into another world.

Pol handed over one of the sleds to Bel before soldiering up a small berm and into the snowy forest. Bel helped Alix and Maddalena pull the sleds up the berm behind him and then followed the deep caverns of Pol's tracks.

Maddalena pulled one sled, Bel the other behind her while Alix bounded back and forth between them. Her feet crunched in the snow when she went to catch up with Pol and ask what he was doing, but he put a finger to his lips and she fell silent. Alix lifted her head, perhaps looking for the same thing Pol was; little flakes of snow drifting down from the canopy above caught in her scarf and eyelashes.

They delved deeper into the forest, Pol's head on a swivel. The man spent more time looking up than where he was going, but he never tripped or faltered. Sometimes Bel forgot that Pol knew the mountain and forest as well as his kitchen, had spent his entire life here on the mountainside. Pol was always quiet, of course he was, but there was also a stillness to him here, a calm he exuded as he slipped amongst the trees. If he didn't leave tracks to follow, Bel thought they might have lost him, a nymph slipping back into the wilds.

Bel's thighs began to burn as the snow grew thicker and he picked up a little more weight on his boots with each step. His body pulsed with warmth beneath his layers, and when they stopped to catch their breath, and let Pol inspect a possible tree, Bel pulled the scarf from around his neck. The cold air slicked along his skin, making him shiver involuntarily, but it was a nice sensation after having the wool stick to him.

As Pol continued to chip away layers of snow and ice from the tree's trunk, Maddalena reached into one of the satchels and pulled out a small pack. She held out a strip of meat jerky to him, and Bel took it gratefully.

Never one to ignore food, Alix flitted over, wiggling her fingers until Maddalena put a sizeable hunk of jerky into her palm. She gnawed on it much like a wolf pup Bel had seen one winter, all sharp canines and hungry gusto. Maddalena just rolled her eyes and took a smaller piece for herself.

The three of them chewed their jerky as they watched Pol, the only noise the occasional crunch of snow and wet smack of mouths. Bel swirled a bit of jerky with his tongue, letting it warm and moisten in the hot well of his mouth.

"What's he looking for?" Maddalena finally asked. Both she and Alix turned curious eyes to him for explanation.

Bel just shrugged. "The right tree I suppose."

Alix huffed and Maddalena gave him a droll look, making sure he was watching when she rolled her eyes.

Bel shrugged again but smiled. "Probably something big enough to be worth our while but not too big that we'll be here all day just cutting it down or have to bring it back in sections. Something not too close to other trees, with a good place to bring it down and then work."

Maddalena and Alix shared a look, smiling as they bit into more jerky.

Pol backed away from the tree he'd been inspecting and headed off again, leaving Bel and Maddalena to scramble for the sleds as Alix bounced after him.

As the day wore on, the bank of clouds burned away, leaving an almost painfully blue sky. Golden daylight shone down on them through the frozen branches in thick slants and shafts, glittering on the pristine, fresh snow. It seemed almost wrong to make footprints and sled tracks through it.

It didn't take Pol long to find another possibility, and he was soon making little circuits around it and knocking off ice. He waved at Bel and Maddalena, who brought up the sleds and started unpacking the saws and axes. The tree was thick but not nearly as tall as its neighbors and stood a fair distance on one side away from the others.

Once he'd knocked away all the ice on the trunk, Pol waved Bel over. He signed what he was doing then began to make a sharp, diagonal cut into the tree.

"He's making a top cut," Bel narrated. "And then a perpendicular cut to make the notch. Then that's where we come in."

With the notch made, Pol stood back with Alix at the sleds and ate his own portion of jerky as he signed and waved Bel and Maddalena over on the opposite side of the tree from where he'd made the notch.

Start swinging, he instructed, mouth full of dried meat.

Bel and Maddalena exchanged looks before he shrugged and picked up the bigger of the two axes. Maddalena joined him after exchanging her mittens for work gloves.

After pointing out a few spots along the trunk, Pol eventually gave them the sign for *yes*. Maddalena nodded at the tree, so Bel drew the axe back and made the first chop. A disappointingly small wood chip fell off.

Bel worked the axe free of the thick, frozen bark, his ears growing warm and red from the snickering behind him.

"Is this why you wanted me to come?" he asked Maddalena.

She cocked an eyebrow at him as she wound up her own swing. She too dislodged a small wood chip before having to work her axe out of the tree.

"So you wouldn't be the only one looking ridiculous."

"Oh!" she laughed. "You've seen right through my plan."

Bel's smile grew as he took another swing. He and Maddalena traded off, giving each a moment to reassess and catch their breath. Clouds of steam puffed from their mouths as they worked themselves into a rhythm. When they made it past the bark, bigger wood chips began to fly, and Bel's heart began to race, pumping with the hard work and the thrill of doing something he never had.

With their rhythm came a pleasing harmony, a drum beat that matched Bel's heartbeat. It thrummed through him, the movement eventually settling into something like an *ariant* form, his muscles learning how to move, appreciating how Maddalena's mirrored his.

Even their breaks took on a rhythm, coming at steady intervals. Pol plied them both with food and water whenever they broke from their trance, and as Bel shoved as much ham and cheese into his mouth as would fit, he became even more aware of the work he was putting his body through.

He nearly hummed with it, already an ache growing in his shoulder blades and wing bases. But it was a good ache—at least for now—and Bel stripped off his outer coat and cap when he and Maddalena returned to chopping. She too had begun stripping layers off with each break, their bodies nearly steaming with the harmony of their tandem. He admired the strength of her shoulders and curve of her back as she swung, felt a sense of...pride at how strong she was. It pleased him that she was so strong, that she asked him to stand beside her now or opposite her in a sparring match and demand he be just as strong.

She noticed his staring, and he didn't think he imagined her flushed cheeks growing just a little pinker. One side of her mouth kicked up into a smug, insolent sort of grin, and Bel felt himself thrumming again, as if the world had stopped to watch Maddalena too.

"You getting tired?" she asked.

Bel stood up straighter, his wings giving an indignant little flap.

"Just making sure you weren't," he replied.

She laughed, more of a huff as she took long, panting breaths. She wiped the back of one hand across her forehead, swiping away sweat and a few tendrils of flyaway hair. A droplet escaped from her hand, trailing down the side of her face, climbing the rounded cut of her cheek to run down her jaw to her chin, where it pooled precariously, unwilling to leave her skin.

For a moment, one that felt scalding and a little like madness, Bel wanted to trace the drop's path with his fingers, maybe even his tongue.

He blinked, only managing a weak smile when Maddalena waggled her eyebrows at him and started again. He forced himself to follow her back into the rhythm of it, though he couldn't help feeling the stiffness creeping into him.

As the afternoon peaked and waned, they cut through the tree, making a harsh gouge in the trunk. Pol waved them off as they neared his notch on the other side, taking over the chopping. He made a few precise cuts and started using wedges as Bel and Maddalena retreated to the sleds.

They watched Pol as they ate the last of the food, the cook moving deftly around the near side of the tree. A great groan echoed through the forest, a few creaks and snaps wafting down from the canopy above. The tree seemed to shiver, and then began to sway.

Pol backpedaled, eyes never leaving the tree.

It groaned and swayed again before, with branches snapping every-where, the tree came crashing down.

Alix hooted and Maddalena gave a whooping laugh, reaching out and clutching his arm.

The touch burned through Bel, his eyes snapping to where her hand grasped him. She didn't seem to notice, watching as the snow settled again and the echo reverberated further away through the forest, but Bel couldn't look away.

She touched him so easily, and not in violence—not even mock vio-lence.

He didn't think about doing it, just watched as his hand took hers, squeezing it gently. Maddalena squeezed back.

His heart swelled again, but this time it wasn't sweet. This time it burned with something hot and dark and velvety, something that carried the hint of danger. He knew Maddalena had never ceased being danger-ous, but as their hands gently, loosely held one another, Bel thought this danger wasn't bad. It was...exciting.

His heart skipped a beat at the thought. Danger that was exciting; not the kind that would hurt him or threaten him, but the kind he wanted more of. He didn't know he could ever want more of something that promised danger, that he could ever want the thrill of uncertainty and excitement.

There were words for this, he knew there were, but it took a long while for them to surface in his head. There was so much to see and feel and wonder about. The warmth of Maddalena's hand, the soft rasp of calluses on the palm. The slight hitch in her smile, how she hadn't pulled away yet.

Attraction.

The word panged within his heart. He was attracted to her, as they stood steaming together in the snow from their teamwork.

The feeling was familiar and strange all at once, like an artifact from another life. It hadn't meant anything before Maddalena. It'd gone unused since his time as a prince, a young male just beginning to understand what it meant.

It washed through him, as if encouraged by having its name back, and Bel nearly went to his knees with the strength of it.

Alix was saying something, hopping about and being a helpful nuisance to Pol as he inspected the tree.

Maddalena slowly pulled away, glancing at him from the corner of her eye before joining the others. She took with her some of the feeling's intensity, but it still echoed through Bel as sure as a fallen tree.

Bel swallowed, feeling the rough pull of his dry throat. He busied himself by taking a drink from one of the canteens, all the time repeating the word that now consumed his thoughts. *Attraction.* To Maddalena.

Hell, what did he do now?

28

Lena couldn't say what woke her—the rustle of fabric, the strike of a flint—but she was awake now. The second thing she noticed was a cold creeping in against her naked back as her eyes, still in sleepy slits, took in the thick canvas wall of the tent.

Carefully, she rolled onto her back, only slowly realizing that there was a symphony of small noises all around her; the soft tread of feet against the tent's thick carpets, the swish of water falling into a basin, the grating scrape of a razor across stubbled skin. Noises of preparing to meet the morning.

The sleep finally retreated from Lena's weary mind, and she blinked to clear her eyes of it too. Two braziers had been lit. A fire laid. And the bed beside her was empty.

Lena sighed and climbed from the bed, not bothering to be quiet. The time for that, apparently, had passed.

She silently cursed herself as she worked her stiff legs into her stiffer trous and boots. She turned away from the glow of the fires and the man shaving in the corner to don her long-sleeved linen undershirt. She didn't feel up to facing the crown prince without it.

Lena stood, wincing at the soreness between her legs. Memories of the previous night flitted through her mind, making her cheeks redden. There had been something intense and frantic about their lovemaking, something that made the blood pump faster and every caress feel laden with finality. It could be like that, on campaign, where death was always a possibility, sometimes even a third bedfellow. But this...this had been different, and Lena's gut twisted with unease.

This was why she always made a point to be the first one up, to leave the tent long before Arion ever woke. There was something about their affair that she thought best suited for the amber of candlelight and blue of deep shadows. In the gray light of morning, things could seem very different.

It was always in the cold mist of morning that Lena told herself it must stop, that no matter how the prince smiled or joked with her or made her feel like she wasn't just a body to get shot up with avian arrows, he was still the Crown Prince of Vagora. And she was just Lena. She might have been a knight and a Montcaer at that, but she knew none of that really counted when put alongside Arion's birthright.

She knew, deep inside, that this wouldn't last. She would never be deemed acceptable anywhere but here, in an army camp. Here, in this artificial life of prolonged campaign, few cared who was warming whose bed. A soldier knew comfort was taken where it could be in the moments between boredom and bloodshed. There were those who frowned upon the crown prince lying with one of his guards—namely, the captain of the guard, Joran—but no one would stop it or begrudge them.

But the morning always brought that reality back to Lena. Sometimes the truth burned away with the day, and in the haze of sunset, it didn't seem true anymore, that she could have what she wanted. Just a night happiness, of forgetfulness. Sometimes she thought it was the only happiness she had, being with the crown prince, and the thought of having nothing at all, of wasting her downtime with meager card games that had already been played and campfire stories that had already been told, just waiting for the next battle to start, to hear the *whiz* of arrows raining down as thick as a swarm, invited madness. She returned, time and again, to get just a taste of what it was to not be here at the base of this forsaken mountain.

Arion's head tilted toward her at the squeak of her boots. Still patting his freshly shaven face with a rough towel, he turned to her.

Lena didn't need to see his mouth to know he was smiling. It was in his eyes. The prince was one of those fantastical people who could smile with every part of himself—mouth, eyes, shoulders, hands—so that you only had to see some of him to know he smiled at you. Lena wasn't immune, even if she knew that smile was also for the world outside this tent.

"I didn't want to wake you," he said.

"I should've been awake long ago." She shifted her weight from one foot to the other, wanting to look away from him but not able to. With his smile came that magnetic pull, something Lena had seen rouse thousands of troops. Arion drew people in and put them at ease, pulling them into his orbit like a celestial body. He was Matella, and Lena, and all the rest, were his Maidens, circling, waiting, anxious to see his golden brilliance. With the golden hair and eyes of his mother, but a warm smile that was less leonine and more welcoming, Arion was the stuff of old ballads about handsome knights conquering the dangerous land for their loves. Men had no business being as handsome and charming as him, and Lena knew she had no business being around such a man. She knew being so close to a sun would surely burn.

Arion tossed the towel on a nearby camp chair to await cleaning and folding by his valet.

Lena watched as he crossed to the table, pouring water into two goblets. She scuffed the heel of her boot, knowing she didn't want to take the goblet; it would mean she meant to stay when really she needed to flee to her own pallet. There was enough talk about them. If she lingered too long, if he saw her too much, people would begin to think she was a kept woman. It was a sword's edge they walked, Lena knew this, but still she came back, even if the idea of being a kept woman burned through her belly.

No one cared who warmed whose bed, but when it was the same person over the whole three-year campaign, people began to talk. And soldiers were the worst gossips.

Lena could do nothing but croak a thank you when Arion handed her the water. She took a long draught, wetting her dry throat and giving her something to do other than watch Arion by morning light.

The prince picked up an apple and began to peel it with a small knife. Lena finished the water, watching him. He seemed a little subdued. Not that she regularly saw him at this hour or watched his morning ablutions. Yet the sun of his golden eyes seemed banked behind clouds, there but hidden, distant.

He's melancholy.

The word hadn't come immediately to her, for even in the hellish life they led here at the base of the avian stronghold, waiting perhaps for a miracle, that Hadria would all just come sliding down to them in a heap of rubble, the prince always found a way to be affable. In the first years Lena had been assigned to Arion, she'd thought it all affectation, a way to get what he needed from those around him. But as the years passed, Lena came to realize that no, he was good and affable to his core. He listened when someone spoke to him, from his generals to his valets, and had the uncanny sense for when his soldiers needed him. He fought alongside them—much to Captain Joran's chagrin—walked amongst them, and made sure the supply lines and the coveted rotation home was on time. It'd taken her a while, but Lena finally saw that Arion *cared*.

It made guilt churn in her gut for wanting to be away from him now.

His melancholy made her a hair curious, but more wary than anything else. This wasn't like Arion. Though he stood still, gazing intently at the apple he worked in his hands, Lena knew his tells by now. It was the same restless energy that overtook him whenever he had to deliver bad news to the troops. He always needed something to do with his hands.

Lena waited quietly, unwilling to be the one to break the silence. She hadn't enjoyed the years squiring out with her mother, but she'd learned a great deal. One of her mother's lessons was to wait and let the silence stretch. People would always fill it, usually with the truth.

"Old Jarrett swears winter is going to be upon us soon. Fortnight or so," was what he finally said.

"The quartermaster's stiff joints are oddly accurate," she offered weakly. She didn't usually like or welcome Old Jarrett's predictions. To know that winter came, that they would soon be in feet of snow on top of the usual grime and blood and refuse, didn't improved Lena's mood.

"Two more supply caravans should get through before the roads ice up."

She made a noncommittal noise, waiting.

Was he going to end...whatever this was between them? He was never so withdrawn about battle plans or even his worries about the campaign. He asked hard questions of his generals and told Lena his troubles. What was this, then, that he couldn't quite dislodge from his throat? All she could think of was that this, whatever it was, was coming to an end.

The thought jounced around her brain, making her gut twist again in a painful give-and-tug of despair and relief. She scuffed her boot again.

Arion's gaze rose from the apple to stare at some indistinct point on the far side of the tent.

"I've had word from Highclere. My father wonders why this continues, why so many soldiers are dying for inches. He wants us to push in the spring, to find another way in."

"We've searched for the mines," she said to no one in particular. After the first year of the campaign had withered away any remaining sense of triumph from capturing Aeriand, the prince had quietly ordered his guard to poke around the mountains and see if there was any truth to the legends of Hadria once being a mining complex. Lena had done her share of scaling rock fall, scrabbling through crevices, and sloshing through murky water that could be a foot or a thousand feet deep. She had heard enough water dripping and bats screeching and the hurried, panicky breath of her fellow guards in dark, closed quarters to know that they'd never successfully get the whole army through the caves.

Arion shook his head. "He has something in mind, though he's yet to enlighten me or any of the generals. But he wants this over come next spring. Forces will be shored up. There's only one last rotation going home. After that..."

Lena sucked in a pained breath, her heart aching for all the soldiers who waited anxiously for their chance to go home. It became a lifeline in this blasted stalemate, knowing if you only survived another season, you'd eventually see the great rolling hills and golden vineyards of Vagora soon. They'd been at the foot of Hadria so long nearly everyone had already rotated home and come back again.

Lena was one of the few who hadn't yet. Return to what? She received a letter from her mother every month, like clockwork, advising how she, Lady Margot, would run the avian campaign differently—and therefore better. In fewer words, her mother thought herself wasted at the southern front and that the prince had had his chance in the east.

She received a letter from her father, too, almost every other week, and those were much more welcome. But sometimes it pained her, reading about Lindenfaire. He rarely asked about her situation at Hadria, just that she assure him she was hale. He talked about the day she would return to Lindenfaire like it was a given, like it was her destiny, but even here in these rocky mountains, Lena didn't find Lindenfaire the sanctuary her father seemed to.

So, Lena hadn't returned, for what was there to return to? Arion was here; her duty was here.

"They won't like it, but the soldiers will understand. Eventually," she said, thinking to ease his pain at delivering such unwelcome news.

Arion pulled in a long lungful of air, and Lena watched as his chest expanded with it. She had always loved his chest, not just that it was muscled and golden-skinned, but that it was warm. Sometimes it felt as if the divot bisecting his breast had been carved just to fit the curve of her cheek. She stared his chest now, a place that had brought her such comfort in the past years. He sucked in air, and it was as if he could keep going, could suck all the air from the tent, from the mountain, into his chest before finally, it came out on a sorrowful sigh.

"Lena, I must tell you...I've put you on the last rotation home."

The blood rushed through Lena's ears, and she clutched the goblet in her white-knuckled hand, trembling with the force of her grip.

"What?"

Arion shook his golden head. "I haven't gotten all the details from my father, but this could be suicide. Longer and slower than usual but suicide, nevertheless. I won't let that be your fate."

The goblet bounced on the ground, a spray of water splattering her cold boots, but she didn't care. She took two angry steps, advancing on him, and could feel all the heat of her body pooling in her cheeks and chest.

Arion stood taller, shoulders squared, prepared to take the brunt of her anger. "The rotation leaves at first light tomorrow," he said. "You have to get out before the snow comes. I've arranged for your reassignment with the War Minister. Lord Balderak's is a quiet demesne. A few border skirmishes now and again, but it will be safe." Another sigh left him, and even in her rage Lena could see the heavy lines of worry and tiredness pulling at his face, making him more like a cloud than the sun. "I need you safe, Lena. I couldn't bear it if something happened to you."

"You can't—" Lena nearly choked on her rage. "You can't do this!"

Arion closed the distance between them in three long strides and snatched up her hands in his, pressing her palms to his cheeks so that she held his face in her hands. She tried to pull away, but he gripped her wrists.

"I know, Lena, I know. But I can barely think knowing you're in danger, let alone lead a campaign. I can't stand the idea of you being hurt or—"

"Too bad!" she cried, trying again to yank her hands away. "That is your burden to bear, not mine! I'm a trained knight and we are at war. My place is here."

"It'll get worse before this is over," he said as if she hadn't spoken. He pressed her hands all the harder to his face, and she thought he must feel it, feel the pressure of their hands pressing down on him. His face was turning red, either from the pressure of their hands or the emotion burning hot in his eyes. "This won't be won with bravery but with blood. There's no winner in a numbers game. I won't let you become a casualty, Lena."

"It's my job to protect you and yours to lead this campaign. You will do your duty and let me do mine!"

"Your duty now is to live."

She finally wrenched her hands away. "That isn't your decision to make."

"I've already secured your place on the rotation."

"I won't go."

"I'm not asking you to. I'm ordering it."

"No other guards are being sent home. What will they say?"

"I don't care as long as you're safe. They aren't—*Lena*—!" But she had already stormed from the tent, too disgusted to remain.

Lena felt herself steaming in the chilly mountain air as she stormed back to her meager tent. Hot puffs of air misted across her face with each ragged breath, and her fists shook with the effort of keeping them closed. She wanted to throttle something.

A little cough, barely anything, had Lena stopping in her tracks, sending pebbles flying. Her cheeks paled and cooled just the smallest bit as the cold gray eyes of Captain Joran surveyed her.

He stood as he often did, arms and hands folded neatly behind his back. It was one of the guards' favorite whispered jokes, that someday his arms would get stuck like that and he'd have to hold a sword behind him forever. Dark flecks of black hair dotted his scalp, the gray patches growing ever more prominent, especially around his temples. The captain suffered no nonsense and found hair to be exactly that; he cut and shaved down to his scalp, the little tendrils of sprouting hair just barely breaking the skin.

Joran had always been a demanding captain, but a fair one. He didn't play favorites, and Lena had thrived under his leadership, his quiet words and occasional bark a welcome relief from her mother's running narrative of how she was doing it wrong and could be better. But he didn't approve of her and Arion; it was always in the long look he gave them when they slipped into Arion's tent late at night and the downward slope of his mouth whenever he saw her leaving again in the morning.

His face was a weathered one with large features; large forehead, large nose, large chin, but together it looked right, even gave him a dignified countenance. That weathered face was set in such disapproving lines that Lena had to cling hard to her outrage to not buckle and wither under it.

"Did you know?" she said.

"It's what's best."

Lena turned away but saved her huff of disappointment until he couldn't see her face. There had been talk, a few years ago, that she might reach the rank of lieutenant, *his* lieutenant, but all that had gone quiet when she'd taken up with Arion. She didn't know what she expected from the captain, but...

She'd hoped at least that her service would speak for itself, that the warrior wouldn't suffer because of the woman. *Just because Joran didn't seem to have any human needs...*

Her little tent sat waiting for her in a row of identical tents. She slapped the entrance flap aside, taking in her weapons and armor and personal effects, neatly arranged. Unseeing, she grabbed the nearest satchel and began packing.

The heat in her had pooled again, this time in her nose and eyes, but Lena refused to weep. She would not cry over this, wouldn't make it seem like the prince had ended what was between them and sent her away. Her heart burned at the thought, that all her years of service could be overlooked as a lover's tiff, a good story. And Arion, to dismiss her even though it was her sworn duty to protect *him*—oh, yes, she could just throttle him. All her work, her sacrifice, to be dismissed like this! As if she were a castoff bedmate!

Damn him! She should hate him, should march back and demand he treat her as just another guard and respect her choice to put herself in danger, for the sake of him and Vagora. She should—

Lena pawed at her eyes and took a wobbly breath. *This wouldn't do.* She wouldn't let herself fall apart.

And so Lena packed, shoving everything into her two leather satchels, pushing everything, all of it, down, down, down. She would not cry. She would not be the story they would tell about her. And she wouldn't forgive Arion for this, for folding under his own fear rather than trusting her courage and skill. No, she could never forgive him for that.

29

Spars blurred into days that turned into weeks, and in that time, Bel knew it—he was getting better. He could feel it in the way his body moved, how his wings became weapons rather than hindrances, how it took more and more matches before he was even winded. When he smiled, it was a ferocious one. He hadn't felt this way since sparring with Eamon in the last days of his training.

Like a warrior. Like someone who could fight and win.

He ducked, avoiding Maddalena's practice sword, and swept her legs with one of his. With an *oof* she went down, only to roll in a backwards somersault and pop up again. He was right there when she did, launching a series of quick jabs that had her retreating towards the east hearth.

From the sidelines, Alix catcalled as if this were a spectator sport, but Bel barely heard it. All he could hear was the clatter of swords and the rush of blood in his ears. All he could feel was his body, moving as it never had before, and his strength, growing every day. And all he could see was Maddalena, parrying his thrusts and darting away.

He followed her, his heart beating faster, in a rhythm that was unique to their battles. It wasn't tiredness or exertion that had Bel's blood pumping. No, he never felt tired, not around her. It was as if his attraction had gained power now that it had a name; he suddenly noticed things, about her and about himself, that couldn't be unnoticed. The curve of her cheek, the strong line of her back, the glossy shine of her hair in the firelight. Her fairness in all things except chess and cards, her patience, her goodness to Alix and Pol and the horses and to him. And his desire for more of it, *all* of it.

They were in their fifth match of the morning, and Bel wanted to win. He'd won one already, but he wanted another, wanted to see more flush in her skin and gleam in her eyes. She'd never admit it, he knew, but she preferred to be a little on the ropes, on defense. She liked the challenge of coming back from the edge, of saving herself. Bel was happy to oblige, but he was also happy not to and win.

Maddalena feinted to the right, and Bel was ready. She liked that move and sometimes he let her get away with it because it meant this would last just a little longer. But this time, Bel didn't want that; he wanted to win, to prove to her and himself that he could.

He caught her practice sword with his, spun it away in a wide arc, and used their momentum to spin her into his space, within his reach. Within his very arms.

She stilled, feet planted, and looked at what he'd done.

He'd caught her up in a hold that, despite her boiled leather cuirass, or its metal battlefield counterpart, with enough pressure would have broken her back. But this wasn't the battlefield. Here, it wasn't a threat. Here, it was almost an embrace.

Bel smiled, ferocious again, all teeth and a little cockiness.

Maddalena arched an eyebrow at him, her smile rueful, and Bel held his breath as she seemed to move and shift infinitesimally closer. He could smell her now, taste her too, took in the sweet-spiciness of clean sweat and rosehip and woman. His blood rushed again, but not so much in his ears as other places, and Bel felt as if he grew, readied, waited for just a sign—

For what? He didn't know, but waited, watched her eyes to see if she waited too, if she felt it too.

Humans kissed.

The thought zinged through his mind like an arrow hitting home. When human lovers drew close to one another, they touched lips. He'd read enough of their poetry and ballads to know this, to know that it often led to something. Avians showed the same affection in other ways, but would she know this? Would she know what it meant if he ran his nose up one side of hers, over the bridge, and down the other? Would she understand if he drank in her scent where it was strong, just behind her ear?

Bel nearly quaked at the thought. Somehow, doing any of that was even more terrifying than kissing. But her cheeks flushed how he'd wanted, and her eyes gleamed with something, but he didn't know what.

He tightened his hold just a little, then even more when she didn't protest or move away. Each inch he claimed was as good as winning one of their matches—no, better. He wanted to ask her what he should do, what she wanted him to do, but the words wouldn't come. The tactile feel of her cuirass under his hand, her body so near their warmth mingled and heated, demanded all his attention.

He could feel it, the anticipation of this mysterious thing hovering over them, making his lips and fingertips tingle. He wanted to see what it felt like to have her pressed up the whole length of him, to share her breath and the heat of her skin. He felt every year, every day that he had been starved of such sensations, and his lips part at the thought of finally, *finally* knowing again what it felt like to hold another close. To hold attraction so near.

An undignified snort pierced the warm bubble he and Maddalena were cocooned in. A sharp, lewd whistle followed, and then a small towel hit the side of his head and neck like a horseshoe.

"You looked sweaty," Alix said, her smile wide and feline.

The scrape of Maddalena's boot drew his gaze. She'd angled slightly, not away from him but no longer fully in the curve of his body.

Bel let his arms fall away, feeling their shared heat dissipate. He was aware of the cool slickness of his own sweat on his neck, and he dropped his gaze, pretending to suddenly be fascinated with the flagstones of the floor.

The noises of Alix and Maddalena packing up equipment echoed around the hall, but Bel didn't move to join them. He tried to swallow his dread down a dry throat. What had he been thinking? Kissing Maddalena...what if she'd refused? What if she'd stood there, lips clamped shut, waiting for it to end?

What if she'd responded? Opened her mouth and taken him inside?

His body hummed with the thought, but Bel still couldn't quite meet her eyes when he finally went to put his practice sword away. It was a risk he'd almost taken, claiming a kiss. How could he be sure she'd even wanted it? He realized now that while this attraction made his heart beat fast, made him feel taller, stronger, more assured, it also made him question everything.

His dread pooled in his stomach, gnawing away at his guts. How would he ever know if she wanted such a thing from him? And what could he give her in return? It was one thing to have these feelings, quite another to act on them. It would take a courage he didn't know if he possessed. He didn't know if he was strong enough to feel the aching sting of her rejection.

"Bel."

He looked up to find Maddalena offering a tankard of water. He felt his cheeks staining with red as he took it from her with a grateful nod.

"Where did you learn to do that?" she asked, nodding at where they had stood only moments ago, almost in each other's arms.

For a terrible moment, he couldn't imagine what she meant. She couldn't mean kissing—he'd only been thinking about it.

"Thought of it just then," he said finally, about his surprise maneuver. "You've done something similar a few times."

"Mm. Similar but not quite. Me doing that would be pointless and leave my flank unprotected."

Alix snorted. "You mean you've never wanted to crack someone's back?"

Maddalena rolled her eyes. "Wanting and doing are two different things."

"Don't sell yourself short," Bel said, though it felt as if cotton was stuffed in his mouth.

But Maddalena only shrugged and said, "It's a matter of weight distribution and strength. You have me outmatched in that regard."

"You think I'm strong?"

She cocked her head just the smallest bit to the side, as if she thought he was missing something obvious. "Bel, you *are* strong. Look at you. Even without training, avians are bigger than humans, and with it, you've become, well..." Bel watched as a rosy blush warmed her cheeks and held perfectly still, wanting to know what she thought he'd become. "You don't need me to tell you that you're strong. Your arms, your wings, and everywhere else," she said finally without looking at him.

Bel blinked with surprise then had to control himself and not preen. She thought he was strong. Strong *everywhere*. He'd been strong before, in the days and months when he'd served under his brother in the constant ebb and tide of war with the humans. His body had been a hard shell of muscle, honed to do one thing.

It was like that feeling, only different, because he didn't think she just meant the muscle making him strong.

Maddalena and Alix bantered as they did their stretches. Bel, as he usually did, loosely joined them in his *ariant* forms, stretching and challenging the muscles that were growing and fitting into old, familiar molds. Training with Maddalena and Alix made his body *capable* again. He'd grown strong since starting the *ariant* forms, but now, with Maddalena's help, he finally felt strong enough to fight again, perhaps even fly again. Well, that might be farfetched, but Bel had begun to feel as though his body could do more than scribble words on a page, more than wait for and accept every violence done to it. His body could be his once again, could do whatever he needed it to, could even...

Bel caught Maddalena watching him in his fourth *ariant* form. He wasn't too proud to admit he'd been flaunting a bit, ruffling his wings and holding the forms longer than strictly necessary.

He gave a crooked grin filled with much more bravado than he felt and watched in amazement as that same rosy blush crept up her neck onto her cheeks. It was an outlandish thing to think, but he couldn't help but wonder if she was affected by him as well.

The thought made his body hum again, and he went through the rest of the forms, and the morning, in a state of almost numb happiness. There was a word for this...euphoria? Had he ever come close to euphoria before? It was an unfamiliar thought and sensation, but Bel seemed to be having many of those lately.

It was only when he was ensconced in his room, pretending to work for the day, that the feeling finally subsided—rather suddenly at the harsh sound of something *tap, tap,* tapping at his window. Bel blinked and lifted his head, wondering if he'd imagined it. He peered around the room, hearing only the familiar crackle of the fire.

But there it was again, behind him. Bel turned in his seat to squint through the frosted windowpane. A great brown shadow lurked on the other side, shifting the snow on the sill. As Bel stood, he watched the shadow shuffle along the sill, and a scratching noise hit the window again. Then, he stared into the wide, golden orb of an eagle eye.

His heart jumped into his throat, and it was a moment before Bel remembered himself and walked over to the window. He fought with the frozen latch before, with a heave, it gave with a sharp tug. The eagle squawked as it half-fell into the room. Globs of sloppy snow and ice splattered onto the floor as the eagle hopped around, wedging itself through the narrow window.

Bel held out his arm, and great wicked talons gently curved around his forearm. Gingerly he lifted the eagle from the sill and deposited her onto the back of his chair before closing the window and shut them both up inside the warm confines of his chamber.

He turned slowly from the window, his heart beginning to race. The eagle blinked back at him as she ruffled and rearranged her feathers, knocking away snowflakes.

Bel felt the warmth of the morning seep out of him as the eagle extended her right foot, talons caught around two long feathers, one gray, one so dark a brown it was nearly black.

A different kind of dread rose in his gorge. The feathers' colors were achingly familiar, even after all this time.

He held out his hand, and she deftly deposited them into his palm. He immediately felt their weight.

Bel leaned back against the shallow windowsill, holding a feather in each hand. Saliva pooled in his mouth, as if he was about to be sick, as he weighed them in his hands, deciding which to look at first.

The brown one. Get it over with.

Holding his breath, Bel turned the brown feather over in his hands and ran a finger down the shaft, searching for runes with the pad of his thumb. The shaft was smooth and still a little cold from the eagle's flight through the wintry sky, and it wasn't until he'd nearly reached the bottom that he came across one word.

TRAITOR.

Bel didn't need to run his thumb over it again, but he did. *Traitor. Traitor. Traitor.*

He tried not to clench the feather and break it in his hand, instead ran another finger along the barbs. It was the first piece of Dartegn, of his kin, that he'd touched in over ten years. This was the first message his cousin had ever sent himself.

He wanted to crush the feather, wanted to destroy the word written there, but he couldn't. Not when it was a part of Dar he held.

But *traitor* echoed in his head, and it invited *prisoner*, *cripple*, and *coward* with it.

He'd vowed to forget those words, to leave them buried in the snow as he ran to freedom. And look how far he'd come.

Bel shook his head and focused on the gray feather. He couldn't think like that, couldn't let himself believe he'd gotten nowhere. He'd always been comfortable at Finhöln, at least when he was away from the wardens, but in the past weeks, with Maddalena, she'd made this place feel safe, and Bel was...he didn't quite know if he was happy, but at the very least, he was content. And when he looked at his life, at the long stretch of captivity, there was something to be said for contentment.

Shoring himself up with the thought of Maddalena, probably now in the kitchen with Alix and Pol, Bel moved on to the other message.

Unlike Dar's message, this one had so many runes, etched painstakingly small along the narrowing shaft, that Bel had to slowly slide his thumb over it twice before he fully got Eamon's message.

YOU HAVE BEEN IN MY THOUGHTS LITTLE HAWK. YOU ARE WELL? WE ARE HOLDING HADRIA. SUPPLIES AND MORALE LOW. MESSAGE SAID YOU MISTRANSLATE. EXAMPLE? DAR ANGRY BUT—

Bel turned the feather over, amazed that Eamon had been able to etch along both sides of the shaft.

—YOU CAN HELP US. UNIQUE POSITION WITH HUMAN KING. SEND ANOTHER FEATHER WITH MISINFORMATION. VALUABLE WORK. KEEP GOING LITTLE HAWK. DAR WILL COME AROUND. STAY STRONG.

Bel left both feathers on his desk to let the eagle back outside. She gracefully hopped from his arm to the sill, pausing as she opened her burnished wings to look up and blink at him.

He cleared his dry throat to chirp, "Stay in the area, if you could. I might have a message..."

The eagle cawed and then she was airborne, lifting herself over the curtain wall and out into the frozen forest. Bel didn't close the window again until she was out of sight, hoping the cold would get his sluggish, overheated mind working right again.

Bel closed the window and sat at his desk. He leaned his elbows on the table and sifted his fingers through his hair, holding his head in his hands so that he hovered over the feathers. One gleamed in the firelight, but the gray had less streaks of almost-blue in it than Bel remembered, as if the feathers were beginning to whiten with age. The other seemed to absorb the light, like the soft, velvety edges of the night sky.

He wanted to call the eagle back, tell her to go on and find her nest. He hadn't anything to send back. Didn't know if he wanted to send anything back.

He tugged on his hair, trying not to think like that, but the surge of disappointment flooded him anyways, stinging with a sour betrayal. It pooled in him, and Bel let his shoulders and wings droop.

There was nothing on if he should escape or if he needed help. Nothing but empty questions about if he was well.

But then, they'd always been like that, hadn't they? And what could Eamon ever hope to do, anyway?

He told himself these things, but logic was a cold comfort. He didn't know what he'd expected from reopening a line of communication with his kin. It was him who'd offered to feed them information, to serve his people in this way.

They took what he offered and he hated them a little for it, for asking him to stay and do this when he had no other choice, for having him do this and spitting in his face for it.

Well, Dar didn't take what he offered. Dar asked nothing of him except not to exist.

And it wasn't as if Bel had no other choice, not anymore. He was stronger. He tried to cling to the feelings of the morning, to recapture that sense of capability and triumph, but it was like trying to grasp smoke.

Bel could see the future these feathers foretold. He would sit in this seat, before this fire, carving messages into his own feathers as his wings grew limp and weak. He would feed the avians information until he had nothing left to tell them, either because the human king had made him the last living avian, or because he'd be found out. Either way, it ended for him on the wrong end of a sword.

He was ashamed of the hot threat of tears rimming his eyes, and he tried to push them down along with his hurt. This was all his people had ever asked of him and it was all they ever would. This was all the good he'd ever be to them. It was too late to change what had been done.

He knew he was foolish to hope for a scrap of promise or hope from his kin, but he'd do as they asked. He would send them information. He wouldn't be the reason his brother's kingdom fell.

But once, just once, Bel would have liked to read one of these feathers and feel the knot of grief always lodged low in his ribs loosen rather than tighten. To not feel disappointment and not be a disappointment in return.

For once, he wished his people made him strong rather than doubt.

Because instead, he was finding that strength elsewhere. Some of it inside, but most of it from a human. Maddalena didn't ease his grief, but she did fight off the loneliness. She helped him to be strong again, and Bel didn't regret owing her that debt.

If anything, he wanted to owe her more. No, he wanted to *give* her more and take what he could in return.

And what a traitorous thought that was. Bel sank his face deeper into his hands, letting his palms blot out the light of the room. Perhaps Dar, the unwilling king far away in his mountain fortress, knew the truth of it after all. Perhaps, out of everyone, Dar knew him the best. For could there be a worse way to betray his avian kind than care for a human?

30

It was late, probably one of those unmentionably small morning hours, when Lena padded down into the kitchen. Pol would be long asleep, the great hearth fire a meager bed of coals, but Lena wanted to try and recreate that warm drink he always made, with lemon and honey and tea and a little rum.

She hadn't been able to find a comfortable spot all night, rolling back and forth until finally admitting defeat and descending to the kitchen. It would probably help her sleep, plus, she thought she might be coming down with a cough. Alix could be bringing more back with her from her frequent visits to Longbourne to see Violet than just stories.

But if she was being honest, it wasn't the occasional cough that had stolen her sleep. For two nights she'd been kept awake with the mystery of Bel. Particularly, why he was becoming a mystery again.

The snow here seemed interminable, but Lena had thought Bel at least was starting to melt, that enigmatic air he had giving way to some-one who was clever and wry and strong, someone she *liked*. But over the past few days, Bel had drawn into himself.

It was eerie to watch, now that she knew what to look for. It hadn't been so obvious, this shell of his, when it was all she knew to see. But after their truce, after seeing all that he really was and could be, it was painful to watch him slip away. There was an aloofness, a hardness to him that Lena didn't like, not when she had grown used to the smiling

Bel, the teasing Bel, the Bel who blushed and fought and laughed, the Bel who flapped his wings when he was happy or smug, and most especially the Bel who won matches, who drew her close and claimed the distance between them.

Lena blushed despite the cold of the stairwell. She hadn't known exactly what happened during their last match, had only a moment to think that he'd disarmed her and won before he was there, taking up all the space, filling up all her senses. She'd been attracted to him before, had felt the warmth of his skin and the coiled strength of his body before, but it had hit her in force in that moment, tenfold.

It hadn't mattered that Alix stood not twenty feet away, that their people were at war with each other, that outside of Finhöln, she was warden and he prisoner. What had mattered was his pupils dilating, taking up so much of his already alien eyes, his full attention focusing on her. Even if Lena had known less of men, she would have known he thought of kissing her.

And she'd wanted him to—waited anxiously for it.

But he hadn't. And in the days since then, it all seemed to slip away, the heat she sometimes caught in his gaze cooling.

Lena wanted it back. She wanted to see what would happen if this attraction was given its head. But more, Lena wanted to see him content again. He wasn't hiding happiness behind that cold shell of his.

Two days he had withdrawn to his room, avoiding her. Well, he was avoiding Alix and Pol too, absconding from morning training and squirreling away food at odd hours rather than sharing a meal. The first day had been a surprise, the second had made her suspicious. Now, she was only hurt, though she didn't care to admit it aloud. He'd barely even made eye contact. Just earlier that evening, she'd watched him virtually ignore Alix when she tried to draw him to their meal rather than gather up supplies and retreat back upstairs. He'd pretended not to see Pol's flashing hands, and he'd only stopped to give a clipped, "No, thank you," when Lena invited him to the table.

It was as if...

She frowned as she neared the bottom of the steps, the cold of the stone slowly ebbing away. The kitchen was brighter than she'd thought it'd be, and she didn't have to watch her step as she came to the landing.

A small but healthy fire glowed in the hearth, painting the kitchen in warm, somnolent amber tones. Everything was in its place, no cauldron or stew pot hung over the crackling fire.

Only Bel sat at the long kitchen table, a bowl, a few bottles, and piles of clean rags laid out before him.

Lena held her breath as she moved further into the kitchen and the light. She didn't know if he'd heard her coming, but when he looked up to meet her gaze, he didn't look surprised. He didn't look one way or another, really, just mildly wary as he tracked her progress through the room.

She'd come to hate that look, the one that said he was waiting for her to do something, to hurt him in some way.

As she stopped before the cupboard filled with Pol's favorite mugs, a pain filled her chest. It hurt to go back to the way it had been before, and it hurt that though she wanted to fix it, she didn't know if she could. She didn't know how.

Something must have happened. But she had no hope of knowing what, not with his gaze shuttered and his words monosyllabic.

Lena swallowed though her throat was dry. "Couldn't sleep?" she said. She turned her back, going for a mug and the ingredients she would need for Pol's concoction.

"No," he said and nothing else.

Lena clenched her teeth, refusing to say anything as she went through the motions of making her drink. She didn't turn around again until she had the tea steeping, hoping he'd grow a little more companionable.

His shoulders weren't so stiff, and he wasn't watching her warily, but Lena felt almost dismissed as he focused intently on the bottles and bowl before him. He was mixing something, and as she watched his arms move, stirring the liquids together, she realized he hadn't a shirt.

What she'd thought to be a second pile of rags was instead his tunic. His wings covered his shoulders, but the small movements of his stirring fluttered his wings, revealing little swathes of skin.

What in Matella's name was he doing?

She quietly prepared her drink, casting furtive glances his way. When he finished mixing whatever he had in that bowl, he stopped, and in trying not to look at her, revealed that he was paying very close attention.

She could feel his will to have her leave like a physical thing, a phantom push towards the staircase, but Lena only leaned back against the counter, crossed her legs at the ankles, and took a sip of her drink. It went down warm, like a lemon drop but with the spicy kick of rum at the end, and it gave Lena the courage, or perhaps just the stubbornness, to stand there.

When he did look at her, his annoyance clear on his pursed lips, Lena only cocked her brow and took another sip. Perverse as it was, she liked riling him up, liked that she had his gaze, even if it was filled with annoyance. It revealed glimpses of his feelings, his mind behind that stiff mask he'd donned.

Several long moments drew out where the only sound was the crackling fire and an occasional sip from Lena. She resisted the urge to slurp loudly. That'd probably make him snap and drive him away. Not what she wanted.

If he thought she wouldn't win this battle of attrition, he hadn't spent enough time with Alix.

Finally, with a huff, apparently resigned to her being there, Bel turned back to his bowl, dipping a rag into the mixture. Lena watched, suddenly fascinated.

He drew his good wing away from his body, letting it unfurl almost to its full width, the primary feathers brushing against the far counter. Half of his chest was revealed, his skin, while pale, taking on a warm glow from the fire. Lena swallowed her next sip hard, the rum burning a little more than before.

He gently ran the rag along the closest secondary feathers, and from the gleam left behind, Lena realized it was oil he'd been mixing. His gaze flittered to her and away as he continued, methodically running the rag down the length of his inner feathers before returning for a little more oil to do it all over again.

She made sure to meet his gaze every time it skittered her way. She was surprised that he hadn't just up and left with his things when she made it clear she wouldn't leave, but the more he darted glances her way, Lena also realized what this was. A challenge.

Stay if she dared.

He didn't intend to make it easy. He worked in silence, attempting to ignore her, though Lena knew he was very aware of her. It was in his glances, small challenges though they were, the way he didn't angle away from her, how he moved his hands slowly, making it almost...a display.

"Bel, what...what are you doing?" she said through her breathlessness. She didn't know if he intended it to be beautiful, but the soft light of the kitchen made the golden brown of his feather tips shimmer like bronze and the white of the bases almost glow like fresh snow. The oil only drew more light to the down and barbs, highlighting the textures and layers.

"Oiling my wings," he said.

She suppressed rolling her eyes when he left it at that. He was trying to be aggravating.

"Why?"

"It's good for them."

"Why?"

"Keeps them clean. Water resistant."

"And all avians do this?"

The question had his shoulders stiffening, and his gaze shuttered and skittered away again.

Lena bit her tongue, cursing herself. He'd been talking. Sort of. Tersely. In a way, it was like his teasing—Bel liked his word games and ploys. And he hadn't left. Now, as he hunched a little in on himself, his gaze no longer rising to meet hers in challenge, she held her breath, waiting for him to retreat back into the cold night of his chambers.

He didn't. He didn't say anything else, but he didn't retreat, and so Lena didn't push.

She stood there, switching her ankle over the other, and slowly drank her drink.

"Avians..." She would have missed his hushed word if she hadn't been waiting anxiously for it. It was too dark to tell, but Lena thought he blushed a little.

"Avians have an oil gland," he said finally, but barely louder. She had to strain to hear and hold her breath, but she took his words gladly. "Near the wing bases." He waved vaguely over his shoulder at his back, then dipped the rag into the bowl and began methodical swipes down his wing again.

"Then why oil them yourself?" Lena asked, equally quiet.

He didn't flinch at the question this time, but his answer was again a long while in coming, six whole strokes before finally, "The oils are stimulated by flight. The muscles moving in the wing bases during flight triggers the oils, which get worked over the wings."

"And you haven't flown in..."

"A very long time." He dipped the rag into the bowl as his other wing extended. It was no less beautiful to watch, even if it drooped a little and didn't reach as far. He began the process anew.

"Sometimes it works. Training has..." He cleared his throat. "The dry, cold winter can be hard on them, though. Pol got a few special oils on the seasonal inventory that comes for the castle."

"Hair oils?" Lena knew they were popular, especially in the south, and had used some herself when she'd had the luxury.

"Something like that. Pol was horrified when I tried to use cooking oil."

Lena shared in his quiet laugh, letting it settle over them as he continued to work.

This was what she'd wanted. It was almost comfortable. She enjoyed it while she could, letting him work in silence because it was a companionable one.

It was when he neared the ends of his primary feathers that Lena realized he hadn't been able to do his back, the upper wings or the wing bases.

"Would you like me to do what you can't reach?"

He stilled again, but not in the way he had before, not a flinch; instead, it was like he ceased to move, the breath catching in his lungs as he stared at her.

Then Lena heard her own words and she held still too, waiting to see what he would do. She was grateful for the low, forgiving light and hoped it hid the worst of her furious blush.

His throat worked to swallow; she watched the slow bob of it, wondered if he was swallowing words or just hesitation.

Finally, he said, "All right," so, so quietly, but the force of it had her heart racing.

Lena nodded, not giving herself time to think too much about it, not that he was letting her near, not that she would soon touch him, his wings.

As she came to the table, Bel shifted on the stool, turning around to give her most of his back. His injured wing was slightly angled away, but

Lena didn't mind. She was a little frightened too.

"I use a long swiping motion. Not too much oil. Light touch," he said, watching her from the corner of his eye.

"Yes," she said.

Lena thought her breathing overloud as she dipped the rag into the oil. She couldn't tell from across the kitchen, but up close, it had a nutty, warm, aromatic smell, almost like Pol's honey and rum concoction but less sweet.

She tried to be subtle about taking a lungful as she worked the oil through a new patch of rag. She realized she'd smelled this on him before, always subtle, just a hint, and she had to stop herself from bringing the rag up to her nose.

It was a good, rich smell.

Slowly, she applied the rag to his left wing base. A small shudder ran through him, and he rocked forward, but then he stilled, waiting for her next pass.

Lena kept her touch light, as he said. Her breathing remained loud to her ears, but she hoped he didn't hear, hoped that the crackling fire filled his ears instead. She focused on her strokes, making sure not to matt the down to his shoulder or joint while applying a little more pressure, a little more oil to the developed feathers.

This close, he emitted his own heat. She had felt it before, of course, but not like this. She had to stop herself from making too many swipes along the base, just to feel the smoothness of his skin. He hadn't agreed to that.

His back was at once human and not, much wider than a human's with more developed shoulder muscles that piled atop one another into the mound of muscle and cartilage that was his wing base. The dip of his spine between his shoulder blades was less pronounced than a human's, instead only a slight depression as the muscle overlapped his back. His waist was wider than a human's too, even a man's, to support that vast, strong muscle structure that could power him through the air.

She'd never been so close to the naked back of an avian before, never been given the chance to admire the strength and beauty of it. Along the nape of his neck, hair bled into down, tracking in two lines to his wing bases, but that didn't seem strange to her, to see hair and down so intertwined.

She continued to work, a little mesmerized at the glossy shine of his wings. The rhythm of her movements did more to soothe her than Pol's drink.

As she worked, ever so slowly, he leaned into her touch, his muscles easing one by one. It was as if...not that he came apart, really, but that while he warmed, in the firelight and under her touch, he softened. His body seemed to let go of some its tension, almost letting her take his weight. She didn't know if he did it consciously and wondered if his back touched her front if he would snatch himself away, but she wanted him closer, willed him to lean back, if just for a moment.

"Bel," she said, barely more than a whisper, because anything more seemed too much. "What's wrong?"

She heard the long breath he took, felt it under her hands as his chest and back expanded with it. His head tilted all the way back so that his eyes were pointed at the ceiling. A few of his growing gold curls brushed against her cheek, the faintest wisps, and Lena felt herself swaying forward.

She just stopped herself when he said, "Do you have family?"

His question caught her right in the gut, and the breath whooshed out of her.

"My mother and father are alive, yes."

"And have you always done what they asked of you?"

"I...I've tried," she said, the words like untrue ashes in her mouth.

His head came down to nod slowly, and he looked over his shoulder at her with heavy-lidded eyes. He nodded again, as if she said only what he'd expected.

He faced forward once more, to let her continue.

Lena restarted her pattern, gently working further along the wing, trying to get lost again in the movement and the scent, but her thoughts stayed on his maddening words.

His family...

The eagle he'd spoken with flashed through her memory. Is that what he'd been doing?

Did Bel have a family? She nearly blushed to think that she didn't know. It had never occurred to her to ask—mostly because she didn't think he'd answer.

"Do you have family, Bel? Kin?"

"Some," he said on an outward puff of air.

"And they are..."

"Alive."

In Hadria, most likely, but Lena didn't want to think about that dark, rocky place, not now.

"Do you..." She had to lick her dry lips and swallow to wet her dry throat. "Do you miss them terribly?"

Another sigh left Bel, this one longer than the last.

"It's hard to miss what you never had," he said.

His words confused her—*did he have a family or not?*—but then he turned his head again to look at her over his shoulder. His eyes were still heavy-lidded, but there was a brightness in them, as if his words had sparked something.

"That doesn't mean you don't long for it," she replied, not sure where the words came from, not sure she even said them aloud.

His eyes slowly roved her face, the turquoise blue of them darkened to a jeweled sapphire tone in the soft light. His gaze sank to her mouth as she spoke, those wide avian pupils dilating.

Her heart picked up speed again. She'd seen this look before, had craved it since he'd first turned it her way. She felt weak and powerful under it all at once, as if she had and needed everything he was and could give.

A lock of his hair brushed her brow. Her thumb shifted along his wing base, moving past the rag to run along his warm skin.

She was surrounded by him, his wings spread out on either side of her, his heart beating beneath her hand, his scent of male and down and the light oil filling her senses.

They were so close, closer even than before, with his head turned towards her. She was nearly pressed up against his back, she had only to sway forward and then they would meet, would fulfill this dance of a promise they'd been making to each other. She had only to step forward, press her luck, to finally see where this growing, messy mass of feelings would take her.

She had only to push forward...

The thought—*push*—stopped her. He was warm, seemingly waiting for her, his eyes big and focused on her, but what if she was wrong? What if this wasn't what he wanted? What if he longed only for closeness, for comfort? What if she tried to claim something from him he didn't want or wasn't able to give?

It would devastate her.

She wanted him, wanted *this*, but at what price?

Lena forced herself to draw away, only a few inches, but still enough to end this heat growing between them in the warm cocoon of the kitchen. It wasn't about what she wanted. She knew, from these last weeks with him, that Bel had such a great capacity for joy and life, but an even greater capacity for pain and heartache. Something burdened him, she saw it in his eyes, in the downward angle of his shoulders and wings— but more, she *felt* it.

She didn't want to add to his burden, didn't want to force her own want on him. Humans had demanded so much of him, forced their will upon him. In her heart, she knew the circumstances were different, that what she wanted to ask of him would take but also give, would hopefully make him happy rather than hurt. She didn't want, ever, to hurt him.

She wanted him close, but if he needed to be distant, that was his right.

Lena took another mental step back as she made another few finishing swipes over his wing, if only for something to do and avoid his direct gaze.

She'd wait. Let him decide if and when this attraction between them would ever manifest. Let him come to see on his own that she wouldn't be a burden but, if he wanted, would take some of the weight. It pained her, made an ache grow between her fourth and fifth ribs, but she'd do this. She could give this to him, let him hold the decision in his hands. She could only hope he decided soon.

31

Bel spent another two days holed up in his chambers, staring at empty pages and twirling the two feathers between his fingers. At one point he'd carved the brown-black feather into a quill just for the hell of it, to make a piece of the avian king a writing utensil, because he could. But he hadn't liked how the word *traitor* pressed into the flesh between thumb and finger and soon abandoned it.

And now...well, now, Bel was bored.

Boredom had long been his companion, but now that he had the chance, the hope of a real companion, of real companionship, he found his old friend intolerable. It ate at him, picking at his mind.

He couldn't hide out forever, no. But he just wasn't sure he could face Maddalena, she of the soothing hands.

A blush overtook his face as he bundled himself up in a jacket, boots, and cloak. Even now the memory of her hands on his back nearly made him shudder, as if she was still there, just behind him, touching him, standing where he was most vulnerable. He'd gone so long without anyone touching him the way she did. Pol had touched his wings before, had helped take care of him in those early vulnerable years that Bel didn't like thinking about, but Maddalena's touch was more, it was...different.

His huff of agitation flew back into his face as a misty puff of hot air as he trudged through the snow to the stables. He hated not having the words for this, hated that another avian male his age would know what to *do* with it.

The familiar knife of indecision worked its way between his ribs, stabbing at him. He just didn't know what to do.

Did Maddalena feel even half of this longing that constantly ached just below his heart? Did she imagine he was beside her when he was gone, and wish him closer when he was there? Had she touched him that night in more than just comfort? Had she leaned closer in that moment that felt like time ran slow, syrupy, effervescent, waiting for him to lean closer too? Did she think all these things, have all these feelings, but felt them cram in her throat whenever he was near?

He was brimming with questions, so many that they wanted to spill from his mouth in rapid succession. And these questions had answers. Really, the only question was whether he wanted to hear them.

Bel kicked at a pile of snow, frustrated with himself. Bearing the pain of Eamon and Dartegn's messages alone had accomplished nothing. He couldn't tell her of what he'd done, of course he couldn't, but there was part of him that thought she would bear some of this with him. That she could, if not make it go away, make it bearable again.

Pulling away had put into sharper relief that he'd come to rely, however little, on her. On her companionship, the turn of her mind, the soft touch of her hand. All of it, all of her made his world bearable.

It was something of a dreadful thought, and it made his throat catch. If he felt this way now, relied on her now, what would it be like when she left him? It was a cozy little lie they lived in at Finhöln, where the snow walled them away from a world that said all of this was impossible, everything Bel felt was impossible. What would happen when she left? And she would leave, of course she would leave, she belonged out there. People needed her protection. If Bel had learned nothing else about her, it was that Maddalena was a protector. He knew she belonged here even less than he did, but was it so horrible of him to want her protection, her attention for himself?

Such power she had over him, and if he gave in, if he fell, it would only grow. And then where would he be when she was gone?

The thought stole the air from his lungs, making Bel hurry through the frozen stable door all the quicker, out of the cold where he could catch an easier breath.

The musky tang of horseflesh made his nose twitch, and slowly, slowly the panic ebbed. His heart still raced, still banged in his ears, but at least his trembling fingers could unclasp the cloak from around his throat.

He let the comforting sounds of the horses draw him out of his thoughts, knew that thinking the same things over and over wouldn't solve anything. Something would have to be done, one way or another, and Bel dreaded to think that the decision was in his hands. He could pull even further away, could pretend there was a lock on his chamber door and keep out the rest of the castle. Keep *her* out, until she left. Until someone took her place and Bel was alone again.

The thought of that hurt even more.

And there perhaps was an answer for him.

Gray bumped his shoulder when he was near enough, his liquid horse eyes heavy-lidded and sympathetic. Bel ran a grateful hand down the horse's velvety muzzle, letting Gray's hot breath warm his frozen fingertips.

"Can I give you my secrets?" he asked quietly, the soft rhythm of running his hand down Gray's forelock to his muzzle soothing. "I think you can be trusted with them."

"They say horses are the best secret-keepers."

Bel turned on his heel to find Alix in the empty stall across from him, sitting on a few hay bales. She gave him a sheepish half-grin, and Bel tried to return it. He was grateful, really, that she'd spoken up. He liked the girl, could even count her as a friend on her better days, but he didn't know what she would think of the things simmering inside Bel. Alix seemed to like him, but she was protective of Maddalena; he'd never forget the look she'd thrown at the convict when she'd helped truss him up in the kitchen that morning. She hadn't looked like a girl then, hadn't even looked human; instead her face had been a mask of rage and vengeance, like a demon of old, or perhaps a goddess of wrath. Bel knew then, as sure as he knew anything, that Alix wasn't one to cross.

It was when Alix still said nothing that Bel took a longer look at her. The girl wasn't one to stay quiet. He'd seen enough of her and Maddalena to know how Alix's moods shifted, how she quieted whenever she had Maddalena's disappointment weighing on her.

She was quiet now, sitting with her legs loosely crossed. She'd taken off her cloak and unbuttoned her coat, the toggles swaying as she moved. Her hands were busy in little movements, and Bel realized she held something. She watched him take in the thick square of parchment paper carefully but didn't stop turning the envelope over and over in her hands, as if she wanted his attention but couldn't ask for it.

"What is it?" he felt compelled to ask.

"I went down to Longbourne today," she said over Bel's shoulder. "Violet's usually there in the mornings, so I like to go see her. She's nice, we talk and she tells me about Longbourne and the pub and her parents and the mayor—goddess, the mayor. But that's not important."

Bel was wondering if any of it was important, but he stayed quiet, shifting a little closer, leaning against one of the stall posts. Alix swallowed, her gaze caught on the far corner of the stables, the envelope turning round, round, round in her deft fingers.

"Violet said a messenger from Whitewater had come yesterday, had trudged up through the day and her parents put him up overnight. Came with an official royal message, with the seal and everything. Violet said to go look at it, that it was for 'that knight of yours.'" She snorted. "That's what they call her, you know? 'That knight of yours.' Like they don't know her fucking name. Don't know what would've happened if

I hadn't come down. Lena's not going down, and they weren't coming up. It would've just sat in the trading post." Alix looked at the little square, scraping her nail on an edge. "Maybe that would've been better."

Bel didn't understand why the words came rushing out of her, tinged with that low Vagoran accent she sometimes had, nor why she said this without meeting his eyes. But something had upset Alix, and that something she held between her hands. And whatever that letter was, he knew it was for Maddalena.

His mind fluttered with all the possibilities of what it could be, all the horrible things it could say, and his insides twisted in intricate knots.

When Alix remained quiet, he looked at the letter again, finally saw the cracked seal.

"You opened it."

"I was worried," she snapped, defensive, as if he was accusing her of something, when really, he'd made an effort to keep his voice neutral.

He did again when he said, "And is it something to worry over?" He didn't quite understand why he wanted to shake answers out of her, but her manner unnerved him, made him feel as if a sword suddenly hung above their heads.

Alix looked at him, those jade eyes of hers sweeping over him in a quick assessment before she held the letter out to him. He had to stop himself from snatching it, instead moving slow, making sure she wouldn't take it back.

The back of the envelope had that cracked seal, but when Bel looked, it was slightly different than the ones he was used to cracking himself on the human king's directives. The royal crest was there with its crossed sword and stars, but behind it was emblazoned a sun, its nine points spearing the edges of the wax.

He pulled out a piece of paper folded twice, one width and one lengthwise. It was fine paper, the highest quality. But most important, scrawled across the folded face in an elegant hand was the name *Lena*.

Not *Maddalena* or *Lady Maddalena* or *Lady Maddalena Mont-caer*. Just *Lena*.

Something burned in his gut at the sight of it, something that wasn't quite anger, not quite pain or longing, but a mix of it all. His eyes ran fast over the letter, consuming it before he really understood it, and went back for another pass. The heat in him only grew with each word, reddening his cheeks and the pointed tips of his ears.

> *My dearest Lena,*
>
> *I cannot say how it grieves me to be here and find that you are not. It was what got me by, thinking you were safe. But I come home only to find all the wrongs done to you. The first thing I did upon arriving home was ask for news of you, but no one wanted to speak of it. My lord father said little, only spoke of the claims against you. Lena, know that I don't believe a word of it. Balderak is a snake.*
>
> *My father has wronged you, and I want to set it right. Come home to me and let me make this right. By the time you read this, know that I have already started an appeal and will be consulting with my advisors about how to get this overturned. I hope to hand you a clean record when you arrive.*
>
> *Come back to me, Lena, and I will make this right.*
> *Yours, always,*
> *Arion*

Bel read this human man's words and finally knew what it was he felt. *Jealousy*, hot and cutting. It had been a familiar feeling to him growing up, watching everyone claiming Maddok's attention, leaving none for him, the spare, the prince that should not have been.

He knew of this human male, knew what the seal and the given name meant together. Crown Prince Arion. The man's family had taken Bel's home, his brother, and now the man himself wanted Lena.

"It's from the crown prince. Of Vagora," Alix said unnecessarily, ignorant of the stinging pain claiming the center of him. "He and Lena were...*close* during the last campaign. She was one of his guards, and..." Her gaze flicked to him then away again in an instant, but Bel suspected she saw enough. He just didn't care. Alix, for all he'd worried over her feelings, wasn't going to take Lena away from him.

"He wants her to leave her post. Without orders. It was the king who sentenced her here, but it doesn't say anything about being pardoned while waiting for the appeal to go through."

Bel tried to hear what the girl said, tried pulling himself out of the mire of jealousy. He knew the feeling was like quicksand, all-consuming and suffocating. He couldn't stop it, felt himself sinking into it, but he forced himself to think about what Alix said.

"This is a personal letter. Not a royal pardon."

"Not a royal pardon," she agreed. "Not a royal anything, really. Just a promise."

Bel drew a long breath into himself, trying to cool some of the hurt burning inside him. He knew how little, how worthless promises could be. Especially from royals.

"You don't think she should go," he said, not a question. It was written in the worry lines etched across Alix's face, the frown that shadowed her eyes. But most telling was the drawn line of her mouth. For all that Alix's eyes were big and bright and expressive, Bel had learned it was her mouth that gave the most away, especially when she didn't speak.

"No," said Alix in an almost-whisper. "She's got strikes against her, you know. They wanted to make her go away. So no, I don't think she should go, not without something...more. It'd just be another strike." *Which would be one too many,* she left unsaid, but Bel understood.

"But he's the prince," Bel forced himself to say.

"And that's a love letter," Alix replied, pointing an accusing finger at the paper Bel wanted to crumple between his hands. "Not a pardon or anything else official."

Bel folded the letter again, not wanting to see those words anymore, and turned it over in his hands, once, twice, again. He could feel it bubbling up between him and Alix, the question he didn't want to ask—should they give it to Lena?

It shouldn't even have been a question, really. It was addressed to Lena, the words were for her alone, and he and Alix were in the wrong for claiming them first. Perhaps she'd welcome the prince's words, would be comforted that someone so important was fighting for her.

And maybe the words would carry her away from here, far away from Bel.

The thought cut through him. Lena leave if she got this letter. He'd be alone again, abandoned here, and he couldn't even blame her for it—the letter promised exactly what Lena desired, exactly what she deserved. How could he ever ask her to give up such a chance?

Breath rushed back into him in a sigh, and Bel forced himself to consider this. How could he, of all people, take away a chance like this? She'd been punished for protecting people, and Bel knew the pain from that punishment was worse even than the trap that had bitten deep into her leg. She'd suffered enough, much more than she should ever have had to, and she deserved the chance to have her name, her honor restored.

Perhaps it was best that he'd pulled away, perhaps it wouldn't hurt as much when she left with the letter's promise. Perhaps that was a lie he told himself, but what else could he do?

Bel turned the letter over in his hands again, feeling the weight of the words. The crown prince's message made Bel think of his own royal missive, sitting on his worktable. What would it be like, to have someone fight for him the way the human prince promised to fight for Lena?

It would be the right, selfless thing to do, to give her up—but Bel... didn't want to be selfless, and he especially didn't want to give her up.

Not now, not when he was so close to having *something*, something good and also somehow right. *He* wanted to be the one who fought for her, whatever that may mean.

He had a chance now to be happy and to make someone else happy in return. He could give her more than a promise, could offer more than words on a page. He could give over his whole self, could take the chance that she would want it. Even if this was only for a while, a preset period of time, wasn't this chance worth it? Couldn't he be worth the trade, this time for the precarious, small chance that an appeal would go through?

He wanted to be worth it, wanted it so fiercely he could taste it, on the back of his tongue. He wanted *this*, wanted *her*. And there was no going back.

"What should we do about it?" Alix's voice brought Bel out of the fury of his thoughts. Alix swallowed heavily, looking between the grim set of his face to the letter he absently mangled in his hands, his churning thoughts no doubt playing across his face.

"Burn it," he murmured, his voice sounding unfamiliar to his ears, harder, harsher.

Alix swallowed hard again, but after a long moment, she nodded.

"I think it's for the best," she whispered.

"Yes. For her," he said, equally quiet, as if their plotting had to be done in whispers, as if there was someone else to hear them other than the horses.

"Yeah, for her." Alix looked up at him, those big eyes of hers wide as she took in his face. He wondered what she saw when she looked at him, if he looked at all like the possessive, jealous beast that writhed just beneath his skin.

He nodded and shoved the letter back into Alix's hands, not wanting to touch the male's words to Lena, words that were too familiar and too dangerous to Bel. "Come on," he said to her, and started putting on his outer clothes again.

The horses neighed in complaint, but Bel and Alix left the stables for the great hall, trudging through the new snow. Bel had spent enough winters on this mountain to know that winter was waning, the worst of it already blanketing the ground. Green would overtake the mountain and the castle soon enough, new grass shoots and pine needles and aspen leaves reclaiming the land. He looked forward to spring, to the promise of it—perhaps he would go *outside* again, with Lena—but he'd be lying if he said he didn't feel an urgency with the lengthening winter. The snow kept the world out, and if he was to act, if he was to take his chance, it felt as though it had to be before their insulation, their protection melted away.

The great hall was empty, though a small fire lingered in the eastern hearth. Lena was nowhere to be seen, the only sounds in the hall the echo of his and Alix's quiet footsteps.

They crept like the plotters they were. When they reached the hearth, he didn't let himself think about it, just watched as Alix took the crumpled letter out of her pocket.

"It's for the best," Alix said again, and Bel nodded.

She took a deep breath, but Bel held his as she tossed the letter into the fire.

They watched in silence as the edges cracked and folded in a black wave before being consumed. The wax seal hissed and bubbled, running through the page into the coals below.

There, it was done.

And Bel only felt a little guilt, for he had too much dread to feel much of anything else. It was like first flight, standing on the edge of the precipice, terrified of the fall but having to trust that his wings were strong enough to catch and carry him. He'd done this, he'd fallen now; there was no giving her the letter if she refused, no pretending that he hadn't done this so that the human male couldn't have her. So that he could. He'd jumped, and now he'd have to trust Lena to catch him.

32

That night, Bel sat before his hearth, going through the motions of making a new fire. He'd already let two flames dwindle down to a bed of coals. His mind had been elsewhere all day, and he'd spent his time staring at empty pages.

Long after the fire had grown to a healthy flame, Bel stared at it, feeling like the flint he held in his hand. He was all potential energy, waiting for the strike to create a flame. He needed to do something, had promised himself he would, but what? He just didn't know the right way to this, to even start.

Burning that letter had to mean something.

Outside, the sky was a mosaic of blushes and golds, with dots of blue and purple clouds as the sun began to dip behind the mountain. The days were growing longer, ever so slowly, and Bel could feel the restlessness in the world, how animals emerged from their winter dens and shook off their snowy sleep, how the trees shed layers of snow and outer, protective bark. Spring was coming, and for the first time in a long while, Bel wasn't sure he welcomed it.

A light knock at the door had him looking up in surprise to see Lena poking her head in. She bore a tray of food and came in when he said nothing, closing the door behind her.

They stared at one another for a long moment, Bel a little shocked to see the blush creeping across her cheeks.

She shuffled her feet before coming closer to deposit the tray onto the far corner of his worktable.

"Pol worried you'd be working late, so I thought I'd bring dinner. To make sure you ate."

"He feeds me enough. If he had his way, I'd never leave the kitchen and he'd constantly be ladling food into my mouth."

She gave him a halfhearted smile for his halfhearted joke, but it quickly faded. She looked at her feet and he heard the small scuff of her boot against the floor.

"He worries about you. We...I worry about you, too."

"I'm sorry," he said, inane as it was.

His gaze caught on her hand, clutched in a loose fist, and he realized she was picking at her cuticles with the nail of one finger. She shifted again and folded her hands behind her, in a pose he had grown very used to. But she soon dropped it, perhaps because it was so formal, and clenched her fists instead.

"Bel, won't you tell me what's wrong? You've been...distant. Did I...?" She didn't blush, but her lips pursed and she swallowed hard.

Bel shook his head to reassure her. But he couldn't tell her, couldn't admit what it truly was that had him so forlorn. She would understand missing family, but then he would have to admit how he'd heard from them in the first place and then, if they knew where he was, why they didn't try to help him and then...then...then she might know who he really was. That was his secret of all secrets he supposed, something he jealously guarded, something not even Pol knew. And he wasn't sure he could part with it yet.

He felt the heavy bob of his throat as he tried to swallow his nerves.

"Memories," he finally said. "I suppose they've made me melancholy. I didn't mean anything by it."

She nodded, he hoped in understanding. "I know how something can...linger." She said the last word with distant eyes.

"Yes."

"I hope...I hope we're still friends."

Bel's brows rose at that, and the impact of her shy but hopeful stare had him leaning forward in his seat.

"Yes," he said again, quicker, with more force. "Yes, of course we are."

She smiled a little in, perhaps, relief, and Bel gave her one to match. His shoulders eased with the movement, like something had been agreed upon and they could get past this awkwardness.

Perhaps he should have felt guilty that she'd taken the burden of the blame for his mood, and perhaps he was, a little, but Bel was more flattered that she cared. She came to assure herself that they were still friends, still had a connection. It didn't feel as good as her hands on his back, soothing oil through his wings, but he would eagerly take any sign of her friendship and affection.

Lena came forward, poking at a pile of papers next to where she'd put his dinner tray. She shifted a few papers while Bel held still, trying his damnedest for nonchalance. He didn't really think there was anything there to give him away; most everything was in some form of runic, which he doubted Lena knew, as so few humans did. It was another one of his secrets he wasn't quite ready to part with yet, certainly not when it could jeopardize all that he'd done and had yet to do.

"I've been in here before and never really considered what all this is," she said quietly. "There's so much of it..."

"Translating takes a lot of paper. At least, that's what I find."

She looked up, surprised. "These are your translations? For...?" *King Artemian*, she didn't have to say.

He nodded. "Takes a while, and a lot of paper, to get things right."

Lena sifted through the papers again, tracing the scrawl of Bel's runic script. The inherent terror of her somehow knowing what he'd done was still there, but there was also something else, something a little like excitement, to see her finger running over something he'd done. The king may want the words for himself, but really, they were Bel's, and he felt a greedy sense of pleasure at having Lena touch his work.

"I suppose I just hadn't considered that's what all this was. Remarkable."

"What did you think I did up here? Hang upside down from the rafters like a bat?"

"No," she laughed. "More like write maudlin poems by candlelight."

They shared a soft laugh as Lena continued looking through his papers. And he let her, because she looked interested, but mostly because she was here and laughing with him.

He couldn't help but wonder, now that she realized what all this was, whether she thought of when she would take these translations to her king, once the time came.

"And what's this?"

Bel peered over at the half-revealed rectangle of paper. He already knew it was a map of the Gogona Mountains, but he still got up and came around the table to look over Lena's shoulder. The thought of leaving had him wanting to be close to her.

"Ah. That's the Gogona Mountains," he said, pulling the paper out from a heap of others.

"This is Hadria," she said, tapping a little doodle of a castle Bel had done to mark the site.

"Yes."

Her eyes swept over the rest of the map. Hadria was at the bottom of the page, while the rest of the mountains curved northeast like a craggy spine.

"I just hadn't considered...there's so much more out there than I thought. I didn't realize Hadria was in the southern part of the mountains, that they extended so far."

"Avians like mountains."

She turned her head to look at him and smiled. "Yes, I see that."

He smiled back, a feeling of lightness and warmth cocooning his chest. He found the curve of her mouth entrancing, but only when he noticed her pupils widen did he realize he stared. He thought, if one of them leaned forward, then he would do something—this is what he'd been waiting for, this—

Lena leaned forward, just the slightest sway towards him.

The breath left him in a hiss, and Bel tried not to gasp for breath as he backed up and swiveled toward the fire.

Hell!

Bel seethed hotter than the fire, gritting his teeth so he wouldn't gnash them.

That was it! That should have been it! Damn, damn him!

Lena cleared her throat. "How long does it take you to translate something?" She didn't sound disappointed, only, perhaps, carefully neutral.

"That depends," he replied, trying to match her tone. He squatted, balanced on the balls of his feet, to stoke the fire. "For a page, probably a few days. Have to make sense of it first."

Bel gathered up what courage he had and stood back up. Turned to her. She was still here, he still had time.

"Is it hard to do?"

He took a sharp breath in spite of himself. "Sometimes."

Another swatch of color bloomed across her face. "I'm sorry, that was insensitive of me. Of course it must be hard."

"It's not...what I would like to be doing." It was about the most diplomatic thing he could manage.

"No, of course not." She frowned down at the pages spread out before her as if they were her enemy too. "It must be...difficult, to work for the enemy."

He didn't know what else to do with her commiseration but shrug. "No one has cared whether I want to do it or not. It's this or my life."

"*I* care. Bel, this must be a heavy burden to bear by yourself."

It took him a moment to answer, for all he could hear was her simple words, *I care*. "It's what I've been doing for a long time now."

Her frown turned indignant, and he thought she wanted to stamp her foot, her look became almost...impetuous. "It's ridiculous that you've been kept here like this. For what purpose?"

"I assumed it was to keep me away."

"Away from what?"

"You. All of you. I've learned much about humans from reading your books and honestly, avians aren't so different."

"Aside from your wings," she said with a soft smile.

"Aside from our wings," he agreed. "I always figured your king didn't want others seeing the similarities, either."

"Alix had never seen an avian before you...few in the south have. You're more a myth, really."

"Or a monster. A rallying cry."

She made an unhappy noise, her look suddenly troubled. Bel knew he was biased but also that she would have to make her peace with what her king did. She'd be in his service again one day. It was enough for Bel to know that she was on his side, even a little, even if it didn't count for much outside this castle.

Lena sighed. "Well, you're doing something not many could. I'm not sure I could..."

His heart gave a painful lurch in his chest. Did she think he'd taken the coward's way out?

She looked up at him when he said nothing to see his grimace of shame. His cousin's message beat at him, and for all the days he'd put between him and it, it still felt fresh in his mind, cutting and sharp.

Lena closed most of the distance between them, a beseeching look in her eyes as they searched his. "Whatever you're thinking, stop it. I meant that you made the decision to survive, Bel. It's not an easy path to take."

"Surviving *is* the easy way out."

"*No,*" she argued. "Sometimes that's all we can do. Bel..." She placed a hand on his forearm, ensuring she had his gaze when she said, "You're a *survivor,* you've done what you've had to, and I...I for one am so happy that you have."

Bel's throat went dry as his heart hammered a rapid tattoo in his ear. He eased forward, reaching for her, and his hands, trembling ever so slightly, gently took her waist. He watched her nostrils flare, but she didn't pull away, just watched him watching her, and Bel filled his palms with her hips and slowly, so slowly, in case she pulled away, in case he was dreaming, pulled her close.

She came willingly, not slowly, stepped into his space and gazed up at him as her hands ghosted over his chest, so lightly at first he could barely feel their weight or warmth. But as he drew her closer, they came to rest along his collar, her fingers teasing the skin above his breastbone.

"Is that what I've done—survive?" he murmured.

"Sometimes all you can do is put your head down and get through it."

"Like you've done here."

He watched her swallow. It was good to know she saw him not as a coward, not as a victim, but as a survivor. But it mattered to him that she didn't see him as just a distraction, just a way to fill idle time. He wanted her time, yes, but he wanted *her* most of all.

"At first," she said. "This mountain was the last place I thought I would ever want to be. But..."

"And now?"

He held her tighter, splayed his hands along her back, as if something just out sight would wrench her away. But she moved closer still, until their bodies pressed against one another, until he felt the swell of her breasts against his chest. She wore only a shirt today, tucked into her trousers; just two layers of fabric separated their skin.

"Bel." Her gaze was intense, focused, as it held his. *Yes*, it said, *yes*.

He leaned down to her, unsure quite what he was going to do once he got there, and had the sensation of falling, of weightlessness. As terrifying as first flight.

The first touch of her mouth to his sent his whole being whirling. It was...well, odd. Not unpleasant but not, perhaps, everything he'd hoped it would be. She made a subtle movement, changing the angle, and Bel held still, unsure what to do, unsure how it was supposed to feel.

It'd been so long since he'd held anyone, had been expected to give pleasure with his touch and receive it in return. He loved the feel of her in his arms, their bodies pressed together from knee to chest, but the unfamiliar sensation of her mouth moving against his made him suddenly too aware of his hands, nearly clutching at her back, and he had to stop from shifting his weight from foot to foot.

A pang of terror lanced through him when Lena pulled back. She looked up at him, another blush coloring her face, but it was coupled with worry. Bel had a sucking sensation in his gut, hating the doubt now creasing her eyes.

"Bel, have you ever...?"

"A long time ago." He swallowed hard. "And...avians don't kiss."

Her expression eased. "Then what do they do?"

"*Ashita*."

"*Ashita*," she repeated. "And what's that?"

Bel opened his mouth to tell her, to explain as a dictionary would, but closed it again with a *click*. He should show her.

His heartbeat picked up again, in excitement this time. He leaned down, and Lena kept still, watching him with an open, curious expression.

He touched his nose to hers, nuzzling, before moving to her cheek. "It's like your human kiss, in a way," he whispered against her skin. He traced the tip of his nose over her cheek before running it up one side of her nose, tracing her brow, then back down the other side. He eased down to her jaw, where he followed the curve to her ear. "It means 'to be close together,' but it's not vague like your kiss."

"Vague?" she said, and Bel tried not to be too smug at her breathlessness.

"Mm," he hummed, tracing the shell of her ear before taking a deep breath from the scent-rich skin just behind her ear. "A kiss can mean many things. *Ashita* is done only in affection, between mates, or those who want to be mates." He whispered this to her before slowly pulling away, making sure to follow the line of her jaw to her chin before leaning back a few inches.

Her face, even her neck, was flushed a lovely rosy color, and she gazed back at him languidly with heavy-lidded eyes. She said nothing about mates and what *ashita* meant between them, but she did smile, wide and beautiful, and he knew that smile would stay with him, seared into his memory like the burning green of the sun on the eye after looking too long.

"I like your *ashita*," she said, her fingertips tracing his collar before she cupped the side of his neck.

He smiled back and hitched her higher against him, standing her on her tiptoes. "Kiss me again."

She arched an eyebrow at him, her smile widening into a lopsided grin that Bel felt through his whole body. His wing bases shivered as she leaned up again.

He was ready this time and refused to let the disappointment take hold when it still felt awkward. He didn't totally understand the appeal of kissing —there seemed to be a lot of working parts. But after a moment, he decided he liked that it was warm and that it brought her body into the curve of his. After another, after her tongue flicked against the seam of his lips, Bel thought he was beginning to understand.

He let her lead them in a rhythm, opened when she asked without words. She coaxed him to chase her, curling her tongue around his to draw it into her mouth.

Bel sucked in a breath when he realized this was a dance, a give and take, push and pull. It was like their sparring matches, testing the other, challenging and teasing and finding what felt right. The thought eased all the others from Bel's mind and finally, finally he surrendered himself to instinct, to paying attention only to what felt right.

Lena showed him what she liked with little noises in the back of her throat that drove Bel a little mad and made his blood run hotter. He loved that it echoed in his ear whenever he ran his nose along the underside of her jaw in a quick, teasing *ashita*. His hands moved almost frantically over her, trying to find ways to draw the sound from her again and again. She shivered when he traced the dip of her spine, more pronounced in her human back. But he got what he wanted when he placed his mouth on her neck, alternating between nuzzling and licking and sucking. He almost lost himself in those noises, almost lost control, almost didn't notice her hands running over him in the same urgent way.

Her hands travelled over his back, fingertips at once light then digging into his flesh, and he waited almost impatiently as she edged up to his wing bases. They were sensitive, always had been, and Bel knew they were pleasure points on most avians, but it had been an abstract thought until now, something that couldn't be true after all the violence done to them. But when her palms closed in a warm clasp around them, her touch washed the memory of that away, alternating between teasing with her fingertips along the underside of the bases before caressing the radial bone and his shoulder blades. Bel's shudder began in his wings and radiated down his spine, coalescing at the small of his back where it hummed and throbbed.

He didn't quite realize he'd done it until the sound of papers and quills and ink bottles crashing to the ground rang in his ears. A large portion of his worktable was swept clear, probably for the first time in years, and Bel wasted no time depositing her there.

Lena spread her legs and welcomed him into the space between. Consumed with the need to feel her skin, he tugged her shirt from the waistband of her trousers. She helped him pull it over her head, and it went sailing over his shoulder somewhere, unimportant in the face of her, bare to him from the waist up.

If words were lost on him before, he was truly speechless now, gazing upon her breasts for the first time. They were neither large nor small, instead, as Bel rushed to discover, a perfect handful. She was achingly soft here, a contrast to her lean waist and strong shoulders. Her golden skin was warm to the touch.

When he felt a tug at the laces on his flank, he stepped back just long enough for Lena to rid him of his tunic. She ran her hands over him, exploring the lines and dips and scars of his chest. He groaned at her touch, leaning in to bury his face in her unbound hair. Bel held his breath but let it out again in a harsh gasp when she traced the waistband of his trousers—but nearly groaned in disappointment when she stopped.

"Bel." She nudged him with her shoulder until he gave her his eyes. He thrummed with need, with urgency, could barely keep himself still enough to meet her gaze, but he did his best at her serious look.

She ran her fingers along his waistband again, and he did groan.

"Bel, is this all right?"

"Yes," he growled, not recognizing his own voice. *Of course it was all right.* The worst thing she could do was *not* touch him.

Lena smiled in the way he loved, brightening her whole face, and she didn't make him wait any longer, delving below the waistband, and took him in hand. He gasped, rocked forward, put all his weight on his splayed palms on either side of her as she made a fist around him and ran it up and down, up and down.

It felt as if this pleasure, this need would surely burst out of him, from every pore, and it nearly did when she stroked him harder and bit the tip of his ear at once.

The animalistic growl that echoed through the room couldn't have been his, but he felt like an animal then. He was quick, merciless in getting rid of the rest of their clothes, desperate to feel the searing pleasure of her skin pressed to his.

But when she was completely bare before him, Bel was able to take in a fortifying breath. He wanted to drink in the sight of her, have his fill. Not rush through it, even if most of him disagreed. If this was to be his one chance, he had to take all of it, scrape the bone and lick the marrow of it so that it would last him.

She held her arms out to him, and he went happily, shuddering again when her hands found his wing bases. She was quick to find ways to please him, and Bel wanted to do that too, make her shudder, make her noises never end.

He began with her breasts, alternating between *ashitai* and kisses, and delighted in making her squirm and groan. When he ran his tongue over her a certain way, she dug her nails into his shoulders and almost made him see stars. He took his time between her breasts, listening and feeling for her reactions, wanting to wring everything from her, wanting everything she could give.

She made another sound in her throat, a needy huff, and took one of his wrists in her hand, guiding him down. Bel sucked in a breath at the feel of her, exploring this new, hot, slick part of her. Human and avian females weren't so different, at least Bel didn't think so until Lena pressed his middle finger to a bit of flesh that had her back arching, driving her chest into his.

Bel teased her with different touches, watching in amazement as her face contorted with abandon and her breath hitched. Pride echoed through him that he could please her so, that he could make her look at him with such fierce need.

He ran his fingers up and down, giving her light touches between more pressure, pleased when she no longer squirmed but writhed. She was slick as river rocks in his hand and hotter than candle flame.

She grabbed a handful of his hair, pulling almost to the point of pain.

"Bel, now, now, please!"

He wanted to touch her everywhere, see what else he could create with his hands and mouth, but he wouldn't deny her—and he didn't know how much longer he could deny himself. He crushed his mouth to hers, uncaring if his kiss was perfect, and sank himself inside.

She gasped against his mouth, and Bel made himself hold still, wallowing in the intense pleasure of her clutching him close. He moved again when she made that noise in the back of her throat, pressing further in, rocking them together until their hips were flush.

"Bel," she murmured, the strain, the joy in her voice making him shiver. One of her hands clutched his back, nails scoring his skin, while the other gripped the hair and down at the base of his neck. She hung onto him, fingers digging in, and Bel felt her everywhere, felt as if she were the one invading him. Her scent filled his lungs, her cries his ears, and Bel closed his mouth around the curve between her neck and shoulder, holding her in place with the light bite of his teeth.

He grinned around her flesh when she gasped.

Her grip tightened as she undulated, making Bel move. And once he'd started, he couldn't stop. He set an almost brutal pace, but she only demanded more, in her cries and shuddering breaths. Her head shook from side to side, spreading the papers of his desk beneath her, as if it wasn't enough. He liked the sight of her there, dark hair spilled across all his papers, the words of his people.

Bel moved his hips, trying to hit that place she so liked, and was rewarded with her cry of surprise and pleasure. He did it again and again, changing his angle, wanting her to fly.

His hips swiveled as he found her neck again, and then, there she was. She screamed, came undone, and Bel watched in amazement, losing his rhythm, losing himself entirely. Her head thrown back, eyes heavy-lidded, she was a goddess made flesh, and he was her willing supplicant. The sight of her, of what they'd done together, had Bel tumbling over the edge after her. Bel would follow this goddess anywhere.

Another animal sound reverberated in his throat at this feeling of total pleasure, total surrender, and the world narrowed to a single point of focus, going dark and fuzzy at the edges as he was reduced to fundamentals. For a long while he was only breath, sawing in and out of his lungs, and heat, emanating from his chest.

He came back to himself in increments. First was his hearing, and most of that was taken up by the rapid, thundering beat of his heart. There was an echo to it, and that's when Bel felt his mind snapping back into place, when he realized his heartbeat kept time with hers. Next came awareness of his own body, still tucked tightly to Lena's, and the sudden, fierce need not to move a muscle.

She shifted against him, and Bel hummed in happiness when she kissed his throat.

Lena straightened enough to bring their gazes even, and Bel leaned his forehead against hers. It was too wonderful for words, too wonderful to let go of. So Bel decided he wouldn't.

She made a sleepy sound of disappointment when he slipped from her. He found a clean rag and gently ran it over them both.

She smiled at him again, the firelight dancing in her sleepy, content eyes, and Bel wrapped his good wing around her. Then he hitched both her legs around him, making sure her ankles were locked at the small of his back before he picked her up off the table and took her to his bed, his nest.

He lay down with her, and in the waning firelight, they slowly learned each other's shape. And when they both tumbled into sleep, they did it with their limbs tangled together and Bel's wing draped over them both.

No, Bel wasn't going to let go, not of this night, not her, not whatever happiness he could find. He didn't know what would happen now, what this meant for them once the sun rose again, but it didn't matter. She was warm and content beside him, and tonight, it was enough. It was more than enough.

33

Something tickled Lena's nose. She blinked blearily into the darkness, the low light and the fog in her mind tricking her into thinking she lay inside a cloud, soft and divinely warm. But then a low, exhaled sigh reminded her what it was, what had happened.

The joint of Bel's wing curved just overhead, canopying them within a bubble of warmth. But it wasn't feathers that had wisped against her face. He sighed again from his place against her chest, his forehead pressed against her neck and his face pillowed by her breast. Her own was buried in his hair, and she couldn't resist running her nose along his hairline and kissing his temple.

Because she could. Because she held him in her arms, and he trusted her enough to sleep beside her. She could see little of him in the darkness, only make out shadows and lines, but she saw that he slept deeply, his large chest expanding and lifting his wing a little with each breath.

Gently, Lena sifted her fingers through his hair from temple to nape, then into the down. Both were soft in their own way, both textures a pleasure to touch. She almost didn't believe her memories, of gripping his nape as he moved inside her. If she weren't so comfortable and tired, she might have blushed.

But she was awake enough now to recognize her body's needs, and slowly, regretfully, she began disentangling herself from Bel. First were her legs, slipping away from the thigh he had between her own. Then his arms, guiding them from around her and down onto the bed. Finally, she eased out from under his wing and landed beside his bed in a crouch.

The cold air slapped her, and she shivered from head to toe. Rooting around in the darkness, she came up with a tunic and pulled it on, realizing only when the hem hit her knee that it must have been one of Bel's.

She made quick work of relieving herself and then set about rebuilding the fire. It had simmered down to a lazy bed of coals and took some coaxing, but Lena soon had new flames crackling away.

The glowing illumination of the new fire cast a thin slant of light into the bedchamber, framing Bel. He'd moved closer to the wall and wrapped his wing tightly around himself. It was dark still, her eyes tired, but she thought he frowned a little now in his sleep.

She watched him for a long while, the only sound the soft crackle of the fire. She stood in the entryway, shivering in the thin shirt, but couldn't make herself cross back to him.

Surrounded by Bel and his warmth, it was easy to forget the world outside Finhöln, the world that said they had both betrayed their kind. She hated herself, standing in that doorway, for getting what she wanted and questioning it, for wondering how long it would last, but could she afford not to? She would carry the memory of Bel and their night with her always, and she suspected it already meant much more than any of her past nights with past men. Even her time with Arion.

Perhaps what she hated most was that it felt right, instinctive to leave, to put on her boots, gather her things, and slip away through the dark castle to her own bed. She had years of practice slinking away in the early hours, that hazy time before it was truly morning but not quite night anymore. Perhaps habit had been why she woke at all.

The thought sparked an ache in her chest, and Lena rubbed at her breastbone.

Bel wasn't Arion. He was...well, he was Bel—cunning, enigmatic, wonderful. And she wanted to see his face when he awoke in the soft light of morning, wanted to hold him as they lazed the day away.

Bel was not Arion, and Finhöln was not the battlefield. Here, she felt as if she could finally have what she wanted. She could stay in bed late with Bel. She could teach him all her favorite ways to kiss and have him show her how best to bestow an *ashita*.

Lena padded back across the bedchamber and slowly lowered herself down beside him. She kept the shirt, as there was still a chill in the air, but inched closer to him, buried beneath his wing. She didn't worm her way back under, just lay quietly, watching the firelight flicker over his features.

He wasn't handsome by human standards, his face too sharp in places, but Lena thought humans had little concept of beauty when she looked at him, for how could there be anything more so?

As if he sensed her close again, Bel sighed and rolled closer to her, pulling her in under the shelter of his wing. His thigh pushed between hers again, and his arm drew her flush against his chest. It was Lena who sighed then, burying her face against his neck as he had with her, and kissed the hollow of his throat.

Bel held her tightly in his sleep, but Lena didn't mind. She had no plans to leave.

•—•◆•—•

She awoke again to the sound of rain. From the heavy pattering of it, it was a steady, soaking kind of rain, the crisp smell of it teasing her nose. She drank in the sound as she slowly stretched her toes and cracked her ankles. There was something soothing about the sound of rain. With snow, unless it was a blizzard, it fell silently. She liked that rain always announced itself.

Her movements were small, the flexes and twitches of coming awake, but they must have triggered them in Bel too, for she felt his skin move against hers and his wings rustled as he rocked a little on his side.

She kissed his throat again before shifting her head onto the pillow beside his.

His eyes were the somnolent slits of early wakefulness, languid and hazy. They tracked her in a slow arc, the blue of them almost incandescent in the soft morning light. Lena didn't know if she'd ever seen a blue like that before, if it even existed in such a pure form in the clearest water.

In the thin light that found them in his bed, Lena looked over what she had only had the chance to touch and taste the night before. His body was hard, a contrast to his lithe wings and soft feathers, a study of muscle moving in very human and inhuman ways. In the right light, his hair looked like burnished gold, gleaming in the sunlight. His hands were square and strong with blunted tips, the veins of his wrists prominent.

Lena liked his textures most of all, liked how they moved from skin to hair to down to feather seamlessly. Her hands couldn't seem to stop moving from one to the next and back again—it was almost too much to take in and she had to go back for more.

But as her hands moved over him, a counterpoint to his own beginning to move over her as well, she started to notice different textures breaking up the smooth warmth of his skin. She traced a line along his back only to find another, and another. They scored his skin, from backside to wing bases. And there were more. Pockmarks and burns littered his sides.

Took a fire poker to the prisoner. Needs to watch that mouth of his.

The words came back to Lena, making her stomach turn. It had been a long while since she'd looked at the warden's directive, but she still remembered each of the detailed accounts of the punishments meted out on Bel's body. They'd been written with such apathy, such dispassion, that Lena hadn't truly conceived what all this abuse would do.

She lightly ran her fingertips over the remnants of those words on Bel's body, and she was ashamed.

But she locked away the hurt that came with it, told herself to think on it later, when she wasn't warm and content beside him. Right then, as his hand moved up and down her leg and flank, she only wanted to feel good things.

He lay there watching her, and Lena didn't want to break the spell. She had little experience with sweet words whispered across pillows. She almost blushed to think about telling him the things she thought, how she liked the slope of his cheek or that his right eye had a fleck of jade just below the dilated pupil or that he was one of the cleverest people she'd ever met. But she wanted to say these things, somehow felt as though whispers and pillows were the safest place to give them voice.

But did Bel want that? She wasn't sure, so she held her tongue and watched him.

Her skin broke out in gooseflesh at his touch, a pleasant shudder. His fingertips traced up her leg and hip, skimming around the hem of his tunic that she wore. It'd been rucked up around her waist as they slept.

He ran the fabric between his fingers, and Lena silently watched him realize that she wore clothes now where she hadn't when they'd fallen asleep. A small line formed between his brows, and for a moment his gaze shuttered.

Lena held still, wanting to tell him no, she was here, of course she was here, but she continued to hold her tongue. It felt important that he come to understand this himself, that he feel her beneath the shirt, in his bed, beside him.

And then Lena watched him realize that she must have left the bed sometime in the night and donned a shirt, but that she'd come back to him.

When she felt the slight pressure of his hand on her back, she happily moved further into the curve of him.

"Were you cold?" he asked quietly, and Lena felt the vibrations of his voice rumble through his chest into her cheek.

"Mm, when I stoked the fire, yes."

"Can't have that."

He drew his wing more securely around her, like a feathered third arm, and Lena had to wonder if this was what a caterpillar felt like in its chrysalis—safe, ready to transform.

They held each other in the quiet for a long while, only languid fingertips and occasionally exploring lips. Lena could feel the morning growing; even with the rain outside, the light began to swell as the sun rose somewhere overhead, but for once, she didn't want to get up.

"I don't think I've ever been this comfortable," she found herself saying, and she stretched like a cat, making Bel chuckle.

"Feathers have their benefits."

"Yes, many."

She traced a few of those feathers, liked watching the shimmer of the barbs as they eased from bronze to white under her finger.

"You...you don't want to get up and...?"

She took her time in answering, too delighted in touching him to break the spell of their quiet. She traced the line between his pectorals, up the column of his throat to his strong jaw, then circled his lips.

"No," she said. "I don't. Do you?"

"No. I want..."

She saw him swallow, watched the bob of his throat and the line crease between his brows again. She leaned into him, running the tip of her nose along the bridge of his, over his cheek, and kissed the corner of his mouth. He shivered as she bestowed her *ashita*, and when she was done, she pressed her forehead to his.

"What do you want, Bel?"

"You." He clasped her even tighter, almost too tight, and shifted to look into her eyes, bringing her almost entirely underneath him.

"I'm right here."

His eyes flicked between hers. "I want you. For as long as I can have you."

It was Lena's turn to swallow, and her throat tightened as the words sank into her as surely as the rain outside soaked into the mountain.

"Then you'll have me," she said, unwilling to think about what *For as long as I can* meant for them, unwilling to consider what would happen when she left.

He let out a shuddering breath, his gaze turning from pensive to warm again. His hand hooked behind her knee and drew her top leg up over his hip, opening her to him. He slid inside in one fluid move, and Lena gasped at the pleasure of it.

"Bel..." She clutched him close, and he came willingly to her, meeting her mouth in a slow slide.

"I think you're in my heart now, Lena," he said as he slowly began to move.

34

For over a fortnight, Lena woke exactly as she had that first morning, surrounded by Bel. It felt like waking into someone else's life, someone who had or could have anything their heart wanted. Sometimes, when she traced Bel's face with her fingertips in those early hours while she waited for him to wake, she didn't recognize the hand touching him, couldn't quite believe it was her feeling the sensations of his skin and his warmth.

It was their secret, guarded jealously between the two of them. They rarely came down to the kitchen together, though Lena didn't know how subtle the looks they shared over the carving table were, not when Alix and Pol shared looks of their own. Perhaps they didn't kiss in front of Alix and Pol, perhaps they didn't touch each other as they did in the quiet of his chambers, but it wasn't because Lena didn't want to.

No, it just felt too precious, too good to share. That somehow, it needed a little longer before other eyes were upon it.

Even so, they spent almost all their days together, whether in training or quiet afternoons of chess and reading lessons or outside the castle foraging for food and supplies with Pol. And the nights, they spent their nights together always, and it was quickly becoming Lena's favorite time of day. She hadn't tired yet of slipping from her room to his, watching that warm, pleased grin break across Bel's face at the sight of her. It was her favorite thing in a long string of good, happy things.

They had agreed to take it a day at a time, to enjoy what they had while they had it, but Lena couldn't help looking forward to the next day and the next when she knew they'd be filled with Bel. It had begun to feel interminable, waiting for Alix to yawn wide and retire too so that Lena could follow Bel up. Sometimes they ate dinner together, sharing a goblet of one of Pol's concoctions and reading from his vast, eclectic library. Lena had been delighted to find that Bel was an excellent bard, reciting poetry like a natural, and he could even sing, his deep tenor a sound that did wonderful and terrible things to her.

Sometimes it was late, and they only had time for quick hands and mouths. And others, there was no time or energy for anything at all before falling into bed, but sleeping beside him, without sex or talk, was plenty for Lena. She was never cold in the night with him, never looking for a better spot to burrow further into the bed. But more, she was content to lay beside him.

Really, she was content to do anything with him. It was good that Bel was relatively judicious, since he could talk her into most anything. Once it had been a drinking game that involved rhymes—she didn't totally remember it, only that she'd lost soundly—another challenging her not to laugh while he tickled and caressed her with his wings from head to toe—she'd laughed until she'd cried then laughed even more.

She felt as though she could deny him, them, nothing.

Which was probably how Lena found herself quite literally rolling in the hay with him one day.

The warmth and quiet of the stables provided a haven for them, and once the horses had been lulled into a doze after a good brushing, it'd been too much to resist, stealing a few moments together.

They fumbled with their laces and buckles before Lena muttered, "Fuck it," and drew him to her with one pant leg still encasing her leg and one boot dangling precariously from her foot. Bel groaned in happiness and moved; they'd gotten much less done on him, and the fabric of his trous rubbed against her inner thighs, creating a delicious counter-sensation.

"Lena…"

"Yes, yes, just like that!"

"I don't think I'll last—"

"Doesn't matter, doesn't—just—yes!"

Bel flicked his finger just where she needed him; he'd been a quick study in what made her quiver, what made her burn slowly, and what made her completely combust. He twisted his hips next and Lena cried out—louder even than the squeak of the stable door swinging open.

They were too far away from the door for the cold gush of air to reach them, but Lena felt a chill run down her spine when she met Alix's eyes.

"Oh fu-uck!" the squire squawked.

"Alix!"

"Oof," Bel grunted when Lena's elbow caught him in the gut as she scrambled underneath him—to do what she didn't know.

"Uh, I, well—" Alix flapped her hands, her cheeks burning red with mortification. But her lips also twitched in amusement. "I'll leave you to it!" And she fled just as quick as she'd come.

Alix took all the air and warmth with her; Lena and Bel stayed perfectly still, the shock of being caught keeping them enthralled. Lena told herself to relax, or at least decide if she was trying to crawl out from under Bel or not, but her body was stiff and locked into place.

Goddess, what would she tell Alix?

They had to tell Alix and Pol at some point, but to be caught so, it was…

Well, Lena's own cheeks were beginning to burn red too.

Little tremors ran up and down Lena's body, and it took her a moment to realize what it was. Above her, Bel shook with trying to hold in his laughter, biting his cheek, and his eyes danced with mirth. His stomach made teasing little points of contact with each chuckle, and his wings even shook and gave a happy flap.

"It isn't funny, it's mortifying!" she grumbled, though she was fighting her own begrudging smile, watching him.

He began to laugh in earnest then, and Lena slapped at his shoulder. Not too hard, but enough to get her point across.

Bel settled down on his elbow so that he could easily run his nose up and down hers to her ear in a short *ashita*.

"I hate to tell you this, but I don't know that this was a great secret."

Lena sighed. "I know, but I'm still embarrassed. I certainly wouldn't want to walk in on her." Her eyes went wide. "Not that she's old enough for that!"

Bel cocked an eyebrow at her. "Haven't you noticed how much she talks about that Violet girl from town?"

"*What?*" came out more as a screech than a word. "She's too young!"

Bel had another fit of laughter, and Lena let him. She was too busy thinking about what Alix had gotten up to in town. She was only fifteen! Lena had a hard time thinking of the skinny Alix as an adult. Not with her exuberance and bouncing, wild hair. She was Alix, her squire, her...

Goddess, she'd need to talk to Alix about this. Lena's cheeks flamed red again.

She sighed. "Maybe we should..." Lena shifted under Bel, drawing her own elbows up to lean forward.

"Lena, wait." Bel eased some of his weight onto her, and Lena fell back into the hay. When she looked up at him, the laughter was gone from his eyes, and he slowly caressed her inner thigh. "Not yet. Please..."

Those eyes of his flicked between hers, searching, asking.

She took a deep breath and tried to swallow her embarrassment. She'd be embarrassed and worry over what to tell Alix later.

Lena ran her fingers through Bel's hair, and the curls wrapped around her knuckles. She had to have this time with him, take all she could get.

She leaned up to kiss him, bringing him back down to her.

Because she could deny him nothing.

———◆———

It was later in the afternoon, much later, later than she'd intended, when Lena found Alix in one of her favorite nooks, up high in the turret of the north tower. She was curled up in the window seat of a broad set of bay windows, a nest of blankets and pillows spread out around her on the sagging seat cushion.

What surprised Lena most was the heavy book propped on her lap, about the size of Alix's whole torso. It wasn't like Alix to read in the afternoons, or voluntarily, and, as she called it, *"waste my valuable time."* She supposed the book must be Bel's, for Lena hadn't hauled anything so big up the mountain with them.

Alix looked up at the creak of Lena's footsteps along the old floorboards. She offered a light smile and shifted her feet so Lena could sit down facing her.

A brief silence stretched between them, and Lena couldn't help but think Alix seemed at her most feline then, curled up as she was in a thin beam of light, surrounded by soft blankets, eyes watchful and slowly blinking, content to wait, and all with an underlying hint of smugness.

"What are you reading?" Lena asked, trying not to wring or knead her hands.

With a heavy *slap*, Alix closed the book and read the cover. "*The Writings of Carrick Fleetwing, Royal Historian to His Highness King Maddok II Adiiron—An Account of Avian Lore and History, Volume Two.* This Carrick guy really likes his proper nouns."

Lena laughed, feeling a little of the tension drain from her shoulders. Alix was joking with her, and she hadn't missed that sharp, catlike grin on her face. She wasn't about to get an argument from Alix.

Not that she really thought she would, but this was serious for Lena, to come to someone as important as Alix with this new, delicate, beautiful thing blooming between her and Bel. They would be asking her to keep its secret, to watch over it, and Lena understood what it was she asked of Alix. Really, it was no more or less than the girl had been asked of before, but Lena keenly felt the girl's age then, the apples of her cheeks rosy, her eyes glittering as she waited for Lena to come out and say it.

"And why'd you choose that monster?" she said instead.

Alix shrugged. "I got through volume one. Thought I might as well continue. And avian history is actually pretty interesting. The Adiirons have just taken over in volume two—that's the current royal family, yeah? King Dar..." Alix rolled her wrist, the name not coming to her.

"Dartegn Adiiron, yes," Lena murmured. "Wait—you already finished volume one? When did that happen?"

Alix shrugged again, avoiding Lena's eyes as she flushed. "About a week ago. Bel started me on it a while back, when your leg still hurt."

"He got you to read all that?"

"Mm. He's a good teacher. Patient." She stuck the tip of her tongue out a Lena. "And I like his books."

Alix, liking books? Lena almost fainted.

"Alix, that's wonderful!"

Alix blushed harder at Lena's choked voice and waved away her words. "Figured you'd be happy."

"I am happy." Lena smiled and, drawing in a fortifying breath, she laid her hand over Alix's bent knee. "I'm so happy, Alix."

The sharp jade of Alix's eyes almost seemed to change color, darkening infinitesimally as she considered Lena's smiling face.

"Are you?"

"Yes."

"You're not just...bored?"

She frowned. "No, Alix. I…I like Bel."

"Do you love him?"

Lena's mouth opened to answer; she could feel the weight of the words, heavy on the back of her tongue, but they slid back down her throat. She hesitated, and she hated that she did, but in truth, she wasn't sure.

She couldn't help picking at her cuticles as she said, "I care for him, so, so much. He's wonderful, Alix."

And it was the truth. Lena loved every minute she spent with Bel, loved being near him and touching him and teasing him and playing with him…she just didn't know if that meant she loved him or, perhaps more importantly, if she could afford to love him.

Alix said nothing about Lena's hesitation, only leaned forward so she could grasp her hand.

"Then good. I've been waiting for you to be happy for a long time."

"I'm happy with him. You have to take happiness where and when you can."

Alix looked into her eyes again before nodding. If anyone knew the truth of this, it was Alix, an orphan of the streets. No matter how her own career turned out, Lena would never stop thanking the goddess for putting her in Alix's path. The thought of Alix's state that day, her dirt-crusted body and matted hair, had Lena pulling the girl into her arms in a rare burst of affection.

Perhaps it was because she'd been sharing affection with Bel for weeks now, but Lena didn't feel as stiff as she might have months ago, taking Alix into her arms. And it shamed her that she once would've been. Her mother was cold, and Lena had never wanted to be like that.

Alix let her have this for a moment before groaning loudly and with relish. She squirmed away to the other side of the seat and huffed, fluffing her curls.

"So does this mean you two will stop sneaking around? It's been downright painful to watch. Pol and I've got a bet going, you know. About where and when you'd finally be found out." That feline smile returned, and Lena wouldn't have been surprised to see a bird feather poking out from those sharp teeth. "I won the pot."

Lena scoffed in righteous indignation before throwing a pillow at Alix's head. By the time they were done with their fighting and fits of giggles, pillows were strewn across the tower room and feathers had gone flying, never to find their way back into the casings.

Yes, if she could spend her days like this, laughing with Alix, being with Bel, Lena would be happy. More than happy. A year was a long time, and she had more than that left. She would make the most of it, take it all greedily. Until then, there wasn't a world off this mountain, only the old stones of Finhöln where, for once, Lena was happy.

35

Bel had known what it was to have a long series of bad days. He knew even better what it was to have a long string of boring days, of days that blurred into a colorless swathe that cut across his life. What Bel hadn't known, not for over ten years, was what it could be like to be happy—not just for a day, or for two, but for many, one after the other. He was beginning to collect them like shells on the beach, beginning to pick favorites and consider what he liked about each.

Of course, what he liked best about each and every one of them was her. Sometimes it was for a color or taste or sound, sometimes for a texture. They were growing in number, beginning to overflow his hands.

Bel watched as his fingers slid between Lena's, dipping to run over the webs, tracing knuckles and dimples and scars and freckles. And as his hands moved one way, hers mirrored them, tracing the lines of his palm while he explored her fingertips. The small, soft movements were entrancing, and Bel liked watching their hands meet, tangle, then come apart for a new angle.

They had begun this small dance of fingers perhaps an hour ago, but it felt longer and shorter all at once. They'd begun the day planning to go foraging; Pol wanted to make a berry pie and with the slightly warmer temperatures, he was sure there were some early bloomers. Bel thought it'd be a sour pie, but Lena had said they'd look for firewood and perhaps any easy game. When Pol had winked at him over Lena's shoulder, he'd realized the berries weren't the point.

He and Lena had walked a few trails, which were becoming more familiar to Bel the more he left the castle with her. As the sun crested overhead in a sky that seemed dizzyingly big and blue, they'd found a place to watch the world for a while in a hollow between two great exposed roots of a tall spruce tree.

The ground was cold, had barely warmed from frozen in the time he'd sat there, but Bel didn't mind. He had Lena laid out between his legs, her back pressed to his chest, and her head cradled in the curve of his shoulder.

What would make this day one of Bel's favorites wasn't the feel of her skin or the hue of her eyes in the clear day, but the ease with which they'd come together. Without real discussion, they'd decided on the place, she'd drawn close, and they'd sat here ever since, easy with each other.

Lena shifted a little, and Bel drew his legs up to bracket her hips. He rocked them back and forth, and Lena made a sound suspiciously like a giggle.

It was heady for Bel, to inhabit a body that wasn't just a broken thing, a site of violence and abuse. With Lena, holding her, being with her, he and his body could give and receive happiness, comfort, pleasure. It was more than Bel had ever dreamed he'd find, and it was a gift to have such a body.

Running his nose along the part of her hair, Bel inhaled and let out a happy sigh.

"From up here, not covered in so much snow, it's actually kind of beautiful," said Lena.

Bel lifted his head to look over the steep berm they sat atop. Far down the slope, the craggy walls of Finhöln broke up the carpet of trees and branches. Some of the snow had melted away under the slightly warming sun, revealing the high arches of the columns ribbing the great hall and the delicately tiled turret towers in the north, south, and west corners.

"Starting to grow fond of the old beast?"

"I'd be pretty fond of anything that kept all that snow out. But they don't make castles like this anymore."

"What are they like then?"

Lena shrugged, making their leathers creak as they rubbed together. "More decorative, I suppose. Less sturdy looking."

"So Finhöln is the work nag of human castles?"

Lena rolled her eyes, but she laughed, and that's what counted to Bel.

"Most of them today are styled after the royal palace. Large basilica instead of a great hall. Lots of columns, different stone. You don't see turret towers like that anymore, either. Though, Lindenfaire does have a few."

"Lindenfaire—your parents' school?"

"Mm. It's technically a castle in the new style. My father had many of the original statues and fountains restored, and for the gardens…"

Bel listened to the pleasant lilt of her voice, the way she rolled some sounds and popped others. She captured the essence of her family's home for him, and he could easily imagine the blond limestone covered in wisteria and ivy, the hills beyond combed into neat vineyards. He imagined the basilica painted in all the colors from the stained-glass windows and the blue plating and tiles that decorated the roof. But mostly, he liked to imagine Lena, smaller but just as fierce, going through her forms with other cadets and besting them all.

"I'd like to see it someday," he said, not for the castle but for the home she described.

Lena swallowed before saying, "Perhaps you will."

She shifted again, but not away, and Bel welcomed her deeper into his arms. Lena twisted her head towards him and kissed the underside of his chin.

"If you could go anywhere, right now, where would you go?"

He raised his eyebrows at her question. It came out of her a little hurried, but Bel took his time answering.

"Part of me would want to go to Aeriand. Just the sight of it would be enough. Otherwise, the eastern sea. My...guardian brought me shells from there but I haven't seen it myself."

"I hadn't even thought of the eastern sea. It's just something I know is there, but it's hard to imagine, so far away."

"They say sirens still haunt those waters."

She cocked one of her eyebrows at him.

Bel cleared his throat. "Eamon said that there are wide beaches below cliffs so white they look like bone. Birds with long legs, like sticks, walk in the shallows."

"It sounds beautiful," Lena agreed.

"Where would you go?"

"Probably the hot lakes at Vasalia."

"Hot lakes?"

"Yes, they're heated from the earth. Whole lakes, some underground. It's like soaking in a hot bath but the water never cools."

Bel groaned his appreciation. "I think yours is better."

Lena laughed. "Well, if we go, could you get these wet?" She ran her finger along the arch of his right wing.

"Of course," he said, pretending offense. "That's what the oil is for."

A lovely flush bloomed across Lena's cheeks at the mention of oiling his feathers, and he grinned before kissing the color. She'd done it for him again just a few days ago, but this time there had been no shyness, no pulling away—he'd enjoyed not only the sensation of her hands coaxing the oil over his feathers but also her skin pressed to his back, caressing wherever she could.

"I'd like to go there with you," he said.

"I'd like that very much." She reached a hand back to trace the point of his ear before catching a curl of hair between her fingers.

"Where else would we go?"

She made a humming sound as she thought. "Well, where would you want to go?"

"Hm, the Wailing Cliffs perhaps." He'd read human texts about the sheer cliffs leagues south along the sea, where the wind was so gusty that a person could step off the edge and the wind would catch them and buffet them back onto the cliff. When he'd read about the winds, he'd let himself fantasize about flying again, even if it was just catching a mighty updraft.

Lena smiled. "You'd like them," she agreed. "I'd probably never get you to come back down."

They spent another hour like that, talking about where they would go if they could leave Finhöln that very moment. If they'd had a map before them, with all the places they would go marked with hashes, there'd be little topography left to see.

"And what would we do afterwards?" Bel asked. He tightened his arms from where they'd been laying loosely in her lap. "What would you want to do—if you weren't a knight?"

Lena was quiet so long that Bel had to stop himself from fidgeting, from trying to draw the words from the air and cramming them back into his mouth.

"I honestly don't know," she said softly. "It's never been something I'd ever considered."

Nor been allowed to consider, he thought, but he didn't say so aloud. Bel didn't know too much about her parents but neither did he think much of them, and it wasn't because they were celebrated knights who'd led campaigns against the avians.

"Well," he said, trying to push the words past his dry throat. "Do all your human cities have mayors like Longbourne? You would make a fine mayor."

Lena blinked up at him. "Truly?"

"You run Finhöln with an iron fist. Why not somewhere else?"

She laughed at that, and he laughed with her, curling himself around her. Sometimes he wanted to meld them together, to see how close he could get to her. Sometimes he wanted to be one being with her, not just in sex but in all ways.

"But you would be, Lena," he whispered into her ear. "Really. Truly. And I'd be proud to see it."

She smiled wide. "Well, I..." Her words trailed off with her thoughts. Her spine stiffened and she leaned forward.

"What is it?"

"Look."

She pointed, but he looked at her face, draining of color, first. His heart began beating a fast rhythm, and his limbs flushed with warmth, preparing for a fight.

Finally, he caught sight of what she'd seen. A crimson banner moved within the walls of Finhöln, a stark contrast to the greens and grays around it. Bel's sharp eyes picked out human riders atop horses. Many of them, at least twenty, circling inside the bailey.

There was something familiar about the banner, but from so far away, Bel couldn't place it.

Lena jumped to her feet and craned her neck, balancing on the edge of the berm as if this would allow her to see further. Bel followed her up, slower, a sudden reluctance weighing him down. He didn't want to leave his spot, instead wanted to draw her back into him; he'd sit back against the tree, turn their faces away, and let the roots swallow them.

She was perfectly still when he came up beside her, only a slight breeze lifting her hair. He touched a hand to the small of her back, ensuring she wouldn't lose her footing on the soft earth of the berm.

Lena didn't pull away from him, but she didn't relax back into his touch the way Bel had become so used to.

"We have to get back."

"Who is it?"

For the first time since she'd spotted the riders, Lena looked up at him, but it was a fleeting glance, her eyes there and gone again.

"They carry the crown prince's standard."

For a moment, Bel's ears snapped with the sound of a crackling fire and the hiss of melting wax. He could see it in his mind's eye so clearly, how the paper of this prince's letter curled in on itself as it burned away to ashes.

"We have to get back," she said again, but it was not to him—to the forest perhaps.

She began down the slope of the berm, but she kept turning her head toward the castle, watching as the horses and men moved like an angry hive of bees under the crimson standard.

And Bel followed her, though his feet felt leaden, though he wanted to stay there and let the roots swallow him, even if Lena wasn't in his arms. Nothing good would come of this, he already knew. But Bel could do nothing but follow her down the mountain to watch it happen.

***

Alix met them when they were almost back to the castle, her hot breaths puffing around her like clouds as she pounded uphill to them. She didn't stop until she had Lena's shoulders clutched in her small hands, and she didn't stop for breath before launching into her news.

"Prince Arion is here and says he's here to see you and I think he wants you to come back with him and he's brought half his guard and they're already looking all over the castle and are looking for you and Bel and and and—"

"Breathe, Alix," said Lena.

Alix gasped for air as Lena turned to Bel. He tried not to react or recoil from the desolate look in her eyes. An hour ago, they had been so warm, so full of light. Now she looked at him as if from a far distance, resignation carving lines around her mouth.

"You have to get back to your room. Don't let them see you. I'll keep them in the bailey as long as I can."

Bel had barely nodded before Lena was urging Alix back downhill, their boots scraping against rock and dirt and moss. He watched them go until they'd disappeared into the thin mist and trees.

He stood there longer still, listening as the silent forest slowly came back to life. Birds started to twitter, and from the corner of his eye, he saw a doe and last year's fawn walk through the heavy brush.

The forest had gone quiet around him, accepted him instead as one of its own. How easy it would be to melt into it, to fade with the mist. The castle was overrun with humans, and in the chaos of conflicting stories, he wouldn't be missed for some time.

But the idea of running this time sat sour on Bel's tongue, and most of him rebelled at the thought of leaving her. If a prisoner couldn't be found, the warden would pay.

Bel drew in a long breath of cold mountain air, tasting the crispness, the tang of pine, for he knew it would be some time before he had good brown soil beneath his feet and smelled the forest again.

He picked his way down the mountain to Finhöln, taking a different route than Lena and Alix had.

⸺⸳⸳◆⸳⸳⸺

Bel didn't return to his room as Lena said.

It would've been the safest thing to do, the wisest, but he felt compelled to see these humans before they saw him, to see the man who would write Lena such a letter. As if a cord connected him to her, his feet drew him closer to the bailey, but Bel maintained some sense of self-preservation. He ascended a narrow set of stairs near the west tower, winding his way through the castle to a small arrowslit window looking down into the bailey. The angle of the window, set into the deep stone of the wall, was perfect for raining arrows down on enemies—or spying on the bailey.

He had to wonder, if they didn't make castles like this anymore, how did the humans do all their spying?

The horses and men had gathered together in a calmer mass than the last time Bel had seen them, grouped near the shallow steps leading to the doors of the great hall. A semicircle of them framed a lone man in gleaming armor emblazoned with the midday sun.

It wasn't the armor or the clean, graceful face or his position at the center of his men that told Bel this man was Arion. It wasn't even his faint likeness to his father, Artemian, whom Bel had only seen once but whose face was etched across his mind, like a sigil stamped on the malleable metal of a coin, the face of his pain and anger and despair.

No, it was much more visceral, the way the eye was drawn to him and him alone amongst so many men. It was there, in the straight cut of his shoulders and the way the others looked to him.

It was the same way Maddok had stood, had drawn the gaze of all those around him, commanding the eye to him.

Bel hated him for it.

And he loathed him more for the hand he had on Lena's shoulder.

She stood stiff before him, back straight, fists loose, but Bel couldn't see her face.

The prince smiled and his hand moved. It was an innocent enough grip, probably looked like a comrade's greeting to his guards, but what Bel could see that they couldn't was how he caressed Lena's neck in small moves of his thumb, as if he had to feel her skin in some way.

Bel hated him for it, hated that he, even now, had the same longing.

"It's good to see you, Lena," the prince said.

"Has something happened?"

The prince's smile was wide and full of blue-white teeth. "I'd say so. I've done as much as I can for now, but I'll need you to see it all the way through."

"What are you talking about?"

That smile froze on the prince's face, and a vicious pleasure coursed through Bel, even over the din of his hammering heart.

"Lena, I sent for you."

"No, you sent me away," she said, barely loud enough for Bel to hear.

"No—" He shook his head. "No, that isn't..."

"You did. For my *safety*," she hissed, spitting the last word.

"I can't do anything about that, Lena. But it was the right thing to do. The campaign..." He gave his head one fierce shake. "But that's not why I'm here. I would've come sooner—maybe I should have—but I thought you would come back."

"Come back? Why would I?"

A frown marred the prince's golden face. "Lena, don't you want justice? To set this whole travesty to right?"

"What do you mean?"

"I've appealed your case—did it as soon as I heard of it. It's back in the courts now. I wrote to you about this months ago. I knew it would take time to get to you, for you to make the journey back, but you still didn't come. So I..."

"So you came here," she finished.

He took a breath, as if fortifying himself, then a step closer, into her space, and Bel's back teeth groaned as he ground them together. The prince spoke low, presumably so only she could hear, but the guards were so close that there was no true privacy. Could he not see how the guards' shifting eyes took in Lena with judgement? Could he not see how tense she'd grown under their suspicious gazes?

"Why didn't you come back, Lena?"

"I never got your letter."

Bel's tongue stuck to the roof of his mouth, whatever moisture there'd been evaporating as he remembered that damn letter, remembered the words themselves that had called Lena back home. He'd gotten what he wanted—more time, and most importantly, time with her. But at what cost?

Hell, how stupid he'd been.

Lena ground the heel of her boot into the ground before she said, "Your Highness, you honor me by coming, but you shouldn't have. The king himself sentenced me. I have to see it through."

Arion shook his head fiercely, indignation burning bright in his eyes. And damn it, Bel hated that they shared in that, an indignation that Lena should ever be sentenced to anything.

"We both know it was asinine. There've been rumors about Balderak for years."

"It was a noble's word against mine, Arion." She shifted again after saying the prince's name when many sets of eyes cut to her.

He smiled then. "I've had a talk with Lorde Merle. It seems that his memory of that night is improving. He says he might remember your squire coming to him with several papers."

Lena held very still, and it was a long moment before she said carefully, "I don't want to put my fate in the hands of someone who can be bought."

But Arion smiled again, waving away Lena's concern. He grew more animated as he talked of his schemes. "I wouldn't have gotten an appeal with just Merle. You're to go to the courts, Lena. It should've gone there in the first place, but tensions were high. And, after approaching a few of the women who you helped, some would be willing to launch formal complaints. You'll have a fair trial with witnesses this time. I won't rest until this is overturned."

"You...want me to come back with you."

"I want you to come *home*."

"When?" she said in almost a whisper.

"Tomorrow," he said with a grin, as if they shared a joke between them, "if you can manage it."

Lena said nothing to that, but Bel held his breath for it, willed her to say *something* as his heart beat, in his ears, his chest, even in his gut. He didn't know if he'd hear her reply over the pounding, the rush of blood that told him to run—away—down to her—to—

"You must be hungry from the climb up the mountain," she said finally, and Bel could read nothing from her tone. "I'll see what Pol in the kitchen can put together."

And then she turned on her heel, passing beneath the window. Then she was out of sight, and Bel eased back from his vantage point. He couldn't feel his fingertips, numb as they were, but not from cold. His heart continued to drum in his chest, riding the knife's edge between agitation and panic.

If he could go back, would he tell Alix to give Lena that damn letter? If he knew it would bring the human prince here, would he have taken his chances and let Lena decide?

He didn't know, and it didn't matter anyway.

He could hear the echo of many human feet tromping through the castle as they made their way to the kitchen, flooding into Finhöln like the invading force they were, and he knew then that his time was up.

He'd lost his gamble.

36

Finhöln wasn't meant for so many people. That became painfully apparent within the first hour of Arion's arrival. Long into the night, the castle groaned and creaked with the many new feet trampling her worn floorboards and flagstones, and Lena had to wonder if the old rafters would just give out with all the armored bodies tramping up and down the different levels, staircases, and corridors.

In the morning, Lena squeezed past two guards heading up as she went down into the kitchen. She avoided their eyes. They were new faces, hadn't known her on campaign, but it was hard to look at the clean lines of their armor, the prince's standard emblazoned across the cuirasses, and not feel shabby in her worn leather. She'd done her best the night before to put herself in order, polishing her boots, brushing out her trous, and this morning, for the first time in weeks, she'd neatly plaited and coiled her hair.

Edging past the prince's soldiers, Lena heard the commotion long before she made it to the kitchen, the layered sounds of too many people in too small a space echoing up the stairs.

The kitchen glowed a warm amber as always, but the shadows of over half a dozen bodies cut the light, making it darker than it usually was in the mornings. The door to the kitchen gardens was open, guards heading in and out, and a chill lingered along the ground as cold morning air crept in. The half-dozen guards in the kitchen tried to move in a concerted way, but the space was new to them and confining, and as they went to see to duties, carry supplies, or grab a meal from a dwindling spread laid out on the sideboard, they kept knocking into each other. They almost looked like an ant colony, but ants were more organized.

From his place at the carving table, Captain Joran pored over something with his lieutenant, occasionally barking orders, as Arion sat beside him, eating a plate of sausage, eggs, and toast.

When he saw her, Arion waved her over. Lena weaved around the assembled guards, catching sight of Pol near the hearth. He was hunched into himself as he chopped something, eyes pointedly watching what he did with the sharp knife, as two guards crowded around him, speaking loudly but not quite shouting.

"I'd suggest you get breakfast," said Arion, following her gaze. "But there doesn't seem to be much left. I don't think the cook was prepared."

Captain Joran turned from the woman he was speaking with to regard Lena. She tried to stave off the shudder that wanted to run down her back. She had respected this man, had gladly served under him in her time with Arion's guard even if he'd vocally disapproved of their relationship, but there was no fairness or understanding in his gaze now. She'd felt his censure before, but sharing the prince's bed wasn't a crime —not like attacking one's liege lord.

What would those eyes of his, sharp and blue like a knife blade, look like if he knew she'd shared an avian's bed?

It didn't bear thinking about.

Lena averted her eyes first, trying to keep the blush at bay. She hadn't allowed herself to think of Bel since the new arrivals had come. If she did, a sucking sensation assaulted her gut, as if she could be swallowed from the inside out. If she thought of him, she would think of how he had looked, gazing down the mountain at human soldiers, at the prince whose father kept him in this place. She would think of how last night was the first in almost two months that she'd spent in her own bed, alone.

Joran cleared his throat, bringing Lena's thoughts round again.

"You speak to him," he said with that deep, reverberating voice of his. It was a voice that could be heard even over the clash and clatter of battle, one that echoed down through the ears into the very bones and could inspire and terrify all at once. "The cook is being obstinate."

"Pol?"

"Is that his name? He hasn't said. We're trying to get a second round of food and establish mealtimes, but he won't speak."

"He's deaf."

"Ah." Joran cleared his throat. "Can you communicate with him?"

"Yes, he has his own hand language. His brother can speak it too."

"The derelict steward. Yes, we've sent someone to collect him. For now, talk with the cook. Get him to understand that we'll need to establish a meal schedule. I also want a thorough report on the stores and how often he goes to town for supplies." With that, Joran turned back to the woman he'd been speaking with, and they bent over a large parchment— plans of Finhöln, she realized.

Arion caught her gaze again with a crooked grin. He nodded slightly at Joran over his shoulder and rolled his eyes.

Lena forced a neutral smile in return then hurried over to Pol.

The cook was red in the face, his body angled away from the guards surrounding him.

"Did you hear me?" said one.

"Goddess, he's useless."

"You deaf?"

"Yes, he is," Lena said.

The guards jumped, having the decency to look ashamed.

For his part, Pol threw her a relieved look and waved her closer.

Never been happier to be deaf, he signed.

I am sorry for them. They did not know to speak with their hands. They did not ask.

Lena winced. *I am sorry.*

Pol patted her forearm. *Do not be sorry. You asked on your first day.* His look turned sour. *Could have had the good manners to bring their own food. Where will I find the food to feed all of them?*

The captain—she pointed out Joran to Pol—*wants to get a schedule made for them. I will help you speak with him. Perhaps we can suggest the knights eat in town.*

Or send them hunting. That should keep them busy. Pol made his huffing laugh.

Lena agreed and accepted the buttered toast Pol had saved for her. He'd even scraped a thick layer of his raspberry preserves she so liked over it.

Licking the butter and jam from her fingers, Lena led Pol back to the carving table, leaving the grumbling soldiers to fend for themselves.

Joran looked between the two of them. "You can speak with him?"

"Yes, sir."

Joran nodded before bringing two fingers to his lips and emitting a harsh whistle. The noise of the kitchen died except for the sound of Arion cutting into a sausage. The prince hadn't looked up or even flinched at the shrill sound, just continued like a rock in a river, letting the commotion flow around him. He'd always had that skill, and Lena supposed it was necessary for a prince, when the whole kingdom flowed around him constantly.

"Listen up!" the captain barked. "Those of you who've been fed, head to your posts. Those who haven't, stick to rations and come back in an hour. We'll have meals figured out by then. Dismissed!"

With minimal grumbling, the kitchen began to clear out, the unfed knights shooting Lena and Pol sneers and frowns on their way. They were too well trained to say anything, or at least had a sense of self-preservation with the captain standing right there, but Lena could feel their resentment prickling along the back of her neck.

Turning on his heel, Joran faced Lena and Pol and, with a flick of his wrist, indicated that Lena should translate. He set about explaining what they would need, a fairly standard soldier's affair, and set the times of day Pol would need to have meals ready for them, starting today with the midday meal.

As Pol looked between Joran's mouth and Lena's hands, his lips continued to thin.

"We'll be having food sent up from the town soon, but for now, he'll need to make do," said Joran in conclusion. The captain then dismissed them with a nod before turning back to his map.

Lena held in her wince. *He will have food sent from Longbourne, but you will have to make do today.*

Pol huffed. *I am not an army cook. How does he think I will feed all of them again in a few hours?*

Lena had no answers for him. *I am sorry, Pol. I will send Alix to you when I find her, and if I can, I will help too.* Alix had been mysteriously absent yesterday, and when Lena checked her room that morning, it'd been empty, the bed unlined and cold. It wasn't like Alix to stay out from underfoot.

Very well. Pol jerked his hand in a way that Lena thought was his way of grumbling. *But keep them out of the good honey and the rum.*

Lena agreed, though she knew it was probably a fool's errand; soldiers were a hungry lot and they could get crafty when it came to sussing out food.

When Pol returned to his chopping, Lena approached the captain.

"Sir, when you told the guards to head to their posts, what did you mean?"

"They're starting repairs," said Joran without looking up.

"Repairs, sir?"

"The castle is falling down around us. This isn't a proper prison." He did look up then, planting his palms on the table. "It needs to get put back in order if it's to remain in use. Repairs must be made, and protocols must be reinstated."

"It eats away at him," said Arion as he put his fork down, "when he sees something that needs fixing."

Lena cleared her throat and folded her hands in front of her on the table, avoiding Arion's joke and his smile. "I see."

"I saw the improvements you did to the hall roof, and I reckon you've done the best you could on your own with your slip of a squire.

But more will need to be done to get this place in order. It's a prison with a hole in one of its walls!"

She'd thought so too at her first sight of the castle, but hearing Joran say it made her strangely irritated. Derelict as it may have been as a prison, Finhöln had kept them warm and safe through winter. She didn't like Joran's disdain, a man who'd only spent a night under its roof.

"He wants to stay," explained Arion with a sigh.

"With a handful of knights, yes. I know this is important to you, Highness—" it was probably from years of training that Joran's eyes didn't immediately cut to Lena, but she knew the implication regardless "—but this is important too. We're talking about a prisoner who does sensitive work. He can't be allowed to escape, not with everything he knows. And what prisoner wouldn't escape with all the opportunities around him?"

Lena tried to keep the grimace from creasing her face. She knew Bel's days under a warden and squire had been bad in their own right, but what would his life be like under Joran and a half dozen elite knights? She didn't think Joran would beat him, he wasn't a cruel man, but Lena knew firsthand that he could make life hell in other ways.

She didn't know all the details, but Joran had helped get Lena reassigned and away from Arion. Why she didn't know—perhaps simply because Joran was a man who lived by the rules, and she'd broken them with Arion. She supposed she should've expected him to punish her for it, just like it was no surprise now that he saw Finhöln crumbling and demanded to fix it.

"He'll need to be confined, no more of this free range of the castle—especially not while repairs are underway," said Joran. "Which means he'll need to be guarded around the clock, in shifts. I'll need knights for that."

"He doesn't need to be guarded," argued Lena, careful not to say Bel's name and sound familiar. "I mean, he hasn't in the time I've been here, nor with the other wardens. His crippled wing has seen to that." The words were like ashes in her mouth, but she forced them out.

The captain considered her for a long moment before he said, "Be that as it may, we can't take that chance. Not with the work he has yet to do."

She watched as a look passed between the prince and his captain.

"It could take weeks to do the repairs," said Arion. "And there's no telling how long he still has left on what my father's sent him."

"Another reason to stay. I will keep him on a work schedule."

"We can't delay for so long. Time is of the essence."

"Highness, you know how long the courts can take. Besides, I'm not asking you to delay for more than a few days. I ask that I stay behind with a few choice knights. Five should be sufficient."

A little thrill of shock went through Lena at their discussion—for some reason, Lena hadn't pictured herself truly leaving, and not as soon as a few days. When Arion had joked yesterday that he wanted to leave tomorrow, she'd taken it for what it was, a playful way to try and give her hope. He'd joked in such a way before and he would again, so Lena hadn't thought to start packing her bags.

But now, sitting across from him, Lena saw the determined line of his jaw as the prince stared down his captain. Arion wanted to save her from all this, and Lena knew that when he had a cause, something to fight for, Arion could be a force of nature. It was one of the many reasons she'd grown feelings for him, but she never wanted to be his cause. She had been once before, and the memory still stung.

Did she want to clear her name and see justice done for the women Balderak had abused? Of course she did. But those desires had been... muted, somewhat, in the haze of happiness enveloping Lena these past months.

Now, it seemed she'd have it whether she was ready or not, and she felt as though she should be guilty for not appreciating all Arion had done and would do for her.

But Bel...she would be leaving Bel. Not only leaving him, but abandoning him to a true prison sentence, confined to his rooms by a taskmaster. She knew it could be worse, knew that Bel had seen his share of monstrous wardens, but it still gutted Lena to think of him cooped up in his rooms, working on those papers day in and day out. And what happened when he finished? What happened when the king ran out of documents, of a use for him?

Goddess, she did feel guilty then, but not for her lack of gratitude. She'd brought Arion here, and Joran by extension, and she'd ruined everything for Bel.

He should have run. When she saw those banners from up the mountain, she should have pushed him into the forest and told him not to look back.

Lena picked at her cuticles until they bled while Arion and Joran continued to argue the point until, finally, the prince sighed and nodded.

"All right. I concede." He peered over at the plans Joran had found of Finhöln. "Goddess knows this place could use the work. How long do you think it'll take?"

"If we can find a mason or two in town, sooner than summer."

"Very well. Do what you must. In the meantime, we'll return to Highclere to see to Lena's case. I'll also be putting in a word with my father about the wardenship. He'll want to send someone up and relieve you, but I want to convince him to send you down with the prisoner. I never understood the logic of keeping someone so important in a place like this."

"Important?" Lena echoed, attention snapping back into place like a reset bone—painfully, suddenly, and with a suppressed shudder.

Arion nodded. "Whoever heard of keeping royalty in a crumbling castle? He'd be more use in the capital—not to mention we'd be able to keep a better eye on him."

"R-royalty?" she croaked.

"Yes." He frowned, taking in her rapidly paling face. "Didn't your orders include information on the prisoner?"

"No. I only learned there was the one when I arrived."

Arion barked a humorless laugh. "Good goddess, what is my father up to here? Not even telling the warden that we've had an Adiiron for over a decade."

Adiiron. She tried to keep the shock from her face, but she felt it move through the rest of her, snapping her spine straight, tensing her limbs, and making a pit of dread open up in the bottom of her stomach. The name of the avian royal family rang in her ears as loudly as if she stood next to a clanging bell. All this time, Bel was a...

Mistaking the reason for her shock, Arion nodded again, this time grimly. "Arubel Adiiron, younger brother of the former king. He was taken in the ambush that killed his brother. Been kept here ever since for some reason."

So that no one sees him for what he is—funny, feeling, clever. Not a monster.

Lena worked to swallow, but there wasn't enough moisture and she almost gave herself a coughing fit when her dry throat closed on nothing.

Arubel Adiiron. So many of the fragments he'd given her began to make sense; a dead but beloved brother, a guardian but no father, no other family to speak of, his training and education, his life in a bed-chamber rather than a cell.

She'd never seen the previous avian king, Maddok, but she'd heard the stories, that you could always tell an Adiiron by their golden wings. Bel's weren't gold; the tips gleamed bronze in the right light, but bronze was not gold. Lena remembered her knighting ceremony, when she looked at the great wings spread over the wall behind King Artemian's throne. Surely it was just rumor that they were Maddok's wings dipped in gold. Surely the flesh and feathers beneath would have rotted away.

Because if not...that was Bel's flesh and blood nailed to the wall. And when she thought that, she couldn't help the image of Bel nailed there instead, strung up like a sacrifice. Her stomach almost heaved.

They kept him here, an avian prince *here*! They could've traded him in a prisoner exchange. They could've brought him to the capital to try for peace. The king could have done so much more, so much better with this. Bel should have been treated like a being with dignity and feeling—

and Vagorans should have been shown what avians were truly like. The king could have sought peace, could have stopped the next ten years of killing.

She tried to listen to Arion as he continued talking, relieved for the noise and his ignorance at the true reason for her shock. But she could feel Joran's stare on her, and she worked to bring her thoughts in order. She cracked her fingers and flexed them beneath the table to try and get blood flowing again.

When she next looked up, she met Joran's gaze.

His face was neutral, a common expression he donned whenever the prince worked himself into a passion, but Lena watched his eyes watching hers. His lips were thin under his large nose, and other than the occasional blink, he held perfectly still. It wasn't the first time Lena had gotten the impression of a leopard waiting in ambush from the captain. He wasn't a threat, not yet, but he always knew how to wait, to watch.

She'd have to be careful, then. But Lena had to see Bel.

━━━━━ ••◆•• ━━━━━

Lena couldn't find a time or excuse to slip away from the buzz of activity gripping the castle until the next night. Joran's repairs were well underway, and with new supplies coming up from town, including a begrudging Malthus, Finhöln had already begun her transformation. The captain kept a steady stream of work going from dusk until dawn, enlisting everyone with a capable pair of hands before she, Arion, and most of the guard departed in a few days' time. After an argument with Malthus, the steward was relegated to the kitchen so he could translate for Pol, and he soon found himself sleeping in the castle he so hated. Joran wouldn't hear of him staying in town.

"*He isn't steward of Longbourne,*" the captain had said.

Finally, with the knights settling into a rhythm and tired from their journey here, as well as all the manual labor, Lena took her chance and slipped upstairs to Bel's room after dinner.

She found a knight at the mouth of the corridor, leaning against the wall so that she could see his door but also the hallway and staircase.

Lena nodded in greeting. "Captain Joran said to go down for your dinner. I'll watch your post while you eat."

The woman regarded her with assessing brown eyes. She had the most beautiful skin Lena had ever seen, with one large freckle below and to the right of her left eye. She'd never met the knight before, and for that she was grateful. She wouldn't know Lena like some of the others did—mainly, how bad she was at lying.

"Thought I'd get it when the next shift came," the guard said.

Lena shrugged. "You can. Pol, the cook, will be asleep by then, so it'll be cold."

Her lips thinned in displeasure. "Well, when you put it like that." She picked up her helmet, which she'd taken off, and propped it against her hip. She nodded back at Bel's door before saying, "Haven't seen the bastard all day. He's a quiet one—been checking on him to make sure he's even there."

Lena made a noise of agreement and was happy to see the back of the woman. She waited until her footsteps faded down into the castle, and then another minute, counting the seconds in her head.

Finally, she crept down the corridor, not wanting to make her own echoes. The door, as always, was unlocked, and Lena softly pushed it open. She ducked inside and shut it behind her before she thought too much about her flimsy plan. She hoped the woman was a slow eater.

She found Bel where she usually did, sitting at his worktable, hands ink-stained, golden curls falling haphazardly across his brow—but no smile graced his face at her entrance, and for the first time in months, his wings were downcast, hidden behind the expanse of his shoulders.

His eyes ran over her in a way that was neither loving nor angry. An assessment. "Are you taking your turn guarding me?" he said softly.

The sight of him, the sound of his voice, sent a pang through her, her heart giving a tug as if to draw her closer to him. All the hours she'd spent with him here now felt like looking at her own reflection in a pond; the likeness was there but distorted, as if it belonged to the watery world below. It almost didn't seem real anymore, like the memories belonged to someone else, someone who knew how to be happy.

Lena didn't think she knew that person—just as she didn't know him, not really.

"When were you going to tell me?" she said.

She watched his whole body tense, starting with his mouth, down to his shoulders and forearms. He swallowed, throat bobbing, before saying carefully, "Tell you what?"

"Who you are."

A surprised breath shuddered through him, the sound like a great tree shaking in a violent gale. His mouth opened once, twice, but he shut it again as a pained frown creased his face. He said nothing.

A potent mix of frustration and hurt stung her eyes, but she blinked back the tears, unwilling to let them fall. Not now.

"When were you going to tell me, Arubel?"

He flinched, eyes cutting away from her to the hearth.

Lena collapsed back against the door. "Goddess. It's true. You're an Adiiron."

Bel shook his head slowly. "No. Not anymore. I'm not Arubel anymore."

"You're the rightful heir to the avian throne!"

She saw a spark of fire in his eyes at that, but he still wouldn't look at her. She watched him bank that fire, throw sand on its ashes and smother it. "No," he said again.

"How could you not tell me?"

"What difference would it have made?"

Words clambered up Lena's throat, but she wasn't sure which, wasn't sure what to say to him. Perhaps it was just noise that wanted to come out, a scream of frustration, of disappointment.

"You should've told me."

"Why?" He levelled a look at her then that she'd never seen before, his lips pulled back in something between a sneer and a snarl. "My name has never done me any good."

"Bel, we—" What? They what? Weren't supposed to have secrets? What a lie that was.

He seemed to think the same thing, and that terrible sneer of his turned into an equally terrible grin. "Apparently you have royal taste in men."

Lena gasped at the slap of his words. "How dare you? You've got no right to judge me or be jealous. It's the past."

"I haven't got rights to anything, remember?"

"Stop it."

"What?"

"Whatever this is. Stop trying to pick a fight. It won't make anything better."

He made a frustrated noise before planting his elbows on the table and burying his face in his hands, his fingers tugging through tangled curls. She wanted to brush it out for him, wanted to draw his hands away from his face, kiss his palms, and tell him something different. But there was nothing she could say.

She was a knight, his warden, and he was an avian prisoner. She couldn't think of a way to change any of that.

If she could, she thought she might do it. At least try.

"Is there anything else?"

"For what?" he murmured from inside his hands.

"Is there anything else you haven't told me."

He went quiet again, answering her question.

"Bel, I can't help you if you're not honest with me."

"Help me?" He looked despondently at her from between his fingers. "You can't help me." He shook his head. "No one can help me."

It made Lena's heart sick to see his back bowed, his wings slumped on the floor. He looked exactly as she'd felt, chained before her king and court. She could do nothing then and she could do nothing now. And it ate at her.

She wanted to tell him how sorry she was, for his being here, for drawing Arion here, for giving him—both of them—hope when really, there hadn't been any to begin with. But she didn't.

She didn't tell him any of it because it made no difference and because he hadn't told her things either. It was petty but she held onto some of her anger; it was easier to bear than the devastation that nipped at her heels and weighed Bel down in his chair.

She left without another word. Perhaps there was more to say and perhaps there was nothing at all, but Lena didn't want to contend with either. All she wanted was to crawl into her bed and not come out.

Lena stopped at the end of the corridor, though, and took up the position. The knight hadn't come back, and she wouldn't leave Bel "unguarded," if only so he avoided trouble.

Goddess, Bel was a prince. The son and brother of kings.

Slumping against the cold stone of the wall, Lena focused on her breathing, trying to soothe the worst of her despair.

She couldn't reconcile the idea of him as someone called Arubel, could only think of the clever, sweet, sometimes taciturn Bel she knew. She wanted *Bel*, longed to go back to just days ago, when that was all he'd been. She wanted to go back.

But she'd wished such things before and knew how useless it was.

37

Lena's last days in Finhöln went by faster than she could have imagined and always with a sense of impending collision. It was as if she rode Yvain blindfolded, the wind whipping her face as she sped blindly by, unable to catch her breath, unable to see the dangers ahead. All she could do was hang on and wait.

It quickly became clear that she was no longer truly needed. Joran had everything in hand, the repairs and the knights and even Pol and Malthus moving like clockwork. She hadn't truly been serving as warden for a long time now but being so summarily dismissed stung.

The day would begin at sunrise, the castle soon filled with the sounds of industry, of sawing and hammering and shoveling and raking and heaving. The kitchen was overcrowded at mealtimes, the knights pouring in to eat and play cards and joke and boast about who'd lifted the heaviest rock or shoveled the most rubble. At night they used all the serviceable rooms in the servants quarters, and Lena could hear the echoes of them snoring, talking, slipping from room to room to see a lover. It was like being in camp again, like being back in the life she had led for most of her knighthood.

She'd rarely been so miserable. And she was in good company. Malthus stomped everywhere, growling rather than talking, with a black look for anyone who tried to catch his attention. Every day the lines beneath Pol's eyes seemed to grow and deepen, and she rarely saw him smile. His hands were always so busy with cooking that he couldn't stop to chat. Alix had become a wraith, there and gone again, and Lena hadn't a clue where she got off to. When she could, she enlisted the girl's help in the kitchen, where she herself had cleaved to, finding the space and Pol familiar and safe within Joran's loud bustle.

And Bel...well, all she knew of him was what the knights who'd just come from guarding him said. It took much of her will, and a badly bitten tongue, to keep herself from demanding they never say such things about him again. That they not even look at him.

Helping Pol feed the knights kept Lena busy and out of Arion's way, and for that, she was grateful. She fell into bed exhausted each night, sometimes too tired to count the days, as Arion did, until they left. He was adamant about helping her and making things right between them. She was grateful, she *was*, but all the hopes in Arion's eyes made her wary.

But Arion and his promises couldn't keep her from thinking of Bel. Sometimes it was in the soldier's talk of him that she so hated or imagining that his feathers brushed against her or seeing his favorite pewter mug. Lena had had to hold back wrathful tears when someone broke the mug one night—she hadn't stopped herself from calling the man a clumsy idiot and to get out if he couldn't manage not to break everything in sight.

It was that intense spark of emotions, always pulsing just beneath her skin, that had Lena staying far away from Bel. What could she say to him like this? How could any of this be put to rights? And what did it even mean to be righted?

She asked herself these things for days, wanting a solution that did not exist, and each night she slipped into bed, tired and aching, she fell asleep to the thought that it was another day gone, another closer to leaving, but another without a way for her to make this right. She knew her time ran like sand through the fingers, but she was still surprised when it came to an end altogether.

At the nightly meeting Joran held after dinner to check on the day's progress, it was announced that everyone had the next morning off to prepare for the prince's departure in the afternoon.

The gulp of honey mead Lena just swallowed nearly came up again at the news, making the back of her tongue tingle with cloying sweetness and bile.

They were leaving. Really leaving. South again.

Leaving Bel. Lena struggled not to choke on the mead stuck in her throat.

"Any other questions?" Joran was saying, looking around the kitchen packed with knights sleepy from the day's work and their full bellies. No one said anything, so he nodded and continued, "Good. That leaves only one issue—the avian's wings."

Joran wasn't looking in Lena's direction, so thankfully he missed how her head snapped up at the mention of Bel.

"I'd like a report from everyone who's guarded and seen the prisoner. How does the right wing look?"

"It droops," said one knight over the rim of his cup. "Never seen one do that before."

It's because he's miserable. Lena bit her abused tongue to keep quiet, but the thin metal of her goblet dented under her fingers as her grip tightened.

"He holds it down, definitely lower than the other," supplied another.

"Always puts himself between you and it."

"But he *can* move it. Not as much as the other, maybe, but I've seen him move it around."

Joran made a considering noise. "It's what I thought. He's reset the break." He looked to Lena when he said, "It'll need to be broken again."

"No."

Joran's eyebrows rose, and Lena made herself release the cup she'd been mangling. She left the indentations of her fingertips behind.

"Lena?" said Arion, trying to catch her eye.

"With all due respect, sir," she told Joran, "the original break has never been reset. The wing *is* broken. It isn't useable."

"The wing should be broken in two places. The directive, which was issued by the king himself, is very clear on this. There are always to be two breaks to ensure flight isn't possible. He's reset the lower break, I'd say months ago."

Lena could feel them, the many pairs of eyes on her, reading the truth in the sharp, stiff lines of her body without Joran having to say it aloud. The prisoner had reset the break and she, the warden, had known about it. And done nothing.

"Sir, as you must have also read in the directive, he's reset that break from the beginning. All the wardens have broken it again, but he continues to set it. But he leaves the other alone. He doesn't leave. The second break isn't keeping him here." *Let him have this, it's so little to give.*

"All the wardens except you, lady. They followed their orders."

Lena's lips thinned. She remembered the sloppy figure of Sir Ollander, the state of Finhöln when she arrived, and took great exception to being thought of as less than *him*.

"It didn't seem necessary."

"Not the point. You had strict instruction—"

"Sir, it's cruel."

A murmur went through the gathered knights, the noise humming unpleasantly in Lena's ears. She knew then she'd lost them—she'd never had them to begin with, but the idea that it was bad to be cruel to an avian was unforgiveable to anyone who'd fought at the eastern front. Lena had tried not to think too hard on why so many of the knights Arion had brought with him were new to her. She tried not to think about whether she'd be with those she remembered, if Arion hadn't sent her back to Vagora when he had.

Joran filled the silence with a sigh. It was not a sound of annoyance or even exasperation. When Lena looked at the captain, she saw a man dearly in need of a good night's sleep. He rubbed his eyes with his middle finger and thumb then folded his hands behind him in a very familiar pose.

"I understand it's unpleasant," he said, not unkindly. "But it has to be done. The precedence has been set and a point must be made."

"He's too important of an asset to let anything slip," Arion agreed, effectively ending the argument. Not that she'd had much of a chance to begin with. "We have to ensure he stays put. If he were in the capital, I'd be less worried, but nothing can be done about that until I speak with my lord father."

The prince and captain shared a nod, and Lena hated how, in their own subtle ways, they were trying to be kind. But there was no way to be kind about *breaking Bel's wing.* Arion only called the king his *lord father* when he disagreed with him, but he would let this happen anyway. Joran would have a guard on Bel always and keep him confined, but he'd still hurt Bel because he was supposed to.

Joran sighed again, and he suddenly looked his age. It'd always been hard to think of him as older than her parents, but right then, Lena could see it, and it made her gut clench.

"Well, no reason to delay. I'll go do it now."

"No." Lena cleared her throat. "No, I...I'll do it. Tomorrow, before we leave. I'm still warden and it's still my duty."

Joran looked her over, took her measure, and nodded. Perhaps it was the low light of the fire and dozen candles, but she thought perhaps the captain looked...proud that she would face this and do what needed to be done.

But his pride only made Lena cold, and when the others were dismissed to their beds, Lena slid from her stool and tried to lose herself amongst them. She didn't want to see or speak to the captain again, not tonight, and she would do her best to avoid him tomorrow.

Arion, though, she couldn't avoid. She felt a warm hand slide around the inside of her elbow, gently steering her out of the stream of knights headed up to the servants' wing.

The others moved around them, too tired to notice or care that she and the prince slipped into an empty corridor.

There was little light here, only what filtered up the stairwell from the kitchen, and Lena could barely make out the contrasting shadows of

Arion's face. His hand slid down her arm to take hers and squeeze. He moved, and then his other hand was holding hers, drawing her closer.

"I'm sorry, Lena," he said. "You don't have to do this. You don't have to break his wing."

"Neither do you. Arion, good goddess, he'll have a guard and be confined to his room. He's had full range of the castle for ten years. Why would he run now?"

"It has to be done. We can't take any chances."

"With what?"

"From what I understand of my father's orders for him, the documents he's currently translating could win us the war."

Lena wanted to scoff. "How's that? He's been here for ten years and hasn't."

She thought perhaps he frowned, for the whole of his eyes and their sockets darkened into great pools of shadow.

"My father seems to think what he's translating will get us into Hadria."

Lena's breath stuttered in surprise. "The mines."

"The mines," Arion agreed.

Lena had seen Bel working at his desk so many times, had looked at the great mass of papers that littered the worktable, yet she hadn't fully considered what it was he translated. Did he know what it was, what it would be used for? Would he truly give his people's secrets away, possibly leading to their own destruction?

No, he wouldn't.

But that would mean...

Arion sighed, the warm breath fanning across Lena's face, and she realized that he'd drawn closer in the dark, their noses almost touching.

"Lena, let Joran break the wing. Please. I don't want this to weigh on your conscience."

It was much too late for that.

When she said nothing, he pressed, "You're compassionate and good, Lena, I know that. It's one of the many things I love you for. But you've got to look forward. This place is your past. We're going to make things right."

Arion's hands, warm, gentle, cupped her face, his thumbs tracing the contours of her cheekbones. She didn't know how he always managed to be so warm. His touch was almost familiar, almost comforting, and it would have been so easy to sink into the memories, to let him make her feel how he once had. He'd been so good at taking everything away, even if only for a night, and with the day that loomed before her, all Lena wanted was to forget.

But she had promised herself, what seemed like a very long time ago, that she wouldn't forget.

She gently took his wrists and drew his hands away.

"It's late, Arion."

"I did what I had to, Lena. But I'm going to make it up to you. I'm going to fix this."

Lena could only shake her head, giving his hands a squeeze before putting them at his sides. "We have to live with what we've done, the both of us."

She left him in the dark, somehow feeling more tired than she had entering the corridor.

She had to stop her feet from continuing to climb further into the castle, to Bel. Part of her wanted to warn him of what would happen. But then, would knowing be better?

Another part wanted it to be his hands on her, wanted to feel their warmth and callouses as he pulled her hair from its tight coil.

But the largest part of her wanted her bed, empty and cold as it may be. That part of her wanted sleep and nothing else, nothing complicated.

She was so tired, so weighed down with what tomorrow would bring, that Lena didn't notice at first that there was already a fire going in her room. Lena blinked, surprised to see Alix sitting not far from the hearth, knees hugged to her chest, cast half in firelight, half in shadow.

Lena didn't need the light to see how grim her face was.

She was curious to know where Alix had been all this time and more than a little aggravated that she never stuck around long enough to be of much help to her and Pol, but right then, Lena just wanted her gone so that she could sleep. There would be time to lecture her later.

It would be almost three weeks of travel back to Highclere.

The thought made her want to flop face-first onto the bed.

"We're leaving tomorrow," she informed Alix. *Which you'd know if you deigned to show up for more than five minutes at a time.*

Alix just stared at her, eyes flicking between Lena's slowly, giving Lena the sense that she had heard but wasn't listening to her.

"Alix, what's the matter?" She was beginning to worry, even in her tired haze.

The girl licked her lips before croaking, "It was me."

"What was you?"

She somehow pulled her knees even closer to her chest. "The prince's letter. It did come. I picked it up in Longbourne."

"When?"

Alix shook her head. "Over two months ago."

For a moment, Lena didn't understand why Alix looked like a dog who'd just been kicked. She sighed, opening her mouth to tell her it would be all right, whatever she'd done, Lena would make it right. In the morning.

But then it struck her like an avian arrow in the chest, whizzing down from high above where she couldn't see or escape it.

Lena gasped. Alix had—

She slammed her gauntlet against the door, the noise reverberating up her arm, into her shoulder, where it burst in a shock of pain. A wail escaped her before she clamped a hand around her mouth.

Betrayal cut a hot swathe through her—how dare Alix take *her* letter? How dare she take away the choice it offered?

Lena slid to the floor, her back braced against the door. The anger left her feeling hollowed out, a shell to be shucked after the nut was scraped away. She watched Alix across the room without really seeing her. The girl looked like a cornered animal, all curled around herself and wary, but Lena didn't have the will or desire to make it better anymore.

"It was for the best," Alix hurried to say. Her eyes caught too much light, the whites rimming her green irises as they opened frantically wide. "It was too risky for you to go back. You'd be leaving your post. It'd look bad. I was trying to protect you."

"You're *fifteen*," she felt the need to remind her. "You don't always know best. Damn it, Alix, I could've written back. I could've *stopped* this. And now I have to…"

"The prince would have come if you'd said no."

"It was my choice to make. Not yours."

"I wanted you to be happy." She scrubbed her sleeve across her face, mopping up tears. "I wanted to give you the chance at least."

"It's too late now." With a soft *thunk,* Lena's head slumped against the door. She closed her eyes, and they immediately started to water, relieving the gritty feel of them.

Perhaps tomorrow she would find her anger again, but for now, all Lena had was disappointment. At Alix for keeping this from her. At Bel for lying to her about who he was—or at least, not telling her the truth. At Joran for hurting Bel, and at Arion for letting him.

At herself for letting hope start to take root. Hope that, somehow, there would be more time with Bel. Time to deepen what they had, let it grow and see what it became. Time, perhaps, for Bel to trust her enough to tell her his full name.

Alix sniffed, and Lena cracked an eye open to see her pushing her hair out of her face.

"We're really leaving tomorrow?" Alix whispered.

"Yes."

She made an unhappy noise. "Lena, you know we shouldn't. It'll look bad."

"Arion's here now," she said mechanically.

Alix snorted. "And you just agree with him always, do you?"

Lena recognized the barb, but she didn't have the will to even lift her eyes in acknowledgement let alone indulge the attempt to bait her.

"He's forcing you, Lena. He's not listening. He's just trying to get what he wants."

"He's the prince, Alix. Of course he gets what he wants. At least he's on my side this time."

Alix made another sound, and Lena agreed, though she wouldn't admit it. She knew Arion was sweeping her wishes aside. Doing what he thought was best, no matter the consequences, was his greatest strength and most painful weakness. She'd lived through it once, had promised herself never again, but then, "There's nothing else I can do."

Alix growled something that otherwise would've had Lena sending her for a run around the bailey, but Lena said nothing. Her stillness finally got Alix moving. She heard her jump up and stomp to the door. Lena didn't move, even though she should've, and instead took petty pleasure in Alix's huff of frustration. Alix pulled the door open with effort, moving Lena with it, and slammed it shut.

With Alix gone, the room settled into quiet, only the crackling fire filling the void.

Lena scraped her fingers through her hair, taking a deep breath and holding it. She didn't want to think about this, any of this, anymore. She didn't want to be Arion's cause. She didn't want to forgive Alix or make her more upset. She didn't want to be lied to anymore. And she didn't want to leave like this.

But she was going to. Goddess save her, she was going to leave, because it was all she could do.

<h1 style="text-align:center">38</h1>

Bel found himself in his cell much sooner than he'd anticipated. He thought of the three weeping stone walls and slate of bars across from him as *his* since it was the cell he returned to every few years. Like a horse to its stall. It was the one where he'd spent his first days in Finhöln —he couldn't say how many, really, they'd been a blur of damp and bitterness and pain as Warden Hallan made him understand he wasn't to leave through fists and broken bones.

He was used to the nervous energy that filled not only him but the whole cell, as if just the tiniest catalyst would make the whole place light up like sparks thrown up from a bonfire.

But it was the unknowing that kept Bel on the edge of panic. Before, he'd known why he was here—he expected to see a new face and a hated one, an old warden and the new, before they turned his world into a relief of pain and ache. Before, he'd almost been able to work himself into a defiance, already planning when he'd set this new break. It had kept him strong enough to bear the sharp agony this place always promised.

But this time, Bel didn't know what this meant—hadn't known what anything meant in days. Everything had changed so quickly. And it was worse now. So, so much worse.

It was one thing to go from one misery to the next; he'd come to expect it. It was another to have such happiness taken from him just like that. And it was more than the human prince coming for Lena—that look on her face when asking who he really was…It gutted him. All the hopes and happiness were gone now and the world felt broken. Irreparable.

The manacles on his wrists weren't so tight to be painful but not loose enough to wiggle free of. They each connected to short chains melded with the floor, keeping his arms pinned to his sides. The two soldiers who'd escorted him down here had tried to belt his good wing to his side with thick leather straps, but they'd thought better of it when he gave each a good flap.

He hadn't meant to do it, really, didn't know these soldiers, but instinct told him to expect the worst. Still, something in him had rebelled against letting them touch him like that, letting them strap him down and handle him like chattel. Something inside had just said *no*, something that sounded like Lena.

He'd expected a blow, *the* blow, but none had come. Instead, he'd been left down here, chained, to listen to his own unsteady breaths and the scuff of his shifting feet.

The scrape of footsteps descending the stairs echoed down the corridor, filling Bel's ears and making him cringe away from the sound. He didn't know what he preferred, this or the silence that always came with a sucking nausea that pulled at his stomach.

His breaths came in quick, unsatisfying puffs as he waited, counted steps, waited, ten, eleven—was that—twelve—it sounded like her steady gait, but—thirteen, and—

The man he'd come to think of as the New Warden appeared, his stern face cut into unequal halves by the cell bars. The man had told Bel his name, introduced himself much like Lena had all those months ago, when she'd stood so straight and rigid that her spine seemed a steel rod rather than bone. He looked Bel up and down, eyes taking in the manacles but no belt. His face pinched.

Then he made room for Lena, who walked up behind him.

She too pulled a face, her lips scrunching into displeasure, but her eyes avoided his.

"Locked in?" she said. "He hasn't ever been before."

The New Warden cocked a brow at her. "No? Well, call me cautious."

From a pocket, the man pulled out a key and stuck it into the gritty iron lock. He didn't turn it, though.

"Lena, go join the prince. Tell him it's done."

She turned that displeased look onto the man, and it grew somehow, deepened and hardened. It made Bel's innards, from his guts to his lungs to his throat, clench.

"No. This is my duty and I have to finish it. Sir."

"It's not the same as in battle," he said in nearly a whisper.

"I know that."

"Do you?"

Lena turned to face straight ahead, though she again wouldn't look at Bel, instead stared at something over his left side.

"The sooner I do this, the sooner it's done."

The man made an unhappy noise in his throat. "I'll stay and—"

"No, captain, let me do this. For my dignity. And his." She nodded sideways at Bel.

His eyes cut to Bel in a sharp look before he sighed and walked back to the stairs.

Lena stood facing but not looking at him until the New Warden's footsteps faded up into the castle.

When it was nothing but a heavy silence, Lena finally turned the key in the lock and swung the door open with a cavernous, echoing screech.

His heart made a painful gasp in his chest, and though the only sounds were her boots softly padding across the small room and his erratic breaths, a rush of noise filled his ears, like standing before a waterfall—a pounding sound that drummed into the bones.

She said nothing as she went, and in only moments, she stood behind him. He caught barely a glimpse of her face, set in stony lines. She looked like a death mask. He'd seen many in the old catacombs below Aeriand, of the old kings from when the practice was still done.

The stone effigies looked just like her unforgiving, hard visage, and the memory sent another thrill of cold down Bel's center.

Soon he completely lost sight of her, nothing even in his periphery.

The hairs and down at the back of his neck prickled, and if possible, his breathing grew more labored. Though he drew breaths in, so, so, so many breaths, no air reached his lungs. Dark spots danced around the edges of his vision, and his lips grew numb, his fingertips chill like—

Lena's hand, warm, familiar, awful, gently touched the center of his back, between his wing bases.

A shiver of comfort went through him, followed swiftly by a wave of nausea.

For a moment, not even that, a flash, a heartbeat, Bel thought she would unshackle him. She hadn't closed the cell door. She was here to help him. She would get him out of here, somehow. Away from these men.

He didn't know how they'd make it or where they'd go, but for half a moment, no longer, Bel thought they would.

And then her hand touched his right wing.

He hissed.

She was no different, no better than the rest. She'd hurt him now, hurt him like all the rest—but worse. She would hurt him so much worse and he hated her for it, hated that—

And then her hand slid down his right wing, to the base.

Oh, damn, damn, damn her!

And damn him too. He'd known she would hurt him, known since the beginning, hadn't he, but he'd lied to himself, made himself believe that things could be better, that he could have better, that he *deserved* to be—

He felt no warmth from her when she leaned over his shoulder to whisper in his ear, no heat from her body as he had so often before, with their flesh pressed together in the many dark nights they'd shared. The only hint of her was the clean smell of her hair, orange blossoms as always, and the faint pressure, the *knowing* that something loomed behind him.

"Get it wrapped and bound quick," she said in something even softer than a whisper, barely using her voice at all. "Make it look good."

Bel froze as her hands framed his wing base, pressing painfully into the mangled flesh and cartilage and bone. She grunted, almost pulling Bel out of his fugue, almost making him try to move away, but then she adjusted, brought her elbow down in one decisive strike, and Bel's world exploded into a blinding white pain.

He felt his body give under her hands, so different from all other ways it had before. He felt himself break.

An unholy crack resounded in his ears, reverberating like the frantic beat of his heart. He slumped forward, the pain taking him down as quick and as surely as an undertow. He drowned in it.

39

So high up was Bel's first thought as he stepped up to the sheer drop off.

This wasn't even the highest level of Aeriand; he'd been to the top before many times, had stood inside the spire and looked out over the great riverplain that stretched far from the base of his brother's great mountain city. He'd soared high into the clouds on Eamon's back, and even on Maddok's, chasing wisps of cloud and rainbow tails.

But it was the first time Bel had approached the drop off on his own. He'd been forbidden from getting close to it, and like most good avian fledglings, he'd listened to his elders about this. If there was anything avians feared, it was freefalling, and even the most confident fledgling knew to stay away from the unpredictable updrafts near the edge.

The wind grabbed Bel's hair and sent it flying. The gust caressed the exposed skin of his face, skating across like fingertips, before forcing its way up his nostrils.

Bel tried not to sneeze. And he tried to wipe his stinging, watering eyes in a way that didn't make the curious onlookers think he was crying. He *wasn't*.

He could feel those eyes on him—it wasn't every day that an Adiiron prince took his first flight. But the king wasn't there to see it, it was only the spare, so the crowd wasn't nearly as big as Bel had worried it'd be. Probably nothing to Maddok's first flight.

He shifted his feet nervously but stopped, remembering where he was.

As he continued to lean into the wind, pretending to wait for just the right updraft, Eamon swooped back into view, his great gray wings holding him aloft as he drew even with Bel standing on the terrace.

"C'mon, Little Hawk!" said Eamon with a grin. He threw his arms wide, as if to show how much Bel was missing.

If anything, that was Bel's problem; there was so much—space, air, emptiness, there was just so *much* of it. He could go anywhere, including down.

Bel swallowed, pretending it wasn't a gulp of fear, and took a step back with one leg. He put his weight there, breathed in one two, out one two, remembered his *ariant* training, thought of Maddok cutting across the horizon like a gold blade.

Tears burned Bel's eyes, and he charged for the drop off before the onlookers could see. There'd be no way to pretend it was just the wind.

He got in one, two bounds and then there was nothing beneath him, nothing but Eamon and his great gray wings and further, much further, the earth itself. There was that moment Bel had felt before, where you just hover there, weightless, the air in your lungs and nose and all around and your stomach lurches into your throat and your mind buzzes with a thrill of excitement and dread.

It never lasted; the earth always drew things back down to it. But Bel had been on someone's back for this next part, had had his stomach thrust back down into his chest with the great beat of wings that defied the earth and sky, lifting him and Eamon away.

He didn't have Eamon's back under him this time. They were even for a moment, caught each other's eyes, and then the earth pulled Bel down, down to it.

Bel gasped, arms flailing, forgetting everything, everything he was supposed to do, everything but the ground rushing up to meet him. His stomach didn't go back down into his chest, instead pushed against his throat as if it wanted to completely come out. He wanted to scream, but his stomach was there, blocking the sound, choking him.

He could feel those stinging tears lashing from the corners of his eyes across his face, and wetness dribbled from his nose, running in cold trails around his mouth.

"Flap, Bel, get your wings out and *flap!*" shouted Eamon from what sounded like leagues and league away.

The words didn't make sense, nothing did but the wind and gut-churning sensation of falling, falling, falling down.

He opened his mouth, maybe to scream, maybe to shout something like *Catch me* or *Help* or *I want Maddok*, but nothing came out. Without words, without hands there to catch him, Bel continued to freefall.

It was expected, of course, that fledglings would fall. That was the nature of learning to fly. But the thing about first flight was that there would always be hands, arms, to catch them, draw them close and keep them aloft. Parents, whole families, leapt out into the air to catch and encourage their fledglings, ensuring there was no way they'd fall, not truly *fall*.

But Bel fell, his brother far to the west waging yet another war, and Eamon was now far above him.

The air rushing by made Bel's sob more of a hiccup, and the gasp of air gave him a moment of clarity. He snatched at his thoughts, trying to remember what he was supposed to do. He and Eamon had been training for months. Bel had put off first flight for as long as he could; others his age had been flying for over a year now. He'd hoped Maddok would be back by then, would be the hands that caught him, but there'd been no more putting it off. Eamon had insisted on practicing, and so they had practiced.

But *what* had they practiced?

Bel wiggled in frustration, making a pocket of air hit his wings.

Right, he had to open them. He had to let them carry his weight, had to trust that they were strong enough.

With a yelp, Bel let his wings unfurl. It was a fight against the wind and his angle, he should've done this as he leapt off the drop off, but with three, four flaps his wings were out, the feathers rustling before slipping into place.

Immediately his back muscles contracted and released, the memory from practice, of all his avian ancestors who had come before, locking into place. With another set of flaps, Bel righted himself, wings catching an updraft that bore him up.

The change in direction made Bel's head spin, but he was determined now. His knees locked, making his body streamlined, like an arrow cutting through the sky.

He swallowed his stomach and looked above him, where Eamon waited, hovering in the sunlight. Bel banked softly in the updraft, slowly spiraling upwards until he circled Eamon.

The warrior had a wide grin on his face, proudly watching the strong flaps of Bel's wings. There was barely any gray fledgling down left, instead the white and bronze tips caught the light, almost making them gold, almost the color of Maddok's Adiiron wings.

"You were supposed to catch me!" Bel howled over the wind.

Eamon's grin faltered. "I knew you could do it, Little Hawk."

Bel shook his head but stopped when it altered his course.

"You were supposed to *catch me*," he said again.

Eamon's grin was gone now, and instead he frowned, that pensive look he got when he thought deeply on something. It was usually followed by some sort of "wisdom," but Bel didn't want to hear it. He hadn't wanted to freefall. He hadn't wanted to do this at all, really, without Maddok. But Eamon had insisted and pushed, and Bel had finally agreed, with the comfort that Eamon would be there, that Eamon would *catch him*.

First flight was supposed to be an important step, a new stage in a young avian's life. It was crucial for the *ariant* training, too, and now Bel could move on to the next phase, was that much closer to being a warrior and joining Maddok.

But he didn't care about any of that now, not with his heart hammering with leftover terror.

Banking again, Bel caught another draft and soared out, away from

Aeriand and the few dozen clapping onlookers. He didn't know where he was going, knew he should stay close with his untried wings that would tire soon, but Bel didn't want to go back. Not yet.

He knew Eamon followed him, but for now, Bel pretended it was just him in this wide-open sky, just him and the power of his wings, holding him up. Nothing went as it was supposed to today, but he was starting to like this.

He gave a big flap and careened through the air, whizzing past birds and bugs and he imagined he was just a spec on the horizon to Eamon, the bigger male surely lagging behind, surely not as speedy as Bel was. He looped and banked, getting a feel for the wind beneath his wings, beginning to understand what older avians meant when they said the air caressed the feathers as you soared.

Bel was being hugged by the air, and he let out a whoop, loving the stretch of his wings as they carried him further, higher. Even if they weren't Adiiron gold, they were good, strong wings.

They took him away from Aeriand, away from everyone, and for one glorious afternoon, it was just Bel and the sky and the sun.

40

Like giant's fingers reaching up from the earth, the great spires of Lindenfaire poked the horizon, the blue tiles glimmering in the afternoon light. Flags fluttered lazily in the soft breeze, announcing that her father was there and that lessons were in session for the young cadets.

Lena had always loved the sight. For all that her father's life had changed after the assassination attempt, for all that he hid himself away here at Lindenfaire, he'd still created something wonderful. The estate and grounds were picturesque with their white walls and colored tiles and airy palisades. Lindenfaire was a marriage of beauty and defense, comfort and practicality. Wisteria and ivy hung over the battlements, and sculpted fountains broke up the inner courtyards where the cadets practiced. She saw her father everywhere in the building, his genius and ideas and innovation. She'd long drawn comfort from the sense of being surrounded by him when she was at Lindenfaire, and as she rode with Arion at the head of their weary party, she longed for that comfort.

It'd been over two weeks since they'd left Finhöln, two weeks of shedding the cold and reentering a world Lena had almost forgotten about. Everything seemed so fast off the mountain; even spring itself came on quickly, flowers blossoming overnight and whole fields of crops shooting up a foot if she blinked.

She'd grown used to castle living again, the steady routine of it, and especially having a fire, warm food, and a bed close at hand. Though they marched south to seek justice, Lena couldn't help wishing for Bel's bed back at Finhöln and the thick slice of brown bread with homemade jam that always awaited her in the morning. She was cranky in the mornings, her mouth watering for what it wouldn't have. She was in good company; the soldiers were quiet and sullen, and the only one with any enthusiasm was Arion. He seemed determined to singlehandedly make up for the somber mood of their group—or perhaps Joran otherwise dampened his talkativeness.

From dawn to dusk, Arion recounted their year apart, campaigns, routs, strategy, as well as the march back, court life, intrigues. Lena had no interest in the latter and still too sore about the first to listen with any real interest. But she nodded along, offered words back when they were needed because she couldn't forget what Arion would do for her.

But as Lindenfaire took up her sight, Lena's heart ached. Uncomfortable and drafty as it'd been, she missed Finhöln, and now she hoped Lindenfaire could ease that ache. After everything, she just wanted the familiarity, the safety of its walls and wood-paneled corridors and plush burgundy rugs.

They were all weary from the road, but Lena was *tired*.

The sight of Lindenfaire seemed to buoy everyone's spirits; even the horses began trotting a little faster, somehow knowing a real stable was close at hand. A light chatter hummed in her ears where before it had just been the dusty sound of hooves hitting packed earth.

"Home at last," grumbled Alix from her right.

Lena made a noncommittal noise. She saw the flash of something in Alix's face from the corner of her eye, perhaps hurt, perhaps anger, but Lena was too tired to care. She'd spent two weeks with Alix swinging like a pendulum from snarky grumbling to awkward small talk. No matter her mood, the girl was always beside Lena—not so uncommon for a squire, but for two weeks Alix had been *right there*, never more than a few paces away. She'd had to send the girl away more than once while finding a private spot to relieve herself.

"Have you been here before, Lady Alix?" asked Arion brightly, leaning around a scowling Lena to engage an equally scowling Alix.

As much as her squire had been determined to dislike the crown prince, his usual charms were working even on the hardened street urchin. Alix would have taken being called 'lady' as condescending from anyone else, and most would have meant it so, but not Arion. Lena swore the girl almost blushed, and it just made her grumpier.

Alix and Arion chatted around her about Alix's first visit to Lindenfaire, all those months ago when their path had been northward and the future had been set but so bleak.

Now, Lena didn't know what the future held, but it promised to be brighter. At least, that's what she told herself. It was, as always, hard to argue with Arion's enthusiasm and promises. Not that she fully believed in them, but for now she could do little else but go along with him.

The town of craftspeople that surrounded and supported Lindenfaire set down their tasks to crowd around and watch the golden prince ride through. It wasn't long before flowers flew through the air, landing on the party's saddles and heads. Arion waved, flashing that white smile that always endeared him to the people.

And Lena couldn't even be grumpy about it because she knew he meant it. He was as happy to see the people as they were to see him.

A crowd followed them to the white walls of Lindenfaire, where the gates had been thrown open to welcome them. Little faces poked out of arrowslit windows up and down the turreted gate, eyes wide at the sight of royalty riding in.

As the young cadets came flooding from their practice yards and classrooms, Lena was glad for Arion's escort. No one saw her, the disgraced knight who brought dishonor to the great man who'd built this academy. She didn't have to slink out with the dawn to avoid curious, pitying, disgusted eyes but rode in the daylight up the main promenade. Like she had always done. As was her birthright, as her mother would say.

They passed through the concentric courtyards, through inner walls and gates and the growing crowd of excited cadets, all clad in their blue uniforms with the bright gold buttons. In one courtyard, drills were in session for a newer class of recruits, the wooden swords still crooked in their wobbly arms. They were led through their forms by a tall man with floppy yellow hair. Lena blinked, a memory washing ashore in her mind, but just as he turned around at the sound of the students' delighted gasps, they moved on to the next courtyard and another wave of memory overcame her.

It was just as Lena had left it, the stables off to the east, the kitchen chimneys puffing with the heavenly smell of yeasty bread, the dovecote alive with the coos of little messengers, fat bees buzzing between the flowers and apiary behind the kitchen gardens. They had come early enough in spring to see the new buds of wisteria beginning to bloom, hanging like grapes in light lavender sprigs.

In the center of the academy stood the manor house, her father's house. Shallow stone steps led up to the ornately carved doors, thrown open in greeting. Her father hurried to meet them, his smile wide and welcoming.

Lena's chest warmed despite her churning stomach.

Sir Warrek clapped his hands and beamed up at the prince. "Prince Arion, you're a man of your word—you've brought me the greatest gift," he said in that croak Lena knew so well. She loved the tone of it, no matter how broken or ugly others might find the sound, but the words made her uneasy.

"Indeed I did," replied Arion, turning his smile on her. She watched it change from the smile that was for everyone, the wide one that showed off his dimples, to something much different, a small smile that was for candlelight and telling secrets.

"You knew he was going to Finhöln?" Lena asked her father.

Warrek and Arion shared a look between them, and Lena watched a whole conversation take place in only a moment. It was a language of tilted lips and cocked eyebrows, over as quickly as it'd begun. They'd decided something by the end of it, too.

"Let me look at you," said Warrek, waving her down off Yvain.

Lena bit the inside of her cheek and dismounted, walking into her father's waiting arms. His embrace was firm but brief, a squeeze of her torso and a soft, "My dear girl," and then it was over. Lena clung to him a little tighter, wishing it would last, but then the pat came on her shoulder and she disengaged.

She worked to keep her face neutral as her father marveled at Alix and how much she'd grown. The girl took the fawning graciously, but Lena felt each of Alix's quick stolen glances, trying to gauge how Lena reacted.

After Warrek heartily shook the prince's hand, he ushered them into the front hall. The room was a vast, amber-hued rectangle of paneled walls and checkered floorboards, with a broad, carpeted staircase taking up much of the room and ascending to open galleries on the second floor. The glossy, ornate bannisters of the staircase and gallery shone in the light from the front doors, and not a speck of dust marred the rich burgundy of the carpet. Along the walls hung shields, swords, breastplates, tapestries, and horns, mounted in the center of their own square with raised panels framing each trophy. Her parents' whole lives were detailed in just the front hall, full of glories and gifts.

Her father talked them out of their outer layers before leading them deeper into the manor house to his favorite sitting room.

It was a large, masculine room, full of plush chairs and sofas, gleaming dark woods, and deep hues of green, red, and brown. Tapestries hung from the walls, depicting some of Vagora's favorite legends, including a few that featured Warrek and Margot. Warrek moved to the great stone mantle, where all manner of trinkets, trophies, and oddities stood—Lena had spent many afternoons daydreaming about how her father got each one.

He took flint off the end of the mantle to start a fire. Though it was a warm spring day outside and the sun streaming in from the windows made the wood paneling gleam, the stone manor house was often cold.

When the fire had been stoked and food sent for, Warrek said, "Well, tell me about Finhöln."

The words didn't immediately come to Lena; she could see the castle and her time there so clearly, but it felt almost wrong to speak of it in such a place as Lindenfaire, as if she were gossiping about a poor relation. She didn't know yet how to talk about the people who lived there, didn't know if she could speak of Bel without her voice giving away that she missed him so much that it was safer not to think about him at all.

So she recounted her first impressions of the crumbling castle—Arion emphatically added his own thoughts on first seeing it—and the first days in the small servants rooms, the drafty, empty spaces, and the warm, humid kitchen. She described how cold the winter was there, how the south knew nothing of true winter, and how she and Alix had made do.

Alix interjected now and then with a quip or memory, making Warrek smile. But Lena saw the creases around his canny eyes; he knew what she talked around what he really wanted to know.

"And the prisoner?" Warrek asked.

Lena looked to Arion, unsure how much of a secret Bel was and grateful for an excuse to stall.

Arion returned her gaze with a quick nod and said, "An avian taken years ago. My lord father thought it wise to keep him all the way up there. Joran and I have been driving ourselves mad trying to understand why he hasn't been brought south."

Lena snorted softly. "But then people would see him and that avians aren't mythical monsters," she quipped.

Her comment was met with silence, and she looked around in surprise to find her father and Arion casting her strange looks. Alix's eyes were wide, her mouth pulled into a thin line as if to say *Shut up!*

Lena cleared her throat, trying to think of something else to say, but was saved by the refreshments her father had requested. A serving girl Lena didn't recognize deposited a tray on the sideboard, curtsied, and left, and Warrek moved to pass out mulled wine.

Lena lingered near her father even after she'd collected her cup, a question for only his ears pressing on her tongue. She kept herself from fidgeting by holding her cup in both hands and clenching her teeth.

As Lena hovered, Alix looked between her and the prince before smiling wide. "They don't have things like this up north. I haven't had a decent drink since…" And with that, Alix began regaling the Crown Prince of Vagora with her best stories of pub fights and bar brawls. Lena's cheeks burned, but Arion laughed along with the story, and not just when he was supposed to.

Alix's gaze cut to Lena, to her father, and then returned to the prince, watching him laugh at her last joke. A familiar hurt ached in Lena's heart—her squire had a knack for knowing when she needed a distraction, and the subtle display of loyalty touched her. But where had that loyalty been when Alix destroyed Arion's letter?

Taking a sip to wet her throat, Lena moved closer to her father and pushed those thoughts aside. She pitched her voice low to ask, "How long have you known about the prince's plan?"

Warrek looked at her, thick gray brows arched in surprise. "In a way, it was our plan," he said, equally as quiet. "Arion came to me about doing something for you soon after learning what happened, and we decided you'd need to be fetched from that awful place."

"Why did you go along with it?"

At that, Warrek frowned. "Lena, did you really expect me to leave my daughter up there to rot?"

Yes. You said nothing to stop it. Lena's throat bobbed with a hard swallow, and confusion made her want to spit up the wine she'd sipped.

"But what about the king? My sentence?"

"Did you want to be up there?"

"Well, I—"

"Did you believe you were guilty?"

"No, but…"

"Don't you think you deserve a fair trial, where you can speak for yourself and restore your good name?"

"My orders—"

"Lena," her father sighed, and she bit the inside of her cheek. It'd been helpful when he'd done this learning exercise with her as a child, putting her through her paces with questions until she had reasoned out an answer. But she didn't like it now, didn't like his impatience, as if the answer should be obvious to her.

Warrek patted her twice on the shoulder, offering a small conciliatory smile from under his thick beard. "Sometimes what's done is not what's best. When this happens, we have to put it to rights."

Lena's mouth fell open, a little in shock, perhaps to respond, but nothing came out. What he said could be true for what he and Arion had done too, and it amounted to treason, implying the king was wrong.

Warrek's gaze flicked over her shoulder, leaving their conversation and her surprise behind as he smiled and welcomed someone into the room.

Lena stood woodenly in her spot, absorbing that her father would suggest going against the king so easily. It was hard to reconcile his words with the man who'd taught her the knight's code and who'd stood by the king's side for so many years, battles, and decisions.

Where was this attitude before, when I was jailed and chained and humiliated?

"She'll be happy to see you. Lena! Come see an old friend."

Though her body turned so she could see the newcomer her father ushered in, Lena's mind took a few moments to catch up. It wasn't until she was shaking hands with the tall, handsome man in front of her that she could put aside her father's words.

That half-formed memory she'd had before resurfaced with the man's broad, ruddy face and floppy yellow hair.

"Kerry," she said, a delighted smile overcoming her.

He grinned. "Yes, miss."

The man before her barely resembled the pitiful boy and gawky adolescent she remembered. He was broad-shouldered but lean like the best of swordsman, and he didn't look like he needed her saving him anymore from pirates or vagabonds, real or imagined. She hadn't even noticed much of a limp as he'd strode over to her, shy but assured.

"You remember my daughter, Maddalena."

"Of course I remember Lena!" He smiled wide, dimpling his ruddy cheeks. "Everyone's heard of the brave Lady Maddalena. The students are always asking about her."

Lena's smile turned brittle but she clung to it.

"Kerry keeps this place going. I couldn't do it without him. He's become quite the swordsman and teaches several of the classes," Warrek said, clapping Kerry on the back. "He's indispensable to me and this academy."

"Thank you, sir," said Kerry, blushing profusely. "I help where I can."

Lena reached forward to give his shoulder a squeeze. "That's wonderful, Kerry. I'm very pleased for you," she said and meant it. It was good to see her childhood friend had made so much of himself.

Warrek pulled Kerry into their group, introducing him to Arion. If Kerry had been blushing before, he practically burned red at meeting the prince, even if Arion was mid-chew during the introductions. Arion grinned sheepishly and welcomed him warmly, though Kerry seemed most at ease with Alix. The girl was always easy to talk to, and Lena didn't miss how she slipped a little into her low Vagoran accent while she chatted with Kerry.

Lena was content to let the conversation swirl around her, eddying and flowing according to the others. She was pleased to hear of Kerry's successes here at Lindenfaire, to know that her father and the cadets were in good hands, but she couldn't help the ugly feeling growing in her stomach. She'd never seriously considered living full-time at Lindenfaire, teaching classes and helping her father, but it was nice to think of it sometimes, to know that she had a place if she ever needed it. To hear her father talk, all he needed was Kerry to keep Lindenfaire ship shape.

Kerry was humble, but his easy manner and strong body spoke to the truth of everything her father said. Kerry had made something of himself here, he was strong and accepted and necessary, and that fed the ugliness brewing inside her. It wasn't jealousy, not really—she was well acquainted with that feeling and knew this wasn't it.

She didn't want to admit to feeling disappointed or displaced. Not when she was home. Not when Arion and her father had already done so much for her and were planning to do more. She didn't want these feelings of strangeness, like she didn't know her own home or wasn't part of the group that surrounded her.

She could join any time, jump into the conversation by agreeing with Arion or asking Kerry a question, but she held back. Part of her didn't want to join at all. After the long journey here and all the unfamiliar familiarity of home, she was tired. She didn't want to hear about the running of Lindenfaire or the cadets or even about Arion and Warrek's scheming. For now, she just wanted a bed, a real bed, to lay down on and sleep. There would be time for everything else later.

But the men continued to talk, with Alix making a joke now and again but mostly keeping a furtive eye on Lena. Resigned to wait, Lena reminded herself that these feelings were temporary; she just needed to adjust to Lindenfaire. She'd had similar pangs of disappointment and despair when she first arrived at Finhöln—she'd make the best of it, adjust, just like she always did.

"So soon?" It wasn't her father's words that finally pulled Lena out of her own thoughts but his tone. What had been a light, jovial room took on a nervous energy. Kerry shifted his weight from one foot to the other, his gaze cutting to the window. Alix was trying to catch her eye with a significant look.

Arion, cognizant of the way the air had shifted in the tighter set of his shoulders, shrugged, as if the mood hadn't changed. "Today to rest and then back on the road. I think it's prudent to get to Highclere and the investigation underway as soon as possible."

Today to rest. He wanted to leave Lindenfaire tomorrow?

"The guards should have more time," Lena said, her voice almost croaking from disuse.

"I'm not sure haste is the answer here," Warrek added.

"It isn't haste—this has gone on too long anyway. I want to put an end to it and restore Lena's name. The sooner we get to Highclere, the sooner we truly begin."

Arion's argument made sense, but the idea of leaving Lindenfaire sent a sudden frisson of cold panic through Lena.

"I don't know that I should leave yet," she said, though none of the men were paying attention to her. Her father and Arion continued to argue, and Kerry was paying painfully close attention to whatever was going on out the nearest window.

"If she went now, she'd be arrested on sight," Warrek argued.

"Do you think I'd allow that? Lena would be safe with me. She'll be needed to give testimony to the appellate judges."

"That can be done in writing. We agreed she'd stay here, at least until the way is safe."

Lena swallowed hard. "I don't think—"

"We didn't, we talked about getting the initial steps done quickly so that during the longer appeals process, she'd be safe in the city."

"She shouldn't go somewhere her safety isn't assured. The king won't like this when he catches wind."

"My lord father will have to see reason. And if she stays here, it looks like cowardice. She must be there to defend her claim."

"She will be, but first—"

A heavy clatter made everyone jump, and they all watched with wide eyes as Alix scooped up the empty cup she'd dropped. "Sorry," she said, giving Warrek an apologetic grin.

Right.

Lena cleared her throat. "I think, for now, it'd be better if I stayed here. Showing up in the capital would cause an uproar and you wouldn't be able to get anything done on my behalf. The judges would know of my coming before you could reach them."

"We wouldn't announce your arrival," said Arion, not ready to give up.

"I'm travelling with you and you're always announced," she reminded him gently. "I'd have to sneak in on my own and find you again without being discovered."

"Many know her face," Warrek said. "She'd be away from your protection too long."

"There would be a way. We have time to figure it out."

"It's too risky," her father argued.

Arion sighed and turned to her, eyes imploring, to say, "Just think on it." The words of everyone who wanted to stop an argument but not cede the field.

"Fine," she agreed softly. And she would. But first she'd sleep.

⸺ ◆ ⸺

It didn't change her mind.

Though the bed had been welcome, being in her room hadn't offered the comfort she'd hoped. Often in the night she woke unsure of where she was, and it took many long moments before that shock of unease faded enough for her to slowly go back to sleep.

Despite this, she didn't want to leave Lindenfaire. She might not feel comfortable here yet, but it was still home and offered more safety than Arion could promise.

She hadn't stopped to think on his plan much on their way south from Finhöln, but hearing her father's thoughts, those concerns became her own. For so long, she'd wanted nothing more than her good name and honor restored, but now, as the horses were saddled and the prince, the man who promised to restore them to her, prepared to ride, Lena couldn't swallow her fear of returning to the capital. She couldn't bear to have another hope ripped out of her hands.

It made sense for Arion to smooth the way first. Less risk.

"I want this to happen, you know I do," she told Arion. They stood outside the busy stables, his remaining guards moving swiftly to ready for the road again. They moved with more alacrity with fully bellies and a good night's sleep in them, and Arion would be ready to depart in minutes. He'd even had Yvain saddled for her.

Arion stood with his hands on his hips, a frustrated frown marring his face. Lena had only seen him like this when thinking about how to open the avian stronghold of Hadria to their forces. He was like the sun hidden behind a bank of clouds, gloomy and severe.

"Lena…"

"But my father's right, it's too risky right now. I know what I'm asking, Arion, I do. If it's too much to ask, I understand, but—"

He grabbed up her hands to hold. "Never, Lena, it's never too much. You know I'd do anything for you."

She bit her cheek. "I know."

"Come with me. Please."

"I shouldn't. If anyone discovered I'd returned before you swayed a judge to hear the case…"

"That won't happen. You'll be under my protection, always."

"You can't be with me always, Arion. You have duties beyond just trying to secure an appeal."

"I'll keep you safe."

"How? Hiding me away?"

His mouth thinned into a displeased line, and Lena knew she was right. His plan was to hide her away until it was safe. But who knew how long that could be. Stuck inside the capital, the palace, so close to the king and all those loyal to him, made her throat close in panic.

"I understand your fears, your father's too." He sighed, gripping her hands tighter as if he could will her with just that to come with him. "But I'll keep you safe, Lena, I swear it. Nothing matters more to me."

"And what happens if we're caught? I'd be imprisoned?"

"I wouldn't let that happen."

"Arion—" She lowered her voice and stepped closer when one of the guards looked over at her use of the prince's name. "It's too dangerous to go to a capital where you're my only friend. I know you'd do everything to keep me safe, and that you're well-loved, but Highclere turned on me once. If I go with you now, it will again." *And I can't take another disappointment, another betrayal.*

Arion made an unhappy sound in his throat. "I'd feel better if you were near me."

She squeezed his hands and leaned forward until they shared breath, willing to give him what he wanted for a moment. "I know. But for now, it'd be easier for you without me near."

He searched her eyes for a long moment, probing, but Lena didn't know what he hoped to find. Finally, Arion sighed, and Lena's innards released from their hard clench.

"I'll send word the moment it's safe for you, and I won't rest until it is."

"Thank you, Arion," she said and dearly meant it. She'd been his cause before, had been burned from coming so near the sun, but this time, perhaps it would be all right. Perhaps for once, things would start to go her way.

But she wasn't ready to truly hope yet. She'd leave that up to Arion.

Arion pressed her hands to his chest before stealing a quick kiss. She couldn't pull back before he was gone, striding towards the readied group of guards. She avoided their gaze, only watching Arion as he gracefully mounted and eased his horse forward.

As he passed, Arion reached a hand down to her and she took it.

"The next time we see each other, you'll be a free woman. This I promise."

"Matella bless and guide you, Prince Arion."

He smiled down at her and then his hand slipped away and he passed by, his guards following behind him. He rode out of Lindenfaire to the din of cheering cadets, who'd all gotten up early to see the prince off.

Lena watched as he smiled and waved at the children. She hugged her arms around herself, hoping to keep the churning mass of worry inside.

Goddess, had she been right to do this, to come south and defy the king? She didn't know anymore—Arion took all the surety with him. What she did know was that she missed Finhöln, missed Bel with an ache that only grew as the days passed.

She tightened her arms, holding herself together, and trudged back into the house.

41

Bel's instinct was to wait until the dead of night to unwrap the bandages binding his wing, to let the deep darkness covering the castle muffle what he did. The want to unwrap his wing itched worse than a healing wound, prickling at the back of his mind, but Bel made himself wait.

It turned out to be at night, but not so late. Bel noticed that at the evening shift change, the soldiers were eager to talk, especially the one left on their own for the night to guard his door. They chatted until the soldier being relieved finally made noises about being hungry and left. Bel estimated he'd have a quarter of an hour.

He waited in his chair, a fire crackling, papers surrounding him. Normal. He even made scratches with his quill now and again, though he hadn't dipped it in ink. He didn't know how much his door deadened the sounds he made, but the soldiers guarding him always stood at the other end of the hall, where echoes had time to gather and grow.

Bel tried to keep from thinking about the stint and bandages by keeping his hands busy. He made invisible patterns on the parchment with his empty quill, and in the other, he rotated Pol's note with his thumb and middle finger.

He hadn't seen his friend in weeks, confined to his room. The New Warden had him on a strict schedule, disliking that he hadn't been able send Bel's important work on with the prince and Lena. Now Bel would fill his time with only work. Without the distraction of company or happiness, he was making good time.

Pol made his meals, but they were sent up with the shift changes. But Pol, always wily, found ways of sneaking him things. Notes were often stuck to the bottom of mugs and goblets. Once, he'd even covered the outside in wax and put it at the bottom of Bel's mug. Bel hadn't noticed until he'd drained it that there was an odd lump at the bottom that when chipped away revealed a tightly folded note. Pol had even baked gaming pieces into bread to give him something to do.

The notes were mostly stories of how the castle was changing under the New Warden. Pol complained about the work it was to cook for so many soldiers; even though many had left with the prince, there were still many more hungry, demanding mouths to feed than Pol was used to. He complained about Malthus, too, who hadn't taken his return to Finhöln well.

One thing the notes never mentioned was Lena. Pol had written once about how he missed Alix bouncing into the kitchen each morning, but he was careful not to say anything about Lena, her departure, or where she might be now.

Somehow, that the notes didn't mention her only highlighted her absence more. He felt it in the way the castle remained cold, even as spring valiantly fought its way up the mountain. The castle had never felt homey, but it had been a good existence with her there.

And just because Bel was confined to his room didn't mean that he was free of her, free from the places she haunted. She'd spent so much time with him in his chambers, almost every night until the prince arrived. The place beside his on his bed had just the slighted dip to it from her body where she'd lain. It had imprinted her form, if only slightly, and Bel had to sleep with his back to it to avoid the temptation of curling up in her shape.

He couldn't blame her for leaving—he knew how royals drew others into their orbit, how it came with the feeling of power but took away choice. But more, he couldn't blame her for wanting the chance to clear her name. If he'd learned nothing else about Lena, it was her goodness, her fairness, and she deserved to have her honor restored. She never should have been sent to Finhöln, not by the standards of the other wardens.

Alix had told him once that the people needed knights like Lena. Bel thought he now understood what she meant.

He wanted her name cleared, he wanted her to go on to do all the things she'd wanted and dreamed of. But it was cold comfort, and he couldn't help the tang of bitterness that always seemed to soak the back of his tongue. She'd been given a chance, and she'd taken it.

He was trapped in his room with the memory of her and what they'd done. What she had done and what she, perhaps, hadn't done...

Bel shifted impatiently, listening hard. Still there was no sound of the changing shift, so he waited.

Pol's latest letter had only confirmed something for him that he'd begun to suspect, and it made it all the more necessary to be rid of the bandage and see what had to be done.

They think because I can't hear that I don't listen, Pol had written, *but I can see them talking of the capital, perhaps taking you with them. The prince was unhappy with the castle and thought it would be better to have you in the south. The captain seems to agree. The soldiers talk of nothing but going back to the south, though they don't like the prospect of having you in tow. I will tell you if I find out more.*

Bel had known of the prince and captain's displeasure at Finhöln and the state of his prison. There was little he didn't hear from down the corridor; the humans would have to talk in very hushed tones, and even then, he'd probably still get the sense of talking, of the sound of a voice being used, even if the words were indistinct.

The prince wanted him moved further south, as did the captain, so that this *"joke of a prison,"* as the soldiers like to call it, could be done with completely. Bel assumed they waited on word from the prince, but when that would come he didn't know. He had no sense of how far it was to the human capital, nor how long it would take for word to come back. He also didn't know how long the captain's patience would last.

He'd begun to suspect that the moment the ink was dry on his translations on Hadria, all of them, including Bel, would be headed south.

And south was somewhere Bel couldn't go. Not if he ever wanted to be free again.

But he was getting ahead of himself.

A small scuff whispered through his door, and Bel held his breath, relieved when the sound of the new guard echoed down the corridor. The soldiers traded greetings and insults, and Bel got to work.

Bel stood silently and padded around the table to stand before the fire. It provided ample light and anyone coming in the door wouldn't immediately see him.

With shaking fingers, Bel untied the knots. His chest eased, ribs moving to find more space as he unwound the tight bindings. Round and round, feathers rustling. Gauze pooled at his feet, and Bel was almost lightheaded as he came to the end of the bandage.

Bel stood up straight, gazing unblinking into the fire as he rolled his shoulders back and forth, left and right.

His heart picked up speed, his mouth going dry as feeling rushed into his wing bases in pricks of awareness. He worked through it, continuing to roll his shoulders until he was almost doing small flaps of his wings, up and down, working blood into his back.

The bones of his right wing base creaked and popped and ached, sore as a toothache, and Bel cried with pain and joy.

It pained him like any healing wound.

But it was reset.

Lena had reset the wing base. Oh, she'd broken it first, but after years of healing improperly, there'd been no other way. She'd broken it so it could be right again.

Bel's mouth stretched in a fierce grin and he had to hold in his whoop. Hot, incandescent joy burned through him, scorching him from the inside out, nearly making him want to jump from his window that moment. To reclaim the sky, to rediscover the horizon and the wind and his own freedom.

He didn't, though; he knew his wing wasn't nearly strong enough. Perhaps it never would be for flight. But he knew what this meant, knew now what Lena had given him.

A chance.

If there was talk of taking Bel south, he'd need to be ready before then. And now, he would be. He had a chance, a real chance at escape now, of finally being a true avian again.

He'd take that chance.

42

Not for the first time, Lena woke with a start, unsure where she was. She searched the gloom, seeking something familiar. When she recognized the shape of the window, outlined through the thin gossamer curtains by gray dawn light, the rest fell into place.

Lindenfaire. Da's house.

She sank back into the soft mattress, rooting around in the blankets until finally comfortable again.

But she couldn't go back to sleep.

This had been her room once, so different from the little cell bunks of the other cadets. She'd slept in this room so many nights, on all her visits home during her squiring years, even on her way north to Finhöln, and rarely slept so well anywhere else.

Not so much these past nights. She blamed it on the unfamiliar shadows; a tree that'd been planted in the small private courtyard of the manor house had grown, its branches finally surpassing Lena's third-story window. She'd enjoyed watching how the light split through the fluttering leaves in the late afternoon, but at night, it created shifting pools of darkness and rattled against the windowpane. The bare walls of the room offered a large stage for the dancing shadows.

All her things had been packed away in the large trunk at the foot of her bed, everything elegantly folded or stored in smaller boxes. She hadn't really noticed it when she and Alix were last here, trudging north, but now it was hard to ignore.

Sitting on top were her spurs. In an enamel box, the blue-gray silver still shiny and sharp. Lena had stared at them longer than she'd care to admit her first night, had nearly pricked her finger on the symbol of her knighthood.

Once the birds woke and began their morning greetings, Lena left her bed. Thinking about her spurs and all her things tucked away wouldn't do any good. Instead, she made quick work of readying; just neat trous, tunic, and braid were all she needed to be presentable at home.

Nobody was in the dining room when she got there, but the cooks had already laid out the sideboard. She swallowed her disappointment at not seeing her old Cook, Kerry's beloved but tyrannical mother. Cook had always been kind to Lena, and she was saddened to hear from Kerry of her passing the previous summer.

It felt odd to rarely see the servants, to not speak with them or know their names. Lena filled her plate with eggs and sausage, avoiding looking at the puffy pastries her father loved but Cook had refused to make him more than once a week, and decided that's what she'd do today, introduce herself to all the new faces and learn their names.

She was halfway through her breakfast and thinking of a plan to greet the staff without getting in their way when Alix wandered in, eyes bleary and curls pillow-flattened.

"Morning," she mumbled, making straight for the food.

"Good morning. Early, isn't it?"

Alix grumbled in acknowledgement, focused instead on collecting a squadron's worth of food. She set down her two plates and bowl across from Lena.

The girl had grown as large of a sweet tooth as her father, it seemed. Thanks to the new cooks, she'd discovered syrup; it covered everything on her plates—the eggs, bacon, sausage, toast, it all had an amber shine to it.

Once Alix was a few mouthfuls in, she looked a little more alert.

"Early lessons today," she said.

Lena nodded. The cadets' day started early at Lindenfaire except for their designated rest days or holidays. She remembered it well, had learned early that she had to be up before everyone else. She'd gotten rising and readying down to an art, able to arrive only a few moments before the others housed in the barracks—too early and everyone laughed at her, too late and everyone resented the headmaster's daughter.

"Are you...liking it? The new classes?"

Alix shrugged. "They're fine."

"And your classmates?"

"They're..."

"Different?"

"I was going to say doughy."

Lena's sip of tea almost came back out her nose.

"You know what I mean," Alix said around a mouthful of toast.

Lena shook her head while coughing up tea. No, she certainly didn't know.

"They're just all so bright-eyed. Happy to take orders and vomit up whatever the teacher just told them."

"Well, that's..." She was going to say that's what school was like, but honestly, she hadn't known any other kind of school. It was hard to imagine anything other than a day of learning segmented by drills and combat training.

"No sense of humor," Alix continued, smiling at her own assessment, "and always so serious. Kind of like..."

Lena met Alix's startled gaze, saw her flush as her eyes flitted away. Alix stirred her syrupy porridge and cleared her throat.

"Not what I meant..."

Lena nodded, took an uneventful sip of tea, and let the room lapse back into silence.

She had nothing really to say about it—Alix was right, the cadets were like her because they were formed and instructed by the same people, same system. Children came from all over Vagora to be taught here, but few were like Alix, plucked from poverty and the city. The majority of cadets came from families with enough resources to spare a child from household duties. Lindenfaire was meant to turn out cadets who would become worthy squires and eventually go on to become celebrated knights like Lena.

Well, maybe not so much like Lena.

After another few bites, Alix finally looked in Lena's vicinity, her cheeks still pink.

"How long do I have to take classes?" she asked quietly.

"What do you mean?"

"How long are we going to be here? When will I start *my* lessons again?"

It was Lena's turn to turn away. She was ashamed that she hadn't thought about what Alix would do or should be doing in a long while. She hadn't thought about the two of them as *we* and *us* since leaving Finhöln. She hadn't even arranged for Alix to start taking classes with the cadets, her father had made the suggestion and gotten Alix placed the day after they arrived.

"If you like the classes, perhaps it's best if you continue them," she said vaguely.

Between her poor mood and the possibility that she may have to leave for Highclere eventually, perhaps it was best that Alix not rely on her for now.

"I'm already a squire, so why take classes for cadets."

"There's always something to learn. It could do you good, offer you some opportunities."

Alix sneered at that. "Opportunities for what? To become someone else's squire?"

The question, the very idea of Alix not being her squire, made her chest seize, but all Lena could say was, "I don't know."

Alix's mouth thinned. "You don't mean it."

"I know my own mind better than you, Alixandre."

"Not sure that's true. I don't think you know what you want."

"Oh, I see, and you do, is that it? Alix the All-Knowing."

That earned her a scowl.

"What I know is that you're letting yourself be pushed around. Everyone's doing it and you're letting them."

"Including you?"

"I'm the only one who's got your back," Alix said through pursed lips.

"You just don't like that others are trying to manage me. I don't need to be managed, by you or by anyone."

"I'm not…" Alix huffed, crossing her arms and slumping against the chairback. "I'm trying to help you. You're like the cadets, thinking the world is a just place if only you believe it enough. Well, it's not. I don't want you to get hurt when you figure that out."

Lena laughed humorlessly. "I'm not a child, Alix, I know how the world works."

"Maybe this world." She twirled her finger in a circle, indicating Lindenfaire. "But out there, not as much."

"And you're going to protect me from it?"

"Someone has to."

"I'm the adult," Lena said, feeling less so by even having to say it, "I'm the one who takes care of you."

"How is dumping me here taking care of me? You think those cadets will accept me?"

Nothing came out of Lena's open mouth, and her stomach churned at the idea of Alix hating this place, of having no friends, of being seen as different from the others, never accepted. She knew what that was like.

Warrek bustled in, snapping Lena's fluttering thoughts. Both she and Alix watched him collect pastries and a few scoops of porridge for his breakfast.

He greeted them both, asking how they slept, before sitting down and tucking into his meal. His gaze bounced between the two of them, sensing something, but neither would look at the other and give anything away.

Warrek cleared his throat after another bite of sweet bun and turned to Alix. "Well, m'dear, ready for another day?"

She managed a weak smile.

"You starting classes here has gotten me thinking, there must be many more children like you, children from the cities just hungry for the opportunity."

Lena cringed, remembering just how hungry Alix had been when she'd tried to pick Lena's pockets.

"I was thinking," Warrek continued, not seeing how Alix's tepid smile had turn into something feral. "What would you think of a scholarship? Find children of talent and bring them to school here and at other academies? Give them the opportunities they need to make something of themselves."

It wasn't a bad idea, and Lena would happily support any plan that got children like Alix off the streets and into safety and security, but Warrek apparently didn't hear how condescending it sounded.

If Alix had been a cat, her hackles and tail would be standing straight in indignation. Lena was a little surprised she wasn't spitting and hissing.

"Scholarship's the only way kids like that would make it up here," was all Alix said, nearly toppling Lena over in surprise at her diplomacy.

Warrek nodded. "Yes, exactly, we should make the most of it so that they can make the most of it."

Alix and Lena watched him cut open and butter another sweet roll wordlessly.

"That wasn't all my ideas this morning, either," said Warrek, casting a sly smile at Lena.

"You're full of them today," she said as lukewarmly as Alix had smiled.

"Mm," he hummed around a bite of bun. "Now that you're both settled, I think it's time for you to find your place here, Lena. In fact, you've come home at the perfect time. We need more anointed knights teaching the cadets, and you know Lindenfaire's system."

"You want me to teach classes?" she said slowly.

Warrek's smile grew wider. "Not just that. I want you to help me run Lindenfaire. Be my right hand."

Lena could see her father's excitement, the impatient glint in his eyes as he waited for her reaction, gave her space to gasp and agree and thank him, promise him she'd do her best and make him proud.

But all she could say was, "But Kerry's already your second."

Her father waved away her concern. "Kerry's a fine young man and done an excellent job. He's done well in the interim, but it's time I get a trained knight in the position. Someone with more..."

"Status?" she offered through gritted teeth.

"Experience," Warrek countered.

"You just said Kerry's doing an excellent job. The cadets love him. Why change that?"

"A place like Lindenfaire should be run by knights. It's a school *for knights*. I will be the first to applaud Kerry's skills as a swordsman and teacher, but he doesn't have what you have, Lena."

"A blacklisted name and a criminal conviction?"

"*Experience*. A knighthood. The Montcaer name."

"Ah."

"What is this tone? I thought you'd be pleased, we'd always planned this for you, to have you help run Lindenfaire and eventually take it over."

Had they? Lena always knew it was an option for her, to come back to Lindenfaire and teach not a few squires but hundreds of young cadets. She liked the idea of helping the young ones find their strengths, liked the manor house and the surrounding lands. But there were so many other things she wanted to do first.

"You shouldn't choose my name over Kerry's merit."

Warrek gave an exasperated huff. "And what about your own merit, Lena?"

She just shook her head.

Alix made a little cough, stood, and cleaned up her plates before announcing, "I'm off to classes." She threw Lena a significant look before beating a retreat.

Lena sighed and stood too. "I should start my day."

Warrek watched her clean up, letting his disappointment and dis-approval permeate the air.

Before she could follow Alix out, Warrek said quietly, "Lena, we will discuss this further."

"Fine."

She strode quickly through the house without seeing, without a des-tination. She just wanted to be far away from her father's suggestion.

It was perhaps a smart move, ensconce her at Lindenfaire, give her a position, let her prove herself in the safety of the family demesne. Per-haps she could win over those parents who'd shudder at sending their child to a school run by a discredited knight in time.

But all of this would take years, not to mention a determination and desire that Lena just didn't have.

Lena hadn't truly realized just how much her father entrenched himself here, behind the beautiful walls and fountains of Lindenfaire. Here it was safe, controlled.

Safe, shelved, stuck in one place.

Her father offered her this life. Bel had had it thrust upon him.

Lena wanted none of it.

She ended up spending her day making loose circuits of the grounds. Accomplishing nothing but letting a frustrated listlessness grow deep inside. Lena didn't want the position, didn't want what her life would surely become if she took it. The problem was it was just another thing she *didn't* want. "*I don't think you know what you want,*" Alix had said. And she was right.

43

Lady Margot Montcaer never really came in, she *arrived*.

Lena sat in the library, surrounded by the quiet friends she had in her father's books, leafing through a beautifully illustrated ballad about the famous battle where her parents had met. Without having met before, only knowing each other by reputation, each had been put in charge of a battalion and in a spontaneous pincer move, had attacked the enemy on both sides and met in the middle. The ballad went on for a full page about how it was love at first sight for the Montcaers, how it was a love never known before.

She was less interested in that than admiring the gilt embossing and colorful etchings that decorated the margins.

The book in her hand began to quiver, and Lena looked up to see the clatter of approaching horses. From the library's second-story bay of windows, she watched a party of at least a dozen flood into the courtyard below, bringing with them a cloud of dust and a few curious cadets.

It was easy to identify who headed the party.

Lady Margot wore no armor or weapons, but there was no mistaking the straight cut of her shoulders and stiff back. The dapple gray of her horse caught the light like sunshine over rippling water. Her mother always rode gray horses; the effect of it and the gray steel of her eyes had long ago earned her the name the Gray Dragon.

Lena hadn't meant to copy her mother with Yvain, though many had said so in whispers behind their hands. She'd just liked Yvain.

As cadets and valets hurried to help the knights dismount and see to the horses, Lena turned away from the window and sank further into the plush green armchair.

It'd been over a week since her father had brought up becoming his second. She'd avoided the subject by avoiding Warrek as much as possible. When it was mentioned, Lena asked if her father thought Arion would be back in Highclere by now.

Surely he would. He'd send word any day now. Perhaps it was best not to make plans before hearing from the crown prince.

That's what she told her father, anyway. Whether or not she'd hear from Arion soon she didn't know and didn't want to hope for. Perhaps a letter would come soon but not with good news. Perhaps it would take months, even years to get the process started. Perhaps the king would catch wind of it and put a stop to Arion's plans. Perhaps her own mother had come to arrest her again.

Lena remained in her comfortable chair and sipped tea while the house grew louder. The sounds of people coming and going, opening and closing doors, echoed up to her, but she didn't leave. She wasn't truly reading either, but the thought of facing her mother sent a shudder through her.

But as it always went with her mother, Lena couldn't escape her for long. It took Margot under an hour to suss out her daughter's whereabouts. Lena didn't even jump when the library door flew open, all the announcement Margot needed.

"*There* you are," she said, entering the library with the force of a hurricane. Her hair was unbound and waved away from her chiseled face, falling down her back in brown-gray ringlets. She'd changed into fresh clothes, and her face had been scrubbed, eyes bright and lips slightly chapped from the road.

She planted her fists on her hips, taking in Lena slumped in her chair, surrounded by open books.

"Well? Not even going to get up and greet your mother?"

"Hello, mum," Lena sighed.

Margot gave a half-exasperated, half-amused snort. She hated being called mum.

"How was the journey?" Lena asked by rote.

Margot waved a hand and came further into the room. She was tall for a woman, all long, wiry limbs and strength, yet her straight back and perfect posture always made her seem twice as big, taking up more space than anyone else. She'd commanded armies this way to great effect for years, most recently the southern campaign for the River Dyne.

That conflict must have simmered down for Lady Margot to leave the front. Lena supposed she should be flattered.

"Dusty. Uncomfortable," answered Margot, stepping around the library to inspect a few books and look out the windows. "We made good time up from the south, stopped in Highclere and reported to the king on our success."

Lena nodded along but didn't listen to the details of her mother's rout of the southern tribes. Apparently there was peace for now, hard won by Lady Margot and her troops—but this was just another way of saying a stalemate. Despite her mother's efforts and continued shows of force, the southern border would remain a battleground. If the king and Lady Margot hadn't solved it by now, Lena doubted they would.

"Well?"

Her gaze snapped up to her mother, and a light sweat broke out over her forehead at the sight of one of Margot's notorious raised eyebrows. Grown for years and still that look could make Lena squirm.

Margot humphed when Lena said nothing and asked again, "And you? Tell me of the north."

Lena told the short version, describing the starkness of Finhöln, the boredom, the mundanity of day-to-day life. She spoke briefly of the one prisoner and her cordiality with the cook, but that was all.

Margot listened without interrupting, though her frown deepened at the mention of Finhöln's one prisoner and the state of the castle. It was the same look Captain Joran had, and it made her heart give a painful lurch for Bel.

Things would change for him. She'd given him what little she could, but it was up to him now.

Margot made an unhappy sound when Lena finished. "I see. Well, I'm happy you're out of there—goddess knows you shouldn't have been there in the first place."

Then you should've stopped it. Lena clenched her teeth until her jaw ached.

"But that doesn't explain why you're here with your father. When I stopped in Highclere, I met with Prince Arion and he said you'd resisted coming with him though he was adamant you should."

"We'd discussed it and I thought it was better to remain here," she said, focusing on a spot over her mother' shoulder.

"Good goddess," Margot muttered, rubbing her temples.

Lena crossed her arms over her chest when Margot clasped her hands together and pointed them at her.

"Lena, why would you think it's smart to let your best chance of redemption *leave without you*? This is your case, the prince is doing you the favor. *Hells.*" She popped her hip and planted a fist on it. "I wanted to know your reasoning first, that's why I came here, but being scared isn't good enough. We're leaving for Highclere in the morning to rejoin Prince Arion and ensure we get this done."

"I'm not scared," she retorted on instinct.

Her mother arched another eyebrow, and Lena felt all of six years old again.

"Either you're scared or you're stupid to have stayed behind. Which is it?"

"Neither," she snapped, back straightening to lift her out of the cushions. Her mother looked almost proud.

Warrek's head poked around the library door, and he cleared his throat while coming in.

"Here you are," he said. "Catching up?"

"I'm trying to convince our daughter to start packing. We need to leave for Highclere tomorrow."

Warrek frowned. "Oh, I'd thought—"

"And I was telling mother that I didn't think it was a good idea then and I don't think it is now. It's too risky. Arion hasn't sent word, it's just ideas and determination right now. I don't want to wait for an appeal in a cell."

"There's never gain without risk," insisted Margot.

"It's my life to risk."

Warrek cleared his throat again. "I agree with Lena, my love. She's safer here, and while the prince's intentions are good, he doesn't have a solid plan yet. Let's wait for him to write and see what's been done. In the meantime, I'm instating Lena as my second."

Margot sighed. "Warrek, we talked about this, she can't stay here forever."

"Not forever, no, but it's the safest place for her."

"Perhaps, but nothing can be done for her here."

"She can make a name for herself here, prove her loyalty by teaching the cadets. It's the safest way to go."

"And what if the prince loses interest? What if he gives up on her? Out of sight, out of mind. She wouldn't be safe then, and it'd hurt the credibility of Lindenfaire if she was kept on."

"Thank you for the reminder that my whole future rests on the whims of one person," Lena muttered.

Margot turned a fearsome frown her way. "Your future *does* rest with the prince, so why you aren't with him is beyond me. This is all about him, anyway; he's the key here."

"What do you mean?"

One of Margot's brows ticked, and she cleared her throat. "Nothing," she muttered.

Swooping in, Warrek insisted, "She'll do wonderfully here, Margot. You'll see. We'll get her started on—"

"I haven't agreed to it yet, Da."

Both her parents frowned at that.

"Well, I haven't. I'm still thinking it over. I agree that I'll have to go to Highclere at some point, and I don't want to be a burden to the academy, so I'm not sure it's right to be your second. And Kerry—"

"Never mind Kerry," grumbled Warrek. "This is about you."

"Indeed. This is all for you, Lena. All our plans. Yet you don't want to do anything. What exactly is it that you want? You wouldn't go with the prince to Highclere. You don't want to come with me. You don't want to be your father's second. What do you want, then? Hmm? Please, tell me, so I can make sense of you right now."

Lena's mouth opened and closed like a fish just pulled from the sea and gutted.

Everyone seemed to be asking her this. Everyone wanted to know the answer.

She did too.

Margot threw her hands in the air. "You have no idea. Fine. That's fine. Then step aside and let me fix this."

"Margot..." Warrek tried.

"No," she said, waving her hand in Lena's direction. "She's being impossible right now." And she turned on her heel and left the library, leaving with as much force as she'd blown in with.

Lena huffed and grumbled, hiding her hurt away and sinking back into the armchair as her father went after Margot, arguing his point.

Her mind tumbled and her gut churned in ways only her mother could inspire. She gave up trying to read and instead sat sulking, licking her wounds in the quiet of the library. Noises eventually drifted up to her from the rest of the house, the manor alive again with the whole family and her mother's party now in residence.

She picked at her cuticles well into the evening until summoned for dinner. It was an unavoidable inevitability—when they were all here, they all ate together. She wasn't ready for it; she knew Margot wouldn't give up, even if there were half a dozen other knights at their table to watch.

Gritting her teeth, Lena trudged to the dining room like she would to meet her executioner.

———— ·•◆•· ————

She survived dinner, barely, and the next day, too. But as the hours dragged on without Lena dragging herself onto a horse, Margot's patience drew thinner.

Lady Margot was a renowned hunter and tactician—she could outwit and outwait anyone it was said. She ordered, she guilted, she flattered, she coaxed, she promised, she threatened. And as Lena continued to resist, she started to feel like a walled fortress her mother had besieged, and it was only a matter of time before the strategy got dirty.

Lena tiptoed through the house when she couldn't be out on the grounds, but more often than not, Margot found her and delivered another argument, another demand that they leave immediately for Highclere. She'd begun to suspect her mother had spies everywhere and couldn't trust even the cadets.

On the second day, Margot cornered her on the second-floor gallery late in the afternoon. It was the fourth time that day she'd demanded Lena decide on a course of action, and as Margot stood there, imposing and frustrated, arms crossed and eyes sharp, arguing her point yet again, Lena eyed the banister and wondered if she could make the jump.

"*Lena!*"

Fingers snapped just under her nose, and Lena jumped.

"At least do me the respect of paying attention. I'm trying to help you," grumbled Margot.

"You don't need to fix anything," Lena insisted, so tired of this. "This is my life, not a broken saddle to be tacked back together."

Her mother snorted. "Oh, I wish it was that easy, Lena, but you've insisted on making it complicated like you always do."

"I do *not*," she said, trying to keep the whine from her voice.

"You were perfectly happy to let the prince go off and handle this for you. You don't want to do the work? Fine, then *I will*, but you'll damn well do as I say to get it done."

"I didn't ask Arion to do this. I'm grateful to him, but I won't wait for an appeal from a cell."

"Tell her why, Margot."

Lena and Margot unlocked horns long enough to look across the gallery to see Warrek emerge from his study. He crossed the gallery to them, a shrewd look to him as he assessed them both.

"Tell her what you told me," Warrek insisted. "About the prince."

"Warrek, it won't—"

"If you insist on taking her to Highclere, she should know what she'll be up against."

Lena's guts twisted painfully as she watched her parents have one of their silent conversations, passing secrets with cocked brows and twitching lips. The longer Margot remained silent, the colder Lena grew, starting in her fingertips and working up her arms. When her mother finally looked at her again, it felt like walking into the heart of winter up in Finhöln without any wools.

"Crown Prince Arion is in love with you, Lena."

Those guts of hers twisted and pinched.

"He was. Maybe."

"No, Lena. The prince's feelings for you haven't faded. While stopping in Highclere, I learned that someone close to the prince reported back to the king about you and Arion's affection for you. How attached he'd grown. So he was encouraged to send you home. And when you arrived, you were sent far away from the capital, to a lord who'd keep a close eye on you."

An indignant sound echoed across the gallery, so close to her own feelings that Lena thought for a moment it'd been her.

Across the gallery, Alix emerged from the shadows, her arms crossed over her chest. She didn't join them, just stared from across the way, but her feelings were clear in the fiery set of those jade eyes.

Margot grumbled when Alix didn't leave but continued. "You were supposed to just fade away. Go on with your life and let the prince forget you. But then you—" Margot let out a sharp huff, shaking her head.

"I did as you'd taught me, what the knight's code taught me," offered Lena weakly.

"You made a mess of it," Margot corrected. "You gave yourself up on a silver platter. The king couldn't have his son in love and wanting to marry a knight, no matter whose daughter she is. He needed to be rid of you."

Lena's heart pounded and her lungs burned even though she sucked in great gulps of air. She couldn't get enough—couldn't—

"He couldn't kill or maim you, not if he wanted to keep the loyalty of his son, but you had to leave."

"Didn't you think it was odd, your punishment?" said Warrek. "Warden of a prison no one's ever heard of, so far north it's barely Vagora."

"Get rid of you before the prince returns, sully your name and disqualify you from ever being considered suitable. It was all planned, Lena. You stumbled into their politics and they spat you back out."

That's exactly how it felt, chewed up, mashed, and spat back out. Lena wrapped her arms around herself, a new habit of hers it seemed, and squeezed, trying not to dissolve into tears.

"Which is why," Warrek said, "she should stay here. If she's with the prince, that's exactly what the king didn't want. We don't know what he could do if he found out."

"It's exactly why she should go. The prince cares for her, she should be with him defending her name, showing she *is* suitable."

Lena laughed humorlessly. "You want me to make me a princess now?"

Margot threw her an impatient look. "I'm just saying nothing should be ruled out."

"I could never marry Arion," she said, incredulous it even had to be said. She'd always known she and Arion would never have forever. And she hadn't wanted it, either. She'd known his life in Highclere was one of politics and intrigue and she wanted none of it.

"For once, Lena, you need to seize an opportunity, especially when it's put right under your nose."

Lena shook her head, hot tears sliding down her face and running from her nose. She couldn't stop them, her hands busy, clasped around her waist to hold everything in place. Dredged up from a dark place full of broken childish dreams, she wished she could stop the dam breaking inside, but it all came pouring out, a gush of grief and despair that had sunk like a cold river stone to the bottom of her gut and stayed there for months. But it wanted out now, any way it could.

"Why didn't you say anything?" she murmured.

"Because I knew you'd be upset," said Margot, misunderstanding.

"No. Why did you let them do it? They wanted to blacken my name—why didn't you defend me? Why did you let them turn everyone against me?"

"Dear goddess, Lena," Warrek said, "we've done everything for you."

"We didn't know the king's mind then, so don't you dare blame this on us. They seized on *your* mistakes."

"I'm what you made me!" Lena shouted, the force of it reverberating in her chest. "You made me into what you wanted but when it went wrong, you threw me away. You didn't defend me. You just watched as I was punished for doing *what you'd taught me to!*"

Lena's words rang through the hall, echoing off the ornate eaves and hanging in the air as Margot and Warrek gaped at her.

"And what were we supposed to do, Lena?" asked Margot through pursed lips.

"Something," she sobbed. "Anything!"

"The king had already decided on your sentence, one that mostly spared you, I might add. But he needed you gone. What could we have done?"

"But you're my *parents.*"

"And he's the *king.*" Margot made a sound that was part sigh, part huff, and all exasperation. "You're being impossible. I can't—I won't have this argument again," she said before turning on her heel and marching down the stairs and out the hall.

Margot took the bottom of Lena's stomach with her, leaving behind an awful sucking sensation that threatened to buckle Lena's knees. Her mother spoke as if there had been an argument before, as if the one time Lena pled for her mother to intervene as she waited for her trial, stuck in that cell in Highclere awaiting the king's judgement, had been an argument. It'd been no such thing, only a scared, whispered, *"Can't you help me? Mother?"* Margot had pretended not to hear. *"And as if this trial wasn't bad enough, they're threatening to knock your name from the registers. What were you thinking?"*

Warrek sighed, pinching the bridge of his nose.

"What a mess," he sighed. He rubbed his eyes before pegging her with a firm, disappointed stare. "You shouldn't speak to your mother and I like that, Lena. Not after everything we've done to help you."

"We both know nothing you've done has really been for me, Da. Not my training, not Lindenfaire, not this."

Warrek frowned, a terrible thing that had terrorized whole armies, and Lena shivered as it turned on her.

"I didn't raise you to be such an ungrateful—"

"You raised me to be a knight, to follow the code and do right. That's all I've ever tried to do. And for what?"

Warrek blinked in shock, but Lena was done.

She pushed past him, stalking across the corridor without seeing, still clutching her sides.

"Lena..." She heard Alix hurrying toward her but put on speed, the roiling mass of disappointment and heartbreak writhing its way out of her. She wanted to be by herself when it came out.

Her room was blessedly quiet and empty, but it offered none of the comfort it once had. Lena slumped down the closed door and drew her knees up to her chest, using all her limbs to keep herself from cracking to pieces.

It started as a trickle, but soon Lena was sobbing, crying out her hurts as she stared at that one damn trunk that held her entire childhood. That's what she amounted to in this house, one box's worth.

44

Lena emptied herself of tears that first night. After that, she watched the shifting shadows of the tree outside her window as the days blurred by. She liked how the shadows danced along the blank wall in the afternoons.

It was easy to sink into her bed and nest among the blankets; even in the warm afternoon, she covered herself from chin to toes, rubbing a corner against her cheek.

Moving had become an effort, so Lena just didn't.

A nameless servant brought in her meals and took out the untouched one from a few hours before. Lena had stopped asking for names.

She knew her mother came in at some point from the angrily gesticulating shadow that took up most of the far wall. There was a long, impassioned speech, something about Lena being ungrateful and willful, how she shouldn't just lie there and do nothing. She needed to *do* something.

But listening was an effort, so Lena didn't.

With a huff, the aggravated shadow disappeared and so did the annoying noise it came with.

She eased deeper into the blankets and rubbed a corner against her cheek. It was soft, but she wished it was softer, like...

She told time by the shadows, their length and depth. Two days passed in bed, but she didn't have the effort to care. Her teeth were fuzzy, her skin had a sheen, and whenever she shifted the blankets around, she caught a whiff of herself.

But caring was an effort, so she didn't. She was an oyster scraped of its meat and pearl, just a shell with nothing left to give.

On the rare times she thought to get up, the blankets grew heavy atop her, weighing her down. They coaxed her to stay, to forget, and Lena was easily swayed.

She was tired of the betrayal, the disappointments, the expectations. Her bed and blankets were none of those things.

She reckoned it was the third night when the door creaked open well past midnight. Dinner had already cooled and congealed and wouldn't be taken out again until morning, and the tread across the floorboards was too soft for the maids who brought meals.

A little intake of breath, not quite a sigh, told her it was Alix.

The other side of the bed rustled and dipped as Alix climbed in. She didn't get under the blankets, Lena had pulled most of them into a thick cocoon, but instead spread her own over herself. She moved this way and that, getting comfortable, and Lena tried not to be annoyed.

Annoyance was a feeling and she hadn't any of those left in her.

Alix settled down after another few moments, but her breathing continued to hitch every few beats. Lena waited her out, quiet and un-moving, and eventually sleep took Alix.

All was silent again, but she couldn't not be aware of the other body so near hers, distracting her from the dancing shadows. This late, they were nearly invisible in the inky blue of the night, but Lena liked to look for them anyway.

Watching the shadows quieted her mind so that she didn't have to hear herself think. If she did, she'd hear her mother asking if she was scared or stupid. She'd hear her father's scoff. She'd hear her king passing sentence. She'd feel the bones of Bel's wing base breaking under her hands.

They were all memories she didn't want.

She'd retreated to her room and under the blankets like the child she felt like and hadn't come out. What was there outside but more disappointment? In her parents, her king, herself.

But Alix's presence had her heart aching and her mind working again, slow and clumsily.

At first only feeling came back to her. She hesitated when it rushed her, wanted to sink back in to the blankets and forget again. Sadness came first, pulling her into its undertow to sink and drown. She shed a tear for Bel, stripped of everything but his life, another for all she'd hoped they would be but couldn't. She cried for all the good men and women who'd met their end in the crags of Hadria, and for the avians too, who'd watched their city burn. And she wept for the world that had never been, the one she'd thought was real but was really the stuff of storybooks.

But eventually the sadness ebbed, spent with the tears she shed.

Then came exhaustion, wide and deep. She was tired of not being grateful enough for the things she'd been given. She was tired of being scolded and ordered around and condemned. She was tired of doing what was right only to be told it was wrong when she knew, *knew she was right*.

Next came resentment, fierce and stinging. At her mother, who even now wanted to bully her and throw her to the lions in Highclere. At her father, for letting that assassin take his courage years ago. At Arion, for dragging her into this and not preparing her. And at her king, for not being that glorious, fair sun god he dressed up as.

Finally, small and achingly sweet, came longing. To belong. To do right. To be important to someone, not for what she could do but for what she meant to them. To have a purpose again. To be who she was meant to be...whoever that woman was.

She wanted...

She rubbed the blanket against her cheek again. She wanted this blanket to be softer, like feathers. She wanted to feel the softness of Bel's wings run up the length of her, feel the warmth of his skin against hers.

The blankets were warm, but they weren't like sleeping beside him, and she missed the weight of his arms as they held her.

Goddess, she missed him.

Being with Bel had given her what she needed, had shown her a vision if only she opened her eyes to it. She wanted him, wanted to give him a chance at a life.

He deserved that chance. He never should have been held, *tortured* like that for years.

There was no reason to it, just cruelty, to Bel and to Vagora. Bel wasn't some monster to fear from the night sky. The avians weren't evil and they didn't deserve to be wiped from map. She didn't know why the king renewed this war nor why he took it so much further than any of his forebears...but Lena no longer trusted the king's reasons.

But in wanting Bel, she sacrificed her only chance. She'd never be welcome in her land again, would never reclaim her name or honor from those who'd schemed to take it. All Arion's efforts would be for nothing. Everything she'd done to become a knight...nothing.

She wiped at her damp cheeks. That was the way of it, wasn't it? Nothing was ever truly free; everything had a cost. But did that mean that the cost wasn't worth the price?

She took a deep breath, felt it rattle around in her lungs and expand her chest.

But Lena had her honor. It wasn't something that needed to be trumpeted and cheered for. It just needed to be *true*. And it could only be taken from her if she let it be.

There was no honor in what had been done to Bel. What had been done to her.

And the last thing Lena felt in that bed was resolve. It pushed her up, up from the blankets, up from her nest of tears and self-pity. She rubbed the center of her chest, heart swelling with purpose, sweet and intoxicating.

Her head swam when she reached for her boots, her stomach rebelling at the move. She thrust her foot into a boot even as she swayed, swallowing her stomach's next gurgle.

The blankets rustled behind her.

"Where are we going?"

"You're not coming," she whispered but with no heat, no snap. This was dangerous, what she planned to do, and there wouldn't be a way back.

"Like hells I'm not!" Alix leapt from the bed and tackled her own boots.

"Alix…" Lena stood and her back snapped and popped, making her wince. "I'm going north. You can't come."

"North!" Her eyes shone with excitement. "Finally! We're—"

"You're staying here, where it's safe. This is…there's no going back. It's the right thing to do, but I won't ruin your life for it."

Alix snorted, bent over her second boot. "You're not ruining anything."

Lena put a hand on the girl's shoulder. "Alix, listen, this will be dangerous, and I won't risk you. Stay here where it's safe. Finish your training, become an amazing knight. The world will need knights like you."

Alix stared up at Lena for a long moment, face so childlike but fierce even in the dark. Lena stood her ground, though.

Finally, Alix stood, a defiant frown on her face. "You think I care about becoming a knight?"

Lena's mouth opened and closed.

"Well, I don't give two shits about becoming a knight. Never have and never will."

The child in Lena, the one who had tried so hard to please her parents and dreamed of being the best knight Vagora had ever known, moaned in horror.

"But you…"

Alix shrugged. "It was a good offer. Came with learning to fight, free food, clean clothes. Get off the streets." She took a step closer, invaded Lena's space. Her low Vagoran accent thickened as she said, "But I didn't take it because of that, either. Plenty of fucks who'll give kids like me that kind of thing, for a price. But not you. You didn't want to use me. You wanted to help. You cared."

Lena was shocked as a small tear collected at the corner of Alix's eye. Alix sniffed and pawed at it before it could fall.

"I don't care about being a knight. Not one of them ever stopped to help me or any other kid like me. Not one knight stood up to Balderak or the other rich fucks who abuse their power. But you did. I don't give a fuck about being a knight, but I sure as all seven hells give a fuck about you. So if you say you're going north, then I'm going too. If you say you're going to cross the eastern ocean to pull out mermaid hair, then that's where I'm going too. And if you're going to Highclere to marry the prince just to piss off the fucking king, then I sure as hells am going with you so I can—"

Alix hiccupped trying to speak and breathe all at once.

"Alix, all I did was give you the chance. You did the rest yourself."

She shook her head viciously, curls bouncing. "*You* did that for me, you made it happen. Now I'm going to do this for you. I don't care about pledging myself to king and country, but I promise—where you go, I'll go; I'll watch your back and defend you 'til the end. You're my friend, Lena, and I protect my friends."

Even with little light filtering into the room, Alix's eyes shone with a fierce belief in all she'd said. Open and wide, they were a window into the boundless, vulnerable loyalty she promised.

How could Lena refuse it? How could she possibly deny this girl, a true knight in heart and soul, from pledging her loyalty? It didn't matter if Lena felt unworthy or unsure—it wasn't for her to refuse.

Sniffing back her own tears, Lena gathered Alix close. She hooked her chin over the bouncy froth of curls and felt Alix's tears slide down her neck into the loose collar of her shirt.

"I, Maddalena Montcaer, recognize Alixandre of Highclere as knight of the realm. May she serve with heart and courage. May she be the people's shield and the people's sword against all those who would do them injustice."

Alix leaned back an inch in surprise, and Lena smiled down and wiped away the tears.

"I accept her pledge of loyalty and return it tenfold."

Alix flung her arms around Lena and hugged her back. Lena held her through a few sobs and thumbed away stray tears.

She couldn't have fathomed this, all those months ago, when she caught a little dirty pickpocket trying to rob her. She'd taken a chance on Alix. She'd helped her and been returned many times over. She'd do whatever she could for Alix, everything in her power to make sure this girl could take on the world and conquer it.

She wanted the same for Bel.

With a shaky laugh, she dried their tears again and said, "Let's go north, then."

"Yup. But first, you need a bath."

Lena truly laughed and agreed. While Alix gathered their things, she drew herself a bath, enjoying the manor house's piped hot water for probably the last time in...well. A while.

When she finished, she loosely coiled her wet hair atop her head and dressed in her things. The shirt and trous were crisp and clean, her boots sturdy, and her cuirass fit perfectly to her form.

Night still clung to the edges of the sky as Lena and Alix collected what they'd need. No one saw or stopped them as they gathered stock from the kitchen, blankets and clothes from the cupboard, and extra weapons from the house armory. Alix made off to the stable with bulging saddlebags as the sky began to gray with the dawn.

Lena took one thing from her father's study, a hidden purse of coin that Warrek had told her was for emergencies. She weighed it in her hand, knowing her father certainly wouldn't consider her purpose an emergency, but she left with it anyway. She didn't know where or how far she needed to go, but the purse would see her some of the way.

As Alix prepared the horses, Lena did a final sweep of the house, listing things in her head. When she descended the grand staircase to the bottom level, a giddy terror stole over her, doubt sucking at her stomach. It wasn't enough to make her turn back, but she took a long moment to look around at the place that made her. This had been her life, but not anymore, and it was time to leave.

It was time to do right, by Bel and by herself.

Just one last thing to do—Lena left her spurs on the mantel in her father's favorite room, in pride of place.

45

A waft of cold air caressed Bel's sweat-soaked back, making him shiver. Another drop fell into his eye, the salt stinging, but he held the tenth and final *ariant* form.

He was taking the forms a little faster than he should, but he couldn't get over the pleasure of feeling his right wing stretch and flex through the movements like it was supposed to. It quivered just being held up, barely strong enough to make it through the forms, but it *worked*.

An excited, hopeful part of him thought the wing might soon be strong enough to bear weight. Perhaps nothing more than a short glide, but it was something. Maybe, one day, if he worked hard enough, he'd fly again.

Lena did that.

He flushed at the thought of her and straightened out of his form.

Training again gave him purpose, allowed him to sometimes escape the cluttered confines of his mind, but others it only reminded him of her, of the way they sparred and moved together across the training mat. And then he couldn't help but think of the way they moved together in bed, and he'd make himself go through the forms again if only for something to do, to make his body and more importantly his mind settle.

It'd been easier before, so much easier when he shied away from pleasant feelings. He still had vivid memories of all the good things he could feel, most of them with her, and it made it harder to bear all the bad. When he thought of her, his body buzzed with unspent energy, making him want to crawl out of his skin. It didn't help that he was kept to his rooms; his world had become so small, so hemmed in.

So he trained, did his forms. Made his wing stronger, which was all thanks to her. And he began thinking of her again, and so the cycle went.

Bel sucked in a long breath, just to feel his lungs and chest expand, and gave his wings one big flap. The fire across the room sputtered and paper went flying, making him grin.

A loud screech made him jerk.

A shadow lurked just outside the bay window, barely distinguishable from the gloomy night, but the light caught on the yellow eyes and feet. A hawk sat clawing at the window, wings beating against the casement.

Bel hurried to the window as the impatient bird began to squawk.

Frigid air and fluttering wings met him when he threw the window open wide. Though the snows had stopped, the nights were still unforgivingly cold on the mountain, and another shiver skittered down Bel's back as the sweat on his bare chest quickly congealed in the cold.

The hawk perched precariously on the ledge, panting through its open, wickedly curved beak. It blinked up at him indignantly, squawking again.

"Shh, my friend," he whispered, trying to coax the bird inside.

When the hawk just shifted weight from foot to foot, Bel changed tactics and went for the gray feather it held. The hawk moved to stand on his hand amenably but shifted weight as Bel began to bring him inside.

He was young and ruffled his feathers, making his wings hit the window casement. He screeched, batting his wings more to get out of the tight space.

Bel clamped his hand on the bird's feet, making the creature fight to fly.

"Quiet, friend, you'll—"

But the bird was deaf to his chirps, clawing at Bel. He screamed and boxed Bel's head with his wings.

"All right, all right, just—"

"What's all that—?"

His door banged opened, colliding with the wall, as one of the human soldiers barreled in, shocked at the scene in front of him.

Bel's heart skipped a beat, and the hawk clawed his way free and jumped into the air, screaming his anger. The soldier looked from the bird, now circling the rafters, to Bel and back again in disbelief.

The young hawk dropped the gray feather on the ground.

Bel lunged halfway across the room for it.

With a yelp, the soldier followed him down, whether to get him or the feather Bel didn't know. They landed hard, shoulders crashing together, but more important, Bel grabbed the feather.

He rolled away from the confused soldier, running his thumb down the shaft.

LITTLE HAWK, SOMETHING HAPPENING SOON. HUMANS PLANNING SOMETHING. WILL—

"What in the seven hells—"

Another soldier appeared in the doorway, taking in Bel and the first guard on the ground and the unhappy hawk flying around the rafters.

Cold dread sucked at Bel's stomach and made his fingers numb when the New Warden entered too, those shrewd eyes taking in everything with no astonishment or confusion, just assessment.

"He's got something," the first soldier said, pointing at him, "that damn bird brought him something!"

Bel stood up, feather clutched in his hand.

With a nod from the warden, the soldiers closed in on Bel, grabbing for his arms.

He pulled away, wings fluttering, heart in his throat. He'd sat patiently through so many broken bones, so many punishments, but something inside rebelled against being restrained. It was too much like that whipping post, ten years ago.

Bel didn't put up a fight, but he didn't let them easily restrain him, either, flexing his arms and chest so they knew he was strong.

One pressed against his wings, making Bel grimace with an awkward twinge of pain, and together the soldiers held him fast in a firm grip. They didn't hem him against the wall, but they used their weight and size to ensure he didn't move forward as the warden approached.

Bel gritted his teeth, trying to calm his racing heart. The warden reached for his clenched fist. He again didn't fight, but he didn't give in either, keeping his fist closed and forcing the warden to work it free.

The man huffed in exasperation, shooting Bel a disapproving look before holding the feather up to the light.

He frowned at it, and Bel watched, heart pounding in his ears, as he turned it one way then the other.

Finally, the firelight caught on the edges of the inscribed runic, high-lighting the dark gouges that made up the script.

The warden's eyes widened infinitesimally. "There's writing on it."

"*Fuck*," breathed one soldier.

"He's been communicating with *them* this whole time."

The warden turned his frown onto Bel. "So it would seem. Goddess, what a mess."

Bel's chest went tight as he watched the warden put the feather into an inner pocket, a fierce possessiveness overcoming him. That feather, those precious words were *his*. The feather, the runic were his people's and all he had of home—what right did this human have to take that from him?

The warden sighed before giving Bel a hard, considering look. "Confine him. We leave as soon as we can for Highclere. I'm not waiting for the prince to clean this up."

It felt as though the floor opened up to swallow him, like that terrifying freefall of first flight but there was no updraft, no wings to catch him. His heart drummed in his ears, quick breaths sawed in and out of his lungs, yet it felt as though he couldn't breathe, couldn't move with the sheer terror of the idea of south.

South was somewhere Bel absolutely couldn't go.

The terror coalesced into a ferocious panic Bel had felt only once before, the night Maddok had died. The night he failed.

If he was taken south, he'd never be free. He'd never fly, never be able to help his people. He'd fail as he always failed.

He'd have to fight, he decided. And that scared him almost as much.

The panic warmed his body, giving him strength and turning his thoughts to shattered, jagged pieces of feeling, just—*he would not go south*.

The warden was inspecting the feather again, the soldiers looking to him for orders—none expected the sudden, enormous flap of his wings, his great, strong wings. With one, the men teetered, their weight thrown forward. With another, they toppled over, grasping at him, fingers digging into the meat of his arms.

He kicked at one, swept the other away. The soldiers cried out in shock, trying to roll away from his many attacking limbs.

The one still clinging to his arm he heaved into his table, sending bottles and parchments flying, and papers cascaded into the fire. Bottles and books and candles fell from the mantle, splattering and shattering on the ground.

The soldiers groaned, slow to get back up, but the warden was ready when Bel came for him, an animal going for the only thing between it and escape.

The warden blocked his first, second fist and ducked to avoid a sweep of his wing. He went for the dagger at his hip, but Bel was there, knocking his arm away.

They fought with their hands, the warden keeping him away from the door and Bel fighting to get to it. This wasn't like sparring, no camaraderie or appreciation of his opponent's moves. Every block was another moment of danger, each parry another inch away from the door, the way out.

The warden was skilled, his many years of training showing, but Bel was younger, stronger, and wanted it more. This wasn't Lena, he didn't have to check his strength or play fair. In a move he'd done a few times with Lena, but not nearly as gently, he hooked the warden's shoulder with his wing, spun him, drew him into his circle. The man grunted at the impact of Bel's chest, and for a moment Bel had total dominance over this human man caught in his arms and wings.

But there wasn't time to break his back, what the move was created to do to an enemy, so Bel shoved the warden into the far wall, away from the door.

He heard the crunch of the warden's nose as he hit the wall, but then that was an echo, forgotten under the sound of his pounding feet. He was out the door in three bounds, running running running.

The castle was dark, but Bel didn't need to see. These halls were his, he knew every wall, every turn.

"Get everyone up! *Up!*" ricocheted down the halls, and Bel picked up speed.

He slid around the next corner, catching himself on the threshold to a set of stairs. He took two at a time, climbing, his panic and will buzzing in his ears.

"That way, the north stairs—"

"Cut him off!"

He climbed the castle itself, going higher and higher, and the soldiers knew it, their shouts almost as loud as their slapping feet as they chased him up winding stairwells like a pack of starved, howling wolves.

He skidded to a stop and doubled back to another staircase when firelight spilled through the doorway at the end of the hall.

Another flight, up, and then he'd be—

"The east wall! He's going for the east wall!"

He didn't know it himself until he heard it, but there wasn't a choice, not anymore. He'd never make it any other way.

The last door, the one between him and escape, was rusted shut. With a yelp he put his shoulder into it, one, two slams and—*crack*! He clawed his way through, breaking off the top hinge and climbing over the bent, crooked door.

He didn't feel the stab of cold on his bare chest and feet when they met the outside. Melted snow and grime squished between his toes, and the chill stung his lungs. But none of that mattered, only the crumbled edge of the east wall did.

He picked up speed, wings unfurling.

A shout from behind him and below in the courtyard.

But he wouldn't stop. Not now, not ever.

One flap, two, and he ran faster than a human ever could. Three, four, his steps turned into bounds, gaining speed and momentum.

A crossbow bolt whizzed past his leg, but it didn't matter, only—

Another flap, another, and then his foot was on the edge and he was jumping, no time to think, no time for anything else. There was only him and his wings and the sky.

He pumped his wings and kicked his legs to add momentum.

The sky opened up around him, wind rushing against his skin, tossing his hair, punching up his nostrils. He fell, and the sky caught him.

A gust lifted him, filled his wings, and for the first time in ten years, Bel was airborne.

A cry ripped from his throat, and the wind slicked away his tears. He burst with something raw and wild, the purest kind of joy.

He adjusted his wings, trying to feel for the ridge lift that had to be somewhere along the mountain face. He needed up, further into the sky, away from Finhöln, away from humans. He was a son of the sky, and nothing would take him away ever again.

A twinge brought him back into his body, a sharp pull on his right shoulder. He clenched his teeth, flapping faster, desperately searching for that up thrust of air.

Pain ripped through his right side, the wing going limp for a whole horrid second before he could get it moving again. But it was too late, he careened to the right, his wing unable to keep up. The wind whipped his hair in all directions, and his own tears blinded him.

All he could make out was the sharp stab of the trees reaching up like grasping fingers to drag him down. His wing gave out again and he screamed, screamed into the sky, then into the trees that took him down.

46

Lena ignored the way her legs twitched and cramped in her position, crouched behind brush under the shadow of Finhöln's east wall. She'd been watching the castle for hours now, looking for movement and gleaning what she could.

They'd made good time on their way north by avoiding towns. The two of them and their four horses made much better time than Arion and his guard, and Alix never complained about rising before dawn and not stopping until the moon was high. Sometimes they rode through the night if the light was good enough.

Eleven days it took to get here again. It'd felt interminable at the time, as if a force drove her north, to *hurry*, but she always felt too slow. The road here hadn't mattered, only that they get here in time.

For what she couldn't say. Just that they get here.

At first it had been to outrun anyone her parents sent after them. They'd run into Kerry in the stables and made the excuse that Lena was headed to Highclere to rejoin Arion. It wouldn't fool her mother long, but Lena hoped it was enough.

As they'd neared the mountain, the pull had grown stronger, a constant buzz in her head. Something had happened and they needed to get there.

Dusk settled early over the mountain despite signs of spring, turning the moss and undergrowth and earth a muddied brown only disrupted by shocks of white, hard-packed snow clinging to shady patches of ground. Lena blinked a few times, letting her eyes adjust to the haze.

She had a few moments before the cobalt of early night settled on them, and then she'd need to move.

Shifting her weight slightly so she could look over her shoulder, she glanced back at Alix, crouched nearby. Face stiff with determination, those jade eyes of hers were bright despite the dusk.

"If I'm not back by midnight, head into Longbourne," Lena whispered. "Find Violet and ask her for help. Lay low."

Alix's mouth settled into a flat line. "I still think I should come with you."

"Too risky. We'll need you out here, ready."

"Fine," Alix sighed before giving her a jaunty little grin that looked out of place with the flinty hardness of her gaze. "Getaway person is the most important job, after all."

Lena returned her grin, even if she didn't feel it. She hadn't felt much but a hard, knotted bundle of nerves writhing in her stomach for three days now.

What if something had happened? What if she failed?

She shook her head, at Alix and herself. "I'll be back soon."

No words of encouragement from Alix, no blessing or wishes of luck, just a firm, confident nod.

It shored up Lena's hopes more than words could. Alix would be here waiting for them, no matter what. She'd do right by Alix, she swore it, to herself and to the goddess. She hated having to put her in danger now, but she had to do right by Bel, too. She'd give that loyalty to him, too, if he'd take it.

Lena eased from her spot and made her way up the slope, feet light and silent, avoiding any patches of unfrozen mud or crunchy snow. Her heart pounded as she traced along the castle's foundations, slowly making her way toward the south garden gate.

The iron-wrought gate stood open just a few inches. She pushed it gently with a finger, waiting for the awful screech of the hinges. Before it could get out a proper wail, she held the gate fast and slipped through.

She stalked around the garden to the kitchen, hoping no one else could hear her hammering heart. It gave her an unpleasant sensation, walking through Finhöln like the wraith in the night she was. Not long ago, this castle had been hers in a way, and having to sneak around felt like petting the wrong side of velvet.

She'd encountered no one so far, but that meant little as she approached the kitchen. Dinner should be over by now, everyone except the night shift of guards soon to seek their beds, but Lena still pressed her ear to the closed door, listening.

The wood muffled most sounds, but she didn't think it would completely muffle the chatter of soldiers eating and gossiping. Holding her breath, she cracked open the door.

Warm amber light spilled across the frosted ground, and a familiar smell of jam and yeast greeted her on a hot gust of air. When she didn't catch sight of anyone sitting at the long table, she eased the door open and took a relieved breath to find the kitchen almost empty.

Pol stood with his back to her, a washrag in his hands.

Lena crept inside and shut the door softly behind her, waiting. No noise echoed down the kitchen stairs, the plates and cups had been neatly stacked near the sink, and Pol was almost finished wiping down the counter.

She waited a moment and then another, expecting soldiers to swarm down the steps or jump from the pantry. None did, but she still kept her eyes on the thresholds as she crept to Pol.

Not wanting to startle him, Lena moved into his peripheral vision, coming up slowly. Pol still jumped and stared at her through owlishly wide eyes when he finally noticed her standing beside him.

Pol let out a muffled groaning sound before grabbing Lena's face in his hands.

He looked her up and down in shock before drawing her into a back-cracking hug. He made tutting noises in his throat, and Lena couldn't help but throw an arm around him and hug him tight.

Happy to see you, she signed.

He looked at her with happy, teary eyes before asking what she was doing here.

Here for Bel.

His brows climbed halfway up his forehead, and Pol took a moment to take her in. Hair tied tightly back, steel cuirass, dark leathers and trous, sword strapped to her back, and rope hung across her chest. Daggers littered her belt and he couldn't even see the two tucked away in her boots.

A devilish grin spread across Pol's face.

Good. I always knew you were good, Lena.

She swallowed down the sweet ache of his words, wished she could bottle it and keep it forever.

Where is Bel?

Pol's expression dimmed, and he told her grimly, *Locked away. There was a fight, and Bel tried to escape. He fell and they caught him before he could get up.*

Fell? she repeated.

He nodded, raising his hand and then bringing it down to his other, quick as a whip.

Jumped off the east wall and tried to fly. He didn't make it far.

Her insides twisted thinking of how desperate he must have been, to try to fly away. Her heart broke, knowing how excited he would've been to be in the air, only to have everything come crashing down.

She had to make this right.

How long ago?

The day before last. They are planning to leave with him tomorrow. South. He clasped her hands in one of his, eyes grave as he told her, *You must get him out. He won't survive the south.*

Lena nodded in agreement. He'd never have a chance of freedom again, so far into Vagora and she'd have no chance of helping him, let alone ever seeing him again.

Where is he?

Locked up, in the cells.

She couldn't help the grimace.

Of course this wouldn't be easy—sneaking up four levels to his tower room wouldn't have been easy, but to break him out of a guarded cell...

Pol read the worries on her face. He raised one finger, telling her to wait, and hurried into the pantry. She heard him rummaging before he came back with a triumphant grin.

The thing about these old castles, Pol signed with a wink, *is they always have extra keys around somewhere.*

He offered her a worn, dusty key. One of the four teeth looked chipped, but she had to hope it'd work.

Lena clasped his shoulder and squeezed. *Thank you, my friend.*

Pol nodded before handing her more old iron bits, a pair of rusty pliers, what looked like a set of pins, and a small hammer.

I don't have anything for the lock on the chains, those came from the south long ago. You'll have to use these.

I will make it work.

Pol smiled and took her face in his hands. He patted her cheeks gently and in a slow, slurred speech, he said aloud, "You are a good woman, Lena."

At her shock, Pol nodded, patted her cheeks again, and signed, *He needs you. Take care of him, take him far away from here where no one can hurt him again.*

Pol's earnest eyes bored into her, reached into her chest, and pulled at her very heart. They drew each other into a quick, tight embrace. This man, who was all goodness and caring, trusted her with what he loved most. He gave over Bel to her, and she would do all she could to live up to that honor.

I will, she promised, even if she didn't know if it was true. That didn't matter—only that she would try and that Bel would have his chance.

Pol wiped a tear away as he nodded, urging her to hurry.

Can you meet us at the south gate with supplies for him?

Yes, leave it to me.

He clasped her hands in his one more time, and then she was hurrying deeper into the castle.

Lena took the kitchen steps as silently as she could, holding her breath when she passed the landing to the servants quarters. With any luck, the soldiers were still bunking there, including Captain Joran.

There was little light to guide her, and Lena wasn't stupid enough to light a torch. Her months at Finhöln guided her along the cold, dark corridors until she made it to the yawning hole in the rock, with stairs leading down into the mountain.

Bel would be down there, and so would at least one guard.

Her hands twitched with wanting to draw her sword, but the clanging of a swordfight would draw everyone in the castle. Instead, she drew the rope over her head and kept it in a firm grip as she took the stairs slowly, one by one.

Light began to filter up from below, illuminating her way, but Lena kept to the curved, shadowy side of the stairwell. She slowed on the last pair of steps, crouching to see over the lip of the stairwell threshold.

Steady noise echoed down the narrow corridor. She put a foot on the last step, searching for the noise, and saw, all the way down the room, the guard pissing into a bucket. The sound was unnaturally loud, or perhaps that was just her anxiousness, but Lena moved before overthinking.

Feet silent—*heel toe, heel toe*—she unwound a length of rope, letting it hang in front of her as she breathlessly stalked across the room.

The pissing stopped. The man straightened. Lena sucked in a breath and leapt.

The rope swung around the guard's head. Lena pulled, drew him down and herself up, making him arch his back. The guard yelped, gurgled, groaned, hands clawing at the rope around his neck.

Lena held the noose fast and leapt onto his back, bringing the both of them down to the ground as the guard struggled. She grunted at the swift elbow to her side, her ribs, her kidney, the guard wriggling and fighting, trying to dislodge her.

She managed to get a leg around him, pulled him in close and tightened the rope.

She couldn't see much of his face, didn't want to either, but when his ear and temple grew redder, she knew it was over.

The guard gave a breathless wheeze that made her want to vomit before finally slumping into unconsciousness. She waited a few more moments to be sure he wasn't acting.

Slowly, Lena eased the rope away and got up. With short, efficient movements, she bound his arms and legs with the rope and used his own cloak as a gag. She looked around for keys but found none, only the guard's half-eaten dinner on the lone table in the narrow room.

She didn't let herself stop, searched until she saw the bright flash of wings in the second-to-last cell, and dragged the guard to it. Pol's old key took a little jiggling, but it did the job, and the door creaked open. Lena dragged the guard in and put him on the far side.

Then, finally, she turned to Bel.

The breath whooshed out of her at the sight of him. Pol had told her of the fall, but she hadn't really guessed what that would look like.

He sat slumped against the far corner, legs sprawled out in front of him and hands clamped together in crossover manacles. He only wore a pair of torn trous, leaving his chest bare for her to see all the angry scratches and bruises littering him. Streaks of grime and dirt camouflaged even more wounds.

Both shoulders slumped and his wings carelessly lay on the ground. His head rested against the wall, slightly tipped back, and his eyes remained closed. Hadn't he heard all the noise?

"Bel," she whispered, unsure now what else to say. He was here, and she was indescribably relieved to see him, but the state of him made her feel like she'd already failed.

His eyelids cracked open into bleary slits. The blue of his irises seemed almost murky, like rough, churning waters. She watched the ball of his throat bob as he swallowed, and his chapped lips opened as if to speak, but he said nothing at first.

He moved to shake his head and winced.

"Didn't think I'd hit my head hard enough to have delusions."

Lena barely kept back the pained sound that clawed up her throat. "What happened?"

He looked at her but didn't really see. "I flew. For a moment at least...and now..."

His whole body shrugged, and she finally noticed how he held his right arm close to his chest, as if it or the ribs beneath were broken. And his wing...his left wing, the one always whole and animated, drooped at an angle, the radial bone out of place and feathers missing.

"Oh, Bel..."

She sank to her knees before him, but his eyes kept that unnerving, glassy sheen.

"They caught me quick enough," he recounted. "Threw me in here until they're ready to go south." A tear escaping his right eye. "I can't go south."

"You won't," she insisted. Unable to help herself, she reached out to cradle his face in her hand and wipe away the tear, smearing grime across his cheek. "You're coming with me."

He licked his cracked lips, his gaze frantic. "That's why I tried to escape, tried to fly. Knew it was too soon, knew it was stupid, it *was* stupid, broke my wing because of it, but I can't—I can't let go south. I won't ever—"

"Shh," she soothed. "That won't happen. I won't let them take you south."

He blinked several times and finally eased into her caress. He searched her gaze, and light, *recognition* slowly bled into his eyes. The tightness in Lena's chest loosened with it, and she smiled.

"You came for me," he murmured.

"I shouldn't have left."

He frowned. "What could you have done?"

She shook her head. *Something*. But it didn't matter now. She was here for him, and he wasn't going south. And she wasn't going back.

"Alix is waiting outside with horses. We just have to get out unseen. And then..."

She didn't know what then, but really, she couldn't think beyond getting him out of Finhöln.

"You came for me," he said again, as if he needed to taste the words.

"I'm sorry it took so long. I...I don't want to leave you ever again."

He lifted both his hands, locked together as they were, to gently touch her face, as if he still couldn't quite believe she was there.

"You fixed my wing. And now you're here, for me."

"We'll fix you up again, I promise."

He glanced over her shoulder at the guard who lay bound and unconscious. "You attacked your own people."

She didn't want to think of it like that. She didn't want to consider helping him a betrayal. Helping him would never be wrong.

"I couldn't leave you here."

Another tear tracked down his face, his eyes full when he said, "I've missed you so."

He shuddered and cupped the back of her head, pulling her down to him. She threw her arms around him and kissed his temple, his ear, his cheek, everywhere she could reach with his face pressed to her throat. She felt him take a broken breath, a sob stuck in his throat, and she whispered to him, burying her fingers in the soft hair and down at his nape.

She'd missed him so terribly, his voice, the feel of him. She'd been so numb before, unable to care or feel much of anything, but feeling flooded back to her now; she felt every nuance of his warmth, listened for every sound he made. She loved that place on his neck, where hair met down, and she couldn't stop touching it.

"I'm still not sure this is real," he said.

Lena gave a watery laugh. She pulled out the few tools Pol had given her and grinned. "I'll prove it to you."

She gave him a swift kiss before getting started, gratified when he made to follow her for more. One more kiss, all right then two, and then she got to work.

Alix had given her the basics of how to pick a lock, though they'd had nothing to practice on. She remembered their talk the night before, huddled around a small campfire, as Alix explained the feel of a lock and how to go by instinct. *"You gotta feel it and listen to it. Close your eyes if you need to. Feel the mechanism, listen for the right click."*

The moments rolled past as she worked the pins around. She supposed they could take the small hammer Pol had given her and smash him free, but Lena couldn't bear breaking anything else of Bel's.

Sweat tracked down her forehead, and she swore she could see the guard beginning to twitch out of the corner of her eye. Bel waited, breathless, the weight of his gaze heavy on her hands.

Lena took a breath and reminded herself to think, to remember what Alix had said about the unlocking mechanism. She resisted just rummaging around and felt for the hole she needed. Finally, a little *click* had them both gasping.

She met his gaze, fierce and blue, and they shared a smile so wide it made her face ache.

Lena jumped to her feet and pulled him up with her.

Before she could hustle him out of the cell, up the stairs, and into the night, he held her face in both his hands. It did something to her, seeing him standing straight and taking up so much space. Though it must have pained him, his wings folded neatly against his back and his shoulders were squared. This was how Bel was supposed to be—tall, big, glorious.

She gripped his wrists and let him search her face. Adrenaline pumped hard and fast through her, urging haste, *escape*, but Bel seemed to need this, his pupils blown wide and his breathing quick. He needed to see or understand, so she gave him that. She always wanted to give him what he needed.

"I owe you everything," he said, his voice low and eyes the blue of an electric storm. It electrified her, lips and fingers left tingling.

"Good, because I want everything."

He made a growling sound she'd only ever heard him make in bed.

A frisson passed between them, a claim, a promise, and Lena's heart pounded with it, anticipation and joy clenching her gut. She smiled at him and tugged at his hand.

They closed the cell door behind them, locking the guard in, and then she led him up the stairs and away. She didn't need to hold his hand, he knew better than she where to go, but she wanted that connection, the feel of him in her hand, never to be taken away again.

As they slipped through the castle, the tightness in her chest faded away, and a calm settled over her instead. It was a rightness, a sense of purpose, and she knew she'd never regret Bel.

47

Bel ached in a hundred different ways—the broken bones in his wing and arm, the bruises that dappled his body, the splitting headache leftover from the fall. But those aches didn't seem important anymore, fading with every step he took up the stairs, away from Finhöln's dungeon.

His heart ached, too, feeling too full for his chest. His lungs burned as excited breaths sawed in and out, the anticipation, the *longing* to be free making them come quick and shallow. His lips still tingled from being pressed to Lena's, a show of affection and tenderness he'd thought never to have again. His entire being vibrated with a bittersweet ache, still a little unsure if this was truly happening.

It was too good for him.

But he put one foot in front of the other, kept pace with Lena and squeezed her hand when he needed a reminder of what she'd done for him.

When they made the landing, she glanced at him over her shoulder, gave him a quick smile, and then pulled him down the dark corridor. That smile lit him up inside, and he hurried to keep pace, the adrenaline beating hard through him. He wanted to run faster, wanted to fly, wanted to pin her against the wall and kiss her until she understood what this meant to him because surely she couldn't—

A metal gleam, there and gone again in the inky dark, wiped everything from his mind.

Bel snatched Lena back by the waist, hauling her against his chest. She let out an *oomph*, the air knocked from her, as Bel scrambled backwards.

A sword emerged from the darkness at the end of the corridor, followed by the grim face of the New Warden.

Lena tensed. "Captain Joran."

"Maddalena. I worried about you. I'd hoped I was wrong."

She drew in a sharp breath and held it, as if those words pained her, and Bel tightened his grip around her waist. They weren't yet in the warden's striking distance, but he wouldn't allow anyone to harm her in any way. Not now, not ever.

Joran stepped further into the corridor, what little light there was only highlighting the thin set of his lips and his steady gaze.

Bel drew half a step back and took Lena with him, not liking him getting closer. A possessiveness roared in the center of his chest. He kept his arm around her waist as a claim, a statement that he was for Lena.

"There are two of us," said Bel quietly. "Just let us pass."

"Captain, you know this is wrong, he shouldn't have been kept."

The warden frowned at both of them. "Keeping him here was wrong, I'll give you that. He should've been taken south long ago. We'll all go at first light."

Panic skittered down Bel's back, making his wings twitch.

"I won't let you take him," Lena said. "Please, we don't want to fight."

"Neither do I," said Joran, surprising Bel. "But I'm armed, and when I call for my knights, you'll be taken back down to the cells."

Lena shook her head before squaring her shoulders. Bel didn't know what decision she'd arrived at, but in two quick movements, she'd drawn the sword from her back and pressed the hilt of a dagger into his free hand.

"I'm not leaving without him, captain."

"You only have five soldiers besides yourself," said Bel, watching the warden's brows creep up in surprise. *Good.* "And one's already tied up."

He finally released Lena and took a step forward, putting himself between the two humans and twirling the dagger in his hand so the warden saw it. "Four soldiers, disoriented from sleep and in *my* castle. I know everywhere to hide, to ambush. Do you really think they have any advantage? Think of your soldiers and let us pass."

It was dark and the captain was a seasoned knight, but Bel could still see the way his shoulders stiffened.

"We just want to leave," said Lena, her voice even and reasonable. "You've wanted to be rid of me for good and now you can be. I just want him to be free."

The warden huffed. "It wasn't personal, Lena. You're a good knight who served her country well. But you forgot your place. And now you've...for goddess's sake, he's the enemy. Listen to yourself. You're throwing everything away for an *avian*."

Bel's breath stuttered to a stop, and he couldn't help glancing at Lena. Joran was right, she was giving up everything; there'd be no turning back from this.

But Lena just looked on calmly, no hesitation or uncertainty, and it soothed the franticness in Bel that still thought escape, freedom, Lena were all too good to be true.

"Everything I've done has led me to him. You don't have to understand, captain, you just need to let us pass."

"You know I can't."

"Yes." She gave him a curt nod. "Tell Arion I'm sorry."

And then she was a flurry of movement, and the clash of metal echoed down the corridors. It was a thing of beauty, watching Lena fight. Not just sparring or training, but their culmination. For a moment, Bel stood in awe of her efficiency and strength.

The warden was a strong man, well trained and cunning, but Lena was younger, faster, and most importantly, when she spun away, she had Bel.

He drove Joran back into the wall, catching his sword thrust with the dagger, and tossing them away. He ignored the cry of his broken limbs, using what he had to against the man standing in his way. It was just this one man—for the first time, Bel could taste freedom, true freedom, and this human wasn't going to stop him.

"Guards! Awake!" Joran yelled into the dark castle.

Bel shoved at him, and when Joran thrust again, he spun and Lena was there, beating him back.

They drove the warden back into a corner, the two of them blocking off escape and crowding him, making his sword almost useless.

The pulse in Bel's ears beat rapidly, a reminder that each passing moment meant the promise of more soldiers. Someone must have woken by now.

Bel dove for Joran, knocking his sword arm away and overwhelming the man with limbs. The crooks of his wings beat against the man's head, stunning him, as Bel worked his arms around Joran.

An elbow hit then dug into his side, and Bel groaned but didn't let go, kept moving until he had an arm around the warden's neck.

The man began to struggle in earnest then, but Lena was there, striking him in the gut with her sword hilt. The air whooshed and sputtered from his lungs, and Bel tightened his grip. A hand clawed at his arm and feet tried to stomp and unbalance him, but Lena was there, knocking the sword away and restraining his arms.

Together they held Joran as his struggles weakened. It wasn't pleasant, and Bel tried to ignore the feel of Joran's hot, clammy flesh as the breath left him. Lena caught and kept Bel's gaze, and they waited it out together.

It felt like a small eternity before the man slipped away into unconsciousness. Bel held him a few moments longer, just to be sure, before they eased him to the ground.

Bel collected his sword as Lena stared down at the warden.

He took her hand in his and gave a gentle tug.

They took the fastest way down to the ground level of the castle. Bel tried to listen for the sounds of soldiers rousing but could barely hear anything over their hurried steps and his pounding pulse.

No one met them in the corridors, and before Bel could comprehend it, they were outside, clinging to the shadow of the south wall. He was dimly aware of the stinging cold on his bare feet, old snow and frozen mud squelching between his toes, but he relished the bite of cold air, tasted it on the back of his tongue.

A familiar figure stepped out of the shadow of the south wall near the gate.

Bel's heart squeezed, and he didn't miss a step, just ran up to Pol and embraced him.

Pol made a garbled croak and pulled Bel into a hug so tight his bruises and bones protested, but Bel didn't care. Pol rocked them back and forth, and Bel sank into the comfort and relief. It still didn't seem real, but he felt Pol's warm body against his, felt Pol's happy tears fall onto his own skin, and he began to believe.

When Pol stepped back, he beamed a smile so wide that even in the shadowy night, it glowed.

Didn't I tell you she was a good one?

Bel laughed as Pol wiped away his tears. *You were right. You're always right, my friend.*

And don't forget it. Pol's smile turned wistful, and more tears ran down Bel's face. *This is everything I hoped for you.*

Bel's face crumpled. Freedom had always been something to dream about—he'd never truly thought he'd ever leave Pol. It'd been a comfort to know the man would always be there, would never leave him, and it devastated him that he was now the one to leave Pol.

Pol eased him back and wiped his tears again. *Enough of that. Here, get into these.*

Come with us, Bel tried to sign as Pol and Lena hustled him into clothes. A shirt, tunic, and coat were pulled over his head, his feet shoved into boots, and his wings folded under a cloak.

My home is here, Pol finally signed after wrapping a knit scarf around Bel's neck. *You're meant for out there. Go. And fly again.*

More tears threatened, and Lena put her hand in his, giving it a squeeze and him the reassurance he needed. This was what Bel needed and what Pol wanted for him. All that was left to do was see it through.

I'll miss you, my friend. Thank you for everything.

Pol huffed and sniffled. *Fly high and fly free, A-r-u-b-e-l.* He smiled at the shock on Bel's face and said aloud in that slurred speech of his, "Come back and see me. But not too soon."

Bel knew they needed to hurry, but he couldn't help but embrace Pol again. This man had been everything to him for so long—friend, healer, mentor, guide—it pained him that freedom came at the price of leaving Pol. He'd made Bel's years here bearable, and there was nothing in this world that could repay him for that.

I'll see you again one day, Bel signed.

Pol smiled before turning and patting Lena's face. *Thank you. Take care of him,* he told her before waving them through the gate and out into the dark forest beyond.

He shut the gate behind them, careful of the squeak. He smiled through the iron grates then disappeared into the shadow of the castle.

Lena tugged Bel along when he would've stood rooted to the spot, transfixed by Finhöln's dark silhouette. It was Lena who kept them moving, as Bel felt lost, swimming through their short journey down the slope and deeper into the trees. The forest, the air, Lena's hand all seemed syrupy and dreamlike.

A soft neigh brought his focus back, and from among the trees, Alix appeared with horses. She winked at him, and he smiled up at her.

"You look like shit," she quipped.

Bel made a face at her that she returned, and he couldn't help the laugh that came, a carefree, joyous sound that began clearing away the last cobwebs of disbelief.

Lena was all efficiency, quickly mounting Yvain and bringing him around for Bel since he couldn't ride on his own. Bel patted the gray beast's neck and thought he saw recognition in those liquid brown eyes.

He mounted behind Lena awkwardly, unused to gripping an animal and hanging on with his legs. He almost let his wings out from under the cloak for balance. But then Lena drew him forward a few inches, closer to her, and she grounded him.

With subtle movements of her legs, Lena directed Yvain to turn around and head deeper into the mountains.

Even the tallest spires and towers of Finhöln quickly disappeared behind the trees, and then all Bel could see was in front of him.

He wrapped his arms around Lena, no matter how it hurt. He needed to hold onto something, to hold *her*. His world was broken but somehow expanding, like an egg that needed to break for the bird to be free. Redemption, rebirth, he didn't know what to call it, but the truth of it sunk into his flesh, making him shiver. *Freedom*.

A breath shuddered through Bel, his hands trembling as he held her close. Burying his nose in the knotted braid of Lena's hair, Bel took a deep breath until the tremors stopped.

"Where are we going?" he whispered.

"East," she said. "Away from here."

Bel tightened his arms around Lena. She touched her hand over his where it rested against her stomach, and he ran his nose up the side of her neck in a small *ashita*.

East. Away. Everywhere he'd wanted to be. He lifted his eyes to the dark horizon, imagining for a moment that he could see it, could see east to Aeriand, his home in another life. He'd see it again. He'd see his brother's city and perhaps his people again. And he wouldn't be alone.

He didn't even feel the ache of it when he drew his wings out from under the cloak and encircled her in them, holding her tight with arms and chest and wings.

"Thank you," he murmured into her hair. "Thank you."

She looked over her shoulder at him, and he just caught her smile in the hazy dark. "Always."

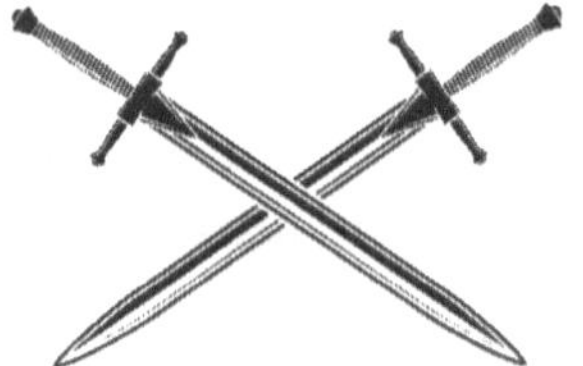

Author's Note

Whew! Mind that cliff! Well, not really a cliff...more like a shallow berm, right? Don't be mad at me!

Hello hello! I'm so glad you chose to pick up *Aerie*! I hope you loved Lena and Bel as much as I do. These two had a rough road and it was sometimes hard as a writer to put them through it all, but they're on the right path! It was sort of a ride into the sunset for them, which was amazing for me.

Lena was a difficult character to write; she may not be the most feisty or adventurous main character, but I loved her all the same. She really does just want to do right and be accepted. I just wanted to reach through the pages and give her a hug.

And Bel. Oh Bel. Talk about someone who needs a hug. Bel for me was the perfect amount of sensitive and brooding, beautiful and scarred. He was an amazing character to write and I'm so glad he's getting his chance ;)

Putting these two in an isolated castle together was both perfect and awful. They had to find things to do! But I loved getting to play with the *Jane Eyre* and *Beauty and the Beast* vibes. So fun!

Lena and Bel will be back in *Haven*, the second book of their duology. They've ridden off into the sunset (forest), but what happens when a new day dawns? I guess we'll have to find out!

If you enjoyed Aerie, please consider leaving a review! Reviews and word of mouth really do make the indie author world go round, they're so important!

Thank you for reading!
—S. E.

If you'd like to stay in touch, come on over to socials and say hi! I'm around on most platforms as se.wendel.author, and I'm most active on Instagram. Come check it out to find out about what I'm working on, get some reading recommendations, and get spammed with pictures of my cat. What's not to love?

You can also check out all my books, commissioned art, and book merch shop on my author website (www.sewendelauthor.com)! Lots of good stuff over there!

I've also started up a monthly newsletter. You can subscribe on my website to keep up with me and my news.

OTHER WORKS

A Time of War and Demons (House of the Rising Sun, Book 1), fantasy romance novel

Aerie (Broken Wings Duet, Book 1), fantasy romance novel
Haven (Broken Wings Duet, Book 2), fantasy romance novel

Stone Hearts (War of the Underhill, Book 0), historical monster/fantasy romance novella
Heartsong (War of the Underhill, Book 1), monster/paranormal romance novel, February 2026
Heartsworn (War of the Underhill, Book 2), monster/paranormal romance novel, October 2026

Halfling (Monstrous World, Book 1), monster/fantasy romance novel
Ironling (Monstrous World, Book 2), monster/fantasy romance novel
Sweetling (Monstrous World, Book 3), fae/fantasy romance novel
Faeling (Monstrous World, Book 4), monster/fae/fantasy romance novel
Changelings (Monstrous World, Book 5), monster/fantasy romance novella collection, Autumn 2025 + Spring 2026
Foundling (Monstrous World, Book 6), monster/fae/fantasy romance, Summer 2026

ABOUT THE AUTHOR

S. E. is a California native who grew up with animals; her ginger tabby is her current writing partner and lets her know when it's time to take a break (by laying on her keyboard). She graduated from the University of California, Davis with a master's in creative writing and uses all her available time to build worlds, characters, and their stories. She enjoys animal rescue shows, almost everything in Trader Joe's, and all the beautiful landscapes of California.

www.ingramcontent.com/pod-product-compliance
Lightning Source LLC
Chambersburg PA
CBHW022015300726
48970CB00003B/905